Cosmic Soul

Cosmic Romance 2

Mars Quinn

Editor: Andra Moon

Cover Artist: Etheric Designs

ASIN: B0DCGCLJZL

ISBN: 978-1-961972-04-9 (Paperback)

Content Notes

The following is a list of what you can expect in my book. Some of these are triggers that may bother certain readers, and some are *massive* spoilers. If you have no triggers, please feel free to continue. If any of the following bother you, please skip this book. Your mental health is of the utmost importance.

**Please note that I am human. I tried to list everything, but if you're concerned about a particular topic or trigger, please DM me.

- Discussion of death
- Death of a family member
- Swearing
- Depression
- Suicidal ideation (there is no attempt)
- Parental and domestic abuse (side character—none shown on the page)

- Mentions of past bullying
- Explicit sexual content (all consensual)
- Spectrophilia
- Light exhibition
- Piercings
- Spanking
- Biting
- Licking
- Body dysmorphia
- Sensory overstimulation
- Chronic pain
- Ableism
- Abliest culture
- Light political unrest

Happy reading!

Chapter 1

BACK AT THE START AGAIN.

Caleb

Being dead wasn't so bad. Was it ideal? No, but honestly, it really wasn't *that* bad. I'd medium recommend. Besides, everyone had to die at some point, so why complain? My death hadn't been traumatic or anything. I fell down a staircase and cracked my head open. One second, I'd been laughing with my brother Matt; the next, I was standing over my body thinking, "Oh, shit."

For whatever reason, my soul refused to move on, head into the light, or whatever. I didn't have any reason to hang around, but hanging around was what I did. I'd haunted my family for a few years. They moved on. All good on that front. Then I'd figured since I didn't explore when I was alive, why not do it now?

The Great Wall? Awesome. The White Cliffs of Dover? A must-see. The Great Pyramids? Not my favorite, but I'd enjoyed watching tourists basically melt from the heat.

Anyway, when I was in Australia, I'd spotted some weird shapes, which turned out to be aliens, of all things. They had toothpick bodies and massive watermelon heads with two conical horns. The little purple dudes wore the worst orange spandex I'd ever seen. Like the eighties had desperately wanted these guys back. They'd had *Ghostbuster* vacuums strapped to their backs with wide clear tubes that sucked up spiders. Spiders! Why would they want those? Who knows, but I'd figured why the hell not jump aboard?

After that was a whirlwind of space stations, ships, and planets.

Eventually, years later, I'd wandered to a space station hovering above the planet Tamkolvanloknol (what a name), home of the Drakcol Empire, where I heard about a plan to go to Earth. It was like a bolt of longing had struck me. I'd wanted to go home. Badly. I'd been desperate to see my family, my home, and my people. The places I knew. Maybe then I'd finally be able to move on.

It hadn't really worked out that way.

Sure they'd gone to Earth, but they didn't land or send a shuttle to the surface. They'd beamed up some dude named Seth Harris because he was Prince Kalvoxrencol's soulmate. Trying to break through the atmosphere had seemed like a bad idea (just my luck, I would've gotten stuck orbiting Earth). When they headed back to the same planet I'd left, I'd gone with them. Now, I was on the Admiral Ven, which was docked at the same space station I'd been at a year ago.

Full circle with absolutely shit to show for it.

What to do? What to do? Jumping on another ship and wandering some more was always an option. Plenty of universe I hadn't seen. A little frown dragged my lips down at the thought. I was… tired, emotionally, not physically, but still. That was why I'd tried to go home in the first place, but that went down the crapper.

I could hang around Seth for humanity's sake and brotherhood and all that. Yeah, he didn't know I existed, but I could make sure he was alright and that Kalvoxrencol was treating him well.

Though from what I'd glimpsed of their romance on the Admiral Ven, he worshiped Seth, and they were mates, maybe not officially—I wasn't exactly sure how it worked. I mean they had a ceremony of sorts with a lighted glass and vows, but that was more of an engagement-like thing. Or had it been a wedding? Honestly, I wasn't sure, but they were together. From what I'd seen, Seth was happy with the arrangement.

Still, he might need me.

Decided, I raced through the halls of the ship, not bothering to dodge the civilians and crew who were disembarking. I slid right through them, making a few people shiver. Amidst the pressing crowd, I spotted a familiar face, Wyn. His bubblegum-pink hair and lavender scales stuck out like a sore thumb.

"Hey, Buddy," I said, falling in step with him. He kept staring at his tablet, grumbling about a phase variance. I was pretty proud of the fact I'd learned to speak Drakconese. I'd picked it up when I lived on the space station, then refined my skills on the year-long journey. There was occasionally a word or phrase I didn't know, but mainly, I understood it all. It was one of the many languages I'd learned over the years.

I wiped an imaginary tear. God, Nana would be proud.

"So where are you going?" I asked him, stepping onto the space station.

I'd wandered the station pretty thoroughly when I was here last year, and it appeared the same. Shops, rooms, laboratories, command, and so much more. The main aliens aboard were drakcol, probably because it orbited their home planet. Some of the other aliens I knew the names of and some I didn't, but they came in all shapes, sizes, and colors.

Wyn didn't pay any attention to the lush plants growing everywhere or the unique items for sale. Instead, he bustled through the crowd and boarded a shuttle.

I recognized a few of the drakcol, all in uniforms, but my attention stayed on Wyn, not only because he was close friends with Seth, but because he'd followed me around the ship during the entire journey, even though he had no idea I existed.

Maybe he sensed me? I squashed that thought like a bug. He didn't. No one did. I was alone, and it was fine.

The shuttle vibrated, not that I felt it, but people shifted with it. I, of course, didn't move. Nothing touched me. Believe me, I'd tried. I was impervious or more accurately, non-existent. Occasionally, if I *really* focused, I could shift or bump something, but it exhausted me, sometimes to the point I vanished, like ceased to exist for a few hours, which was creepy, to say the least. Even when I did manage to touch something, I still didn't perceive it. No texture. No temperature. No nothing. I was a void with no physical sensations whatsoever.

Wyn didn't bother looking up from the tablet when the shuttle landed; instead, he kept tapping away at the glass, claws clicking. He was beautiful, and there wasn't really any other way to phrase it. His hair was short on the sides and longer on top (most of the officers on board had the same hairstyle, probably a military thing). His scales were lavender with hints of gold and magenta skin around them, and they possessed a sheen like a snake. His ears were tapered like elves from the story books and had pink studs in the lobes and golden studs that trailed up to the tip. His heart-shaped face was delicate and his lips full.

He was so pretty that it was a shame I was dead. Oh well.

His long tail, tipped with a thatch of pink hair, thrashed; he was obviously upset. I had no idea what was bothering him, and I couldn't ask. I mean, I could, but the dude wouldn't hear me.

He left the shuttle, and I followed him. Wyn seemed to know where he was going because he didn't hesitate in his step and headed across the fairly empty port to a massive building. The palace was a feat of glass and spires, twisting like dragon tails. It had terraces, balconies, windows with railless verandas, and plants everywhere. Drakcol flew around the palace; their wings spread wide, catching the air.

The sprawling city, just down a steep incline from the palace, was filled with towering glass buildings and lush parks. There would be plenty of places for me to explore when I wasn't haunting Seth like his own personal spector or guardian angel. I grinned. I liked that better. Guardian angel.

Without hesitation, Wyn stepped inside the palace and wound through the halls. Even more plants were inside. The drakcol definitely had a thing for plants from the amount of potted trees, flowers, ferns, and vines growing all over the place. Even the Admiral Ven had plants on almost every surface.

All of the outside walls of the palace had huge windows framed by sheer curtains fluttering in the near-constant breeze. Everything was pretty, airy, and luxurious from the shiny white marble-like floor to the stone walls.

What the palace didn't have was the typical rich people's stuff from knickknacks, pottery, statues, paintings, and unnecessary furniture. You know, junk people collected for no other reason than it was valuable.

We came to an inner hallway that led to a set of stairs with an open channel wide enough for drakcol to fly up or down. Wyn ignored it and walked down the steps, claws clacking away on his screen and tail flicking. As he wound through more hallways, I mentally started to form a map.

Wyn palmed a panel near a door, and it slid open with a gust of air. Inside was a mess of screens on every wall and consoles and terminals crowded every available space. A few people, who were wearing similar uniforms to Wyn, called out greetings, which he acknowledged. He plopped down next to a cluttered console, staring at the screen.

"This doesn't make any sense," he said, fisting his hair. "How is it here? The phase variance is here. How? *How*?"

Yeah, I should've thought of that when he was stalking me across the whole damn ship like an obsessed hound dog. Sometimes my ghostly self messed with technology. Most people either didn't notice or ignored any interference I caused, but Wyn hadn't. Since I was here, it appeared I'd brought the same issues with me.

"Sorry, my Dude. That's my bad."

"NAID," Wyn called.

A face that made me start appeared. An old human woman, though blue, with towering curls, wrinkles aplenty, and a jiggly jaw asked, "Yes?"

"Can you detect the phase variance?"

"Affirmative."

I barely paid attention to either of them, reaching out. My fingers slid through the monitor. Edith Smith.

"Nana." If it was possible for me to cry, I would've started bawling. I had no corresponding physical sensations to my emotions, like the backs of my eyes burning and shit. All of that had died with my body.

It was the same every time I'd seen her on the Admiral Ven. NAID was an artificial intelligence, or some of her had been. It was confusing, to be honest. When I'd been on the station over a year ago, NAID had been a bland, blue drakcol silhouette. But this NAID had been separated from the main hub and had gained sentience. She and Seth were close friends, and to make herself more friendly, she'd chosen a face—a face that happened to belong to my grandmother.

"Why is it here?" Wyn asked, his voice breaking.

"I don't know, unless my coding is causing the error," NAID offered.

"I don't believe so," Wyn said. "It was on the shuttle as well. I'll have to send a report to my superior. Something is wrong."

"Well, that's my cue," I said, heading to the door, though I paused at the last moment because of NAID. She wasn't Nana. I *knew* it, but part of me wanted it to be her because I wanted Nana like I wanted to be able to breathe again.

Shaking it off, I hopped up the stairs.

Chapter 2

YOU CAN SEE ME.

Caleb

I whistled a jaunty tune and began exploring the palace while I kept an eye out for Seth. I couldn't actually lend comfort, but I needed to make sure he was safe. He was the sole human around for who knew how many lightyears.

Bros before hoes and all that. Though, somehow I doubted Prince Kalvoxrencol, or Kal as Seth called him, would like to be referred to as a "ho." God, the very thought of calling him that made me grin. Seth would blush; Kal would stare. I laughed, bouncing out of the palace.

All of the paths surrounding the palace wound in nonsensical curves through towering trees and random ferns. Plants came in as many colors as drakcol did. Bright red bark. Gold leaves. Blue vines. Neon orange flowers. It was an array of colors.

I paused, spotting Monqilcolnen or Monty (Seth really struggled with the long names, though they weren't that hard). His silver-white hair hung around his broad frame and down to his tight ass. He was huge, like many drakcol, well into the six-foot range, probably near seven feet. His deep forest-green scales had a healthy sheen that glinted in the bright sunlight. He was Kal's cousin, and they resembled each other with the same long noses, full lips, and strong jaws, though they had very different coloring.

"Hey, Monty, or Commander Monqilcolnen," I said, voice deepening before I broke into a fit of laughter. "Whatcha doing? Anything fun? Please say yes. Or better yet, take me to Seth."

He didn't reply and his steps remained steady, but I didn't allow that to deter me.

Seth had to be here. Somewhere. He'd left the Admiral Ven about a week ago. I hadn't gone with him, because I missed the shuttle. I doubted Kal had taken him too far away so quickly. I would find him. I had all the time in the world after all.

Monty headed toward an airy cathedral-esque building that gave me the urge to cross myself or say a Hail Mary, not that I did. I was beyond all that, not that I was religious. Nana and my parents were. I'd been dragged to more masses in my short lifetime than I wanted to count.

The building was completely made of glass (drakcol must like light or something) and had a pointed spire in the front that was so tall it appeared to pierce the sky. Even from here, I caught sight of the many plants inside. Maybe it was a greenhouse? That would be fun. I'd always loved nature—being dead hadn't changed that.

When Monty approached, the front wall split in two, forming doors that had been invisible moments ago. I jumped in front of Monty. "Do it again so I can yell 'Open sesame.'"

He of course didn't. Rude.

A drakcol in a white robe trimmed with gold approached. She was old, like dirt and pyramids old, and had jagged scales and wispy green hair. Her pink eyes were covered in a slight film, her steps were shaky, and her wings hung behind her, dragging on the moss-covered ground. I'd never seen a drakcol with their wings out randomly like that. They always kept them tucked away beneath their shirts, not that I'd tried to stare at naked people when they didn't know I was there. I wasn't a creeper. But occasionally, I would pop into a room, and boom, a naked person. I'd gotten used to it.

"Great Mother," Monty said in a reverent voice as he tilted his head to the side to offer his throat. Drakcol did that to acknowledge dominance, like werewolves. Though no one had sprouted fur or howled at the moon. Yet.

"Wayward Child," she replied, tail curling around his. "Finally ready to give up the stars?"

"No. My place is among them. Not here."

She leveled him a look that would've had me cringing, but he didn't back down. "You are the strongest spiritual soul ever tested, Monqilcolnen. You belong among the Ranks. Here."

"I do not. I know this."

The woman, or Great Mother, let him go and faced the massive floating crystal in the center of the room. Like really—how had I missed it? The crystal was over ten feet tall and put off a weird hum that made me twitch. It gave me capital letter vibes. Like it wasn't some crystal. It was *the* Crystal.

"Have you secured our audience with Seth Harris?" she asked.

I perked up. What did she want with my dude?

"Kalvoxrencol will not allow anyone to see him besides family and Seth's friends. He's refusing an audience."

A deep frown tugged on her non-existent lips. "Seth Harris has the purest warrior soul ever tested, and he is not drakcol. He can mind-speak with the prince. We need to speak with him."

"I understand," Monty said, "but I cannot force Kalvoxrencol to allow you or others to speak to Seth. He is protective of his mate, as he should be."

"Ask Seth Harris himself. He can make his own decisions."

He could, but she stood a better chance of hell freezing over than Seth *wanting* to talk to someone. My dude was shy and introverted to the extreme.

Monty's thoughts must have mirrored mine because he gave a scoff that he quickly swallowed. "Seth will not speak to you unless forced."

"Forced?" The old woman practically oozed excitement, which made me glare at her. Nana and my parents might have taught me good manners, but this bitch was lucky I couldn't yell at her. No one was forcing Seth to do jack shit.

"Give them time, Great Mother," Monty said. "They're recently mated, and this is all new for Seth. In time, he may seek the Ranks or the Crystal for curiosity's sake."

Lies. Monty was one hundred percent lying out of his perky ass.

When she seemed placated by Monty's lies, I drifted away. A few rooms were off the main sanctuary, one with monitors and consoles, others led to darkened staircases that appeared to go downward, probably underground. What secrets were down there? Were there bodies? Treasure? Oh my god, I wanted to see whatever was going on down there, and I would, eventually.

Right now, I was more interested in the floating rock. Steps slow, I moved toward it until I was an arm's length away. It felt powerful. Old. And I had the perverse urge to touch it.

It was like a bear or a burning hot coal. I yearned to touch it for some odd reason, even though I *knew* it was a bad idea. I was lucky no bear had ever crossed my path when I was alive because I would have died trying to hug it. Now, I had the same urge.

Sure I was dead, but it felt really *really* dumb to poke the glowing Crystal the drakcol revered like a deity of some kind. I didn't know exactly how it worked, but I had learned that this rock liked to pair up mates, which was why Kal had traveled across the universe for Seth in the first place.

"Don't do it," I told myself. "Don't touch it, Caleb. Don't be stupid." Then I promptly pressed my hand against it. Yeah, I was an idiot. I closed my eyes, added a second hand, and pushed.

Unlike everything else in this universe, I didn't slide through it. The Crystal resisted me. I didn't feel it, but I couldn't move through it. I cracked open one eye, hoping it had changed or reacted to me in some way. It hadn't. The Crystal was the same as ever, floating and glowing in the same creepy way.

I pulled away. Of course, it hadn't done anything to me. But on the bright side—it hadn't done anything to me. It didn't kill me a second time, or rather, scatter my atoms, or whatever I was made of, to the winds.

During my moment of insanity, Monty had disappeared, but I caught a flash of his silver hair heading down the darkened steps. I saluted him goodbye. I would stalk him in the underground area later.

The drakcol in the room with the consoles started mumbling, tail thrashing. Fearing he was picking up the phase variance, I left. I still had to find Seth. My dude was probably lonely.

I went back inside the palace but got distracted almost immediately by a jungle-like garden on a massive terrace out the windows. Seth could wait a few minutes. For all I knew, he would be there, as Seth had liked the atrium on the Admiral Ven.

With nothing for it, I jumped out of the window to explore. A thick canopy of leaves covered the entire garden, blocking a considerable amount of light. Ferns and underbrush grew all over the ground. Multi-colored vines crept up the tree trunks, decorated in bright flowers. Birds sang; small animals darted back and forth, barely letting me catch a glimpse of fur or scales. Butterfly-sized bees sporting barbed stingers near the length of my pinky on their fluffy asses fluttered by.

It was awesome. This place alone would take a while to explore.

Eventually, the meandering path spat me out in front of another church-esque building made completely of glass. This one was way smaller, though. Maybe it held Crystal Jr.? Through the glass walls,

I saw the inside was filled with flowers and plants on tables as well as some floating on nothing but air.

When I went to investigate, the seamless front doors slid open. A drakcol stepped out. His waist-length white hair blew in the wind and around his lean frame. His pitch-black scales had glimpses of silver and white skin around them that I longed to trace with my fingertips. His tail slowly swished back and forth, making me notice his muscular ass. He set down a pot with a bright red flower bush. His long fingers plucked off a couple of decaying leaves before pushing his hair behind his tapered ear, smearing dirt over his scales. Gold earrings and cuffs adorned his ear and one golden chain with an emerald on the end brushed his neck.

"There you go," he said in a steady voice that drew me in like a moth to the flame.

Damn, he was lovely. His strong features, long nose with his septum pierced, and full lips were like candy to my eyes. Every movement was graceful and liquid. What wouldn't I give to shoot my shot with such a guy? Then of course be brutally rejected, but such was life—well, death in my case. No one that pretty was within my league.

Undeterred, I bounced up to him and asked in English, "Aren't you a pretty one?"

He froze and straightened, long hair falling around his shoulders. His deep green eyes stared straight at me. "Little Soul, what are you doing here?"

My mouth dropped open. He saw me? He *actually* saw me. It was like everything came into focus as I looked at him. Someone in this vast universe saw and heard me. Suddenly, I wondered how much my afterlife was about to change.

Chapter 3

THE DRAKCOL MEDIUM.

Zoltilvoxfyn

A human spirit stood in front of me with his mouth hanging open in a disconcerting way. He didn't resemble my younger brother's mate, Seth Harris, but he was definitely the same species.

His light brown hair hung to his narrow shoulders in soft curls, and his blue eyes with round pupils so different from mine stared at me. He was short. I didn't realize humans came that short. Seth wasn't as tall as most drakcol, but this human was even shorter than him with a thin frame. He was clad in odd clothes. His shirt depicted a human with their tongue hanging out and white hair sticking in every direction, and his blue trousers appeared rather stiff.

"Little Soul," I said. "How did you get here?"

He didn't reply, grinning and showing off his even, bright white teeth as well as his unscaled pink tongue.

How had he even gotten here? Tamkolvanloknol was a great distance from Earth, and Kalvoxrencol hadn't landed on the planet when he retrieved his mate, answering the longing the Crystal had instilled in him. So where exactly had this human spirit come from? And how had he gotten here when most spirits didn't wander far from their families or where they'd died?

"Do you understand me, Little Soul?" I asked. He probably didn't speak my language. He might speak the same language as Seth Harris, but from my understanding, there were multiple languages on his planet, unlike my own, which had one. For Seth to speak to this spirit, I would have to explain my inner fire, though Kalvoxrencol might have already done so.

It was my duty to help this soul find peace. I would have to take him to Seth, but I should probably contact him first. He and Kalvoxrencol hadn't been mated long, and they might be engaged in an activity I had no desire to witness. I suppressed a shudder. Watching my little brother fuck his mate wasn't something I wished to see.

"Will you follow me, Little Soul?" I asked, even though he didn't understand me. "You will have to because Seth is the only one who can speak to you."

"My name is Caleb Smith," the human said in passable Drakconese. His voice was higher pitched than any drakcol; it fit his slight frame perfectly.

"You understand me?"

His head bobbed. Seth did that too, and I didn't know what it meant, though I doubted it was him acknowledging my dominance or position. Caleb continued, "I learned. I was on the space station for a while, and then I was on the Admiral Ven."

I crossed my arms, tail flicking. "How did you get to the space station?"

He grinned, eyes twinkling, and it created the oddest swooping sensation in my stomach. He said, "I was on Earth when I followed purple aliens capturing spiders."

"Illegal traffickers," I said. A rather sizable illegal market for spiders existed, but vveki worshiped a goddess whose aspect was similar to that of an Earthen spider, and they considered all of them her sacred children. There was a ban on buying or selling Earthen spiders, as well as a few other planets' spiders, within Coalition space.

Caleb lifted and lowered his shoulders before a torrent of words fell from his mouth. Some were Drakconese, others were human speech. I understood, though, he was on a ship with spiders that had been altered to be significantly larger, from his swinging arms. Said spiders killed the scientists. Eventually, he boarded a passing shuttle.

"Then you came to our space station?"

He waved a hand. "No. I wandered for cycles. Can't even tell you how many. I've been everywhere."

"And you are here now."

"Yep," Caleb said, smiling at me. "I went on the Admiral Ven to go home, but they didn't land, so I stuck around for Seth."

"You know him?"

"No, but he's human."

I didn't know what to say to the wandering soul. He seemed perfectly content as he studied everything. I would've assumed he was alive if not for the slight blur around him as well as an innate sense my inner fire gave me that told me he was a ghost.

"What's your name?" Caleb asked. "I told you mine. It's only fair of you to share. Not that you have to be fair. I mean, I'm dead, but you're the first person I've had to talk to in cycles. So a name would be nice. I can make one up for you, if you'd like. That might be fun, though your name is probably nice. Is it nice? Do you like it? What does it mean?"

My lips quirked at the rambling. "Zoltilvoxfyn. I'm the fourth prince of the Drakcol Empire. My name means precious gift of the Crystal, and yes, I like it well enough, and yes, it is perfectly nice."

"You're Kalvoxrencol's older brother," he said.

"I'm three cycles older."

"Brothers are awesome. Not just brothers. Siblings are nice. I like siblings. It's fun to see how blood plays out in people's appearances, you know? My brothers look nothing like me, but one of my cousins is practically identical to me, even though she's a girl. Weird, right? How can you see me?"

This soul talked. A lot. "My inner fire."

"What? What does that mean? Are you special? You seem special."

"My inner fire. Each drakcol has one, but type and strength is determined by family lineage. Mine allows me to see the spirits of those who have died. Kalvoxrencol has the gift of light. My other brother Dontilvynsan can read minds. Serlotminden can create fire. Hallonnixmin is persuasive."

"That's sweet," he said. "I'm jealous. I would love to move things like I had the force."

What did sweetness have to do with anything and what was this "force?" While he spoke my language, Caleb said things that didn't make sense. "Why are you here on this plane, Little Soul?"

His shoulders lifted and lowered again. "Just am. Never left."

Souls always had some idea of why they lingered: loved ones, unfinished business, revenge, or any number of reasons. I'd never met or read about a spirit who didn't know why they were here. Then again, I'd never met a spirit who'd wandered this far.

"None?" I questioned.

"I stuck around. Why wouldn't I? There's too much to see." Caleb skipped toward my greenhouse. His blue eyes with their strange, round pupils swept the windows. "This place is..." He broke off into human speech.

"I cannot tell from your tone if that is good or bad."

He beamed at me, which caused the same swooping to occur in my gut. "Good. All good."

Caleb slid straight through the glass, and I frowned. I didn't allow anyone in my greenhouse, barring my brothers on rare occasions. It was my sanctuary. A place to be alone with my thoughts when I needed it, though sometimes that wasn't a good thing. My mind was often my worst enemy.

I followed him inside. The humid air clung to my scales, and the hot temperature pressed against me. Flowers of all kinds, mainly my rarest plants and hybrids, greeted me. Light floral scents mixed with fresh dirt and fertilizer. Caleb raced around, a bounce in each step, as he studied my hard work.

Caleb was like no other soul I'd met. He exuded life. He wasn't perturbed about the fact he was dead; though from his words, it had been some time now. Also, spirits did not travel the stars.

Apparently, the normal rules didn't apply to Caleb.

Helping him find peace was my responsibility. I'd never met another medium. It was a rare inner fire—one of the rarest. But there were logs from the previous ones in history, and in them, mediums were mandated to bring restless souls to peace. I hadn't assisted many spirits in crossing over, since most left without aid, but I would have to help this one. How though?

I had no idea, but it was my duty.

Chapter 4

IS THAT A SMILE?

Caleb

This greenhouse was sweet. Definitely in the top ten of things I'd seen in my journeys. Every plant was alive and flourishing. Pots floated in the air, wandering around the greenhouse on their own, like magic... though knowing drakcol, it was "science" or some shit.

Flowers ranged from the usual reds and pinks, but I spotted flowers that started out as blue in the center and turned violent yellow on the jagged edges. There were ferns with spotted leaves or stripes or both, coming in neon colors to purple so dark that it was almost black. One plant was a deep blue and glittered like it was alive with stars and had blood-red blooms that shimmered in the light.

Everything was new and interesting.

Near the back was a fern-type plant, but its leaves curled and unfurled on their own, like they were beckoning me. I leaned closer and spotted delicate white flowers near the base. I brushed a finger over one light green branch.

"Careful," Zoltilvoxfyn said. "It will grab you and its leaves are sharp."

I laughed. "I'm dead. It can't touch me. Stop worrying."

"I forgot. My apologies."

Zoltilvoxfyn was lovely, but he was rather staid. His voice was wonderfully deep, but it lacked inflection. He needed some lightening up. But hey, that was a snap judgment. Though, honestly, he could be as boring as paint drying and it wouldn't matter. He was the one person I'd ever met who saw or heard me.

"I would like to help you," he said.

"With what?" I didn't need anything, unless he was volunteering to take me back to Earth. That would be nice of him, though part of me felt bad I was even contemplating leaving Seth.

"Find peace."

"Oh." He saw souls. It was probably his job or something to see me to the Great Beyond or whatever he believed in. I wasn't necessarily opposed to passing on. I mean, I was tired, like hecka tired, but at the same time, I wasn't upset about sticking around. There was a lot to see in this world.

"I'm good," I told him, turning back to the numerous plants.

"Excuse me?"

"I'm fine," I reiterated in case the Drakconese words I used weren't correct. I never knew. I would think some word would mean one thing, but then someone would say it in a different context than I was used to and confuse me. I didn't have a teacher; I'd figured this out as I went along. "I don't need any help, but thanks for offering.

It's sweet of you. Really sweet. Or nice? Does sweet mean the same thing as nice? I've never been sure, and now, I can ask."

He ignored my rambling. "You don't desire to pass on?"

"Nope. I'm happy here for now. I mean, why not? There's stuff to see and places to explore. I have nothing but time."

His mouth fell open, showing off his scaled black tongue and sharp canines. "That's not right."

I shrugged. "Don't care and not my problem."

Not bothering to wait for him to respond, I stepped through the glass. Zoltilvoxfyn rushed to follow me, his every movement graceful. It wasn't fair. When I was alive, I'd been clumsy as hell. I *had* died by tripping over nothing and rolling down a staircase.

Whistling, I took off into the jungle garden. Part of me didn't like leaving Zoltilvoxfyn behind, because it was nice to have someone to talk to, but I didn't want to listen to him lecture me about moving on. I already knew that. Maybe after I knew Seth was alright and I'd explored this world, I would pass on. What was a few more years in the face of eternity? Nothing. Literally nothing.

"Caleb," he called from behind me, plants rustling as he chased me. "Come back."

I paused because I heard the desperation in his voice. "I'm not going anywhere, just looking around."

He came closer, smoothing his black clothes that clung to his muscular form. The sleeveless tunic with the high collar showed off his muscular arms, and the tight trousers hugged his thick thighs. Once again, not fair. He had no right being this attractive when I could do nothing about it.

"You need to move on."

My head fell back as I groaned. "Zoltilvoxfyn, I'll move on when I want to. Right now, I'm going to explore."

"Maybe we should talk to Seth."

My smile grew. "He's still here? In the palace, I mean. Kalvoxrencol hasn't stolen him off?"

"Yes. He's here."

I skipped toward him. "I would like that. He won't be able to hear me, though."

"I will convey your words."

"Really? That's so sweet… or is it nice? You never did answer that question, which isn't really fair. It's not like I can ask anyone else, so you should answer. Though you don't have to. I don't want to force you into doing something. If you get what I'm saying. Nevermind. It doesn't really matter. Thank you, Zoltilvoxfyn. I've been wanting to talk to Seth for forever."

Zoltilvoxfyn gestured to the bark path that I didn't need to stay on—it wasn't like I was hurting the plants. Whatever. I hopped beside him to make him happy and followed along. My gaze kept gravitating to him like he was a magnet. He was tall, over a foot taller than me, which wasn't hard because I was ridiculously short.

Being a short guy growing up had been unpleasant, to put it mildly. My older brothers and cousins (not to mention countless bullies) had teased me mercilessly about it, but eventually, I'd gotten over it. I couldn't change the fact that I was shorter than average. Hell, I was shorter than most women. It was what it was.

Besides, when I came out, I'd quickly realized there was a benefit to being small. Some guys really liked twinks.

When we reached the edge of the forest, Zoltilvoxfyn stopped and removed a glowing blue stone—a touchstone—out of his pocket. "I best make sure they're available."

"Good idea. I don't want to walk in on them having sex. Been there, done that. It was awkward, to say the least, even though they didn't see me. Still, there was a lot of skin and scales and moaning. So much moaning. I did *not* enjoy that. I wish I could burn it from my brain, you know?"

The slightest smile curled at the corner of his lips.

Hold on just one second, he had a sense of humor. It must be buried. Of course, he didn't know me from Adam, not that he knew an Adam being drakcol, which might be part of the problem. Unfortunately for him, he would get to know me, and I was a talker. Silence was about to become a thing of the past. I had years worth of built-up words, and he was going to get them all.

"Kalvoxrencol," he said. After a moment, he continued, "Pest, I need to speak with your Seth."

Zoltilvoxfyn stopped talking, and I didn't hear anything, not that I'd expected to. I'd seen other people using touchstones on the Admiral Ven, and I never heard the other side of the conversation.

"It's important," he said. "I didn't want to interrupt anything, though."

"They were fucking, weren't they?" I asked. "I bet they were. They do it a lot. Like all the time." Rabbits fucked less than they did.

He choked in what sounded like an aborted laugh, but he got control of it too fast for me to know with any certainty. "I'll be there shortly." Zoltilvoxfyn tucked the touchstone back into his pocket. "This way."

He gestured to the wide, arched doorway, and I bounded inside.

Chapter 5

A FORMAL INTRODUCTION.

Caleb

As we wandered upstairs, I peered around, taking everything in. Once again, I was struck by the lack of typical rich people junk like artwork, statues, and useless furniture. It wasn't only rich humans who liked excess. It had been the same pretty much everywhere I'd wandered, though there was a lot of universe that I hadn't seen.

But people liked things. What they hoarded differed from species to species. The garmiqi hoarded the skulls of their enemies, and on the same planet another race, the kheekii, hoarded shells, pink being the most treasured. Another, the sidlis, treasured the most perfect leaf during autumn from each tree—it was like gold. Each prominently displayed or traded the items for other valuables, some with obvious uses… others not so much.

"Where's all the artwork?" I asked.

He peered around the empty hallway before he answered shortly, "Drakcol are not, as a whole, an artistic race."

Zoltilvoxfyn stopped in front of a wooden door enhanced with a carving of a tree—the first sort of artistic thing I'd seen in the palace. He palmed a panel glowing with blue light the same shade as NAID and waited. A moment later, the door popped open, and Kalvoxrencol stood in front of us. His long silvery-blue hair hung around his muscular frame, and his amethyst eyes focused on Zoltilvoxfyn.

While they were different colors, Kalvoxrencol steel-blue with purple and bright blue accents around his scales, they were obviously related. They shared the same long noses, full lips, and wide foreheads.

Kalvoxrencol held the door open. "Come in."

I slipped inside, passing through Kalvoxrencol, who shivered in response, his wings rustling on his back before tightening to the point they were invisible. Seth sat on the long backless couch in their apartment, a book in his hand and a black cat on his lap.

I could stare at him forever. Seth wasn't particularly handsome. Like if you looked up average in the dictionary, a picture of Seth would be right there. But he was so human. The first one I'd seen in years. I loved his round face, deep brown eyes, and soft brown hair. He was husky with a paunch, and he had broad shoulders and wide hands.

Seth smiled shyly at Zoltilvoxfyn as he clutched the book, making it shake. I immediately rushed over to pat his shoulder, even though he didn't know I was here. "Don't worry. I won't let him be mean to you," I said, shooting Zoltilvoxfyn a look. He raised an eyebrow in response.

It hadn't taken me long to figure out Seth had anxiety, and I wanted to protect him, though he didn't truly need it. Seth didn't hear my words or react, which oddly poked at me. I longed to be able to talk to him, hug him, and hang out.

Kalvoxrencol settled next to Seth, draping an arm over his shoulders. "What's going on?"

Smoothly, Zoltilvoxfyn sank onto one of the stools facing the couch, his tail flicking faster than normal. "I wish to speak to Seth."

Kalvoxrencol grinned like he couldn't imagine anyone *not* wanting to speak to Seth, which was fair. I wanted to. Who wouldn't? Seth, on the other hand, paled, dropping the book to the couch and fisting his hands in his hoodie pockets. The black cat on his lap started to purr, but she kept glaring at Zoltilvoxfyn.

"Why?" Seth asked in a strained voice.

"Be nice," I told Zoltilvoxfyn, who flicked his tail at me but otherwise didn't react. It had to have taken years of practice not to respond to the random dead people who talked to him. I would've been hella bad at it. I would've jumped at every noise and chatted with ghosts all the time. Hello, padded cell. Room for one.

"Has Kalvoxrencol told you about my inner fire?" he asked in his steady voice.

"Yeah," Seth said.

My head tilted toward him. It was nice to hear him speak in English. NAID translated Kalvoxrencol and Zoltilvoxfyn for Seth, but she couldn't do the same thing for me, because no one knew I was here. I'd had to learn Drakconese, and trying to mimic the guttural noises was hard. Listening to English was achingly comforting.

As Zoltilvoxfyn explained in more detail about his *magical* gift that wasn't actually magical, something about brain chemistry yada yada, and how it worked, I tuned him out and explored.

Two tall windows with sheer white curtains were directly across from the door. They led to a railless balcony covered in potted plants. Between the windows was an overfull bookshelf stretching to the high ceiling.

I wandered past the couch and around the cut-out wall carved with vines. An easel that had a painting depicting what appeared to be an outline of Seth sat on the other side. A low dining table framed by woven mats was near two doors. One bedroom was completely empty; the other was full of childhood junk like clothes, toys, and books.

Still ignoring the conversation, though my ears perked whenever Seth spoke, I went to the door on the other side of the apartment. This was obviously Kalvoxrencol and Seth's bedroom. A huge canopy bed, with colorful vines coiled around the posts, stood in the middle. The three windows had the same sheer curtains as the living room. Clothes, books, and cat toys were scattered around.

There were two paintings of Seth, one on the wall and the second on an easel. The first was a portrait, chest up, of Seth done in shades of red. The other was also in shades of red, but it was a full-body painting of Seth. Naked. While it wasn't completed, it showed exactly what Seth was working with.

I pushed my head out of the door and commented, "Seth, my man, Kal is obviously obsessed with you. Paintings everywhere. I would say it was a bad sign, besides the whole soulmate thing."

Zoltilvoxfyn broke off mid-sentence and cleared his throat. Kal's eyebrows lifted, clearly wondering why his brother had stopped talking.

I peeked over my shoulder at Zoltilvoxfyn who watched me. "Your brother is lucky as long as he didn't exaggerate Seth's cock. Nice and big."

A strangled noise came out of his lips, which sounded suspiciously like suppressed laughter. Zoltilvoxfyn definitely had a sense of humor. He just needed something to draw it out. It would be the mission of my afterlife: Operation Make Him Smile. He needed it. Hell, he deserved it. The dude saw ghosts. It couldn't always be rainbows, sunshine, and unicorn shit.

"What's going on, Zoltilvoxfyn?" Kal asked. "I doubt you came to talk about your inner fire."

"A soul recently came across my path."

I snorted. I'd called him pretty to his face, but whatever. Sure, I'd crossed his path. Like a cat.

Seth sat up straighter, petting Lucy who continued to purr. "A ghost?"

"Yes."

"Are they see-through?"

"No," Zoltilvoxfyn said slowly. Obviously, Seth was working off Casper-type images. I looked like me, just dead.

Lucy nudged Seth, and he started petting her again, not meeting anyone's eye.

At the thought of cats, I crouched in front of Lucy. Some animals saw me. Spiders did, which was terrifying. Images of genetically modified black widows the size of German shepherds came to mind. I shuddered, pushing it away. That had been a bitch of a nightmare to escape.

Cats were hit or miss for me. Some reacted, while others ignored me entirely. Cats were assholes, so it was hard to know one way or another if they all saw me or not. Lucy had ignored me back on the Admiral Ven, even when I'd rolled on the floor in front of her or tried to play with her. I'd even focused as hard as possible to throw one of her balls, and she'd ignored me. Though I'd paid the price by vanishing for a couple of hours.

"Hello, Chunky Bunky," I said in a baby voice, wiggling my fingers right in front of her, then gave her a loud smooch. Lucy's eyes grew wide. She arched and hissed before darting under the couch.

Seth started. "What the hell?"

"She can see me," I yelled triumphantly. "What an asshole to ignore me for months. Do you know what I did to try and get her attention? Lots of things. Embarrassing things. She ignored me the entire time. I could've been playing with her."

Zoltilvoxfyn released another cough, which made me grin. I moved to his side, and he tracked me the entire way.

"The ghost is here right now," Kal surmised.

"Yes," Zoltilvoxfyn replied.

Seth sat up straighter. "Here?"

"Yes."

I patted Zoltilvoxfyn, sliding through his shoulder. "Tell him about me. Hurry up. I want to talk to him."

He glanced at me before focusing on his younger brother and Seth. "His name is Caleb Smith."

Seth's mouth dropped open. "He's human?"

"Yes."

"How's that possible?" Kal asked.

Zoltilvoxfyn answered, "The story is Caleb's to tell."

Seth nodded.

I bounced on my toes in excitement. I was going to speak to Seth. He was the first human I would talk to since my death. Yes, it was via Zoltilvoxfyn, but I didn't care.

A sudden longing started, making me ache, like a physical ache, which had never happened before. I *felt* something. *Physically.* It was so distant and faint that it took me a bit to identify the emotion attached to it. Loneliness. I was lonely.

The prickle disappeared as quickly as it came, leaving me wondering if it had happened at all. I'd probably imagined it. Feeling something physical was impossible.

When Zoltilvoxfyn stared at me, gesturing to Seth, words clogged my throat. I was desperate to speak to him, yet at the same time, it wasn't actually him I was lonely for. I missed my family. My brothers. My cousins. My parents. My nana. I wanted to be on Earth. I wanted to be alive again, but that would never happen.

Swallowing it down, I focused on Seth. A human was here, in front of me, wanting to talk. Instead of being sad about my death or not seeing my family, I was going to seize this opportunity and talk to him.

Chapter 6

TWO HUMANS CONVERSE.

Zoltilvoxfyn

Caleb beamed at Seth, and something dark and hot curled in my gut at his expression. It was possible that Caleb had grown fond of Seth over their six-month journey from Earth on the Admiral Ven. Maybe more than fond. The tightness returned with more force this time, but I banished it.

Seth was mated to Kalvoxrencol. That would never change. Drakcol mated for life. That fact didn't comfort me. Though why would his possible infatuation with Seth bother me? It shouldn't. It didn't.

"Tell him I said hello," Caleb said.

What an illustrious start to a conversation, but I dutifully translated.

"Where is he?" Seth asked. I gestured to the space beside him, and he said, "Hi. How old are you?"

"Twenty-one."

"I'm twenty-nine," Seth replied. "How long have you been dead?" He paled. "I'm sorry. That was rude. You don't have to tell me."

Caleb patted his arm, though his fingers slid through Seth's bulky black jacket. "Don't worry about it. I'm not sure how long it's been. The cycles have blurred together."

"What year did you die?"

He rattled off some numbers that had no meaning to me, but I told Seth, who bobbed his head. "So twenty-three years depending on what time of year you died."

"It's been that long?" His eyes turned distant while his voice radiated sadness.

Unable to stop it, I slid off the stool and crouched in front of him. "Are you alright, Caleb?"

His gaze lifted to mine, and a sudden urge to cup his cheek or wrap my tail around his wrist burned through me. My hands fisted at my sides while my tail flicked. Touching him was impossible.

"I'm fine," he said. Caleb turned toward Seth, who stared in his general direction. "What do you miss most about Earth?"

Seth leaned against Kalvoxrencol, who in turn wrapped his arms around his waist. "It's hard to pick. I miss a lot, and not so much, if that makes sense."

"It does." Caleb bounced, standing in front of Seth. I pointed so Seth would know where he was. "I miss…" I had no idea what that word was, but I did my best to imitate the same sounds, forcing out a *beear*.

Seth frowned, clearly not understanding. Caleb put his thumb to his mouth, three middle fingers curled to his palm and littlest finger out, and swallowed. I copied the motion.

"Oh, beer! Yeah, I miss that. Oh god, I miss food from Earth."

"Me too," Caleb said.

Snuggling against Kalvoxrencol, Seth said, "I miss a lot."

My brother winced, and fiery anger pulsed in my chest at Seth's careless words. He was distressing Kalvoxrencol. My little brother acted more sure of himself than he actually was.

"Surely you don't miss that much," I snapped.

Seth started, and Kalvoxrencol growled at me, his tail winding around Seth's wrist. "I miss a lot, but I'm happy I stayed," Seth replied, shoulders tense.

"Leave him alone," Caleb yelled. "He's allowed to miss home."

Caleb started crowding Seth while Kalvoxrencol glared at me, but I returned his look. Kalvoxrencol was my little brother, and I would protect him whenever possible. For most of our lives, he'd protected me, even though I was older. Now, I would make sure his mate's callous words didn't injure him.

Kalvoxrencol whispered something in Seth's ear, and he relaxed.

"At least you have Lucy," Caleb commented.

Seth glanced at Kalvoxrencol. "Kal brought her with me."

"We could hardly leave your house god behind," he said with an equally fond look at his mate.

"House god," Caleb repeated. "Am I understanding that correctly? A house like a dwelling and a god that is worshiped?"

"Yes," I said.

"The cultural law of Earth. You can't move a cat when they're sleeping on you. It doesn't matter if you're going to work or have an appointment," Kalvoxrencol explained. "It's quite the epidemic, as I understand it. Shouldn't you know that?"

Caleb stared at Seth, who looked at the floor, cheeks bright red. A sly smile pulled at Caleb's lips. "Yes, I remember. It has been so long since I was on Earth, so I forgot for a moment."

"I understand," my brother replied.

"Yeah, humans worship cats," Caleb said. "One of our cultures even has massive statues of cats. Humans are all about cats. I always wanted one, but my parents were... I don't know how to say it. They couldn't healthwise have one."

"Allergic," Seth supplied.

"Yep," Caleb said. "I don't know the Drakconese word." I supplied it for him, and he continued, "So am I."

"It's sad your parents and yourself are allergic to your house gods," Kalvoxrencol commented.

"Yep," Caleb said, still looking at Seth, who was red. "So sad. So very *very* sad."

Clearing his throat, Seth asked, "How did you get here?"

Plopping onto the floor, Caleb crossed his legs and began to tell his story. "So I died young, and after I haunted my family for a while, I decided to explore Earth. Why not, right?" He lifted and lowered his shoulders. I needed to ask Kalvoxrencol if he knew what that meant. "I was exploring, and there were these aliens with oblong heads literally sucking up spiders. I took one look at their ship, and I knew I had to see what was out there. So I jumped aboard."

Seth's mouth fell open. "You went aboard?"

"Yep," Caleb said, knees bouncing. "They hung around Earth for a couple of weeks putting more spiders in containers, then they left. Their ship made awful noises as they traveled. A few minutes later, they arrived at a space station."

"A few minutes?" Seth asked. "It took us six months to get here from Earth."

My brother replied, "Some species travel faster than we do. I believe Caleb is describing the xoi. They have slipstream technology that allows them to travel faster than anyone else."

Caleb started talking again. "I was on their space station for a few months. No one was coming or going. They were doing experiments on spiders. They made them the size of..." he trailed off. Instead of saying anything, he formed an approximate shape that was more than twice his width and about half his height.

Seth shivered.

"The spiders killed everyone. The main power on the ship failed. I spent months running in the dark from the spiders. Even though they couldn't touch me, it was terrifying, because they saw me. Different types of aliens came, trying to contain them, but they all died. Eventually, one alien got away, and I joined him on his shuttle."

"That's horrifying," Seth said.

"Yep," Caleb replied, but he grinned widely like he enjoyed scaring Seth. "After that, I wandered around for cycles apparently until I came to the space station orbiting Tamkolvanloknol. When I heard about Kalvoxrencol going to Earth, I jumped aboard to go home."

"Then we came straight back here," Seth finished.

"I didn't have a chance to get to Earth."

"I'm sorry."

Caleb said, "Don't worry about it. It might take me a few more cycles to make it home, but it doesn't really matter."

His words picked at me. Caleb had been dead for a long time, longer than any other soul I'd heard of. Most didn't remain on the mortal plane for much time before they continued on their journey. Also, the prospect of staying here for even more cycles didn't bother him. This was a problem. It might be impossible for him to leave.

Maybe he was untethered?

Most souls were tethered to either the place they died or their family; Caleb had clearly left both with no issues. When a soul releases their mortal concerns, they untether and move on, but maybe Caleb had always been untethered. So he wandered with no end, unable to leave.

"How did you die?" I asked, hoping Seth's presence would aid in Caleb's desire to talk.

"I tripped."

"Tripped?" I asked, after sharing his words with Seth and Kalvoxrencol.

"I tripped over my own feet and rolled down a staircase. I cracked my head open. I died instantly."

Seth scooted to the edge of the couch, his eyes not quite on where Caleb sat. "I'm sorry."

Once again, Caleb dismissed his concern. "It's not a big deal. I've been clumsy my whole life."

So it wasn't his death that kept him around. Sometimes when a person's life was cut short, they clung tighter to the mortal plane, but Caleb was unbothered.

"Did you leave someone behind?" I asked, though saying the words felt like ingesting glass for some reason.

Caleb glanced at me, forehead creased. "What do you mean?"

"A lover. Child. Someone that you cannot let go of?" I explained. Seth turned bright red at my blatant words, though I didn't know what that color change indicated.

"My family. But no. Why?"

I translated his words for Seth and Kalvoxrencol but didn't answer Caleb's question. Another reason why his soul lingered disappeared. He didn't have anyone holding him back, which oddly relieved me.

Caleb said, "You're trying to get me to move on."

"Yes." It wasn't a secret. This was something Caleb had to do. This plane was for the living, not the dead.

He crossed his arms. "I told you, I'm not ready."

Kalvoxrencol asked, "What's going on?"

"Caleb is upset because I brought him to meet Seth in the hopes it would help him move on."

"That's his choice, isn't it?" Seth asked carefully.

Caleb stuck his tongue out at me. "Seth gets it."

My soul pounded and my breath sharpened at the sight of his pink tongue, so different from my own. It appeared so soft and delicate. What was it about this human that drew me in? I didn't understand.

"It is," I conceded, keeping my voice even. "But this is not the place for him." I told Caleb, "You need to move on, and I will help you."

"Well, I'm not ready." Caleb didn't bother waiting for me to respond. He fled, disappearing through a wall.

He would be back. Caleb obviously cared about Seth, and I saw and heard him. That knowledge didn't stop the instinct to chase him and confirm for myself that he was safe.

"He's gone," I told them.

"Will he come back?" Kalvoxrencol asked.

"I believe so."

Kalvoxrencol held the back of Seth's neck, muttering something. Seth bobbed his head and gave me a wave, going to the bedroom. I crossed my arms. I knew my little brother planned to lecture me about snapping at Seth. Kalvoxrencol was protective of everyone he loved, Seth more than anyone. Even though he was a creator soul, Kalvoxrencol got more overbearing in his protection than most warrior souls.

"Do not yell at my mate," he growled, approaching me.

I got to my feet, not backing down. Kalvoxrencol was a better fighter than me, but I didn't think he would attack me. He never had in the past, though he was now mated. That changed things.

"He injured you," I said.

He paused, and I scoffed. Kalvoxrencol acted as if I and the rest of our older brothers didn't know him as well as he knew us, which was a lie.

"Unintentionally."

"He should've been more careful with his words," I said.

"He's my mate. He can say whatever he wants." Kalvoxrencol glanced at the shut door and closed the distance between us. "You are to never tell anyone what I'm about to share with you."

I tilted my head to the side, exposing my throat in concession.

He shoved a hand through his long hair, his eyes remaining on the door to his and Seth's bedroom. "Seth was abused by his caregivers and by past partners."

My soul froze before speeding up. "He was hurt?"

"Yes. Do not yell at him, Zoltilvoxfyn. It scares him, then he retreats deep within himself where I struggle to reach him. It makes him question his value when he's afraid. I know you understand that."

"I do," I replied quietly as an ocean of guilt flooded me. I had a chemical imbalance that led to a deep moroseness. I got injections and spoke to someone about it, but it wasn't a cure.

Kalvoxrencol's tail curled around mine. "He's similar to you, which I think is one of the reasons I fell in love with him. He has *anxiety*, and while I don't understand the word, I understand what it is. Everything is threatening to him already. Please don't add to it."

"I won't. I apologize."

Kalvoxrencol was shorter than me or any of our other brothers, and he seemed so small, reminding me of the child he used to be. My brothers and I had spent cycles trying to help when Kalvoxrencol was lost, but he was finding his way.

"I spoke before thinking," I said. "I don't like you hurting."

"I know."

"I will be careful with your Seth. I would like to get to know him."

Kalvoxrencol beamed, and light began to pool beneath his scales. My eyes widened. I'd never seen his inner fire activate from joy, only anger or fear. The sight made me relax. He truly was happy with Seth.

Chapter 7

A NEW CITY TO EXPLORE.

Caleb

I raced out of the palace. I understood his need for me to pass on or whatever—it was his job after all. Despite that, it annoyed me that the reason he brought me to meet Seth was for information, not because he was nice or some shit.

But it didn't matter.

He couldn't make me leave. I had to make sure Seth was alright, maybe hang out with Wyn more, and explore Tamkolvanloknol. It was a pretty planet, and it was new. How was I supposed to leave when there were things I hadn't seen yet?

Pushing Zoltilvoxfyn out of my mind, I wandered the grounds, all the while searching for Wyn's bright pink hair. He was around here somewhere. If anyone else was going to figure out I was hanging around, it would be him. Then I wouldn't have to talk to Zoltilvoxfyn. The problem—I didn't see him as I headed toward the sprawling city in the distance.

Whatever. I had all the time in the world.

The city was a mass of glass and metal spires that looked luxurious and ethereal. Plants were everywhere from flowers and trees, to bushes lining the copious amounts of balconies, terraces, and numerous parks. Not all of the parks were on the ground either; I spotted ones on terraces connecting buildings. Drakcol flew through the air in a multitude of colors, scales winking in the bright sunlight. They could be any color, unlike humans, from Wyn's lavender to Monty's forest green. All of the drakcol were tall with muscular frames (hello gym rats).

I wove through the mostly empty, but surprisingly clean stone streets, making a map in my head. I did catch sight of a few other aliens, some I recognized, like the tree-esque sidlis with bark-like skin and green hair full of glass beads walking beside a drakcol woman. Others I didn't, like the squat alien that was purple in color and covered in spines.

Aliens came in all shapes and sizes from towering over me to reaching my knee. Some were humanoid in their appearance; others resembled reptilians or jellyfish. All were fascinating with their own cultures and languages and with the different things that made them tick.

Every so often, I saw drakcol on the ground. When I was on the station orbiting Tamkolvanloknol and on the Admiral Ven, no drakcol flew—a restriction probably due to the cramped spaces—but here, everyone flew, landing on balconies and slipping into open arched doorways.

A hulking green form with bristle black hair appeared in my vision. They carried several bags, displaying their muscular tattooed arms; a wide grin pulled on their thick lips, exposing the two tusks that curled over their top lip.

"Urgg," I called, even though they couldn't hear me. I came to their side, having to jog every couple of steps to keep up. Urgg was a barbarus that was mated to Captain Talvax who'd led the expedition to Earth. They were also friends as well as a mentor to Seth. "How are you?"

They didn't respond. If I'd been alive, I would've felt a stab in my gut, maybe a quickening of my pulse or something, but I didn't. Oh, I still had emotions, like right now it hurt that Urgg couldn't hear me, but there was no physical correspondence. No body, and all that. My emotions were fully functioning, though muted. It sucked ass.

I fell silent and followed Urgg through the city, examining the stone streets and the tall buildings covered in open windows with balconies. The street view was rather boring with a few plants and wide tree trunks (though one tree trunk was blood-red with black veins; if I hadn't been with Urgg, I would've studied it).

There were doors for people who didn't fly to enter what I assumed were shops and apartment complexes, but they were plain and unadorned. The windows held nothing interesting, but I saw glimpses of the shops displaying items for sale higher up, clearly catering to the drakcol populace.

What I didn't see anywhere were billboards, like displays or advertising. No shop had outward signage besides small screens near the entryways displaying their names (I thought. I couldn't read

Drakconese). There were nooks with flowering vines and ferns that had blank screens in them. When a drakcol alighted on the landing, they activated and scrolled through what appeared to be a list. It was difficult to ascertain exactly what was happening from where I was on the ground, but I was pretty sure it was a directory terminal.

So no advertising, but plenty of directories or maps were placed around. Though I didn't spy any on the street level, which sucked for the grounded populace.

With Seth mated to Kalvoxrencol, I wondered if that would change? Would the shops try to appeal to the wingless patrons? It would probably depend on how much shopping Seth did, which was probably going to be minimal. I couldn't picture him spending much time wandering around the city.

Urgg's destination was a building with arches and planters overflowing with bright orange flowers resembling lilacs, but they grew straight out of the ground like asparagus. Unlike many other buildings, this one had elaborate double doors framed by white pillars with thorny blue vines coiling around them.

Urgg stepped inside, then immediately moved to the side because a busk, who was exiting, grunted at them. The alien was over seven feet, maybe even eight feet tall. They had dark brown fur covering their corded muscles, and pink spines ran down the length of the spine to the tip of their tail. The busk's arms were so long that their hands dragged on the ground.

After the busk left, Urgg stepped inside. A staircase and a tunnel went straight up into the ceiling for the drakcol to fly up to other levels. A sidlis came down the stairs, acknowledging Urgg with an arrogant nod, wispy clothes floating around their lean body. Urgg said something, and the sidlis replied in their flowy, lyrical language. I wasn't fluent in Leyasian by a long shot, but the sidlis was giving Urgg a traditional greeting.

Metal doors with glowing blue labels on the upper right corner lined the hallway. More aliens exited and entered the doors, most non-drakcol. When another alien exited, I peeked inside and paused at the living room setup.

It was an apartment building. Talvax and Urgg must live here. Captain Talvax had to be on shore leave, waiting for the Admiral Ven's repairs and updates. That meant she and Urgg would be in the capital for a while. Seth probably liked that.

I followed Urgg until they reached a door on the seventh floor. Man, I was glad I didn't feel my legs anymore or they would be burning. The drakcol needed to invest in elevators or escalators. Yes, they flew so it was unnecessary for most of them, though they had elevators on the spaceship and station (probably because drakcol couldn't fly on board), but it would be nice for everyone else. Besides, there had to be drakcol who couldn't fly due to age or injury.

I slid in through the door when Urgg went inside. The apartment was spacious with a massive terrace spreading all along the back wall, which was actually one long window. Talvax was sprawled on a backless couch, wings spread. Her bright orange hair was mussed and standing up straight. She lay on her stomach, reading something on her glass tablet.

Urgg planted a sloppy kiss on her head, and Talvax's brown scaled tail swiped at their backside. Urgg said something, and I listened intently. I hadn't learned whatever language they spoke, because there had been only a handful of barbarus on the Admiral Ven.

Talvax dropped her screen and placed a kiss on Urgg's wide palm. "Thank you, Mate."

They said something else before scooping Talvax into their arms. She wrapped her arms and legs around Urgg before capturing their lips with hers.

"Whelp," I said, wheeling around. "That's my cue to get the fuck out of here. You kids have fun." I bolted out of the apartment, trying to ignore the groans that were coming from behind me. I headed down the stairs, though I could throw myself down the shaft in the center. The fall wouldn't injure me. It's not like I could die again.

A drakcol flew up the square shaft, their deep green wings spread wide. They grabbed the railing covered in flowering vines on the floor above me and swung over, vanishing from sight. The drakcol were so graceful, and I was supremely jealous.

Many of the apartments had potted trees and flowers in front of them. The ceiling was coated in creeping green plants with bright pink flowers. The drakcol had to not get allergies, because from the amount of plants everywhere, the pollen must be killer.

A door suddenly opened, and a harried woman, with steel gray scales that had pink and gold accents, rushed out. Her long green hair was pulled back into a messy braid, showing off her tapered ears lined with gold studs.

She ran down the stairs. "I'm late."

With nothing else to do, I followed her. Where was she going, and why was she giving me white rabbit vibes? I had no idea, but I chased her, intrigued, as I thought over and over again, *I'm late. I'm late.*

The woman was over six feet, sporting a broad frame and thick muscles. Her green eyes stayed focused ahead of her as she dashed down the street. She wore plain black pants and a tunic that had a patch on her shoulder. I couldn't read Drakconese, despite my best efforts, though I assumed it was maybe her name or a company logo.

It was oddly human, seeing a patch denoting what business I assumed she worked for. I'd seen other species that did something similar because why would humans alone have something like that? Still, the patch, for whatever reason, felt so human, like Tamkolvanloknol wasn't so different from Earth.

A shadow crossed over the street, and I instinctively ducked. A drakcol flew over us, leaving a sinister shadow on the ground. Okay, so maybe it was somewhat different here.

My shoulders hunched as I chased her. Whenever a drakcol flew above me, I flinched, unable to shed that prey feeling. One of them could swoop out of the sky and pick me up like they were a hawk and I was a squirrel. Not that any drakcol had a reason to, or that they could, you know, see or touch me.

The drakcol woman I was stalking darted between buildings and broke through the tight alley to a wide port in the middle of a ring of buildings, surrounded by huge trees with blue-black trunks and vibrant red leaves.

Shuttles lifted and lowered at regular intervals while people dashed on and off. She boarded a shuttle that might as well have been a gray box, and I followed her. I hesitated at the ramp as the drakcol woman continued inside. What if she went too far away, and I couldn't get back to Zoltilvoxfyn? What if he was lost to me?

I forged forward. It would be fine. I'd wandered the universe. I didn't need him. So what if he saw me? It didn't truly matter unless I had the urge to talk to Seth again or I got bored of no one talking back to me, so I should be good for another twenty-three years, right?

Chapter 8

ANOTHER GHOST.

Caleb

People were crammed into the shuttle, most were drakcol but not all. My friend, I guessed I would call her, sat in the back, her foot tapping on the smooth metal floor.

"What's wrong?" I asked her, taking in her pinched expression and tense muscles. Her tail slashed the air, smacking the person next to her who growled in warning. She quickly apologized. "I wish you could hear me. Whatever's wrong will be okay."

I mean, I didn't know that, but I hoped for her sake it would be.

When the shuttle landed, it jarred everyone besides me inside. The woman leaped to her feet and pushed her way through the crowd, sending off rounds of growls that she ignored. I trailed her, sliding through people, leaving a wake of shivers in my path.

She rushed down the street, and I paused in my step for a moment. This part of the capital, if we were still in the capital, wasn't as nice, not that it wasn't beautiful or was rundown by any means. The buildings were shorter, though they still had spires and plenty of windows framed with balconies. Plants were still plentiful, but they weren't as prominently displayed, and many drakcol wore uniforms versus street clothes.

My friend ran down the street, feet pounding with every step. She stopped in front of a wide building with numerous windows and terraces that wrapped around each level. The glass doors slid open, seamless with the windows beside it, and she dashed inside.

One look was enough for me to realize what kind of business this was. Injured people sat on metal stools while harried people ran long instruments over them and asked questions. The walls and floor were sterile gray without a trace of plants anywhere.

It was a medical facility.

The woman headed down a hallway without any bland artwork or even boring scenery pictures to liven it up, then started up a staircase. Like the apartment building, it had a wide square space for drakcol to fly up, but she ignored it. On the third floor, she stopped in front of a door and palmed the panel next to it, making a bell chime.

The door slid open, and an older drakcol with jagged pink scales sat next to a desk crowded with tablets. His hair was steel-gray and cropped close to his head, and he wore the dullest, most boring, gray uniform. It was like a onesie made of scrub material that had a high collar and no sleeves, showing his thin arms. He gave her a small smile, revealing his toothless gums. That, plus his jagged scales, told me this dude was old. Like dirt old.

"Tinlorray," he rasped, waving her in. His claws were so long they were curling back toward his skeletal fingers. "Enter. I thought you weren't going to make it."

"Sorry I'm late, Dr. Maklownil." She tilted her head to the side, offering her throat, which he ignored.

"Let me see them," he said, gesturing to the stool in the cramped office.

Tinlorray spread her gray wings that each had a single talon midway down the bony ridge on top. The reason why she walked instead of flying became immediately apparent. An angry red stretched over the delicate membrane, and her right wing was oddly crumpled, the bone broken. The doctor tutted as he examined the massive wings that nearly spread from wall to wall, knocking some screens off the desk, which he ignored.

He ran a long wand with a wide flat tip about the diameter of a baseball over one wing, then the next. Dr. Maklownil grunted at whatever the readings were on his tablet, bony fingers clacking on the glass. "Your left wing should heal normally with some scarring. The right..." he trailed off.

"It won't recover, will it?"

"Not without reconstructive surgery," he said.

"Which is something you can't do here."

"No, this facility is not equipped with the necessary surgical suites. We can send an appeal to the Seeker Council for a medical facility in the capital to do the surgery, but they are busy. It will take time, though you will have the surgery eventually. This is a delicate procedure and will require an expert. I would be honored to help you file the necessary paperwork, of course.

"But more than that, you have my apologies. I can keep treating it so it doesn't pain you, but your flying days are over unless you have the surgery, even then the nerve damage may be too severe."

"I understand," she said before biting her thin bottom lip. "How is he?"

The doctor stood, exiting the cramped office. I followed the two of them down the hall and up to the fifth floor. They eventually stepped into a long room with a window opposite of the door. The never-ending breeze fluttered in, stirring the sheer curtains and the green ferns on each side. More plants filled the terrace as well as a couple of stools. Four beds lined either side, and monitors, flashing with blue lights and unreadable symbols, hung above them.

A mountain of a man lay in the bed nearest to the window. The drakcol had dove-gray scales accented by shoots of emerald green and gold. His reddish-brown hair was shaved on one side, revealing a massive scar that ran from near his temple all the way to the back of his head. The skin around it was mottled with the same green and gold around his scales.

He was handsome with his long face, thinner top lip and plump bottom one, and wide forehead, but something was wrong. I couldn't put my finger on it, but something was off. It was like he was empty.

Tinlorray stopped at his bedside and grabbed the lifeless man's hand. "Doctor?"

"Yolkeltod has no brain activity. He's gone, Tinlorray. No matter what I do, I cannot bring him back."

Her chin trembled, and she smoothed the deep blue blanket over him. "My little brother will be fine. He has to be. He's a warrior soul, a fighter."

"There is nothing to be done. We are merely keeping his body alive."

"No," she snarled.

The doctor didn't act bothered, standing beside her, not speaking, as tears rolled down her cheeks.

My jaw worked side to side. "I was wrong. It won't be okay. Nothing will be fine."

A man came up behind Tinlorray, his long brown hair hanging in a sheet down his wide back. I started when he looked in my direction. I was seeing double. The man in front of me was the same as the one in the bed. His blue eyes stayed on me and his nose crinkled.

"Who, or better yet, what are you?"

He was dead or rather a spirit like me. Yolkeltod wasn't the first ghost I'd met before. They were few and far between, shockingly. Most people didn't hang around long.

"I'm Caleb Smith. Human."

Yolkeltod jerked. "You can see me?"

"Yep. I'm dead, and so are you, I guess. Sort of. I mean, maybe you're not. I'm not sure. I'm not an expert. But you're here and there, so... yeah. Dead."

He chuckled. "Like I hadn't figured that out."

"Yeah, sorry."

He lifted his palms, which I was pretty sure was the equivalent of shrugging. "It's not your fault."

Tinlorray sniffled and drew my attention. I stepped back; whereas, Yolkeltod crowded her, trying to soothe her. She didn't sense his presence and kept straightening the blanket over Yolkeltod's body.

Dr. Maklownil slipped out, leaving Tinlorray to her grief.

I watched, feeling voyeuristic. The longer she cried and the more Yolkeltod tried to comfort her, the more my emotions swelled. I wanted to go home. It had been years since I'd seen my family. However, even if I had been there, it wouldn't have changed anything. Their grief had long since subsided; I was a distant memory now.

Zoltilvoxfyn. He heard me. Suddenly, I needed to see him. Talk to him. Have him talk back. A real conversation, not my empty babbling. Maybe I shouldn't have run off. I mean, moving on wasn't the worst idea. I *had* thought about doing it when I headed to Earth.

It might be time to consider the idea once more.

When I started to back out of the room, Yolkeltod called out, "Wait."

"What?"

"Can we talk? Please. You're the first spirit I've seen."

I nodded, which made his forehead crease. Nodding didn't mean the same thing in Drakcon culture. I figured it out pretty quickly when Seth had kept doing it and confused the hell out of everyone.

I said, "We can talk."

"Thank you."

Chapter 9

A DEAD GUY WHO'S NOT DEAD. INTERESTING.

Caleb

Yolkeltod and I stepped into the hallway. It would've been weird to have a conversation next to his crying sister and lifeless body. Or at least, I would've found it weird. Maybe it was a normal Tuesday for him. I didn't know what the hell he did with his time.

I sat on the floor near the wall, so people wouldn't traipse through us. Yolkeltod hovered over me, his tail lashing.

"Sit down," I said with a wide grin to soften my order.

I didn't know for sure if drakcol took being ordered well, especially with him being a warrior soul. Drakcol believed in four soul types: warrior, seeker, spiritual, and creator. Warrior souls were more aggressive, I assumed. Once again, no one had explained it when I was haunting them. It was infuriating to know bits and pieces, and not know if what I thought was true was actually correct.

Anyway, him looming over me wasn't a great way to talk, and this wouldn't be a fun conversation. I remembered when I'd run into my first ghost.

She'd been an elderly woman in the same neighborhood who passed away a few days before me. She'd been extremely sweet, explaining what she knew, which hadn't been much. It had been stressful, and I'd been a bastard to her for the simple fact she heard me. I took every ounce of anger I had out on her. I'd demanded answers. The why of everything, and she of course hadn't known, which pissed me off.

She passed on a few days later.

Stiffly, Yolkeltod sank to the floor across from me. His tail didn't stop moving, and he crossed his arms over his broad chest. He was a massive dude in height and width. Well into the six-foot range, maybe even seven foot, and had muscles upon muscles. I appeared positively puny next to him.

"You can ask me anything," I said. "My Drakconese is really good."

"How long have you been dead?"

"Twenty-three cycles," I replied while saying a silent thank you to Seth.

"Why?"

I knew what he meant, but I still asked, "What do you mean?"

"Why me? Why were me and Tinlorray in that shuttle accident? Why can't I get back into my body? What's the point of everything?"

"Well, you don't ask small questions," I commented, not surprised. I'd asked basically the same thing. Death was apparently the same for humans and drakcol. People were people. Strip away the casings and we all hungered to know the same things.

"I wish I could tell you," I replied. "I really wish I could, but I don't know. I'm not some afterlife guide. I'm just a guy who happened to be walking by. I have no answers for you."

His tail went lifeless by his thigh before curling around his calf.

"How did you get injured?" I asked.

"A couple of months ago, Tinlorray and I took a shuttle into the capital for work, and it malfunctioned, crashing. We were among the few survivors."

"I'm sorry."

"It's not as bad for me. I worry about my older sister. I'm all she has."

"I'm sorry," I repeated. Those words were incredibly small in the face of what he'd revealed, but I didn't know what else to say.

"Do you have any idea how I can get back into my body?"

"No," I said, but Zoltilvoxfyn surfaced in my thoughts. "But I might know someone who does. We can go meet him."

"Where?"

"He lives in the palace."

Yolkeltod said, "I can't leave."

"What?"

"I can't leave. I tried. I can't get past the door of the hospital. It's like a shield is stopping me."

"Really?" I asked. "It must be because your body's here. I have no trouble wandering around, and trust me, I'm not from around here."

"I would have never guessed."

I laughed.

A slight smile pulled on his lips. "You must be good at this spirit thing. Can you touch stuff?"

"Not really. If I focus incredibly hard, I can move little things, but I can't feel them. Though be careful doing that. If you expend too much energy, you'll vanish for a while."

His expression fell—something I understood. I craved to feel something too. Anything. I scooted until we were right in front of each other. I wished to pat him or give him a hug, but ghosts were unable to touch each other, which sucked. I was a tactile person. I loved hugging, high-fives, and snuggling. None of which I could do as a ghost.

In an effort to lighten the mood, I said, "But you can pass through walls or jump out of windows."

"How am I not falling through the floor?"

"Because you expect not to. You're used to gravity and the normal rules of the world. It takes a while to unlearn it." I focused on the floor, and slowly, I started to sink, disappearing. Yolkeltod cried out, and I chuckled. "Don't worry." I concentrated, and I sat solidly once again.

"Can you teach me that?"

"Sure. It takes a while to forget all the constants you're used to running your life."

"How long will it take?"

I shrugged. "I don't know. As long as it does."

His eyes gravitated to the doorway again. "How long will I be here?"

"I don't know. I've never had the urge to move on. Most spirits I've met, which haven't been many, left within a few days of their deaths. But you're not dead."

"The doctor said I had no brain activity."

"Yeah, because your soul is wandering around here," I argued. "Don't give up. I'll talk to the person I know who can see me. Maybe he can help."

Yolkeltod's head cocked to the side, allowing me to see the black cuff near the tip of his ear and the chain that threaded through the cartilage down to his lobe. "You said the person was in the palace. You're talking about Prince Zoltilvoxfyn, aren't you? Are the rumors true? He can see souls?"

I nodded, then stopped myself. "Yes."

"How did you meet him?"

"I wandered around the palace, then went straight up to him and called him pretty. This was before I knew he could see me," I said, laughing.

His mouth hung open. "You flirted with the prince?"

"Unintentionally."

Yolkeltod smiled, which stretched his lips wide and made his eyes close. It was such a joyous expression that a grin grew on my own face. He chuckled. "You flirted with the one person who can see you." His smile dimmed. "One of the people who can see you."

I had no way of comforting him. I wanted to say the right words to make it all better, but I couldn't think of any besides empty platitudes, so I kept quiet.

After a few moments, he asked, "How did you get here?"

"It's a long story. I've been wandering the universe for cycles, but I decided to stay here because of Seth Harris," I said, then quickly added, "The human who married Prince Kalvoxrencol."

"I might be brain-dead, but I know about him. He and Prince Kalvoxrencol have been the main news for months, and the prince left over a cycle ago to travel to Earth," he remarked, tail lazily moving. When it neared me, the tuft of hair at the end of his tail disappeared into my knee. I didn't react, because I doubted he meant to do it.

Yet again, his gaze gravitated toward the door where his body was, and I didn't blame him. He swallowed, his throat bobbing in his long neck.

"You can tell me anything." I'd heard or said it all before.

"I'm scared."

"Of?"

"Leaving Tinlorray. Death doesn't bother me, but she'll be alone if I go. We don't have parents or other family members. All we have is each other."

"I will do whatever I can to reunite you with your body. There has to be a way."

"I don't believe that, but thank you." He started toward the door as if he was pulled by a string, and I followed him stiffly. The edges of his soul were starting to blur while color leached out of him, turning him transparent. I recognized what was happening. I'd seen other ghosts pass on, and Yolkeltod was about to leave.

"Give me time to talk to Zoltilvoxfyn," I pleaded, following him.

Tinlorray sat next to his body, holding his hand in hers.

"Don't go." I didn't want to be the only one here.

He looked back at me, the light from the window growing as he blurred, becoming even fainter. "I'm glad I met you, Caleb Smith. I think all I needed was to admit I was afraid. Maybe that's all you need to do as well."

"I'm not afraid," I replied honestly. "What about Tinlorray?"

"Watch out for her, please."

"I can't."

"Please," Yolkeltod said, growing brighter and brighter. He smiled, radiating happiness. "I think you're special, Caleb Smith, and what she needs."

"I'm not."

"Promise me you will take care of her."

The words spilled from my lips. "I promise."

He grinned, and from one breath to the next, he was gone.

Chapter 10

WELL, MAYBE IT'S TIME FOR ME TO GO.

Caleb

I sat on the ground next to Yolkeltod's bed, leaning against the wall with my arms resting on my bent knees. My gaze never wavered from Tinlorray, and she never looked away from her little brother. He was gone. Everything that made Yolkeltod *Yolkeltod* was no longer here.

It hadn't taken much for his soul to pass on. It was like that for most ghosts; well, every ghost I'd met except me. I didn't understand how they all moved on when I couldn't.

Right after I died, I'd tried to pass on to whatever, if anything, follows this existence, but I couldn't. I didn't have any urge to move on. Why that was, I had no idea. Every ghost I'd talked to had known what held them back. Yolkeltod had stayed because of his sister. When he finally let her go, he'd left.

What was I holding on to? I needed to answer that question if I ever hoped to leave this place.

As the sun sank in the horizon and the three moons started to rise, Tinlorray stood, her movements jerky. I followed her out of the hospital and down the street to a building resembling the apartments in the capital, though shorter and it had purple flowering trees growing on the flat roof. Like every other building I'd seen on this planet, it had plenty of windows and balconies.

She entered through the door on the ground, went up the stairs, then stepped into an apartment with two bedrooms, spacious living and dining areas, and a generous balcony covered in plants. Tinlorray must not live in the building I'd followed her from. Perhaps she worked in the other building?

Tinlorray promptly collapsed onto the couch and began to sob. I settled beside her. I wondered if she knew he was gone. If the grief was finally becoming real now that Yolkeltod wasn't beside her? Maybe after she let it all out she would be able to release his body.

"I'm sorry," I told her. "I will watch over you, like I promised, but I don't know what good it will do."

I stayed by her side until she cried herself to sleep. When I reached the street, I hesitated. I had no idea where I was or how to get back to the palace. Tinlorray had taken a shuttle, which meant the palace was probably quite some distance from wherever this was.

My best bet was to wait until morning and hope Tinlorray traveled the same way she had yesterday. I sat on the ground and leaned against the building, blindly watching the city and the people rushing by until everything went quiet and the moons hung overhead.

The image of Yolkeltod vanishing wouldn't leave my thoughts. I tried to think about something, anything else, but my mind circled around it, replaying it over and over again. He wasn't the first ghost I'd seen vanish, but I hoped he was the last. I hated watching others leave when I was stuck here.

My eyes lifted to the gleaming stars in the sky. It had been so long since I'd been on Earth that I'd forgotten what my own sky looked like. There were a lot of things I'd forgotten. The feel of the wind in my hair and the sun on my skin. The taste of food. The smell of fresh-cut grass in summer. The sound of my family laughing. Hell, I'd forgotten what my own face looked like—I hadn't seen it in over twenty years.

A dim ache grew within me, so faint it was barely present, but it was there—I was sure of it. I missed my home so badly, but the chance of me seeing Earth again was slim. Not many people traveled that way, and I couldn't expect Zoltilvoxfyn to journey across the universe to take me home.

The night passed quickly with me watching the stars and the world moving around me while I stayed the same. When morning came with a burst of light and the warbling cries of birds, Tinlorray exited the apartment building. I dogged her steps. Her shoulders were hunched and her tail was lifeless on the ground.

I wished to speak with her, but what would I say? I had nothing. Man, too bad Nana wasn't here. She always had something wise to say. Something to help. A sad smile twisted my lips as I thought about when I came out to her.

I'd been worried that she wouldn't love me anymore. That me liking guys would somehow preclude me from her affection. Nana had yanked me into her arms and told me how much she loved me, then promptly said that if some guy broke my heart she would smack him in the balls with her cane.

Tinlorray headed to the same port as yesterday and boarded a shuttle, so I was hopeful it would take me back to the capital. She sat on a stool near the back, shoulders slumped. It was a miracle she even got on a shuttle with the accident that claimed her wings and her brother hanging over her.

When the ship docked, I caught a glimpse of the palace spearing the sky in the distance. So I was back. I took note of the shuttle markings. It had to be a bus-like system. I would need to ask someone, probably Wyn or Urgg through Zoltilvoxfyn, about it so I could see Tinlorray again. I'd made a promise, and I intended to keep it.

I followed her until she rounded the corner, then I headed to the palace. If I was going to pass on, I would need Zoltilvoxfyn's help. No doubt he would be smug that I'd relented so easily. Then again, he might not be. I didn't know him well.

Before I went, though, I would make sure Tinlorray was alright, Seth was safe, and Zoltilvoxfyn found his smile.

Zoltilvoxfyn

My eyes were heavy as I plucked withered blooms off the bush. I was supposed to be in hand-to-hand combat class right now. Kalvoxrencol had come to pick me up, leaving Seth to some much-needed alone time with Urgg, but I turned him down.

I'd been unable to sleep, spending the whole night in my greenhouse or the terrace garden waiting for Caleb to return. He hadn't. Retiring had been impossible because Caleb didn't know where my quarters were and he wouldn't have been able to find me if he needed me.

Now, I worried he wasn't going to return. I'd pressed harder yesterday than I should have. I barely knew him; I couldn't predict his reaction. Still, I'd pressed. I tried to defend myself with the thought that I'd never met a spirit who didn't know why they remained on the mortal plane, but that wasn't enough. I should've known or been more sensitive to the possibility of him being upset, but I hadn't been. Caleb had fled, perhaps for forever. The mere thought of that sent my soul racing. I'd never met a spirit who called to me like he did, and it frightened me.

He was so alive, even in death.

My fingers moved automatically as they cleaned the bush of wilted flowers and dropped them into a metal container for composting. A weight pressed down on my shoulders and strangled my throat. I couldn't stop thinking about every single thing I'd said yesterday and how I did it all wrong. Mistakes. So many mistakes. I scolded myself viciously. I'd been an idiot, a horrid idiot. I should've known better. I shouldn't have pushed Caleb or used Seth to get him to open up. And Seth. I'd scared him.

I yanked off a dead flower and berated myself. I desired to be friends with Seth, and this wasn't the way to start.

A worthlessness grew in my mind with every passing moment and made me curl inward. Intrusive thoughts about running away or disappearing bloomed like malignant weeds, fueled by my guilt. My white hair hung around me like a shield, and I kept my face downward to hide the growing tears. If any of my family saw, they would worry. Another thing I had to feel guilty for.

"Zoltilvoxfyn," a hesitant voice said.

I whirled around, tail thrashing. Caleb stood at the entrance of my greenhouse. His hands were shoved in his trouser pockets and he rocked forward on his toes, looking anywhere besides me.

"Caleb." I dropped the container, sending ruined blooms tumbling across the moss ground. I rushed toward him, scouring his thin frame. "Are you well?"

His head bobbed. "I'm fine."

"Where were you?"

"I went exploring, and things took an odd turn."

"What things?" I asked, stopping right in front of him. My tail swished in his direction, quaking with the urge to curl around his ankle. I paused. I wasn't a physically affectionate person, even with my family, but for some reason, I longed to touch Caleb.

His gaze skittered to the side, and I shifted until there was barely any space between us. I needed to move back, but I couldn't force myself to. Even though he was dead, there were still permissions, such as personal space, which needed to be discussed if I was to move closer.

My stomach dropped and my soul pounded. I wanted to move closer. Caleb was a spirit, but I yearned to stay right beside him. Why?

Not many mediums had been recorded in Drakcon history, and I'd read each of their logs and everything they'd written. All of them had said basically the same thing. It was our responsibility to help wayward souls, but we shouldn't get attached to them, because our presence might become a hindrance to their journey.

I forced myself to take a couple of steps back from Caleb, though it physically hurt to do so. "What happened, Little Soul?"

"I was wandering around the capital and saw Urgg."

I didn't know why that was a problem. I knew Urgg well. They were mated to Captain Talvax, who was a friend of the family—Talvax had grown up with my mother. She and Urgg were staying in the capital until the Admiral Ven's updates were completed, and I expected to see them often, especially since Urgg was Seth's oravirven—the one who would guide Seth through being a Crystal-bound mate with Kalvoxrencol.

"When I was leaving their home, I saw a woman," Caleb said, staring at my plants.

"And?"

"She went to a medical facility, and I saw a ghost."

"Was the spirit mean to you?"

"No," Caleb said with a shake of his head. "His body was still alive. Brain dead, the doctor said."

I'd read about something similar from one of my predecessors. They'd tried for months to reunite the body and soul, but nothing worked. Eventually, the soul had passed on.

"He was upset," I surmised.

"I couldn't do anything to help, but he needed to talk, and he..."

I waited for him to continue, but Caleb remained silent, which was odd for him. In the short time I'd known him, he seldom stopped talking. "He what?"

"He moved on. Right in front of me."

Once again, I approached before I'd even thought about it. "Are you well?"

He lifted and lowered his shoulders. I desperately needed to ask Kalvoxrencol if he knew what that meant. I would research it myself, but the Cohort and the Council of Seekers had restricted access to the knowledge taken from Earth. Those mated to humans, Kalvoxrencol, and select scientists, such as Doctor Qinlin who was caring for Seth's medical needs, were allowed access to the information. In a few months, or perhaps in a cycle, the information would become available to all.

"He asked me to watch over his sister." His blue eyes met mine, so full of sadness and guilt that my instincts demanded I gather him into my arms and soothe away every line of stress. "If I had managed to convince him to stay, would you have been able to... I don't know, shove his soul and body back together?"

"No," I replied instantly, trying to lessen his guilt. "There is no way, as far as I'm aware."

Caleb sagged. "Thank you for that."

"You don't need to thank me." My wings rustled against my back.

His face lifted, and I swallowed, looking down at him. "I do," Caleb said in a low voice. "I felt horrible all night, and now, you made me feel better."

"I'm glad," I choked out and swayed toward him, mouth dry. My chest brushed his, and a cold, fizzy feeling started, hardening my nipples, which brought me back to reality. I was crossing a boundary. I stepped back, hands fisting. "I need to apologize."

"For what?"

"For pressuring you yesterday to move on. It's your decision. We'd barely met, and I tried to force you to do something you weren't ready for. I must apologize. I would like to help you, though, in whatever capacity you need, Caleb."

"It's fine," he said. "We're getting to know each other. It's not a problem. There are bound to be snarls."

What did growling have to do with this situation? Unless he was angry? He didn't act mad.

"But," Caleb continued, "we'll figure it out. It'll be fine. I have so many questions, and no doubt some will be inappropriate, so I'll have to apologize. It's normal. I think. I mean that's how it was with my friends back when I was alive. We're people, and we're doing the best we can. At least I am. I think most people are."

Something relaxed inside of me. He was talking again.

"Besides—" he broke off.

"Yes?"

"I think it might be time for me to move on. Meeting Yolkeltod made me realize that I can't watch ghosts vanish time and time again and that I don't want to be stuck here forever. It's time for me to go to whatever comes after this, even if it's nothing."

Something hard formed in my stomach at the thought of Caleb disappearing, but I said, "I will help you."

Chapter 11

WHAT'S MY TETHER?

Caleb

Zoltilvoxfyn worked around his greenhouse, dragging with each step. He'd agreed to help me, and shockingly, he hadn't lorded over me the fact I'd changed my mind so quickly. He must be nicer than I'd thought. I mean, I didn't know him. Maybe he was a saint, who knew? I would, soon, of course, because I didn't plan to leave his side all that much, barring stalking Seth and Tinlorray—not stalking, guarding, protecting. Whatever.

I skipped after him, whistling. Every pressure that weighed me down yesterday had vanished as soon as I talked to Zoltilvoxfyn. He'd banished my guilt with a few simple words. He was like a beam of sunshine breaking up my cloudy day. I felt nothing, but I swore warmth came off Zoltilvoxfyn, and I wanted to bask in it.

When he almost dropped a potted succulent that, I kid you not, was neon orange with green polka dots, I asked, "Are you alright?"

"I didn't sleep last night."

"Why?"

His tail slashed behind him. "I was worried you wouldn't come back, and if you did, you don't know where my quarters are."

"I'm not helpless," I commented. Besides, what did he think would happen to me? A monster that ate souls would swoop out of the sky or something? Like really, what could happen? "I would've waited for you here or wandered around the palace."

"I don't think you're helpless. I was simply available if you needed me."

"Thanks." An urge to hug him swept through me. God, I missed touching people. I was starved for it. I would give almost anything to curl up against his broad chest.

He cleared his throat and went back to work, but his tail kept twitching incessantly while his wings rustled on his back. What did they look like? I imagined his wings were no different than any of the other drakcol's I'd seen, but I wanted to see *his*.

"I'm going to have to give you an endearment," I announced. Drakcol didn't have nicknames the way we did. They didn't shorten their names, because they had some kind of class structure attached to them, which no one had explained. But they did give fun endearments, like Kal's brothers calling him "Pest."

"Why?"

"Your name is too long."

"I am a prince."

Like I'd said, class structure. "So I can't give you one?"

Zoltilvoxfyn peered over his shoulder. "What name?"

My lips pursed as I thought it over. His name left a lot of choices for nicknames, the most obvious ones: Zol or Fyn. But I didn't want to shorten his name like a human, but rather call him something another drakcol might.

Suddenly, I bounced up to him. "Sunshine"

"Excuse me?"

"I'm going to call you Sunshine." He was my light now.

He stared at me with his impossibly green eyes, and I held his gaze. Eventually, he replied, "Fine."

"Sunshine," I said. The Drakconese word was three syllables and hard to pronounce, but if I said it in English, he wouldn't understand me.

He muttered, "At least it's longer than what Seth calls Kalvoxrencol."

"So how do I move on to the Great Beyond or whatever you call it?"

"I do not know."

"Seriously? Aren't you my guide to whatever comes next?"

"I haven't met many spirits, and they all knew why they were still here. You have no idea?"

"Nope. None. Absolutely blank. I'm floating around, basking in the cluelessness of my existence."

"Interesting." He started toward the door of the greenhouse. "If you don't mind, I would like to eat while we talk about this."

That sounded suspiciously like a date, which oddly made me feel rather light, like I could fly. Ooo, flying. That would be cool. I'd tried again and again to fly, but I couldn't unlearn gravity's control on me.

It was too constant, and my soul refused to let go. The most I'd been able to accomplish was floating, and only for a little bit. Not even close to actual flying.

"Sure," I said. "I don't mind." *A date with a hot drakcol*, I sang in my mind, though I couldn't stop humming.

We left the terrace and went to a different part of the palace I hadn't seen. His suite was on the other side of the palace from Seth and Kalvoxrencol's.

Two arched windows were across from the door, overlooking the garden; the balcony off them was covered with even more plants. The living room had a divan on a thick rug that spread over the floor. Plants filled every available space, including light green and blue vines covering the ceiling. To the right was a wide open space with a cylindrical dummy that I assumed was for fighting. A half wall separated the living room from a space with a low table and woven mats. Much like Kalvoxrencol and Seth's rooms, two doors were off the dining area.

To the right of the front entrance was another door that probably led to his bedroom. I peeked at Zoltilvoxfyn, then back at his room, fighting the urge to explore. Sunshine would see me, though, and I might make him uncomfortable if I looked at all of his stuff.

Since I died, I'd become extremely nosy and lost most, if not all, of my manners. No one ever saw me, so peeking inside people's medicine cabinets wasn't rude. Well, it was, and Nana would've scolded me something fierce, but no one knew. So no harm done. Besides, it was interesting to learn what different aliens kept in their private spaces.

Zoltilvoxfyn changed that. His presence stopped my normal snooping and subsequent commentary about whatever I'd found.

He went to the dining area and thumbed through the choices on the dispenser before coming my way with a plate covered in fruit, bread, and meat (a normal drakcol meal as far as I'd witnessed). He sat on the couch, crossing his legs and resting his plate on them.

"You can sit next to me if my eating doesn't bother you," he offered.

I plunked down next to him. "So what do I do? How do I move on? What's wrong with me? Do you think something's wrong with me? What if I can't move on? Will I be stuck here forever? Oh my god, what if I'm cursed? Do you even believe in curses? Does curses even mean the same thing in Drakconese?"

"Well," he said, taking a bite of a purple fruit and showing off his gleaming canines, seemingly unbothered by my chatter, "we need to ascertain what your tether to the mortal plane is."

We. He'd said we. I liked that. A lot. *We.* I stifled a giggle. I sat crisscross-applesauce and scooted as close as possible before my knees brushed him and ruined the illusion that I was alive and this wasn't a date. I would've never had a chance with him if I was alive. And, let's be honest, this wasn't a date, but I had to get my kicks from somewhere. Zoltilvoxfyn didn't need to know.

No harm, no foul.

"How are we going to figure that out? Do you have like a..." I stalled, unable to think of a Drakconese word for "ray" or "sensor," so I settled with, "prodding technology?"

"No. There is no technology that will aid us in this. I will read through all of the previous medium documentation, and you will tell me about your life and afterlife in the hopes we can figure out what it is."

My knees bounced. "I can do that. Talking is my *jam*."

His forehead furrowed at the last word. I'd said in English because I didn't know the equivalent in Drakconese. Zoltilvoxfyn ignored it and said, "Tell me about your family."

"What's to say? They moved on already."

He took a bite of flatbread. "That's not talking, Caleb."

So I proceeded to talk. My family was ordinary. My parents had been office workers, I was the youngest of four kids. I'd had plenty of cousins and aunts and uncles. Nana, my dad's mom, had been a huge part of my life. I'd spent every summer with her in Bakersfield.

Sunshine listened, tail smoothly sliding back and forth. Occasionally, he would pose a question, then fall silent again. His head cocked to the side as he listened. My gaze landed on the studs in his tapered ears and down to the long earrings in his lobes. The golden chains twinkled in the light as rough-cut emeralds brushed his neck. My fingers twitched, longing to touch them, to trail them down to his long neck.

Unbidden, my eyes flicked to his chest. Maybe he had other things pierced. I swallowed. I was unlikely to find out, unfortunately.

"Caleb?"

I started. "What?" I asked thickly.

"You stopped talking."

He'd distracted me. The piercing in his septum distracted me too. I had a random urge to flick the golden ring with my tongue, which was new. Jewelry had never been a turn-on for me, but Zoltilvoxfyn wore it well.

"Caleb," he said again, his head dipping to catch my eye. "Are you well?"

No. I was pretty sure I wasn't. I was pretty damn sure I was developing a crush on Zoltilvoxfyn. Whether it was because he was hot or because he was nice or because he saw me didn't matter. It would never work out. I was dead.

"Why do you wear so much jewelry?" I asked.

"Excuse me?"

"Every drakcol I've seen wears a considerable amount of jewelry."

Sunshine took another bite of food. "I've never even thought about that. It's simply a part of our culture. If I had to guess, I believe it came from when we were warring clans before the Crystal chose the first empress who united us. I know jewelry was taken as spoils of war. When we killed an enemy, we would strip their bodies of valuables, claiming them for ourselves. The more jewelry signaled who the greater warriors were. We no longer do such, but we all still wear jewelry."

My eyes ran over his multiple piercings, longing to kiss them, tug on them, play with them. The knowledge I couldn't, in no way, dampened the desire.

"Little Soul, you stopped speaking again. Are you well?"

I forced a smile to my lips. "I'm fine."

"Then continue."

"I'm bored of talking about myself. Tell me about you."

"Why? You're who's important right now."

His words burned my soul. "Because I want you to."

He turned on the couch, resting his back against the tall arm. "What do you wish to know?"

Everything, honestly. But I had to start somewhere. "When did you start seeing ghosts?"

"I always remember seeing people that others did not. I told my parents and many others when I was young, and I spent some time in different medical facilities getting tested."

"They didn't know it was your inner fire thing?" I asked.

"Mediums are rare, exceedingly so. One of the Crystal's priests was the first to figure it out when I perfectly described his older sister who'd died. She had a message to pass on to him, which I did."

I shifted nearer to him, needing at least the illusion that I could touch him. "What happened after you found out?"

"It was nice in some ways," he said, elbows resting on his knees. His hair covered him like a cloak, distracting me as I followed the white strands hanging around his body. "Before I'd found out, people thought I was insane, and many children teased me. I was odd. Though after my inner fire was known, many people still poked at me."

"Being the butt of the joke is never pleasant. I was teased because of my height."

"So you *are* short for your species?" he asked, and I couldn't help but laugh. He asked it in such an earnest way like he'd been truly wondering.

“I’m shorter than average for men. Seth is about average height for human males.” Well, in the US, but my Drakconese wasn’t good enough to explain the different countries and ethnicities Earth had.

“I like your height.”

I practically preened. “Thanks. I love your gift.”

A laugh, a real one, tumbled out of his lips, sending a thrill through me as toasty sunlight rushed over me. True warmth. It was distant, but there. I was sure of it. New, but oh so real.

“I’m sure you do,” he said, practically bent in half as he chuckled.

“Why did people make fun of you for it?”

He sobered up so fast that I instantly regretted the question. He said, “They thought I was lying, and I was different. People don’t treat different well.”

“It’s the same on my planet.”

“Humans and drakcol are more similar than I would have guessed. Though I should have known because Seth and Kalvoxrencol are able to mind speak.”

“What?”

“Drakcol who are bonded by the Crystal can speak mind to mind. Usually, it doesn’t work with other species, but Seth and Kalvoxrencol can.”

“Aren’t all drakcol mates bonded by the Crystal?”

“There are two different types of mates: chosen and bound. Chosen is when a drakcol starts to perceive someone as their mate, usually after they have fallen in love. The mate bond naturally forms. Bound mates are when a drakcol seeks the Crystal for their soulmate, if they have one. The soulmates are genetically linked in a ceremony, then reaffirm or shatter their bond in front of the Crystal."

"That's awesome."

"It is," he replied.

"Why doesn't everyone do that?"

"Not everyone has a soulmate, and learning that you don't have one is hard to accept."

I got that.

"There is also the fear of what might happen."

"What do you mean?" I asked.

"Whether bound or chosen, we brave the threat of rejection or death," Zoltilvoxfyn said. "Drakcol don't often survive the loss of our mates. We love too wholly and completely. If our mate rejects us or they die, chosen or bound, we most often wither away. Mates are important, and we mate but once."

That was so romantic and yet sad. To have your whole life dependent on another like that was terrifying. It was a wonder any drakcol fell in love or sought the Crystal.

"So," I said, changing the subject, "you have four brothers?"

"Three older. One younger."

"I have three brothers, all older."

"So you are the pest for your family?" he asked.

I chuckled. "Most definitely."

When his eyes crinkled in humor, I swore I felt something again—something soft and slight, but so warm.

The three moons and unfamiliar stars hung over me. I was sitting on Zoltilvoxfyn's balcony, watching the city that was full of lights. The glass spires twinkled in the moonlight, giving it a magical air. He'd told me I could stay here overnight, and I got the impression from the way he insisted, multiple times, that he would feel more comfortable if I did.

Would I sit here every night? No, I would not. It would bore the ever-living hell out of me. But it wouldn't hurt to sit here for the first night to make him happy.

A breeze blew through the leaves, rattling them, and I pretended it ruffled my hair, even though I'd forgotten what that truly felt like.

Twenty-three years was a very long time.

I was pretty sure that I hadn't imagined feeling something before. It had been more than emotional phantoms. It had been physical. A whisper-soft touch on my hand when Zoltilvoxfyn stared at me, and then the warmth when he laughed. I felt it. Truly. Faint and basically non-existent, but it was like a brand burning my memories.

I burrowed against my knees, hiding a smile. It was ridiculous, this blooming crush, but I couldn't stop it, and if I was going to be honest with myself, I didn't want to. How long had it been since I'd cared about someone?

Yes, I cared about Seth because he was a human far from home, but I didn't know him. Wyn seemed nice, as did Captain Talvax, Urgg, and Commander Monqilcolnen, but I didn't truly care about any of them on a personal level.

Sunshine was different.

Somehow, though, I doubted he was interested in dating a ghost.

Chapter 12

POOR WYN FINDS OUT THE TRUTH.

Caleb

I sat on the ground right outside of the greenhouse, watching Zoltilvoxfyn give Seth a potted plant. He wouldn't meet Seth's gaze as he explained its care and what type of hybrid it was. Seth nodded along, eyes equally on the ground, and one of his fingers traced the round, spotted leaves, the stark pink a drastic contrast against his pale skin. Kal was nowhere to be seen, which surprised me. He seemed incapable of leaving Seth for more than a few minutes at a time, but I supposed miracles did happen.

Carrying the dark blue pot, Seth asked, "Is Caleb around?"

"I'm here," I shouted, even though he couldn't hear me.

Sunshine started, which made me laugh. "He's over there," he replied, gesturing to me.

Seth turned in my direction and waved shyly. "Hey."

"Hi. What are you doing today? Anything fun? I hope you are doing something fun," I said, bouncing, and Zoltilvoxfyn dutifully translated.

"I'm going to see Wyn and have a conversation with NAID in front of a group of scientists."

"That sounds awkward."

"It is," Seth said as his free hand burrowed into his hoodie pocket.

I couldn't know for certain, but from the bright sun and cloudless sky, I assumed it was too hot for a hoodie, but maybe he was one of those people who was always cold. *That* had never been my problem. I was a born and bred Californian—flip flops and shorts forever.

You'd never know from my jeans, t-shirt, and tennis shoes. I hated that I couldn't change my clothes. It wasn't like I'd known I was going to die that day or that I'd be stuck forever in the same clothes.

"Can I come?" Wyn would be there, but more than that, NAID was there. While she wasn't Nana, NAID wore her face and had her voice. It was better than nothing, and nothing was all I'd had previously.

Seth tensed, clutching the potted plant to his chest. "You want to come?"

"It sounds fun."

He stared at the ground, not responding. Zoltilvoxfyn glanced at me, and I shrugged. I didn't have to force my way in; if I followed along, they would never know I was there, but it would be more fun if Zoltilvoxfyn came along to translate my words.

"Maybe this will help Caleb find his tether," Sunshine offered.

"Tether?" Seth asked.

"To move on, he needs to find what ties him to the mortal plane, so he can break it and depart."

"How will this help?" Seth asked.

"My thoughts exactly," I added. Zoltilvoxfyn glared at me, and I chuckled, understanding. He was trying to force Seth to let me come.

"I do not know," he answered.

Seth squeezed the plant to his chest, studying the ground, clearly planning on saying no.

"It's okay. I can come another time," I relented.

"N-no," Seth said, though he looked like he wanted to take it back the second the word was out of his mouth. "It's fine. I need to take the plant to my apartment first."

"We can follow you," Zoltilvoxfyn said. "Or meet you at NAID's hub."

"I'll meet you there." Seth slipped into the trees in the direction of the palace. A drakcol with dark gray scales, who was staring at a screen, peeled off from behind a tree and followed along. Neither Zoltilvoxfyn nor Seth noticed or they didn't care. Their glazes slid over him, as if they couldn't see him.

Maybe he was a ghost like me? I immediately rejected that thought. The drakcol had a tablet, and Zoltilvoxfyn would've known if that dude was a spirit. Still, no one paid any attention to the drakcol as he followed Seth from a discreet distance.

Shaking it off, I moved to Zoltilvoxfyn's side, and his tail flicked in my direction, hovering near my ankle before sliding away. I wanted his tail to touch me, even though I wouldn't perceive it.

"I feel bad," I commented.

"Why?"

"Seth didn't want me to come, but we forced our way in."

Sunshine pushed his long hair behind his tapered ear. I swallowed, eyes locked on his elegant fingers, then to the earrings he wore. The golden cuff on the inner part of his tapered ear was oddly sexy and highlighted its length.

What was it about this dude? Every movement pulled me in. Another brush went across my arm, as if fingers ran down the length. I shuddered at the almost imperceptible touch, trying to cling to it, but it vanished impossibly quick.

"We could not go," he offered.

"We could, but I really want to."

"Then we will go this time, and maybe not again. I do not wish to stress Seth out, and if I do, it will be hard to become friends with him."

"You will. Soon. I know it. The two of you will be great friends." I bounced on the balls of my feet, aching to hug him or at least pat him.

"Perhaps."

Zoltilvoxfyn

We met Seth downstairs near NAID's private hub, which was separate from the main. The Network of Artificial Intelligence for Drakcol or NAID was a single entity that had many different parts connected to the main hub, but this NAID was different. The

Council of Seekers wasn't exactly sure what had happened, but she'd gained sentience.

Some scientists believed Seth Harris was responsible for the sudden change. No NAID had gained self-awareness yet—she was the first—but he'd claimed that NAID had done it all on her own. There was another theory that because she hadn't been connected to the main hub when the Admiral Ven left for Earth, she became her own entity.

In the end, no one was certain.

Kalvoxrencol was in charge of her independence project, and Seth played an integral part because she showed more independence when she spoke with him than anyone else. They were friends.

When Seth saw us, his expression tightened and his hand slid into his oversized black jacket. I'd expected to see Kalvoxrencol trailing him, but Seth was alone—again. I wasn't sure where my little brother was, but it was hard to imagine him leaving Seth alone this much.

Something must be happening that I wasn't aware of; something that Kalvoxrencol wasn't telling me, and that made a worthlessness grow inside of me no matter how much I hoped to banish it. I needed my brother to rely on me as much as I depended on him. But he never did—none of them did.

Caleb skipped toward Seth, beaming brightly. My jaw tightened. I didn't know why Caleb liked Seth so much, but it bothered me. It shouldn't, yet it did for a reason I couldn't explain.

"Seth," Caleb called, and I reluctantly told him.

"Caleb. Zoltilvoxfyn," Seth carefully said my name, drawing it out.

"Tell Seth he can call you Fyn. He struggles with your long names," he said, then added in a rush, "Nobody else gets to call you Sunshine. You're my Sunshine. No one else's. Just mine. Not that I'm being weird or anything. Don't read into it. It doesn't mean anything. I promise."

"I will not tell him," I replied, ignoring the fire that burned in my gut from Caleb's subtle claim. As he said, it didn't mean anything.

Seth blinked. "Excuse me?"

"My apologies. I was speaking with Caleb. He gave me a shortening and told me to share it with you."

Seth laughed. "Your name was too long, huh?"

"Told you," Caleb shouted as he jumped. In the short time I'd known Caleb, he didn't do anything by halves. He was so loud and exuberant, moving incessantly. He was so alive, even if he no longer breathed.

"I shortened Kal's name pretty quickly as well."

"I call him that too," Caleb said, though he quietly added, "Not that he can hear me."

His obvious sadness tugged on me, so begrudgingly, I said, "Caleb calls me Fyn."

"Cute," Seth said.

"It is," Caleb replied.

"We should go in," I said, ending the conversation about my drastically shortened name. I wasn't particularly fond of it, but I had a hard time saying no to Caleb for some reason.

The lab was decent-sized with screens on every wall. All, except the large monitor in the center of the room, was full of code readouts. The center monitor displayed an older human woman with a tower of curls on her head. She was perfectly blue like NAID normally was, but her unique countenance was different from the usual silhouette.

A group of scientists hovered near the monitors. A few I recognized in passing, but I didn't recall their names. One of the scientists stood out from the group. I'd never seen him before; I would've remembered. He was shorter and leaner than most drakcol, but what caught my attention was that he was the most attractive person I'd ever seen in my life.

He had soft pink hair that was cut in military fashion—short on the sides and longer on top. His light purple scales had slips of gold and magenta skin showing around them. His wide blue eyes roved over us as his full lips pulled into a smile when he saw Seth. The scientist drew Seth into a hug as his tail curled about Seth's wrist.

"That's Wyn," Caleb said. "He was on the Admiral Ven. Seth recommended him for this position."

"Interesting," I muttered. Normally, I didn't speak to spirits when other people besides my family were present, as strangers tended to react badly, but I didn't want Caleb to think I was ignoring him.

"He followed me around the ship."

"How?"

Caleb leaned closer to me, almost touching. "He was chasing a phase variance, which was me. Or rather, I was causing it. Sometimes I affect technology with my ghostly self."

"Interesting," I repeated, and he grinned. My tail shifted in his direction, but I stopped the motion. A swooping sensation, as if I was free-falling, went through me, and I ripped my gaze away from Caleb, then started. The whole lab was staring at me.

I looked at the ground, hair falling around me like a shield; darkness swelled in my chest and spread like a miasma, coating my cells until I felt as if I was wading through mud. Each breath was slight and rough, like something pressed against my chest, grinding my lungs into my spine.

They all thought I was insane. I straightened, bracing for the inevitable whispers. One of the scientists muttered something to their colleague. My gut tightened and my tail coiled about my ankle, but I forced it away. I would show no weakness.

Kalvoxrencol might have been the royal troublemaker, absorbing the eyes outside of the palace, but everyone within the palace stared at me and whispers followed in my wake.

Seth stepped forward, fisted hands shaking. "Prince Zoltilvoxfyn has a guest with him today. A ghost from my world named Caleb Smith." One of the scientists scoffed, and Seth's expression turned harsh. "If anyone has a problem, they can leave and be reassigned."

My soul clenched. My family always protected me, but I hadn't expected Seth to do so.

Wyn moved to Seth's side and offered me his throat. "Prince, where is Caleb Smith?"

"Right next to me."

He looked at the space next to me, but on the wrong side, and said, "Hello, Caleb Smith. I'm Wyn."

"Hey," Caleb said. "We've met. Sort of. I mean, I met you, not that you know me. I was on the Admiral Ven. Both trips. Tell him it's a long story. I don't want to get into it again." I relayed his words, trying to ignore the blatant staring from the rest of the group.

Wyn's forehead creased for a moment before his mouth fell open, tail thrashing. "You're the phase variance."

"Yep," Caleb replied.

"I was chasing you." Wyn shook his head, tail writhing in agitation. "I can't believe it. My superiors thought I was incompetent with all the reports I sent. They are doing a system purge on the Admiral Ven as we converse because we figured it might be a coding error. Though I did track the phase variance here as well."

"I came down on the shuttle with you," Caleb explained.

Wyn scrubbed his hair, making it stand up straight. "Well, that explains everything." He turned to NAID. "Are you sensing the phase variance?"

"Yes," she replied, and Caleb tensed beside me.

Wyn said, "I wonder if we can somehow project Caleb or find a way to be able to hear him. Our technology can perceive him, so perhaps it's possible."

"It would be fascinating to try," NAID said, her disembodied head bouncing on the screen in a way that made me distinctly uncomfortable. "I would be happy to assist you."

"Then I could talk directly to Caleb," Seth said, smiling. "I would like that."

"Me too," Caleb said, but his eyes never left NAID.

When Seth and Wyn refocused on NAID, I leaned toward him, my hair disappearing into his shoulder. "Are you well?"

"No," he said. "That's my grandma."

"That's NAID," I said. "She doesn't have children, let alone grandchildren."

"I'm not an idiot, Sunshine. I'm talking about the face she's wearing. That's my grandmother."

My soul stilled, and I looked at NAID again. I'd seen her once or twice, but I'd never given much thought to where her human aspect came from. This face, though, belonged to one of Caleb's family.

"Shall I ask her to change?"

"No," he said. "It's fine."

"I would ask for you, Caleb."

"Thank you, but it's nice to see her, even if she's not my grandmother."

For the rest of the session, I stayed quiet, except for when Caleb talked. Instead of listening to Seth and NAID converse as they apparently did on a weekly basis, everyone was more focused on Caleb and how to reprogram the sensors to perceive him. I didn't know if Wyn and NAID would succeed, but I hoped they did. Caleb deserved to be seen and heard by others.

Though, perversely, I craved to keep him all to myself. I liked his focus being entirely on me because mine was certainly on him. Every bounce, smile, and word drew me in. He was like a star that I was helpless to orbit.

Chapter 13

SOUL TYPES ARE ODD.

Caleb

I sat on one of the many tables in the greenhouse as my Sunshine puttered around. He was quiet today, which wasn't odd in itself—he was always quiet. But this silence was heavier than usual, and I didn't know why. Maybe he was finally growing tired of my endless chatter. It had only been a couple of days, and I had a *lot* more words stored up.

With as much control as I possessed, I shut my mouth and stared at the plethora of plants around me. Colors ranged from pale greens, pinks, and blues to vibrant reds, purples, and oranges. Plants floated above me. The air had to be humid because of the beads of liquid gathering on Fyn's scales and the plant leaves.

"Why did you stop talking?" Fyn asked as he skillfully transferred a snapping, biting plant to another pot without a single scratch.

"Hmm?"

Fyn faced me, tail flicking faster. I swear their tails were like barometers for their emotions. “Caleb, are you alright?” He abandoned his plant, stopping more than an arm length away. I wanted to hook my legs around his hips and draw him flush against me. I suppressed a lurch of sadness. It was what it was. No point in being upset.

“I’m fine,” I said, sitting crisscross-applesauce, knees disappearing into several plants. “I was giving you a break from my talking.”

“I don’t mind it. I quite enjoy it.”

“You do?”

“It’s soothing.”

“Soothing?” I asked.

“Like the sound of wind in the trees or the crash of the waves.”

White noise. He thought my talking was like white noise. How complementary. It’s what every dude wanted to hear from their crush: you sound like white noise.

The smallest quirk tugged at the corner of Fyn’s lips before he tilted his head down and his silky hair covered him.

“You're teasing me,” I shouted, leaping down and crowding him. “Sunshine, you’re teasing me.”

He grinned. An actual fucking smile. A tooth bearing smile. Sultry heat slid down my spine like fingers whispering over me. So faint. So barely there. But it was enough to sear me.

His expression softened the longer I stared at him. I shifted closer, unable to help it. What was it about him? Why now? Why after wandering for so long did I feel something?

The door opened, and we both jumped. Seth peeked in, expression tight and face pale.

Fyn tensed. "Seth."

"Hey," Seth said, voice soft.

Where was Kal? He rarely left Seth alone. Like ever. Though I *had* seen Seth the last couple times without Kal, which was weird. The dude was obsessed, like obsessed *obsessed*.

"Be nice," I admonished. "He's obviously upset."

"How am I to know? He's the first human I've met," he said back.

"Because I just told you," I snapped. True. Seth was the first human he had experience with, but he could be nice.

Fyn glared at me, and it didn't upset me in the slightest. Instead, I liked it. A cute little divot between his eyebrows appeared and his full lips pursed attractively. I liked it way more than was healthy. But I was dead; I didn't have to worry about my health anymore. Perks.

"Should I leave?" Seth asked, fidgeting like he was about to bolt.

"No," Fyn said. "I was arguing with Caleb." He waved Seth in. "I normally don't allow anyone, even family, in here."

Seth froze, as did I. Fyn didn't care, or at least didn't act like he cared, when I was in here. My romantic soul hoped it was because it was me, but in reality, it was probably because I wasn't truly here.

"Are you sure I shouldn't leave?" Seth asked, hesitating in the doorway.

"Come in, please," Fyn said, and Seth slipped the rest of the way inside. "Where is Kalvoxrencol?"

"My thoughts exactly," I said. "He never leaves Seth alone. Like ever. He practically stalks him. On the Admiral Ven..."

Seth started talking, oblivious to my chattering. "He's fighting with your dad."

"Why?" Fyn asked, head cocking.

Seth played with the zipper of his hoodie. I patted his shoulder, and he shivered, blinking. "Tell him I'm here," I said.

Fyn frowned for the barest moment before he told Seth I was right next to him. Seth glanced toward me and smiled, but he shifted to the side.

"What's going on, Seth?" I asked, and Fyn dutifully translated.

"I'm not sure yet," Seth said. "Someone is insisting on meeting with me, and I don't want to. Kal is protecting me."

"It's the priest people with the glowing Crystal," I commented.

After Fyn told Seth what I said, he asked, "What are you talking about, Caleb?"

Even Seth was staring at me; well, in my general direction, but it so counted. "You saw the Crystal?"

"Yep." I told them both about how I'd followed Monqilcolnen and the conversation I'd overheard.

My Sunshine crossed his arms. "That makes sense."

"What makes sense?" Seth asked.

"You have the darkest warrior soul ever tested. Warrior and seeker souls grow darker with the pureness of their souls; whereas, spiritual and creator souls grow lighter when they're purer. Warriors are important to drakcol, and you are the purest one in recorded history."

Seth gaped at Fyn, and I was certain my expression was the same hooked-fish one like his. Don't get me wrong, Seth was awesome, but why would he be the best warrior? And even if he was, why did anyone care?

Fyn sat down in the middle of the greenhouse and motioned for me and Seth to follow suit. After telling Seth where I was, he started speaking. "When we turn ten, we are tested by the Ranks to find out what type of soul we have. As I understand it, you humans do not have the same thing."

"We don't," I piped up.

"Originally we were tested by touching the Crystal itself, but now we use a piece of crystal that connects to it," Fyn said.

"Interesting," Seth remarked, though he didn't sound interested.

"It's important to us. The Crystal has been a part of our culture longer than we have written history. How and when it was discovered has been lost to the ravages of time, but its significance has never dimmed.

"Warriors," Fyn said, gesturing to Seth and himself, "are the most venerated because we were and still are, in many ways, a warring species. Royal children have always been warrior souls until Kalvoxrencol. His showing as a creator soul was quite shocking. Creators have never been valued because what did they contribute to war?"

I scoffed. Sure things like books and movies were unneeded, but war was fantastic. That sounded healthy.

"Spiritual souls are the rarest type, and they are treasured because of their connection to the Crystal. Seeker souls found their prominence with the rise of technology. But creator souls." He shook his head. "Many question their value.

"But now Kalvoxrencol, the first royal creator soul, has a human mate who is the purest warrior soul ever tested in recorded history? Kalvoxrencol has the gift of light that was said to be the same inner fire of the legendary first Empress of the Drakcol Empire. Of course, they want to speak to you, Seth. You two are special."

"Not really." He tugged hard on the zipper, making the elements clack.

"You are. We believe Crystal-bound mates are two halves of the same soul. You are a warrior, and Kalvoxrencol has the empress's gift of light. You are special. You can always speak to Monqilcolnen if meeting with the Ranks is overwhelming," Fyn said.

"Why?" I asked at the same time as Seth.

"Monqilcolnen is the purest spiritual soul ever tested in recorded history. His soul is almost pure white. He didn't join the Ranks as people assumed he would," Fyn answered. "But he is still connected to them. He stays in the caves when he's here, not in the palace, though he does have a room."

"Caves?" Seth asked.

"Beneath the sanctuary is a series of caves for the Ranks. It's the order's headquarters."

"That sounds like fun," I said as thoughts of exploring the winding caves flitted through my mind. What did they have down there? Bodies? Catacombs always had bodies. I'd almost forgotten about the tunnels in my distraction of Fyn.

"Caleb," Fyn growled in warning. "No."

"What?" I asked, giving him my most innocent smile that Nana always said was fake as American cheese. "No one will see me."

He frowned.

Seth laughed, and I started at the deep rumbly sound. He said, "You're like Kal. He hates it when I'm away from him too."

Fyn appeared positively struck; whereas, I beamed. I liked that. Fyn cared if I disappeared from his sight.

"Look at him," Seth teased, glancing in my general direction. "I fucking shocked him."

I chuckled, going for a high-five, but Seth didn't see it. My humor vanished, and I lowered my hand to my lap, fisting it.

After Fyn collected himself, he said, "You don't have to speak to anyone you don't wish to, Seth. Kalvoxrencol will protect you, as will the rest of us."

"Thanks."

"You're our brother."

His eyes turned wet as he cleared his throat. "Thanks."

I quickly told Fyn, "Talk about something else. I don't know about Seth, but I hated crying in front of other people. It's a human male thing."

Sunshine stood. "Would you like to see my plants?"

"Yes," Seth said, practically leaping onto the conversation change.

I followed behind them while Fyn talked about his different plants. He even snagged a tablet, showing Seth his copious notes on caring for each and every rare plant and hybrid. Seth and Fyn would become friends—I knew it. This way when I left, Seth wouldn't be alone. Fyn smiled softly at one of Seth's questions. Neither would my Sunshine. Neither of them would be alone.

Chapter 14

TIME TO DO MY STALKING DUTY.

Caleb

It had been over a week since I'd come to Tamkolvanloknol, and we had yet to discover my tether. Fyn had asked me all manner of questions from about my family to past relationships to my interests, but there was no lightbulb moment. I had no idea why I was stuck here, but it was fine.

I was less tired than before. Fyn made me feel alive. He talked to me and treated me like everyone else. Fyn and I spent almost every moment of every day together, and I liked it—I more than liked it.

Seth and I would often hang out, chatting in Zoltilvoxfyn's greenhouse, chilling in his apartment, or with Wyn and NAID. Kal would often leave Seth with Fyn when he was off arguing with people and probably threatening violence—that was a usual response of his from what I'd witnessed. Apparently, he didn't trust anyone to keep Seth safe, except his brothers.

Sometimes Kal would join us when we all hung out, which was fun. He treated me like I was alive as well, laughing and joking with me. He found me funny, even when Fyn and Seth didn't.

Wyn and NAID were trying to find a way to be able to communicate with me without Fyn, but they weren't optimistic it would be anytime soon. I hadn't told anyone besides Fyn about NAID wearing Nana's face either for two reasons. One, she would feel awkward, and two, I liked seeing Nana even if it wasn't her.

I had yet to be introduced to Urgg, and I really wanted to meet the barbarus. They seemed like fun, and since I didn't understand their language, it had been next to impossible to learn much about them.

But it had been a few days since I'd seen Tinlorray, and the guilt was beginning to grow. I *had* promised Yolkeltod to check in on her, but I'd been busy. Well, that was an excuse. I kind of felt like a peeping tom or something when I watched her grieve. I hoped she'd let go of Yolkeltod's body now that his soul had moved on, but I didn't know if she actually would.

Grief was a funny thing. It rooted us in place and refused to let us move on, even when we wanted to.

I glanced at Fyn, then quickly away. He was wearing a tight gray tank top and red leggings that clung to his muscular legs. His long white hair was tied into a messy knot. Unable to stop myself, I peeked again. He was drinking water, scales shinier than usual. The apple in his throat bobbed, making me swallow a groan.

I'd gone along to observe when he went to his combat class, even though there was plenty to explore. The whole time I'd been unable to look away from him. His broad form as he stretched. The way he laughed occasionally with Kal. The way he moved when he fought. The strength of his tail. His serious expression when Kal or the instructor would comment on his form.

It all captivated me.

I'd barely paid attention when he introduced me to his eldest brother and crown prince, Hallonnixmin. I'd clocked dark blue scales, messy purple hair, and nothing else. Same with Hallonnixmin's mate, Gilvaxtin. She was pink—pink hair and scales. I had no idea what else. I'd given no more attention to Monqilcolnen who remained beside Hallonnixmin and Gilvaxtin, making light jokes. Instead, my eyes remained fixed on Fyn.

When we came back to his apartment, I'd barely spoken because I'd been embarrassed by the amount of staring I'd done. I didn't think Fyn noticed my blatant ogling, because he hadn't said anything. Besides, if I'd opened my mouth, words about what I'd felt watching him would spill out.

Obvious thy name was Caleb.

Pulling my gaze from his throat, which bobbed as he drank water, I said, "I think I'm going to go to the city today."

He lowered the glass. "What?"

"I need to check on Tinlorray."

"I will come with you."

"I don't think that's a good idea. You're a prince. I can't imagine she would be comfortable with you randomly showing up."

"True," he replied slowly.

"I need to make sure she's okay, then I'll be back."

Sunshine stared at me, his claws scraping against the glass. "Do you have to?"

"Yeah." I moved until I was in front of him. I peered up at him, wanting to close the distance between us and press my lips on his.

His jaw clenched, tail writhing. "Will you come back?"

"Probably not tonight. It depends on the shuttle schedule." I'd asked Wyn and NAID about the schedule through Fyn, and they'd pulled it up for me to memorize. It had been easy enough.

"I would..." he trailed off and swallowed, making that alluring knot in his throat bob. "I would prefer it if you came back tonight."

I grinned, unable to stop it, and went up on my toes. "I will try my best."

"Thank you."

Butterfly wings fluttered in my midsection, accompanied by a soft beeping noise. Both were gone in a flash, but I rested a hand on my gut. It had been there. Beaming at Fyn, I knew he was my sunshine, bringing this new cozy summertime into the winter of my afterlife.

I stepped onto the shuttle that would take me to one of the satellite cities of the capital. It was quite some distance away, but the shuttle made the trip short and relevantly convenient. When it landed, I slipped through the crowd and wound my way through the streets. I had to backtrack a few times before I found the hospital.

Finding Yolkeltod's room was harder than I would've guessed. The search took over an hour before I stumbled upon a familiar hallway. I stepped through the door, and Yolkeltod's lifeless body was still in the bed near the window.

The machines attached to him via cords and tubes beeped in a consistent rhythm. There was a new square device on his forehead that had nothing on the minuscule screen. I couldn't say what it did, if anything, because it looked like a black box stuck to his forehead.

Tinlorray was nowhere to be seen.

I plopped onto the stool next to his bed and stared at him, tracing the planes and angles. He felt oddly empty, which, I mean, he was. Yolkeltod was no longer here. He'd moved on to whatever came after this.

Some of the lingering guilt of his easy passing had vanished when Fyn had told me there had been no way to reconnect his soul to his body. Despite that, it would have been nice to reunite the two. Yolkeltod was all that Tinlorray had.

The longer I stared at his body, the more uncomfortable I grew until I was fidgeting on the stool like a kid in church. I was in the same room, basically, with a corpse, which shouldn't bother a ghost, but it did. Sure, he breathed and all that jazz, but everything that was Yolkeltod wasn't here anymore. So he was a corpse. A zombie. Though he didn't hunger for brains.

Oh my god, what if he did wake up and crave brains? Zombie apocalypse on an alien planet. Visions of hordes of lumbering drakcol who grunted for brains pranced around my mind.

Thankfully, the door opened and distracted me from my random thoughts. Dr. Maklownil strode in followed by another person. The doctor's jagged pink scales appeared even rougher next to the other drakcol. She stood straight, her fern green scales shiny with youth, and her deep brown hair was neatly braided down her back.

Her claws clicked on a tablet as she asked, "Has his sister or guardian approved yet?"

"No, their guardian has deferred to Tinlorray in this matter," Dr. Maklownil replied as he moved closer to Yolkeltod's bed. He peered at the monitors before focusing on the blank black box, then frowned. "She hopes he'll come back. He's a warrior soul."

"Soul type doesn't matter in this situation," she said, voice laced with kindness.

"I've explained that to her multiple times, but the anomalous readings stoked her hope again, not that she needed much assistance."

"How much longer can we cater to her protectiveness? He will not awaken, and yet I understand her need to keep him like this."

Dr. Maklownil lifted his palms.

"I will talk to her," she said, tapping on the screen. "The hospital can offer her a..." She broke off into a word I didn't understand. I repeated it over and over again, not knowing what it was, but from context, I assumed someone to help Tinlorray. "Perhaps that will help." The woman tucked the screen under her arm. "It doesn't seem right to keep him like this."

"It's not," the doctor said.

The new woman was probably hospital administration checking on the situation. Yolkeltod must be a long-term patient. They chatted for a few more minutes before departing.

Bouncing, I stared out the window and watched the potted ferns wiggling in the wind. There was nothing to do. All the other beds were full of drakcol, but none of them had visitors, nor did they talk. I turned back to Yolkeltod and patted his arm without knowing why I did it, my fingers slid through it like they did everything else.

Man, I missed touching people. Hugging or snuggling. It was the simple things in life. Interacting with the world and being a part of it. I truly wasn't here. I had one foot in this existence and one foot in the other.

Which was why I needed to leave.

Fyn had been right when he said this plane was for the living, not the dead—not me. How to leave was as much of a mystery today as it was last week. What my tether might be was anyone's guess. Still, I would have to try to find and break it.

A twinge pulled in my chest.

What was that? Pain? That was new. Faint. Barely more than a needle prick.

My Sunshine's smile popped into my thoughts. He was finding his smile—maybe it hadn't been lost in the first place? Even with Seth, he'd been relaxing. They would be okay without me. They had each other, Kal, and their other brothers.

Another twinge stung my chest. Gone as quick as it came.

Zoltilvoxfyn, I thought. This crush had refused to dim; instead, it grew steadily under his shining light. Hugging myself, I tried to force away the thought. I couldn't stay here because I liked him. Fyn had told me to pass on; that was his whole purpose.

Still, I didn't want to leave him.

I lifted my hand to the light, pretending to feel it, and I froze. I could see through my fingers. I'd never been able to do that, except when I extended myself too far and vanished. My skin always looked like it had when I was alive, but right now I was blurry to the point I saw the green of the ferns on the balcony. I shook my hand, like that would help, and watched until I solidified once more.

Tucking it against my stomach, I locked any and all worry away. It was all fine.

The sky had started to darken by the time Tinlorray arrived. She was even more worn out than the last time I'd seen her. Her tail was lifeless on the ground, her hair limp, and her scales dull. She trudged across the room and flopped onto the stool, not giving me enough time to leap out of the way. I passed through her, making her shiver.

"You need to let him go," I told her when she grabbed Yolkeltod's much larger hand. She didn't hear me, but I couldn't help telling her. "He's gone, and he's never going to come back."

Tinlorray brushed his reddish-brown hair behind a tapered ear, then tugged the blanket up over his broad chest. She smoothed the blanket over him as she said, "Yolkeltod, you need to wake up."

The uncomfortable curl returned with a vengeance. This was a private moment, but here I was watching it like a voyeur. I *had* promised Yolkeltod, but there was nothing I could actually do.

With a slight grimace, I sat on the edge of his bed. "He's gone, Tinlorray, but you're all he cared about. You were his tether."

She didn't respond; instead, she kept straightening and tucking the blanket around his still frame.

I stayed with Tinlorray the entire time she was at the hospital, even though it made me feel icky. I tracked her to their apartment and watched her crash onto the bed, crying. I patted her back, fingers disappearing into her.

Tinlorray shivered, then paused, head lifting. "Yolkeltod?"

I yanked back. "Shit."

"Yolkeltod, that's you, isn't it?"

"No. No, it's not."

Tears slipped down her cheeks. "I knew you wouldn't leave me."

"Double shit. The worse shit in the entire fucking world."

A shaking hand stretched in my direction as if Tinlorray sensed me. I scrambled back. This was bad. Like really bad. I hadn't thought about the fact I often made people shiver. No one had ever noticed before. But, of course, she would think it was her brother, not some random ghost hanging around her like a creeper.

"Yolkeltod," she cried. "Don't leave me. Please. I need you."

"Fuck." I placed my hand on hers.

Her breathing quickened. "Yolkeltod."

"This is bad. Really fucking bad," I said, but I didn't draw away.

Zoltilvoxfyn

I paced the shared space of my quarters, wings out. I'd tried to keep them tucked against my back, but they slipped out without my permission. My eyes flicked around for the hundredth time, searching for Caleb. The hour was late, and he hadn't returned yet. I needed him to come back.

My tail lashed as I swiveled around again. I should go to bed, but sleep wouldn't come even if I tried. Worry pulsed with each beat of my soul. Where was Caleb? Was he safe? Had he moved on?

The very thought of never hearing his exuberant voice or seeing his beaming smile made ice course through my veins. Life without Caleb would be very dull.

When I turned yet again, I paused. Caleb stood near the door without his usual smile. In three steps, I stood in front of him. My hand lifted of its own accord before I stopped the movement, my fingers curling into a fist and falling to my side.

"Caleb, what's wrong?"

"I made a mistake."

"What?" I asked, tail twitching, and stepped even closer. I shouldn't. Just because he was dead didn't mean I had the right to invade his space. We hadn't discussed permissions. Not friendship… or other ones.

He peered up at me, chewing on his bottom lip. I swallowed at the sight of his blunt, white teeth digging into the plump pink skin. Caleb shouldn't be allowed to do that.

"What?" I asked again, my voice deeper.

"I went to see Tinlorray again, the older sister of the ghost," he explained.

"I remember."

Caleb's shoulders hunched. "I…" he trailed off, then shook his head. "I patted her. I was trying to help, I swear, but she shivered and thought it was her brother. I couldn't leave her, and she kept reaching for me, crying. I-I touched her again. She thought it was Yolkeltod."

My mouth fell open before I snapped it shut. "That is not ideal."

"What do I do?"

I froze under the weight of his large, hopeful eyes. I had no idea what he should do. I hadn't helped many spirits cross over, and none of them had been complicated like this. I swallowed the self-loathing swelling in my chest, growing like a weed. This was my gift. I was supposed to help, and I couldn't do anything. I wasn't worthy of this gift or Caleb or anything else.

Chapter 15

MAYBE WYN CAN DO THE IMPOSSIBLE?

Caleb

A few days ago, Sunshine had said he would come up with a plan for the Tinlorray situation, but he'd said nothing about a plan since. In fact, he'd been quiet, sad even, as he stayed in his greenhouse, missing combat classes and any other activities with his brothers.

Hallonnixmin (or Hal as Seth called him) had come several times to check on Fyn, as had Kal. He'd ignored them both, which made both of the brothers frown. They'd both asked about his appointments with his doctor, and Fyn had told them he wasn't going. I wasn't sure why he saw a doctor, but it was probably important.

Even when Seth came to see him, Fyn had sent him away.

I'd hung around him most of the time, chattering about nothing, though I'd left a few times to explore the palace. Every time, he would tense and ask me to come back soon, which I always did.

I wasn't going to leave Sunshine for long. When I returned, Fyn would crowd me, checking to make sure I was alright. I didn't know what he thought was going to happen to me.

Something was wrong with him, and I wasn't sure what.

Today, I was going to convince Fyn to leave his greenhouse in any way possible. He needed it, and so did I. I hated staying in one place, but I felt hella guilty leaving him for long when something was clearly bothering him.

Fyn was meticulously removing wilting blooms from a few of the bushes and pruning the branches back. His white hair hung around his face, obscuring it. His tail was limp near his leg—a definite sign he was upset.

I sidled up to him and hopped onto the table, giving him a wide smile, which he didn't return.

Tough crowd.

"Do you want to see Wyn, Seth, and NAID today?" I asked. Maybe Wyn and the other scientists needed to run more experiments or maybe Urgg was there, and I could *finally* meet the barbarus.

"Do you?"

"Yeah, and I can't talk to them without you."

He moved to another plant without responding.

"It might be fun, and we don't have to stay long, because I know you have your combat-class-thing."

"I'm not going."

"Ah." I couldn't make him go, but I thought he should. Drawing my legs up and crossing them, I said, "Wyn might have an update on getting NAID's sensors to perceive me."

"Possibly."

So this was going well. I had no idea what was wrong. It had started right after I came back from Tinlorray's and told him about my mistake. My knees paused in their bouncing. Was that the issue? My mistake?

Fyn was probably mad at me for my stupid-ass mistake. I'd caused Tinlorray more suffering. I hadn't even seen her in a couple of days, which probably upset her even more, but I didn't know what to do. I was hurting her no matter what I did.

Or was it about how close I kept getting? Fyn wasn't a physically affectionate person, even with his siblings, though he allowed them to hug him or grab his tail occasionally. I needed to stop crowding him, but I couldn't help myself. Everything inside screamed for me to snuggle right against him.

"Sunshine," I said, my voice quiet, "I'm sorry."

Turning in my direction, he asked, "What?"

"I messed up." I kept my eyes on my lap, so I didn't have to see the frustration in his expression. I never wanted to do anything to upset him—not ever.

A thud, like a pot being set down, sounded, and footsteps came toward me. His hands rested on either side of the table, bracketing me. "You didn't make a mistake, Caleb. You had no way of knowing she would think you were her brother."

"Then why are you mad at me?" I hated the needy tone in my voice, but fucking hell, I *needed* him.

"I'm not." He leaned over me, his hair forming a curtain around us. "This has nothing to do with you. I have a mental health condition, Caleb, and sometimes it makes it hard for me to connect or express myself. This was never about you. My apologies."

"You don't have to apologize."

"I never meant to upset you."

"It's alright," I said. "Can I ask what condition you have?" When he looked away, I continued, "You don't have to tell me. I mean, fuck, that was probably a rude question. I'm sorry. I won't ask again."

"It's fine, Caleb. I'm not mad. I don't enjoy discussing it."

"You don't have to."

Fyn swayed toward me before stepping back. "I have..." He said a long word I didn't recognize. He must have seen my confusion because he elaborated. "It's a disorder that influences my brain chemistry. I'm prone to bouts of sadness, isolating myself, excessive sleeping, guilt, and intrusive thoughts to name a few things. It makes it difficult for me to do things or connect."

Depression. He had depression. "I understand. If you ever need a break from me, tell me."

"I never need you away from me, Caleb."

Staring at Fyn, I fought my damn romantic heart that had me swooning where I sat.

"Let's go talk to Wyn," he said, effectively changing the subject.

"Then you can go to your combat class. I like watching you. It's fucking hot." I gave him a wink and rushed out before I saw his reaction.

I stayed ahead of Zoltilvoxfyn until we reached the lab where Wyn worked, embarrassed. I couldn't believe I told Fyn that I liked watching him. I mean, I did. It was the unadulterated truth, but I didn't have to blurt it out. Curse my tongue and my inability to keep quiet.

The door didn't slow me down in the slightest. Wyn was bent over a desk that was one long monitor. His claws were clicking on the glass as his tail flicked. Strands of his bubblegum-pink hair had fallen over his lavender scales.

Wyn was lovely. No doubt about it. But even as I studied him, I started to compare him to Sunshine. My Sunshine was much hotter.

You are dead, I reminded myself.

The door slid open, and Fyn stepped inside. Wyn stood, approaching, while the other scientists called out greetings and offered their throats.

"Prince, it's yourself." Wyn tilted his head to the side, acknowledging his superiority.

Drakcol were odd creatures. Probably had to do with some of the warring clan crap that Fyn had told me about.

"Ensign Wyn," Fyn replied. His tail swished near me, sliding through my ankle. I swallowed. He was so careful to not touch me, like ridiculously careful, and it made me wonder if the tail swipe meant something. God, I hoped it did. I was acting like a teenager, making a production of every little thing. But still, it meant something, right?

"Caleb desired to speak to you and NAID," Fyn said, startling me out of my thoughts.

"Yep," I said, bouncing and making sure my ankle brushed his tail. When a subsequent shiver went up Fyn's spine, I fought a grin; he didn't move away, though. "I'm here to check on the status on making the sensors see or, well, hear me." Sunshine dutifully translated.

Wyn's tail started moving faster. "It's not going as well as I'd hoped. NAID."

She appeared a moment later. The sight of her sent a strong longing for home through me. I missed Nana. I missed my family. I'd been off Earth for over two decades now. Nana might not even be alive.

I stared at the ground, sadness swelling, and a sudden frustration eclipsed it. My eyes didn't burn. My throat didn't tighten. All of the physical sensations that accompanied emotions were not possible. Man, I missed being alive. I missed everything.

A sheet of white hair blocked my sight of her. Zoltilvoxfyn had stepped in front of me, shielding me, even though no one else saw me.

"Progress?" he asked, voice tighter than normal.

Wyn's shoulders hunched and his tail curled around his ankle. At his obvious distress, I placed a hand on Fyn's back. He shuddered and his wings twitched under his tunic. An urge to run my finger over them, to ask him to set them free so I could see them, rushed through me. I suppressed it. Now was not the time.

"I'm alright," I said. Unable to help myself, I trailed up his spine, then over his shoulders, and down his sides, forming a rectangle before resting my hand on his lower back. His frame was so damn perfect.

Fyn rumbled in the back of his throat, then coughed. "My apologies, Ensign Wyn. I did not sleep well."

NAID's head bobbed on the screen, making me grimace. It was odd to watch a disembodied head move up and down. "Sleep is extremely important, Prince. Edith Smith says, 'Lack of sleep can hinder your decision making. Worries. Stress. All of it will keep until tomorrow.'"

I froze, digging my fingers into Fyn. He shivered when my hand slipped through him, making me pull back. How did NAID know anything about Nana? Sure, she looked like Nana, but NAID wouldn't have known her.

"Progress?" Fyn asked.

"I've been researching other species' technology."

"Why?" Fyn asked.

"It was Seth's idea," Wyn said, leaning his hip against his desk and crossing his arms. "When Seth was first brought aboard the Admiral Ven, NAID searched for species genetically similar to humans to help Dr. Qinlin with his medical treatments."

"Amorians," Fyn said. "Father is currently interviewing an Amorian doctor or two who will be in charge of Seth's health."

Wise, but somehow I doubted Seth wanted one, let alone a team of doctors hovering over him and studying him.

Wyn didn't remark on the new doctor and continued, "Seth thought we could do the same thing here. Search for other species that might have sensors to perceive Caleb. He's tangible, to some degree, so he has to be occupying some plane of existence. There are photonic species that we are unable to see. They might have technology that can perceive Caleb."

"It's a good idea," I said.

"I agree," Zoltilvoxfyn added after telling them what I said. "Has it yielded anything?"

"Not yet," NAID replied. "Technology within the Coalition is easy enough to test. It's the independent nations that are proving difficult. They don't share technology. The..." she made a low snap I assumed was the name of a different species, and I tried to silently practice it, "are a photonic species that I believe have what we need."

His back tensed. I slid my fingers up and down, and he twitched before relaxing.

"What?" I asked.

"They are xenophobic. Most photonic species are, except with other photonics," he explained.

"It's a problem," Wyn said. "I sent a request to Prince Kalvoxrencol regarding asking the luxnis if they have any idea of how to help us."

"That's going to take a significant amount of time. The request will have to go to my father, who might wish to bring it before the Cohort before sending it on to the Coalition," Fyn said.

"Yep," NAID replied. "But we'll keep working. Since Caleb is present, we should run more scans."

"I concur." Wyn snagged a few instruments.

I moved from Fyn's side, and his tail tried to curl around my ankle before flicking away. He directed Wyn to where I stood. I shoved my arms out, like it would make a difference. Wyn ran several different instruments over my general area. One had a flat tip with the diameter of a baseball, another had a glowing tip reminding me of *Doctor Who*, and the final one was a rectangle that gave off a blue ray.

Wyn and NAID made comments back and forth about whatever the results were, but I didn't pay much attention. My gaze remained locked on Fyn, who watched me with the slightest quirk pulling at the corner of his lips.

No matter how Wyn buzzed around me, Fyn's green eyes never wavered, and it caused the oddest sensation deep within me. So faint I had a hard time pinpointing it or even accepting it was real, but I loved it.

"We're done," NAID pronounced, making me start and yank my gaze off Fyn.

"That's good," I replied, voice squeaking. I glanced back at Fyn, but he was facing Wyn and NAID.

We left shortly after that. Fyn was still quieter than usual, and I was still worried about whatever was bothering him. At the same time, I was skipping along the halls because he'd let me touch him. He'd acted like he enjoyed me touching him. It was a very bad idea, a fucking horrible idea, to start something with him, but I was beginning to wonder if he wanted to—like I did.

He was a candle in the darkness of my afterlife. Losing him wasn't an option.

I whipped around, walking backward. Sunshine raised an eyebrow, and I grinned, bounding up to him. I saw his throat bob, and my smile widened. "We are going to your fighting class now, right?" I asked, not remembering the Drakconese word.

"Hand-to-hand combat class, and no."

"But I want to watch you."

His throat bobbed again. "Excuse me?"

"I like watching you," I said again. I'd said as much earlier, but maybe he hadn't understood. "Is that bad?"

"No." He stepped even closer, making me look up at him. "It's not."

"Then you should go, and I'll stare at you. You're the only one who will know, though."

"Not if I tell everyone."

"Do you want to?"

"Yes, but I won't."

I replied, "Then I can ogle you in peace."

"You are more than welcome to."

Chapter 16

LIKE MINDS.

Zoltilvoxfyn

I stared at the door, wings rustling. Caleb had gone back to the medical facility to check on Tinlorray and her brain-dead brother. I'd wanted to go with him because, for some reason, whenever he was out of my sight a pit would grow in my stomach and energy filled my veins. I needed to see him. Be with him.

The thought made me swallow and my cock twitch. I looked down. That was unexpected.

"This is not good."

While not many mediums had lived in our recorded history, there had been enough. More than one had documented the danger of growing too fond of a spirit and hindering their journey.

If I tried to romance Caleb, it would definitely be a hindrance.

Did I even desire to court him?

His contagious smile and laugh resounded through my thoughts. He was always bouncing around, interested in everything, no matter how small. There was an energy about Caleb that had drawn me in from my first glimpse of him.

Could I imagine my life without him?

My knees trembled, and I sank to the couch. I placed a hand over my throbbing soul. I didn't wish for Caleb to leave. I hoped to court him. No. That wasn't enough—not near enough. I desired to claim him as mine. It was foolish. It was impossible. Yet that didn't deter my desires.

In the last few days after I invited Caleb to watch me in hand-to-hand combat class, I'd been flirting with him and allowing him to touch me. The soft chill that swept over me whenever he brushed me was addicting, and I craved more.

Caleb made me laugh. He made me smile. He drew me out of my head with an ease I didn't understand.

I yearned for him to be mine, even though I knew in the end, we couldn't be, not truly. This was doomed to end in soul-rending agony.

If I admitted my feelings, especially to him, I could become an impediment to his journey, which was dangerous. If the soul remained on this plane for too long, they faded, slowly disappearing as time passed. It was believed the soul came apart, unable to stay together, and vanished. One of the mediums who came before me had been a spiritual soul who'd written that the vanished soul didn't pass on to the next plane. They were gone. Ceased to exist.

How could I allow that to happen to Caleb? Yet at the same time, how did I let him go?

The door chimed. I didn't want company, not in the slightest. Still, I went to see who was here.

"Fyn," Seth said, hands buried in his thick jacket. Humans must have a warmer planet than ours because Seth usually wore the same cloth jackets that came in a variety of dark colors. Sweat dotted his temple, though. I should ask Kalvoxrencol what temperature humans were used to. While I doubted it affected Caleb much in his current state, I would enjoy knowing.

What I truly needed was to have access to the human database to research for myself. But to be granted that, I would have to tell people of my affection for Caleb, and we were nothing. Not yet at least. Besides, I didn't know if Caleb felt the same as I did. At times, I caught glimmers of attraction in his eyes or detected the fervor of desire in his voice, but still, I remained unsure.

"Seth, where's Kalvoxrencol?" My brother hated to leave Seth alone; something I now understood.

"Meeting with the Ranks."

"Again?"

Seth swallowed. "They want to meet with me. I don't want to. Your parents are trying to mediate between Kal and them. Hal and Gil are there too."

Mediation, I thought, stifling a snort. Kalvoxrencol wouldn't negotiate when it came to the people he loved. Seth was the most important person in his life, and Kalvoxrencol was excessively protective; he wouldn't allow anyone near Seth unless Seth agreed.

"Did he send you here?" I didn't mind protecting Seth.

He lifted and lowered his shoulders. I still didn't know what that motion meant. "I was going to hang out with Urgg, but they're with their mate. Wyn has meetings all day. Kal doesn't want me to stay in our apartment alone in case someone comes. He likes to worry."

"No one, not even the Ranks, would try and force you to leave, Seth. You are safe here."

"I know. Kal was paranoid about leaving me, though, so I figured I would hang out with you and Caleb."

"He's not here at the moment."

"Oh." he said, and I motioned for Seth to sit, but he asked, "Can we go to the garden?"

"Of course." We headed outside as I said, "Caleb went to check on someone."

"What? He's haunting someone?"

Not how I would have phrased it, but it was accurate, I supposed. "It's complicated."

A gust of air tousled Seth's short hair, and I wondered if it was soft. Was Caleb's? It was on the tip of my tongue to request Seth's permission to touch him so I would know more of what Caleb was like, but that was odd.

I opened my mouth to ask anyway because I was a selfish creature, but I paused. Seth's expression was tight as he took deep breaths.

"Are you quite alright?"

"What?" he asked, whipping toward me.

"Are you alright?"

Seth released a long gust of air—another human thing I didn't understand. "No."

"May I ask what's wrong?"

His shoulders hunched.

Perhaps I shouldn't have asked. Guilt prodded me. I didn't want to be a bother to him; I wanted to help. Not that I was much help. I never helped anyone.

"I have anxiety," he said in a low voice.

Kalvoxrencol had mentioned that to me.

"To put it simply, my brain sees threats when there are none. I always think of the worst-case scenario or what *could* happen. I second guess every decision, and making one is extremely hard."

This I understood.

"I'm fighting my brain," he said. "Some days I don't win. Today is a bad day."

"Did you tell Kalvoxrencol before he left?"

He shook his head. "I didn't want to worry him."

I led Seth into my greenhouse. It shocked me that I didn't mind Seth in my greenhouse. I didn't even allow Kalvoxrencol in here very often, but somehow, Seth was different. He wandered around, and I allowed him to explore for a few minutes before giving him a metal tub.

Together we plucked dying flowers off the many plants.

"Do you know why my brothers call me 'Bloom?'" I asked.

"No. Kal's never said."

"I've always liked plants," I said. "Even when I was very small. When I was perhaps two, Serlotminden and I were playing in the garden, and he raced over a flower, crushing it. He's called 'Speedy' because he is always running from one place to another." It was no shock when he became a shuttle racer. "I cried."

"What?"

I repeated, "I cried. Not small tears, but heaving sobs as I clutched the ruined bloom. I was utterly distraught that it was gone, that I couldn't help it. Serlotminden tried to comfort me, but when he couldn't, he fell to the ground beside me and cried as well."

Seth laughed.

What a sight we must have been. "Dontilvynsan found us like that. He was eleven at the time, and his inner fire had already manifested. He knew from my thoughts why I was upset; I was mourning the flower. Dontilvynsan picked me up and grabbed Serlotminden's hand. He told me, 'Don't worry. This flower will go to the ground and be reborn. In the meantime, I will find you another.'"

"That's sweet."

"Dontilvynsan might be the largest of us and a captain in the navy, but he is by far the most understanding."

"Did he call you Bloom?"

"He did," I said, gesturing to the plants around me. "I've always liked plants because I understand them. They don't confuse me."

"I get that."

"I understand fighting your own mind," I whispered. "I understand having days so bad you wonder if it's worth it to continue. If not being here would be easier for yourself and those you love. I understand the fear of every choice. I understand the guilt of every mistake and the worry that you are the worst thing in everyone's life." I took a deep breath to steady the rapid beat of my soul and to silence my words. "I receive injections and speak to my doctor, usually, but it doesn't take them away."

Seth patted my arm, making both of us uncomfortable. "I know. Kal told me you have… I think he called it moroseness."

"Yes."

He said, "You can always talk to me."

"You as well. I would be honored to keep you company on bad days."

"Me too."

"I would like permissions."

"That's right," Seth said. "Friends require permissions."

"So do family. I'm not physically affectionate, but I don't mind if you occasionally hug or pat me like you just did. I don't wish to snuggle or to be touched often, though, especially my tail or wings."

"I'm the same." Seth's eyes darted away from me. "Don't surprise me, though. Sometimes I don't do well when I get randomly grabbed."

Anger curled in my gut as Kalvoxrencol's words came back to me. Seth had been abused by his caregivers and past partners. A burning desire to shred those people apart and keep my little brother's mate, my new mate-brother, safe swept through me. Nothing would ever happen to Seth again. Not ever.

"You know Kalvoxrencol will never harm you, right?"

"I do," he replied. "Trust me, I know."

I started plucking wilted flowers, and Seth followed suit. We stayed silent, but I felt no pressure to fill the quiet. It was peaceful.

Often when people were with me like this, and we weren't speaking, I had the urge to say something, anything, but not with Seth.

A knock on the glass made me start, but Seth leaped, sending the metal compost bin to the ground; dead leaves and withered flowers littered the moss-covered floor. I patted Seth's arm and curled my tail around his wrist, squeezing him, then I turned to the doors, expecting one of my brothers—but it was someone else.

"Urgg," Seth called.

We stepped outside, and the wind ruffled my hair. I hadn't realized how hot the greenhouse was until I was out in the free air. Urgg was dressed in their usual leather vest and trousers, but they were bright orange which contrasted against their green skin and black tattoos.

"Seth," Urgg said, clapping his shoulder.

Seth staggered under the hit, but he gave Urgg a smile.

"Zoltilvoxfyn," they said, not touching me, as I didn't like it.

"Urgg, what are you doing here?" I asked, peeking around for Caleb, even though I knew he wasn't present. He had, on several occasions, mentioned meeting Urgg, and now, he wasn't here when they were.

"I can't visit Seth? He even pinged me earlier, but I had plans with Talvax, who's the best and must come first."

"Naturally," Seth commented dryly. Urgg was effusive in their love of their mate.

"But then Talvax got called away regarding the Admiral Ven. She tried to get out of it, but she had to go. So here I am for Seth. We'll eat, we'll drink, and maybe we'll break something or spill blood,"

Urgg finished with a broad grin, smacking Seth's shoulder again. When he winced, I tugged Seth to my side with my tail around his wrist.

Seth asked, "Do you have a date for when you and Talvax are returning to the Admiral Ven?"

"Not yet," they answered. "But she's hoping soon. She's bored. My lovely Talvax doesn't like staying still. I've been keeping her occupied, though. Very *very* occupied." Urgg wiggled their eyebrows, leaving no doubts about how they were keeping Talvax busy.

"I'm glad you haven't left yet," he said, cheeks full of color, and Urgg ducked their head, smacking Seth's back, making me step partially in front of Seth.

"Ah, you're so nice. After Talvax. She's the nicest."

"Naturally," Seth said again.

I gestured to the path and both of them followed me—-talking. It was nice. Seth fit into our family, and I was glad he was here.

Chapter 17

DO WE BOTH WANT THIS?

Zoltilvoxfyn

After Urgg left, Seth and I returned to my greenhouse, not talking about much, until Kalvoxrencol came. He drew his mate flush against him, and I easily saw the stress coming off Kalvoxrencol as he rocked his mate. When I tried to find out what happened, Kalvoxrencol asked to speak to me later, which I respected. He needed a moment with Seth.

Now, I was back in my quarters, pacing. Caleb was still not home. It was dark, and he wasn't here. While I'd been with Seth, Caleb's absence had been shoved into the recesses of my mind. With no distractions, I couldn't think about anything else. I sank to the couch, clutching my knees.

My Caleb wasn't here with me. Where he belonged.

"Sunshine."

I started, wings sprawling, but I forced them back in place. Caleb bent slightly and cupped my cheek, thumb running over me. A coldness like ice swept over my cheekbone, making me shiver.

Something pulled in my gut, and a growl sounded in the back of my throat, need pulsing inside of me. Caleb blinked and started to move away, but I followed, extending the connection. He returned to holding my cheek as best he could.

I could stay in fear of what might happen or embrace what had started the instant I saw him. Caleb was mine, and I belonged to him. The other mediums had to have been wrong. Caleb wouldn't fade. He'd been wandering for cycles with no ill effect. He could stay with me, if he desired to do so.

"How was Tinlorray?" I hadn't thought of any way to help yet. I truly wasn't sure what to do, as this was a new scenario. Caleb had decided to check on her again to keep his promise, but not to go near her.

"Determined. When I arrived, she wasn't there, but when she came..." he trailed off.

"What?" I asked.

"She kept talking to him, like Yolkeltod was there. Like he heard her. Tinlorray was more put together. When the doctor came in, she said she knew Yolkeltod was there."

"Should I talk to her?"

"How would that help?"

"I'm a medium, Caleb. It's well known among the drakcol, though most don't believe me. I can tell her Yolkeltod is gone. I can tell her about you."

In the past, I'd helped the first two souls I'd met talk to their families. When they moved on, the families had gotten upset and called me a fake and blamed me for their grief. With the other souls, I had them talk to my family, but no one else. I shuddered at the thought of meeting this grieving woman, but I would for Caleb.

"You don't want to."

It was a statement, but I answered, "I don't want to."

"Then it will be fine. She will eventually realize Yolkeltod is gone." When I opened my mouth to protest, his thumb stroked my bottom lip, making it tremble. "I don't think she would believe you, Sunshine."

"If you think so."

"I do. Besides, you don't have to do something you don't want to. It will work out. I know it. Maybe not right now, but..." He lifted and lowered his shoulders. "It will be fine. Everything tends to work itself out, even if it's not how we want it to."

When Caleb bit his lip, I growled. I shifted toward him, then stopped myself. I didn't have his permissions. I'd been skirting propriety and forging closer than was right. We also had never discussed how he felt. Caleb might not desire me how I did him. Boundaries needed to be respected.

Never had I crossed the line before, but I'd never felt this way before either.

"I'm sorry," he said, backing away.

I followed him. "Don't apologize."

"I have to, Fyn. I keep doing this to you. I keep staring at you and touching you. Fuck, you don't even like your brother's touching you, and here I am groping you. I thought..."

Hope burned me like fire racing down my spine. "What?"

He glanced over his slight shoulder at me. "I thought maybe you might, you know, like me as well."

My lips separated as my tail thrashed. He wanted me. My Caleb wanted me as much as I did him.

"I don't know what I was thinking. Of course, you don't want this. Of course, you don't like me. I'm dead. This is weird. I'm sorry. I like you. I know I shouldn't, but I do. I mean, you're so amazing. How could I do anything but like you? But I shouldn't have, you know—"

"Caleb," I growled right behind him. My wings wrapped around him. He could step through them, but he didn't. "Do not apologize. I want this."

He turned around, biting his lip. "You do?"

"Yes. Yes," I repeated, the words ripping out from somewhere deep within me. "I shouldn't, but I do."

"I'm dead."

"Yes," I replied. "I can't change that. And Crystal help me, I don't want you to move on, because I need you to stay with me."

He smiled softly, staring up at me. "You do?"

"Yes." My lips clamped together, but I had to tell him. "You don't have to choose me, Caleb. You can move on. It's what you should do."

"I choose you."

Fire burned along my veins and my cock surged to life. I struggled to keep it from erecting. I only partially succeeded, and I hoped he wouldn't see it hardening in my trousers. "I'm keeping you, then," I growled.

Caleb went up on his toes and said right against me, "Sounds good to me."

Chapter 18

PERMISSIONS AND THEIR PAST.

Caleb

I sat across from Zoltilvoxfyn while he brushed his hair on the canopy bed in the center of his bedroom. Wind blew through the three windows, stirring the sheer curtains and flowering vines that wrapped around the bedposts. From one of the windows on the back wall, I saw the roof of his greenhouse, which made me oddly happy.

Fyn ran a comb through his long, perfectly white hair as he watched me.

"You're gorgeous."

He coughed, comb stalling.

Unfortunately, drakcol didn't blush, but I was certain he would be right now if he could. I said, "It's true."

"Thank you," he said in a tight voice, staring hard at the purple blanket beneath us. "I find you quite attractive as well."

"That's good. I'm sure my round ears and pupils are weird. That's not even talking about my lack of scales or how short I am or my small muscles."

"No," he replied, setting the comb down. "I like them all. You are you, Caleb, and I like you."

"Good." Now, I'd be blushing if I could.

"I would like permissions."

"What permissions?"

"What I can and cannot do? What do you like and dislike? How far do you wish to go at the moment?" he asked calmly, tail swishing.

My mouth fell open, then I recalled drakcol did this. They conversed about every relationship and what the person could and could not do. I had no idea why. I mean it *was* healthy, though it seemed odd to me.

Carefully, I asked, "You know I can't fuck, right? Like I can't even take off these clothes." I was worse than a Ken doll. There was nothing beneath my shirt, let alone my pants.

"I know, but..." he stopped.

It took me a moment to realize what he meant. He could jerk off while I was there. "Ah. Well, I don't want to do *that*. Yet." Though that did sound hot as hell. "As for the other things, you can touch me, and even when you do, I can't feel it."

"You can't?" he asked, forehead creasing.

"Nope. Emotionally? Yeah. Physically? No. I don't have bodily sensations like tears burning or gut dropping or even pressure when I go through things."

"That must be difficult."

I shrugged. I didn't want to talk about it. "But if you like touching me, or well trying to, you can. What about you?"

Fyn's gaze flicked over me in a possessive manner. "I desire everything, but I'm willing to wait. I like you, Caleb. You are..." he trailed off, staring out the window for a few moments, and I waited with bated breath. "You're inevitable."

"What?" I asked, blinking. That did not sound romantic.

"Like the rising of the sun, the coming of the tide, or the passage of time. You were always my future from the moment I saw you. You are my inevitable, and I would not change that, not for anything. You are mine. You always were and always will be."

Man, if I could, I would have a raging boner from those words alone. I had a thing for possessive guys. "Fuck, Fyn." I didn't know what to say—I had no words that would match up to what he'd said (I mean, who would?), so I asked, "Can I touch you?"

"Yes. I like it. It feels cold."

I moved until my knees almost met his. "Anytime?"

"Yes."

"Anywhere?" I asked.

He swallowed, tail flicking. "If you want to start something, yes. My tail is particularly sensitive."

"I'll keep that in mind." I went up on my knees and ran the tip of my finger down the center of his forehead, down his straight nose, over his full lips, and to his strong chin. Fyn released a gravelly groan that put a smile on my lips. Slowly, I dragged my fingertip over his face, tracing every feature, until I moved to one of his ears and brushed the tip.

He jumped.

Hello, there. "Do you like that?"

"My ears are sensitive."

"Hmm," I replied, running my finger up and down the tapered length. "More sensitive than your tail?"

"No. Less," he said shortly.

With a peek at his groin, I didn't see anything, but his tail was moving like mad. I continued to stroke his ear, loving the quiet noises he gave to me. I fed on each one, savoring them like a damn meal. I reached his neck, and Fyn hissed, wiggling.

"Another spot?" I asked.

With jagged breath, he answered, "Drakcol have scent glands."

I paused, wondering if I understood what he'd said correctly. "Like a cat?"

"Lucy has scent glands?"

"If we're thinking of the same thing, yes."

"Interesting."

"You have scent glands," I said, trying to continue the conversation. I was far more interested in him than Lucy. I ran my finger over the side of his neck, and he trembled.

"On my forehead, neck, and sides. I like you touching me there." His eyes were wide as his breath rushed out. I couldn't be giving him much feeling, but he was enjoying whatever I did to him.

"Me? Or anyone?"

"Just you."

Fuck me. Fyn knew exactly what to say. "Why?" I asked, sliding down his side. When I hit the right place, I knew it from his sharp inhale.

"Instinct demands I scent mark you."

I paused. He couldn't, though. Not really. I bit my lip, staring down at the blanket. "Are you sure?"

"About what?"

"Me."

"Look at me, Caleb Smith," he ordered. I did and Fyn bent toward me, leaving almost no space between us. "I am sure. I have never been more sure about anything in my life. You make complete and utter sense to me. We make sense."

"You are so romantic."

He grunted. "Only with you."

"Well, that's good because if you were like this with someone else, I would haunt them until I figured out how to do bad things to them. Like mess up their hair, or delete important information." I told him one hundred percent serious, "I would make their life a living nightmare if they tried to take you from me."

"That will never come to pass."

I glanced out the window at the moons. "You should go to bed. It's late."

"Will you stay with me?"

"I can't fall asleep, but if you don't care about me staring at you all night, then sure." I had zero problems watching him. With Fyn, it didn't feel voyeuristic. Well, it did, a tiny bit, but I liked him enough to ignore it.

"I don't in the slightest. I don't like the thought of you wandering around all night alone."

I laughed. "You know nothing can happen to me, right?"

"You can leave, obviously, but I'd like it if you stayed with me. Though that might be boring. You don't have to stay. I cannot make you."

His voice was so hesitant like he expected me to leave. I rested my hand on his thigh, sinking through his scales. I wished his body pressed back against me, but it didn't work that way.

"I won't be bored."

Fyn climbed under the silky white sheets and purple blanket, stiff and his expression distant. It didn't bother me. I knew he was embarrassed. I lay next to him on my side.

"Sleep," I whispered.

"I'm oddly excited."

"You mean you're horny."

"I don't have a horn."

Sometimes when I tried to say the same word in Drakconese in English, they didn't have the same meaning. "Aroused," I reiterated.

"Yes."

"It's not gonna happen tonight."

He grinned at me, canines gleaming in the low light, and I fought the urge to fan myself. Damn, he should smile like that more. Only at me, though. A gentle, sultry tickle down my spine at his softening smile. A brush of something on my palms while a rhythmic thrum pounded in my ears. I swallowed a groan, unwilling to look away from him for even a second. My Sunshine. My Fyn.

"Sleep."

"I can't."

"Hmm," I said. "Then tell me why you drakcol have permissions."

"Humans don't do that?"

"Not really."

Fyn wiggled until we were sharing the same air. Well, we would be if I breathed. Still, I liked him being so close. Fyn said, "I told you we used to be a warring species."

"Yep."

"Before our people were unified, it was common to take."

"Take?" I repeated.

"We would steal mates, people, possessions, or rather, anything we coveted."

"Ah." That... sucked, but it's not like Earth didn't have the same history.

"We took lives, freedom, spoils, people." He shook his head. "We took and took and took, hurting each other. When we unified, that was one of the first struggles to overcome—our innate fear and distrust of each other. Permissions became the first thing that helped. We try not to touch people without their agreement, but we do not always succeed. The instinct to claim and possess is still strong within us, especially when it comes to our mates."

"So you ask?"

"We ask. It has been a part of our culture for so long it's near instinct now. It's difficult for us when we don't have permissions. We can feel lost without them."

"Which is why you asked for mine," I said.

"Yes."

I ran a finger over him, and he groaned. I smoothed my thumb over his cheek, trying to imagine the scrape of his scales. "Go to sleep."

"Don't leave. Please."

"I won't." And I wouldn't. I never wanted to leave him.

It didn't take long for him to fall into a deep sleep. I traced his face. God, I was so happy. I didn't know if I'd ever been this happy; if I had, I didn't remember it. Zoltilvoxfyn liked me. He wanted this.

I should long to go home. I should miss my family, and a part of me did, but a bigger part wanted to stay with him. There was something about Zoltilvoxfyn. From the moment I saw him, I was attracted to him.

This wouldn't end well. I was dead. Even by his own admission, there was nothing he could do to change that. We couldn't ever be together, and it wasn't about sex. A relationship without sex was as valid as one with it.

It was about what separated us.

Zoltilvoxfyn would age and change. He was alive. And I... wasn't. This would never be more than a half relationship.

A light snore came out of his lips and his tail moved to drape over his thigh. I ran a finger down the length and paused. I saw his scales through the tip of my finger. That was not good, probably. I mean, it might be fine. What did I know? My finger solidified, but the tip was gray, without a hint of color.

My gaze moved to Fyn, and I smiled. Everything was alright, and we would be together. For now. That was enough.

Chapter 19

DATING. WE'RE DATING.

Caleb

I sat on the floor in front of Fyn. Kal and Seth were on the couch directly across from us. Kal had his tail wrapped around Seth's ankle and an arm draped over his shoulders. We were in their apartment, and it was the same as the last time, besides Lucy. She was hiding. That fucker. God, I'd planned to make faces at her. She was too cute.

Maybe I could convince Fyn to get a pet? That would be fun. I could play with them, kiss them, snuggle them, and... Perhaps not. Not all animals saw me, and if I couldn't interact at all with the pet—it would upset me, to say the least.

Something flashed in the corner of my eye, making me peek out the window. I caught sight of someone fluttering in the distance. A drakcol that had black hair and dark gray scales. I was pretty sure I'd seen him before around the greenhouse when Seth was hanging out, but I couldn't be sure

"Mother is requesting a piece of your art?" Sunshine asked, his tail swishing in and out of my thigh. His voice pulled my focus back to the matter at hand.

"Yes," Kal replied, carding his fingers through his silvery-blue hair. "She has decided to—"

"Patron," Seth supplied in English.

"Yes. That. She has decided to sponsor drakcol artists to decorate the palace. She wants to honor creator souls, and she placed me in charge of the project, starting with hanging a painting of mine in the front entrance," Kal said, dragging Seth even closer. Their eyes connected, and they both fell silent.

I didn't think it was a staring into each other's eyes moment, but more of a silent conversation moment. I wondered what it would be like to speak to Zoltilvoxfyn like that. Did Seth sense Kal or was it like a phone call? I kind of wanted to ask, but somehow, I figured it would fluster Seth.

"That's amazing, Pest."

Kal gave him a slight smile that rang false.

"What did she pick?" I asked.

He gestured to the half-finished painting behind him on an easel. It was of Seth in bed. He was asleep on his stomach, sheets twisted over one leg and tucked under his other thigh, exposing the swell of his ass. One hand was next to his face on the pillow and the other was stretched out on the bed. His expression, from what had been sketched, appeared relaxed, and his hair artfully fell over his forehead.

It was like the Renaissance paintings where a woman had her boob hanging out for no reason while she read or some shit. Artistic nudity for nudity's sake. I'm sure there was an *artistic* reason, though, but I didn't know it. A boob was a boob, and an ass was an ass, but whatever.

Seth turned a deep red, covering his face. "I can't believe she chose it."

"I can." I really could. The relaxed position made Seth appear oddly entrancing. I perceived the love, care, and peace of their relationship. "It's truly lovely."

"Thank you," Kal said, looking in my general direction.

"At least your cock's not in it, Seth," I quipped. Fyn choked on his drink but said my words, which made Seth sputter.

Kal pressed against Seth's cheek and whispered loudly enough for me to hear, "While every part of you is lovely, Husband, I wouldn't have allowed her to display such a painting, because I know you wouldn't have liked it." His voice dropped even more, making me move closer to hear. "Though you have a lovely cock, and it would definitely add to the front hall."

Seth's blush deepened.

Kal apparently liked to tease his husband, but from the pleasant look Seth gave him, I didn't think he minded. I sat down again and scooted until I was pretty sure my back brushed Zoltilvoxfyn's knees if his shiver was any indication. His tail swished toward my thigh, brushing me.

God, I wished I felt him. Anything. Even pressure would be nice. But I refused to be bitter about it. I was here with him, and that in itself was a miracle. Like it really was! I'd died years ago on Earth, and now, I was here with him on an alien planet across the universe.

"I wished she'd picked something else. Like one of your abstracts," Seth commented.

"Did you show Mother the abstracts?" Fyn asked.

Seth nodded. "She complimented them, but she chose this one. Kal was working on it when she came in."

"You can refuse her."

Seth looked at his lap. Kal caught his eye, and another silent conversation took place between them. I glanced at Fyn over my shoulder, and he raised his eyebrow. I didn't know what the problem was either. While I'd observed Seth, I didn't actually know him.

That thought oddly stung. The emotion had actual weight, prickling and uncomfortable. For a moment, I swore my heart clenched. But as quickly as it came, it fled, and I was left with my usual nothing. I peeked at my fingers, and while the tips were gray, they were solid.

"Well, I like it," I said to break up the tension. "You're very attractive."

My Sunshine hesitated before he translated my words in a rough voice. His tail thrashed, and I didn't know why. I reached back to touch what I thought was his thigh.

"Thanks," Seth replied, his blush returning in full force.

"Are you coming to hand-to-hand combat class today?" Kal asked.

Zoltilvoxfyn hesitated. I hoped he would say yes. Personally, I thought it was good for him, and I enjoyed leering at him when he worked out. When I was alive, I'd enjoyed hiking, kayaking, and other outdoor activities. Martial arts had never been my thing. For me, physical activity had been pointless unless there was some sort of exploration involved.

"You should," I told him. "Then I can stare at you."

"I will come."

Kal's shoulders loosened. "Good."

I lay on my stomach, gaze on Fyn. He and Kal were both drinking water after their workout. I'd enjoyed watching Sunshine as much this time as last time. His deep green gaze kept flicking in my direction, and I didn't bother to look elsewhere.

I swear death had stolen all of my shame. Embarrassment didn't come easily for me anymore, especially not for something as simple as enjoying watching my boyfriend workout.

Boyfriend. Shit, that thought alone made me roll around, grinning like a weirdo.

"Where's Seth?" Fyn asked as he came to sit beside me. When we met Kal at the class, Seth had been nowhere to be seen.

Kal raised his eyebrows at him sitting on the floor versus the couch, but he didn't comment. "My mate is with Wyn and Urgg this afternoon."

"I missed Urgg again," I shouted. Fyn had told me about Urgg's visit while I was with Tinlorray, and now, Wyn and Urgg were hanging out with Seth? Ugh, I *needed* to meet the barbarus; we *were* going to be the best of friends.

Fyn flicked his tail through my arm, lending silent comfort.

"It's a miracle Kal's not stalking him. They barely left each other's side on the Admiral Ven," I commented. Sunshine smirked at my comment but didn't relay it to his brother, which was probably best. I hadn't intended the remark for Kal anyway.

Once again, Kal raised his eyebrow, probably about Fyn's rare smile. He glanced at the door, tail whipping. "I should check on him."

"He can't go a single day without Seth," I remarked. "Not even a day. Like an hour is too much."

I grinned when Fyn smirked again.

Kal said a quick goodbye and darted off to find his husband. I chuckled at his departure, rolling onto my back. Seth was fine, but Kal was ridiculously overprotective.

Fyn leaned over me, his long white hair surrounding us. "What would you like to do today?"

My gaze flicked to his full lips. Making out would be nice, but that wasn't an option. His eyes darkened. "I wouldn't be opposed to a physically romantic activity, though we would need to have a conversation first."

Of course, he wouldn't be. It was probably a good thing I couldn't touch him or else I would be all over Zoltilvoxfyn constantly. I would make Kal seem positively normal in his clinginess. "Is there anything you have to do today?"

"No," he answered. "The next Cohort meeting is in a month, and I have no charity boards or anything. I'm all yours."

"I like the sound of that."

"It's the truth." Fyn stared at me with his deep green eyes.

How in such a short time had I claimed him? I didn't understand, but I was grateful. We were starting out, and yet, whatever lay between us was more significant than the beginning of a relationship. This bond felt permanent.

"So," he started in his deep voice, "what do you wish to do today, my Caleb?"

"Spend it with you."

"Easily accomplished."

"What should we do?"

"Whatever you want."

"What do you normally do?" I wanted to learn everything about Fyn.

"Working in my greenhouse or in the garden."

"We can do that."

Slowly, he cupped my cheek. I didn't feel it, but Fyn's lips quirked, and that was enough for me. "I wish to do something to please you," he said, voice low.

"Being in your greenhouse would make me happy. I want to see your life and spend time with you. That's all. We're *dating*," I said, then amended in Drakconese, "courting."

"Yes, we are."

"In English, you would be called my *boyfriend*."

His forehead crinkled in the cutest manner as he tested the word out. It was difficult to understand him because boyfriend sounded more like a groaning engine than the actual word. Sunshine repeated it a few times, perfecting his pronunciation.

"I'm your boyfriend," he said.

"Yes." I traced his lips with my fingertip, and he shivered.

"I like it."

"I do too." I truly liked it. More than I should have. There was no happy ending for us. No future. But here and now? It was enough. It was more than enough.

Chapter 20

UNCOMFORTABLE TRUTHS.

Caleb

Fyn was finishing up his breakfast at the table, and I stared at him like the creeper I was. It truly didn't matter what he was doing, I enjoyed watching him.

"What shall we do today?" my Sunshine asked, his tail sliding near my leg.

He'd asked this every day since we started dating. Usually, we remained in the palace. We would spend time with Kal and Seth or see Wyn and NAID. I still hadn't been introduced to Urgg, but they were never with Seth when I saw him; it was annoying as hell.

NAID and Wyn had made no meaningful progress on the sensors being able to perceive me. They'd mentioned some techno-babble I didn't understand, but the bottom line was—the sensors didn't perceive me yet besides the phase variance I caused. Wyn, and several of the other scientists studying NAID, had gotten super into it, though. Apparently, it was a fascinating thing to study, or, more accurately, I was an interesting problem for them to puzzle through.

And we hadn't heard if the Luxnisian Assembly would allow us access to their technology or not. Our request was still waiting for review from the emperor before being presented to the Cohort, if it even was going to. Fyn didn't know if his father would or not, because not everyone on the Cohort believed Fyn about his gift. Asses.

Mostly, Fyn and I spent our days in the garden, or he showed me around the palace. It was peaceful, and I loved it. My wanderlust usually made me seek out new places or explore all the nooks and crannies, but this time, it was different. Fyn had captured my interest so fully, I had no need to wander. He was the only thing I longed to explore anymore—my perfect Sunshine.

"My Caleb," Fyn said, startling me. "Are you well?"

"Of course. Why?"

"You didn't answer me. What should we do today?"

"I should go see Tinlorray." A few days had passed since the last time I'd seen her. I worried she was still clinging to Yolkeltod, thinking he was there because of my dumb-ass mistake. Of course, she'd assumed it was her brother's spirit, not some rando hanging around her. Because, let's be real here, who would have assumed some *other* ghost was hanging around them?

He looked away, and I fought a smile. Fyn liked to worry. Honestly, worrying had to be a drakcol thing. Kal certainly did it over Seth. I hadn't observed (or haunted by any other name) Hal and his mate Gil enough to know if he worried over her or vice versa, but probably. Drakcol were possessive buggers. Not that I was complaining.

I rested my chin in my cupped hands. "I'll be fine."

"I know."

"I promised Yolkeltod."

"I know."

I laughed. "You want me to stay, though."

"I worry something will happen or you will need me, and I won't be there. I don't wish to fail you."

I frowned at his choice of words. "You won't fail me, Sunshine. I'm an adult, and I'm responsible for my own choices."

"I need to protect you."

Yeah, this was definitely a drakcol thing. "You are protecting me, but if something happens, which it won't, trust me to take care of myself. I've been alone for a long time in some very desperate situations, and look at me," I held out my arms, "I'm still here."

There had been many times I thought I'd get stuck on some derelict ship or station. Or that time I'd gotten left behind on the uninhabited planet for at least a year, maybe more. I *was not* going to tell Fyn anything about that. He would worry, which, as I'd established, was a favorite pastime of drakcol.

His tail whipped side to side and his wings rustled on his back, threatening to slide out through the slits in his shirt. Fyn pulled away from me, and I wasn't sure why.

"Sunshine," I whispered, brushing the line of his jaw. "What's going through your head?" He blinked. While my words had been in his language, I don't think I used them properly or they didn't have the same concept attached to the words. Learning languages without proper classes was hard. "What are you thinking?" I reiterated.

He didn't say anything.

Worry plucked at me. Was he mad? Or maybe rethinking being with me? He wouldn't change his mind, right? "We should go on a *date* when I get back from seeing Tinlorray tonight."

"I do not understand that word," he said. His tone still held something that I couldn't articulate, and it made me worry. Like my pulse actually picked up for an instant before it vanished.

I had said date in English because I didn't know the Drakconese equivalent. Was it the same as courting? Probably. Maybe. But that might be focused on us and not an activity. I wracked my brain for a few more seconds, trying to find a word that was similar, but nothing came to mind, especially with the panic he was about to break up with me flitting through my thoughts.

So I settled with: "An outing where we spend time getting to know each other."

"Like we do every day?"

"Not exactly. A date usually involves food or an activity. Why don't you think of something you would like to do, and we'll do it together. It's fun and we get to know each other. I think you would like it. I mean, I like it. I want to date you; you don't have to date me. We can—"

"I want to," he interrupted, making me relax.

Everything was fine.

I stepped into the hospital room where Yolkeltod's lifeless body lay. Tinlorray wasn't there, but it was early in the day, and I suspected she was at work—whatever it was that she did. I had no idea. I clearly needed to stalk her more.

So many things on Earth and Tamkolvanloknol were similar. People had families, lives, and jobs. While the details might differ, people were people. As I wandered the universe, recognizing the similarities between humans and other aliens always shocked me. Yes, the trappings were different, and aliens appeared different and had unique cultures, but all in all, we were the same, at least in some small way.

Though, the technology. Man, I wished Earth had half of the things I'd seen.

Chuckling to myself, I went to Yolkeltod's side. The same empty feeling came over me when I stared at his body. The machines kept him alive and breathing, but *he* was gone. God, it was morbid, not to mention depressing, and I hoped Tinlorray would let him go.

With nothing else to do, I wandered from bed to bed. There were a variety of patients from older people with rough scales to younger ones with the sheen of youth. There were no children. A few visitors would come in and out, but none of their conversations held my focus for long. Most were about the comings and goings of their lives or families, which should've captured my attention, but things were different now. Or, more accurately, I was different.

I wanted to go back to the palace and spend the day with Fyn and assure myself that we were fine. Perhaps I could convince him to wander the city? I didn't know if that was something he was allowed to do. He was a prince. Also, he might not like shopping or chilling in the city. I hadn't asked yet. God, there was so much to learn about him still.

Maybe we could go somewhere else like the forests surrounding the capital? Hiking? Plants? Both of us would enjoy that.

Or an experience—a simulated reality within a suite. They were usually stories, military, or exploration. Experiences, from what I'd seen, were awesome—Kal and Seth had played one on the Admiral Ven. It would be fun to do with Sunshine.

The day passed like it was on fast-forward as I thought through the different options for our date. The longer I was a ghost, the less time meant to me and the easier it was to do nothing. There was literally no rush or pressure. I had nothing but time.

I was so lost in my thoughts about Fyn that I didn't notice Tinlorray until she flopped onto the stool I was sitting on. I quickly stood, and she shivered.

"Yolkeltod?" Tinlorray asked.

"Shit." I'd been trying my best to not touch her, but that plan was clearly circling the crapper. "I'm not Yolkeltod. He's gone."

Tinlorray ignored me, not shocking, and talked to her brother about what was going on in her life, much like all of the other visitors, though I paid far more attention to her. Her hair was clean and neatly braided, her scales shiny, and her clothes without a single wrinkle.

Hope. I'd given her hope, but it was false and I feared, in the end, it would hurt Tinlorray far more than the truth.

"Work is well," she said, smoothing the blanket over Yolkeltod's body. "Tomkin says I'm the leading candidate for the systems programmer. That means no more fixing broken tech all over the city. I'd work near here. I could see you more."

That's why she'd been in the apartment complex; she'd been fixing something.

"The Guard is still holding your place," Tinlorray continued, straightening Yolkeltod's hair. "Two more cycles and you can go to space as a security officer, like you desire, or join the Planetary Navy, if you want to go to the academy first." Her tail flicked. "I know I didn't want you to go, because I'd miss you, but, Yolkeltod, I would do anything to have you back, and if the stars are where you want to be, I will support you."

Everyone had regrets. You said something hurtful that you wished to take back. You didn't support someone because of fear. You didn't talk to someone as much as you wished. We all left this world with regrets for actions not taken and things left undone, but the people we left behind had just as many. It was the human condition—or rather, the price of living.

"Please," Tinlorray said, voice growing in volume. "Please, Yolkeltod, come back to me. I'm so sorry. That fight..."

When she trailed off, I swore my heart fell, but it was so fast, I couldn't be certain it had actually occurred.

"We fought, Yolkeltod," Tinlorray said, tears forming. "We never fight, but you were going to leave, and I wasn't ready. The last thing

I did was accuse you of abandoning me. Of neglecting your duty to our family for adventure."

She cupped her brother's cheek. "Please, please accept my apologies. Please, Yolkeltod."

"Fuck," I whispered.

Tinlorray gripped his much larger hand. "I'm not ready… I'm not ready for you to go, so I need you to come back."

Chapter 21

MY LIFE, MY MATE, MY CHOICE.

Zoltilvoxfyn

Joy pulsed through me as my thoughts circled on Caleb. While he called me Sunshine, he was truly the sun in my life. He brought a tenderness and light I'd never experienced before. So little time had passed since he'd entered my life, and yet, I couldn't imagine it without him. He was precious to me in an indescribable way. It was like my entire universe circled him and him alone.

"You are not listening to me, Zoltilvoxfyn," Kalvoxrencol said, swatting the back of my legs with his tail.

"I am not."

"You have been smiling a lot of late."

"Is there something wrong with that?"

"No. Hallonnixmin and Monqilcolnen both remarked on it as well. Is everything well?"

In the past, I'd often been used as a means to get information from Kalvoxrencol when he was causing problems or hiding from us, but the same could be said about him concerning me. When I was lost in the ebbs and flows of my mind, the rest of my brothers unleashed Kalvoxrencol on me. Like he was with me, I kept no secrets from him—we were the closest of friends.

"Yes," I said stiffly and turned to the ferns outside of my greenhouse. The seedlings were ready to be transplanted. I had spliced this hybrid together so it was hardier than either of the originals, required less water, and produced more oxygen.

I was going to present it to the Council of Seekers for use on long-haul ships once I'd proven the longevity and ease of care for the hybrid species. The ferns were also a most pleasing shade of purple, which wasn't important, but I quite liked the color, as did Caleb. He hoped the black spots of one of the parent plants would grow on the underside of the leaves as the seedlings aged—I wasn't sure, but I was excited to find out.

Kalvoxrencol stared at me, and I ignored him. I wasn't going to tell him about Caleb, because I feared his response. He wouldn't judge the two of us for caring for each other, but Kalvoxrencol would worry about me and mine's future. I didn't. Caleb was mine as surely as Seth was Kalvoxrencol's. I knew it. I felt it.

Though as much as I told myself that, a niggling weed of doubt wouldn't leave me be. It made me question whether I was the best thing for Caleb, whether it was safe for him to remain, or whether it would be better if he left me behind.

"You didn't meet with Doctor Jalnin."

I snapped, "That is *none* of your concern."

He tilted his head to the side and offered me his throat, and I turned away, head lowered and tail slashing. Kalvoxrencol rarely did that. It was hard for him to concede anything to us, even when he was in the wrong.

Guilt surfaced, and with it, self-loathing. I didn't like injuring him, but whether I saw my doctor or not was my personal affair. I *had* missed the appointment because I was with Caleb. Besides, lying to my doctor was counterproductive to my mental health, but I couldn't tell him about Caleb, and all I wanted to do was talk about my mate.

"I care about you, and I want to make sure you're not neglecting yourself," he said.

"I know, Pest. I didn't mean to bite." I moved several empty pots off the electric trolly before sending the cart away. I planned to create another hybrid for Seth. He'd shown me images of a flower called a *rose* on his planet, and I planned to recreate the flower here. No samples had been taken from Earth when Kalvoxrencol went to claim his Crystal-chosen mate, a shame in my opinion, but I had the genetic structure, once Seth had requested NAID send it to me, and believed synthesizing something similar was possible.

"I know I have been occupied with Seth and I was gone for an entire cycle, but you can still speak to me about anything."

"I know, Pest," I repeated. I wrapped my tail around his briefly. "I don't begrudge you wanting to spend time with your mate. I like Seth. I'm fine. I swear on the Crystal's light."

"You are more than fine. You're always smiling."

Without my permission, another smile stretched over my face. Caleb had asked to spend time together tonight when he returned. I hated him wandering the city without me by his side because something might happen and I wouldn't be there to protect him. While I wanted to keep him within my sights at all times, I recognized he'd been on his own for over twenty cycles. He was perfectly capable of taking care of himself. Being with one another all the time wasn't healthy either; regardless of that fact, my instincts demanded I stay beside him for every moment of every day.

Kalvoxrencol stared at me, tail flicking. All of a sudden, a sly grin quirked on his lips. "You met someone."

"What?" I squeaked, then cleared my throat. "What do you mean?"

"You met someone. Who is it?"

I turned my back to him. I wouldn't dishonor Caleb by lying, but I wasn't ready to speak about us.

Chuckling, he said, "I'm right. You have that presence of a new relationship about you. Who is it?" When I kept quiet and continued rearranging the pots, Kalvoxrencol asked, "Is it someone in the palace? You rarely leave. You've been spending copious amounts of time with the scientists studying NAID."

He paused and swerved in front of me. "It's Ensign Wyn, isn't it? I cannot fault your taste; he is quite lovely. I was actually jealous of him spending time with Seth when I first met him."

"It's not Ensign Wyn."

"But it is someone."

I groaned. "Leave me alone, Pest."

"Tell me who it is."

I wouldn't lie and say there was no one, for there was, but how would Kalvoxrencol react to Caleb being the choice of my soul? Not well was my assumption.

"Why won't you tell me? Did I do something wrong?"

The hurt was obvious in his voice, and it sent waves of guilt crashing around me, even stronger than before. I'd never kept a secret from Kalvoxrencol before. We were each other's confidants. When he was returning with Seth from Earth, Kalvoxrencol had confessed his every doubt and issue between him and Seth to me.

He'd trusted me, and now it was my turn.

I took a deep breath, my soul pounding against my ribcage. "It's Caleb. We are together."

"What?"

"Caleb and I are courting."

He looked as if he was about to speak further when he stopped and stared at me.

A cloud began to gather inside of me as the words from my past came to haunt me like spirits that would never depart. Liar. Freak. Attention seeker. I averted my gaze. My hands trembled as I lifted one of the empty pots to my workstation. My emotions deadened when an all-encompassing numbness descended, filling every fiber of my being. I was courting a spirit, and my brother, my dearest friend, didn't understand. If he didn't, no one would.

"Now you know why I did not say anything," I remarked, voice hard. Stars, why was I the odd one of the family? My inner fire, my emotions, and now my romance. I didn't regret Caleb, but I yearned to be normal—I longed for us to be normal mates who were together with no judgment.

"He's a spirit, Zoltilvoxfyn."

A sharp knife forged of ice plunged into my soul. "I am aware."

"You two cannot be together."

"Why not?" I demanded, wings sliding out the back of my shirt. "He is mine, and no one shall take him from me."

Light pooled under his scales, and Kalvoxrencol's wings spread from my aggression, but he didn't move toward me. Though younger and shorter, Kalvoxrencol would win should this end in an official challenge or physical altercation. His soul type might be a creator to my warrior, but he'd spent every day honing his body into a weapon.

He took a deep breath, and his wings dropped to a neutral position. "Did he agree to be yours?"

"Yes. Do you think I would take advantage of him?" I snapped.

"Does he understand what it means?"

"Yes." Caleb had readily agreed to be mine, without hesitation.

Slowly, Kalvoxrencol grabbed my arm, and I bristled but didn't shake him off. "I do not say these things to hurt you," he said. "I like Caleb, as does Seth. But you don't know humans like I do, Zoltilvoxfyn. They are different from us. Does your Caleb truly understand what it means when you say he is yours? Does he understand that you are to be his mate and that *this* is permanent for you?"

Mollified by Caleb being called mine, I actually contemplated my little brother's words. Did Caleb understand? I had told him I would never give him up. He hadn't acted upset. In fact, he'd seemed to like it. But we hadn't known each other long or well, and humans were different from drakcol. He might not have understood what I truly meant.

"I don't know," I finally admitted.

"You need to speak with him. Humans don't mate only once like we do. Caleb might not understand our desire to claim one person."

"I will."

His grip on my arm tightened. "Are you sure this is what you want?"

I brushed him off. "He is mine, Pest. I knew it from almost the instant I saw him."

"I believe you, but he is a spirit, Zoltilvoxfyn."

"So?"

"You yourself told me that spirits cannot linger here because of the threat of disappearing. Permanently. Is it fair to make him stay?"

I'd had much the same thought. "I'm not forcing him. Caleb is choosing to stay. Besides, he has been dead for a long time."

"Please," Kalvoxrencol said, "read what the other mediums had to say again in case you missed something, and please guard your soul until you know he can stay with you."

It was too late for that. Caleb was mine, and I would have no other. "Did you guard your emotions from Seth until he decided to stay?"

His aspect darkened. "That was different."

"Why? Because the Crystal revealed him as your soulmate?"

"Yes, the second I made the choice to seek the Crystal, my fate was sealed. I went into it knowing I could never have another. This is different, Bloom."

"Caleb is as much mine as Seth is yours. I will not waste time or energy protecting myself from him on the slight chance he might decide to move on. I will cherish what we have right now."

Wrapping his tail around mine, he said, "I understand. I will help you however I can."

"Thank you."

"I don't want you to be hurt."

"Like I once told you, if he does decide to move on, I will allow all of you to hold me together until I can stand by myself."

After several moments of strained silence, Kalvoxrencol asked, hip against my workstation, "Is there anything you want to know? I know you don't have access to the human database we took from Earth yet. Hopefully, the Council of Seekers will release it, or you can tell Mother and Father of your connection to Caleb, and you will be granted access."

That wasn't going to happen. "There are things I would like to know."

"So ask."

"What does it mean when he bobs his head?"

He laughed. "That confused me as well."

I listened intently as he explained nodding, shrugging, blushing, which Caleb had never done—he might not be able to—and all manner of other human oddities. I seamlessly transplanted the fern seedlings while Kalvoxrencol spoke. He even told me of things like

Seth marking when he sucked and nibbled on his skin. A hickey, Kalvoxrencol called it. I would have no opportunity to use such knowledge with Caleb, but I enjoyed knowing that and things like their soft, smooth skin, which was cooler than ours, how soft their pink tongues were, and how amazing it was to be inside of them.

As Kalvoxrencol talked, a shot of longing went through me. Sex and physical love would never exist in our relationship. I would still choose Caleb, though, in spite of everything.

Eventually, my little brother fell silent, eyes distant. Was he speaking with Seth? I didn't know how far they could mind-speak or if they even understood each other, as neither spoke the other's language. I was surprised they even could mind-speak as Crystal-bound drakcol mates did. It was rare for another species to be able to; humans had to be more compatible than we had thought.

"Seth is the best thing that ever happened to me," he said.

I had never seen Kalvoxrencol as happy as he was now, so I readily believed it. "I'm grateful he chose you, Pest."

"As am I. I cannot live without him."

"I feel the same about Caleb," I said, not looking at him.

Kalvoxrencol shifted until his shoulder bumped into me. "I believe you."

"Thank you."

"I will give you the same advice that countless people gave me when I was courting Seth: talk to him."

"I will."

Kalvoxrencol stayed with me until Seth wandered into the garden. The second Kalvoxrencol saw his mate, he raced off, scales glowing.

I shook my head when he seized a blushing Seth about the waist and took to the air, heading in the direction of their quarters.

Chapter 22

AN ILL-TIMED INVITATION.

Zoltilvoxfyn

Sitting on a metal stool next to my workstation, I grabbed my screen and began to work on the roses. My claws clacked on the glass, and the world disappeared. It was easy to lose myself in my work, and time passed in a blur of numbers and tweaks.

Cold trailed up my spine, then across my shoulder blades before trailing down my sides in his usual pattern, making me shiver. I turned around, and Caleb stood behind me.

"My Caleb, you're back."

"Yep."

"I missed you." My wings rustled on my back, and I glanced down at my screen. I hadn't intended to say those words, and yet, they were the truth. I'd missed him. Terribly.

A chill brushed my chin, and I looked up. His fingers drifted over my scales. "I missed you too."

I opened my legs, and Caleb stepped in between them, then I enclosed him in my wings. This scene would be odd to anyone besides me, but I didn't care.

"I have a plan for our outing."

"Date," he said in human speech, then his eyelids lowered. "I'm looking forward to it."

The heated look sent a jolt straight to my cock, and it twitched. I longed for the things Kalvoxrencol had spoken of. If I'd had the opportunity, what would touching Caleb have been like? What sounds would he have made? At the mere thought of his warm hole wrapped around me as I slid in and out of him, my cock filled and pushed at the fabric of my trousers.

"Hmm," Caleb said, pink tongue licking his lips. "You have thought of it."

I cleared my throat. "I hadn't thought of that particular aspect, as we haven't discussed those permissions."

"Then what's going on?" he asked. When I didn't respond, Caleb smirked. "Does my presence alone make you aroused?"

"Yes," I replied, refusing to be embarrassed about my need for my mate.

"That's so fucking beautiful. If I could, I'd be hard, Sunshine. Just for you." His fingers crested my forehead before moving over my hair. For the barest moment, I felt him. Not the coldness of his soul, but the true feeling of him—pressure moving the strands of my hair. Foolish, I knew, and yet I couldn't banish the sentiment. It had probably been the wind. Nothing more. Yet I longed for his touch.

Caleb's fingers drifted over my scales in cool waves. Each one sent rapid-fire tingles through my body. By the light of the Crystal, I had never experienced anything like it before. No partner had ever inspired such passion within me from true touches, let alone whispers that barely existed.

"Caleb," I groaned.

A cold brush on the tip of my cock made me fight back a moan.

"I like seeing you like this," Caleb said.

Slowly, his fingers slid up and down my shaft still trapped in my trousers. I had to fight to remain silent. I didn't need my shouting to bring any guards or servants. Such a thought didn't calm my ardor in the slightest. I didn't care who saw me or saw what Caleb did to me.

"Perhaps," he started, voice husky, "we should go to your room before our date and have that conversation."

"I agree."

"Zoltilvoxfyn," a cheerful voice called, and I swallowed a snarl. Serlotminden. I acknowledged him with a flick of my tail before facing the workstation to hide my raging erection.

Serlotminden was four cycles older than I was. He and our other brother, Dontilvynsan, had left right after Kalvoxrencol reaffirmed his mating to Seth. Unlike Dontilvynsan who had military duties to attend to, Serlotminden came and went as he pleased when he was between diplomatic assignments and shuttle races, and apparently, he'd come back.

"We'll finish later," Caleb murmured in my ear, and I fought a protest. I throbbed in need of him, but at the same time, I wasn't prepared to tell Serlotminden about Caleb and me.

"How was your latest race?" I asked, claws clicking on my screen, though I paid no attention to what I was doing.

"Ninth," he replied, tousling my hair. "Not too bad."

Much like me, Serlotminden had pure-white hair, though his was shaved on one side. He shared the green eyes of our mother, and the wide forehead and strong chin of our father. His scales were dark purple while slips of white and gold skin peeked around them. His tapered ears were threaded with gold chains and a single ring pierced his bottom lip.

"Why are all of you so attractive?" Caleb asked from my side, and I frowned, chest rumbling with a possessive growl. He whispered against my ear, "You're the most gorgeous, though."

I swallowed.

"Zoltilvoxfyn?" Serlotminden asked.

I jerked. "My apologies."

"Not a problem. Kalvoxrencol told me you had a human spirit with you." Serlotminden waved in a general direction of the garden, not even near where Caleb hovered by my side. "Hello, human. I am Serlotminden. Third prince, the attractive one, shuttle racer, and the great romantic of the royal family."

I scoffed, but Caleb laughed. "He's funny."

Unhappily I related what Caleb said, and Serlotminden preened like a bird in mating season. Kalvoxrencol and Serlotminden both had had many romances over the cycles—the most of any of us.

Kalvoxrencol, though, wasn't as annoying in his antics when he pursued someone, unlike Serlotminden.

"I'm Caleb. Human, wandering soul, and the most clumsy person you will ever meet."

Serlotminden grinned. "I like you."

"The feeling is mutual," my mate replied with an equally wide grin.

I fought a frown, but I was unsuccessful.

Serlotminden asked, "Are you well?"

"Perfectly fine," I replied through gritted teeth.

"You're lying," Caleb said, brushing my hair. "What's wrong? Sunshine, are you sick? Do you need to go to the doctor? We should—"

"What's going on?" Serlotminden asked, unknowingly talking over Caleb. "Are you having a bad day? Shall we do something together? I can take you flying in my shuttle." He gripped my shoulder while his tail wrapped around mine. "We can grab Kalvoxrencol and Seth. It would be fun."

My lips opened to say no, but Caleb bounced by my side, brushing Serlotminden and making him shiver. "That would be so fun."

"The spirit is standing a lot closer than I thought," Serlotminden remarked, rubbing his arm.

"Caleb," I corrected. "His name is Caleb."

Serlotminden gave me his throat. "You are correct. My mistake, Caleb."

"Not a big deal." Caleb asked me, "Can we go?"

Resigned, I said, "Caleb and I would love to go."

"Can he? I thought most spirits didn't wander very far."

Chuckling, Caleb said, "You're in for a shock."

"Caleb is a unique soul," I said before telling Serlotminden about my mate, my voice growing more animated with each word. When I finally stopped, I looked at my older brother who watched me. I cleared my throat and turned toward Caleb. He caressed my cheek, and I released a low moan, unable to help myself.

"I would like to get to know Caleb. If you will allow me," Serlotminden asked.

Part of me insisted I deny him. Caleb getting to know my handsome, charming older brother almost felt like a threat, even though there wasn't one. I wanted to keep my mate to myself, but that wasn't right. Controlling Caleb was wrong, and I wouldn't do that disservice to my mate.

"I would like that," Caleb said, and I related it to Serlotminden begrudgingly.

"Hmm," my older brother said, studying me. "I shall retrieve Kalvoxrencol and Seth. Will you meet us at the port?"

"Yes."

When he disappeared into the palace, Caleb said, "I'm excited."

I opened my legs for him to stand between, and once again, I surrounded him with my wings. "Haven't you been on a shuttle?"

"Of course. But this will be fun."

"It will," I replied, keeping my face blank.

Caleb's smile dimmed, and it shredded my soul to see him upset. "What's wrong? Did I do something wrong? You've been..." He stopped, shaking his head. "What's going on?"

Two different paths lay before me: lie to my mate or be honest to him. I refused to be dishonest with the one I wished to share my life with. "I'm jealous."

His head cocked to the side, allowing me to see his cute, round ear through his brown curls. "Jealous? You're jealous? That's it? It's not me? What do you have to be jealous of?"

"My older brother. You liked him."

He blinked, then started laughing. Needles poked my soul. Foolish. I was beyond foolish for confessing such. Caleb and I were together, but from what Kalvoxrencol said, he might not even view our relationship the same way. Caleb and I courting might mean nothing to him, and it was idiotic of me to have, let alone admit such emotions.

A cold brush made me look up. Caleb rested his fingers against my chin. "No, Sunshine. Don't do that. I can see you pulling away from me. I didn't mean it like that. I'm not laughing at you. I swear. I wouldn't laugh at you. Well, I would, but not in a mean way."

I didn't respond.

"I want to get to know Serlotminden *because* he's your brother. No other reason. I mean, he seems nice and everything, but mainly, it's because he's your family. I want to know them because I'm with you, Fyn. We're courting. We're boyfriends. Your family is important to you, so they're important to me."

Heat rushed under my scales. My wings rustled, attempting to gather Caleb close, but they slid through him. "My Caleb."

"We don't have to go."

"No," I said. "You want to, and I know Seth would enjoy spending more time with you, as would my brothers."

"I don't want anyone else besides you. I promise."

My soul jolted, racing in my chest, but the pleasant heat turned into something frigid. "Because I alone can see you."

"No, Zoltilvoxfyn," Caleb said. "I like you because you are you. I was attracted to you from the first time I saw you. You were so pretty when you stepped out of the greenhouse. You wiped dirt on your cheek." He brushed my cheekbone. "Right here. It was adorable. You make me laugh. You make me happy. You make me alive, Sunshine." He bit his lip. "I mean, if you hadn't been able to see me, I would have stalked you. No. I don't mean that. I mean, I do. Cause I would have. I swear I'm not being weird."

I swallowed as Caleb continued to ramble about how he would have stalked me, in a non-disturbing fashion.

Caleb took a deep breath, stalling his rapid speech. "I like you. That's what I'm saying. I like you for you. Do you understand?"

"I understand."

"Good." His fingers roved over my face. "When we get back, we should go on our date."

"I would like that." Unable to stop myself, I growled, "You are mine, Caleb, and I will not let you go."

"Sounds good to me."

Chapter 23

COME FLY WITH ME.

Caleb

I skipped beside Fyn as he led me to the port. I recognized it because this was where I first came to Tamkolvanloknol. The wide open space had several sleek silver shuttles, and drakcol in black uniforms darted around doing something important, I was sure.

It took me all of one second to find who we were searching for because there were no shuttles or people around them. Seth stood beside Kal with an arm around his trim waist. Serlotminden was gesturing to the shuttle behind him, beaming. The shuttle, while gleaming silver like most of the others on the lot, looked different. It was smaller and had a sharp nose and slim wings.

"Zoltilvoxfyn," Kal called when he caught sight of us, or rather, his brother.

My Sunshine returned the greeting, tail wiggling in what I believed was agitation. I rested my hand on his lower back before sliding up his spine, over one shoulder, and down his side.

He relaxed under my non-existent touch, which made my heart soar.

Serlotminden rushed to the side of the shuttle as he called, "Let's go."

We all clambered aboard. There wasn't much room inside. Two seats were at the front of the craft, and Serlotminden slid into one. The stool, I guessed was the way to describe it, didn't have a back, but it did have arms as well as buckles. The drakcol needed space for their wings, I supposed.

Kal directed Seth to the two other seats, leaving the co-pilot seat for Fyn. Sunshine glanced at me. There was no place for me, but I could hardly hold it against Serlotminden. I was a ghost. He couldn't see me. Hell, he probably didn't think I sat down.

"I'm fine," I told him before Fyn said something.

"You're not," he replied. Seth glanced at us, but Fyn ignored him.

"I don't need to sit down. Like I don't even feel my legs. I can't even get tired. Trust me, I'm fine. All fine. No issue. The ship won't even vibrate me or throw me around. I'm dead, Sunshine. It's all good."

He jerked back like I struck him. We liked to pretend I was actually here, but I wasn't. I motioned for him to sit in the remaining seat with a bright smile, refusing to allow his reaction or our reality to bother me.

Serlotminden glanced over his shoulder as he flicked several switches and jiggled a yoke. "Is there a problem?"

"No," Fyn said before sitting down.

I stood behind him. "It's fine, Sunshine." I bent to place a non-existent kiss on his head. "I'm fine."

When he didn't react, I stroked the point of his ear, making him shiver. I smirked and kept brushing the sensitive spot until he was wiggling. While I enjoyed the thought of Fyn getting aroused in front of everyone, staking my claim on him publicly, I stopped. I wasn't sure if that was something he liked.

The sleek craft slowly lifted off the ground. Before long, we were whizzing over the trees and steep mountains of Tamkolvanloknol. I peered over Fyn's shoulder at the deep canyon. The walls were sheer, and I didn't see much of the bottom from our angle, but I did catch sight of the sandy ground.

"We're not leaving the planet, right?" Fyn asked.

"Of course not," Serlotminden replied. "I know I can't take you away."

Why couldn't Fyn leave? Kal had. Serlotminden did. Their other brother Dontilvynsan certainly did. I wasn't sure about whether the eldest Hal or his mate Gil left or not. Why would Fyn have to remain planetside?

A silence hung in the air, and I peeked back at Kal who had his arms crossed, and Seth who looked as confused as I was.

"What's going on?" I asked.

Fyn replied, "My parents don't allow me to leave Tamkolvanloknol."

"Why?" Seth asked.

"How can they stop you?" I asked at almost the same moment.

"Caleb," Fyn said after relating what I said to the group, "my parents can keep me here because I'm in the first phase of adulthood until I'm mated. And Seth, they keep me here, in part, because of my inner fire. It is exceedingly rare. And for other reasons."

I stroked his hair, wondering if his depression was one of the reasons they kept him close.

"It's unfair," Kal commented, and Serlotminden gripped the controls, making me think he agreed with Kal.

"You're not an adult?" I asked.

"I am in both body and mind. In my culture, though, drakcol have two phases of adulthood. The first we enter at fifteen when we are fully grown. While in the first phase, our parents or government-appointed guardian control certain aspects of our lives, like large decisions regarding finance and where we live. I can manage my day-to-day money, but I can't purchase something significant without their approval. I can live anywhere on Tamkolvanloknol, but to leave, I would need their approval. It is the same if I were to seek the Crystal for a mate or reaffirm the bond. I don't become a full-fledged adult until I'm mated."

"It confused me as well," Seth said, looking in my general direction. "Kal is now a full-fledged adult. It's weird."

"From what I understand of human biology," Kal said, "us being fifteen is the equivalent to humans at twenty-five. When we are fifteen, physically and neurologically, we are fully grown."

"Ah," I replied, but I didn't exactly understand. Did drakcol age faster than we did or was their planet's rotation slower? But why was mating integral to being an adult?

"Family and children are important to drakcol," Serlotminden supplied, like he'd heard the questions rattling inside of me. "Mates are very special in our culture. It is said you cannot know yourself until you know your other half."

"That's not exactly fair to people who have no desire for romance or long-term relationships," I commented.

"Yes," Fyn said. "There has been pressure on the Cohort to change our governing laws regarding it. The laws have relaxed from what they used to be. In the past, we couldn't do anything without our parents' permission."

"Cohort?" I asked.

Seth said, "It's their ruling body, like England's parliament, though not exactly. The royals here are more than figureheads. From what I understand, one-third of the seats are inherited, and two-thirds are elected. The Chief of the Cohort, who's like the Prime Minister, has to be elected."

"Ah," I said shortly.

The silence continued as we drifted through the sky. I hadn't intended to make it awkward with my questions, but I wanted to know everything, especially if it affected Fyn.

"How about I show you how fast my ship can go?" Serlotminden asked, and the ship jolted forward, driving everyone but me backward.

Seth gasped, and Kal snapped, "Be careful."

"Where is my trouble-making pest?" Serlotminden asked, casting a roguish smirk over his shoulder. The sleek shuttle went even faster, dipping into the canyon and weaving around the rough rock formations. The sleek shuttle zipped through spaces that didn't seem possible and moved at dizzying speeds.

I grinned so wide I swear a distant ache in my cheeks started, even if that wasn't possible. I held Fyn's shoulder as he shifted to lean into the curves. Kal kept growling, and Seth held his hand, but he was smiling.

Serlotminden shot up into the sky, the sun momentarily blinding me, before tilting the shuttle into a spiraling nosedive. The treetops filled the entire front window as we plummeted to the ground. A scream built in my chest, even though if we crashed, it wouldn't harm me. At the last moment, he jerked back on the yoke and we shot to the sky.

Seth laughed, and I joined him. Kal tried to examine Seth, but the G-force kept him in his place. Fyn glanced at me, and at my grin, he flicked his tail in my direction before facing forward.

"Wasn't that fun?" Serlotminden asked.

"You might have harmed Seth," Kal snapped, trembling. He looked frightened, but somehow, I didn't think his fear was for Seth, because my dude appeared completely fine.

Unbuckling, Serlotminden turned around and stared directly at Kal. "I would never endanger your mate, Pest."

Kal frowned, a dim light growing under his scales. Seth slipped out of his buckles. "Breathe, Babe."

Serlotminden glanced at Fyn, tail flicking.

Fyn asked, "Are you well, Pest?"

"I'm fine," he replied. Seth cupped Kal's cheeks, thumb smoothing the tension, as he stared intently at him. Once again, I was struck with the notion that they were having a conversation—that mind-speak thing. If Seth and Kal could, maybe we could. I mean, if I was alive and we'd been bound by the Crystal (I wasn't a hundred percent sure how it worked). God, I would like that. Fyn would probably get annoyed with my every random question. Though, I guessed, it wasn't that different than we had now; no one heard me when I spoke to him.

"I'm right here," Seth repeated over and over again, and the light began to dim beneath his scales.

"What's going on, Pest?" Serlotminden asked, but Kal didn't reply.

Sliding out of his seat, Fyn rested a hand on Kal's knee, tail wrapping securely around his brother's ankle. "Is this about your crash?"

"Crash?" I asked.

He replied, "Kalvoxrencol was in a severe shuttle crash over two cycles ago."

"By the Crystal, Pest, I did not think," Serlotminden said, reaching for his little brother, but there was no space for him in the cramped shuttle to do more than touch him.

Kal knocked them off and hauled Seth onto his lap, cradling him. Seth wrapped his arms around Kal's neck, and Kal rocked his husband as he breathed slowly.

"Was Kal hurt in his accident?" I asked.

Fyn shook his head but didn't respond. He probably didn't want to risk upsetting Kal more. I didn't ask another question, and instead, dragged my fingers along Fyn's back, soothing him as he watched his younger brother.

After Kal calmed down, returning Seth to his stool, and several minutes of Serlotminden flying smoothly over the treetops, Seth said, "That was fun."

"I'm glad you enjoyed it," Serlotminden replied, without even a hint of a smile.

"Is your name really Serlotminden?" Seth asked.

"Yes," he replied. "Why?"

"He's about to shorten your name," Kal warned.

"What?" Serlotminden asked.

"A nickname," Seth said.

"A what?" Serlotminden asked.

The word nickname must not have translated well. It was difficult for me to know what a drakcol would or wouldn't understand because Seth always spoke in English and they always spoke in Drakconese. Around Fyn, I spoke in Drakconese, and English when I was alone. If I had a brain still, I was pretty sure I would always have a headache from the back and forth.

"An endearment, of a sort," Kal explained. "Humans do it. He already is calling Hallonnixmin Hal and Dontilvynsan Don."

"And don't forget Monqilcolnen is Monty," Seth said.

"I call Zoltilvoxfyn Fyn," I supplied, and with a moment of hesitation, Zoltilvoxfyn told them what I said.

"Well, now I'm feeling left out," Serlotminden said, lips pursing in an obvious pout.

"Can I call you Mindy?" Seth asked.

Serlotminden tried the nickname out a few times before he said, "I like it."

"Good. Mindy," Seth said.

Without warning, Mindy pulled Seth into a hug, drawing a panicked squeak from my fellow human. "Another little brother," Mindy said. "I like it, and you're so cute and soft. I could squeeze you all the time."

"Let my mate go," Kal ordered, tail flicking.

Mindy did, but not before patting Seth on the head. Seth rolled his eyes at Kal, who bristled around his brother; though, Seth was a tad paler than normal.

Fyn and Kal were equally overprotective.

I brushed my fingers over Fyn's cheek, commenting, "You and your brothers are very similar."

"I suppose."

"You are, and I like it." It reminded me of my brothers and cousins. The good-natured ribbing. Jokes. Laughter. I missed them.

"They are yours now too. If you want them."

"I do." I ran my fingers along his forehead. I hadn't realized how lonely I was wandering space for years, completely alone, until now, when I finally wasn't.

"They're yours, then."

Chapter 24

I CANNOT HIDE HOW I FEEL.

Zoltilvoxfyn

Serlotminden landed the shuttle in an open space near the roaring ocean. Kal and Seth were the first to leap out of the open hatch. Kal swept his mate into his arms and nuzzled his neck; Seth, in turn, held him in a tight embrace. A shot of longing went through me. My arms ached to hold Caleb.

Caleb grinned at me before racing to the deep blue water. Violent waves crashed onto the purple sand, then swept back into the ocean. "Be careful," I called after him. "I mean it, Caleb. Do not get too close."

He didn't even look at me as he raced along the shore.

The towering trees with rich green trunks and wide black leaves lined the beach. Undisturbed sand, as this wasn't a favorite beach for locals to visit, was decorated with shells in a variety of colors. None of which I could focus on as I usually did.

When my family and I visited the ocean, I normally studied the plant life, inspected the shells, or sometimes I sat beside the water and watched the towering waves. None of that was possible with my mate so close by.

A tail wrapped around mine, and I barely glanced at Serlotminden, keeping my gaze on Caleb. I had to make sure he was safe. The water was full of dangerous creatures and that wasn't even talking about the waves themselves, which were powerful. They could rip a person out into the ocean and drag them under.

I tried to logically parse through my sweeping instincts. Caleb couldn't be injured by the creatures or swept away by the current. But he could, and probably would like to explore the seabed. That was much too far from me to be safe.

"Caleb," I called again when he bent over the water, sticking his feet in. He peeked back at me. "Do not wander from my side. Please." He chuckled but stepped back, earning a satisfied grunt from me.

"You're courting Caleb, aren't you?" Serlotminden asked.

I crossed my arms, wings fluttering against my back. "Pest told you."

"No," he replied. "He hasn't said anything."

"Then how?"

He flicked the point of my tapered ear, and I hissed at the sharp sting. "You did."

I gaped at him, and he laughed.

"I'm not just beautiful, Bloom. I can be rather intelligent, and I know you. You're acting differently. Stars, you are being protective."

Setlotminden gestured to Kalvoxrencol who kept a secure hold on Seth as they approached the water. "You're acting like Pest and Hallonnixmin with their mates."

Kalvoxrencol was exceedingly protective of his Seth, not that I'd witnessed much of their relationship. Hallonnixmin was as protective of Gilvaxtin as she was of him. It was the drakcol way. Our mates were ours. Our other half. We would do anything to keep them safe.

"Yes," I forced out, muscles tightening in preparation for a battle, not that Serlotminden would physically attack me. If he did, we were evenly matched. As my elder brother, though, he was equally protective of me as Kalvoxrencol was.

"You can't make this love thing easy, can you?" he teased, arm coming around my shoulders and tugging me securely against him. He rested his forehead on my temple, but he didn't scent mark me. When we were young, our family members would scent mark us, claiming us. That ended as we grew, usually nearing our tenth cycle; we no longer tolerated it.

"You're not upset?"

"At you? No. Pest? Yes. He should've told me. Don't worry, I shall repay him for that," he said, but his playful grin stole any heat from his words. Serlotminden gently shook me, his wing drawing me even tighter in his embrace. "I worry, Zoltilvoxfyn, as I imagine Kalvoxrencol does. I worry when Caleb vanishes, he will take your soul with him. I can't lose you, Bloom. I love you too much."

Tears burned the backs of my eyes at his admission, but my brother was right. I kept my gaze trained on Caleb as he dashed over the purple sand, laughing. If Caleb passed on, he would take all that I was with him. I couldn't even promise that I wouldn't wither away. Most drakcol didn't survive their mate's loss, and I doubted I would. He was too integral to my existence.

"He's going to stay," I said.

"For how long?"

"I assume forever, but we haven't discussed a timeline."

"Why not?"

There was no answer to his question, so I didn't try to formulate one. There were several conversations that Caleb and I needed to have.

"You cannot avoid the truth with your mate. I might not have the experience that Hallonnixmin or Kalvoxrencol have, but even I know you need to be honest with your Caleb."

"I intend to, Speedy, but we haven't been together long."

He grinned.

"What?"

"At least you didn't hide it from me for very long, then."

I scoffed. The truth would have remained hidden for much longer if I wasn't as obvious with my affections. Caleb laughed, and I whipped toward him as my soul throbbed in my chest. How could I be anything but obvious when Caleb had claimed me so wholly?

Caleb

The stretch of purple sand, which resembled the color of grapes, was a surprise. The water was darker blue than what was found on

Earth, and the looming waves would make even the most skilled surfer balk. I liked it, though. The same peace I had at the beach on Earth wrapped around me here. The ocean was the ocean apparently—it soothed my soul.

My head tilted back as the wind rushed over the shoreline, making the black fan leaves rustle, but it didn't touch me. I could pretend. Why not? I was a ghost; I was allowed perks, even imagined ones.

Feet crushed on the sand moments before Fyn appeared. He was a perk after all—the best one. His tail swiped my leg, and his lips quirked. I wondered what he felt. I honestly had no idea. I assumed cold from the amount of shivers I created when I ran through a crowd.

"Serlotminden knows about us," he said.

"Is that a problem?" God, everyone was going to think he was insane. He was dating a ghost. My poor boyfriend.

"No. He and Pest are both supportive."

Well, his family was nicer than mine. If I had told my family I was dating a ghost, I would've been admitted to a hospital. Though, to be fair, my family didn't believe in ghosts or the ability to see them like Fyn's family did, so it really was like comparing apples and oranges, or more like apples and rocks.

"I'm glad they weren't upset."

His long white hair ruffled in the breeze, flaring out behind him. The moisture in the air clung to his scales, making them extra shiny. Fyn glanced down at me, and I went on my toes, making his lips open as his breathing increased and his tail wiggled.

"Is your hair soft?" I asked.

"Yes."

"What does it feel like?"

"I don't know how to describe it or how your skin would perceive the texture."

"Hmm." My fingers traced along his chest, and his breathing sped up even more to the point his chest heaved. A smirk quirked my lips at his reactions. Never in my life had I possessed such power over a person. Shit, it was a heady feeling. "Try."

"My hair is soft, like," a deep snarl that I was fairly certain was *lukniskil*, "silk. It would slide through your fingers with ease, like water."

"That sounds nice. I would run my fingers through your hair and scratch your scalp," I said, continuing to explore his chest. "What about your scales?"

"Smooth," he choked out.

"Can I feel the ridges around them?"

"Yes," Fyn replied.

"Is your tail smoother than the rest of your body?" I asked. The scales were more tightly interlocked on the prehensile appendage, not allowing me to see any of the slips of color.

"Yes, very smooth and very sensitive."

"Is it?" I muttered, sliding my fingers down his taut stomach.

With each question I asked, the tighter his voice got. I pressed as close to him as possible without actually touching him. "I would drag my nails over your scales before kissing every part of you. I would lick you until you were crying out for me. Then I would ride your cock until we were both sated and shaking."

Fyn swallowed as his cock visibly stiffened in his pants. His wings escaped from the slits in his shirt and encased me, shielding us from sight. "Caleb."

I fought a grin as I relished the power I had to make him so turned on, in front of anyone who cared to look.

"I would make you happy if I could," I said with complete certainty. When I was alive, I hadn't had *that* much experience, but I had enough to ensure Fyn enjoyed whatever we did.

"I'm already happy, my Caleb. I do not need more to enjoy being with you."

I beamed, but at the same time, guilt poked at me. If Fyn was with a living, breathing person, he could've had so much more than what meager scraps I offered. All I had to give was my time. Nothing more. It wasn't fair to my Sunshine. Not in the slightest. And yet I was selfish enough not to back away. Alive or dead, I'd never cared about someone as much as I cared about Fyn. Being with him consumed me, and I didn't want to exist without him beside me.

"I'm excited for our date," I said, changing the subject. "And I am excited for after."

"After?"

I went up on my toes, so I was a hair away from his mouth. "I want to see you and touch you as much as I can. I want to watch you stroke your cock until you're writhing with pleasure."

His throat bobbed. "We need to have a conversation first, but I would like that."

Permissions. The drakcol were very big on communication. Not a bad thing, but it did kill the spontaneous vibe. Whatever. I would give him whatever he needed so he felt comfortable and loved.

Chapter 25

A MUCH-NEEDED CONVERSATION.

Zoltilvoxfyn

The flight back to the palace was a blur. Serlotminden did keep the speed of his racing shuttle to a minimum for Kalvoxrencol, but, despite my brother's reasonable fear, I wanted Serlotminden to hurry. I wanted to go home so Caleb and I could go on our date before enjoying what would come after. I forced my thoughts away from Caleb, for fear that my cock would stir once again. I was desperate, body and soul, for him.

When we docked, Kalvoxrencol bid us a quick goodbye, then he and Seth headed toward the palace, fingers interlaced. Seth appeared paler than normal, and he'd been quiet on the return trip home, not that I'd noticed at the time. Though the further he and Kalvoxrencol moved from us, the more at ease he appeared. Before they vanished from sight, Seth pulled Kalvoxrencol's hand to his mouth and planted a chaste kiss on his knuckles.

Serlotminden started to fuss about his shuttle, wiping everything down and doing his post-flight checks while he cooed at the machine like it was an infant. When I took my leave, he didn't even look up from the open panel.

Caleb bounced along as we headed inside. The sun was setting in the distance, setting the sky ablaze in a haze of gold and orange. It wouldn't be long before the moons started to rise and stole the heat of the day. For a single beat of my soul, the light shone through Caleb, making him appear transparent. I stilled, but it happened so quickly that I doubted what I'd seen.

"What are we doing for our date?" Caleb asked, hopping around me, never staying still.

Planning our outing hadn't been an easy affair. Caleb couldn't do many things. I couldn't take him flying, he couldn't eat, and I wasn't prepared to go to a play or wander the city with him at my side. I wouldn't ignore him, but nor did I want people to witness me talking to nothing but air.

I wasn't embarrassed by my mate nor would I deny my connection to this human soul, but Caleb didn't need to witness how people reacted to my presence, whispering and calling me names. I didn't want him to see any of that yet. In time, he would because it was impossible to hide it forever, but for now, I would cover all of the ugly parts of my life.

"You shall see." I led him upstairs to the royal wing before continuing upward. We climbed the stairs to the tallest spire of the palace, and when we crested the top step, Caleb exclaimed. The spire was completely forged of glass and pierced the sky. Sheer curtains fluttered in the breeze from the surrounding windows. Potted trees with white flowers were perfectly placed between the windows, lending a floral fragrance to the air. In the center was a blanket surrounded by light stones that shone in soft colors ranging from pink to green to orange.

Caleb wandered around, mouth open wide. "Were you expecting us to have sex here?"

"N-no," I replied, brow furrowed. I hadn't planned that at all.

"Soft lighting and a blanket? On Earth that's a (human word) for sex."

"*Koood*?" I asked, trying to recreate the human word. I failed abysmally.

His lips pursed. "Signal, maybe, or sign?"

"Ah. I understand," I replied. "I planned for stargazing. I'm not opposed to having sex with you here, my Caleb, but I would like to talk first."

"Permissions?"

"Yes, but I would also like to know more about you, and there are things about myself I would like to discuss."

Caleb skipped around the room, hovering near the windows. He was incapable of remaining still, and I didn't mind in the slightest. I loved watching him. Every moment drew me in.

"What do you want to know?" he asked.

"Everything."

"That might take time," he said.

"I have nothing but time for you."

Caleb

When Fyn said everything, he meant *everything*. I told him more about my parents, as well as my brothers and my cousins, and all the trouble we got into. He didn't understand all that I said, because I didn't know the Drakconese equivalent of cow tipping or TP-ing the neighbors' yards on Halloween, but his focus never wavered as I skipped around the circular room. Nothing I said was enough, and I talked more than I had in years, which was saying something (like seriously, I never shut up).

Finally, I stopped hopping around and sat next to his sprawled body. Fyn stretched his arms above his head and crossed his legs at the ankle. My eyes ate him up like a fucking buffet. Damn, this man was a sexy treat.

I leaned over him, and he asked, "Why did you stop, my Caleb?"

I brushed my fingers over his cheek. "It's your turn to talk," I said. His expression shuttered, and I frowned, worry plucking at me. "Sunshine?"

"There are some things you need to know about drakcol."

"Alright."

"When I said I was going to keep you, I meant it."

"I know," I replied. "I meant it too."

"You do not understand."

"What don't I understand?"

"First, I should explain the risk of you staying here on this plane."

"Alright," I said slowly.

Why did I feel like he was trying to break up with me again? Oh my god. He was breaking up with me, wasn't he? I shifted even closer, pressing my knees into him. We'd just gotten together, and he'd already changed his mind, which, I mean, kind of made sense with me being a ghost and all, but I liked Fyn. A lot. I swallowed a scoff. It was a damn sight more than like... but we hadn't been together that long, and it was too much too fast.

His eyes remained on the stars above us. "There haven't been many mediums before me, but each one logged their experience. In them, they speak of the danger of a spirit lingering too long."

"What do you mean?" I asked, laying beside him.

"They vanish."

"Pass on?"

"No," he said, voice tightening. "The spirit vanishes. A spiritual soul who was a medium wrote that the spirit who lingers here too long will be unable to endure, and they will rip apart." Fyn finally looked at me, eyes glassy. "If you stay, Caleb, you might vanish."

He wasn't breaking up with me; he was worried about me, as usual. Fuck, he was adorable.

"I have been here for twenty-three cycles. I don't think a few more are going to end me."

"A few more cycles," he repeated.

"Yes."

"You didn't understand what I meant."

"I did. I do. I might vanish or be ripped apart. To be honest, I'm shocked anything came after death in the first place. I'll take the risk. You're worth it, Sunshine."

"I'm not."

"You are." Didn't he understand how utterly amazing he was? I would give up everything to be with Fyn. "I want to stay with you."

"For a few cycles."

Now, I didn't understand. Eventually, Fyn would move on and find someone alive to spend his life with, which was fine (I guessed. I mean, I didn't like the thought of that, but I wasn't going to be an asshole... I wasn't. I *wasn't*). He was alive, and I wasn't. When that day came, I would start wandering again, trying to make my way back to Earth.

"What's wrong, Sunshine?" I asked. "Tell me directly."

"I said I wished to keep you. You are mine."

Where was he going with this? I was fine with being his. I loved possessive guys. I loved the thought of being his. I was picking up what he was putting down. "And I said I'm good with it."

"You do not understand."

"Fuck, Zoltilvoxfyn. What is wrong?"

"You're *mine*. I don't want you for a few cycles. I want you for forever. I will never surrender you. Not ever."

My mouth fell open. I couldn't find a single word to say.

"Kalvoxrencol warned me you wouldn't understand. Humans do not mate the way we do. You can take multiple long-term partners throughout your life, but drakcol take but one permanent partner. You are my mate."

If I had a heart, it would be pounding. "You want me for forever?"

"I have since the moment I saw you, even though I didn't understand until later. You are mine, Caleb. I will have no other, and

I will never desire anyone else. Ever. So when I say you are mine, this is what I mean."

I wished with every fiber of my soul to kiss him, but the risk was great. If I focused hard enough, I could touch him for the barest moment, though I wouldn't feel it, but if I exhausted myself, I would vanish for a few hours to days. If I did, Fyn wouldn't take it well, especially with the talk of my disappearing for good.

I said with all the sincerity I possessed, "I am yours, Zoltilvoxfyn. Not for now. Not for a few cycles. I'm yours forever."

He took a sharp inhale. "Caleb."

"That means you're mine, right? Like I don't have to share you or anything? I can keep you?"

"I am yours alone."

Part of me felt guilty for being so damn happy. Fyn could certainly do better than me. He was choosing to be with me when he could have someone better, someone who would age beside him. Still, I wasn't going to force him away. I'd been alone for a very long time, and I never wanted to be lonely again. It was more than that, though. If I didn't have Fyn in my life, there would be no point. Wandering wasn't a lure for me anymore. He was all I needed; he was my smile; he was my heart; he was my reason for this half-existence.

"I lo—" I broke off. I wasn't ready to say that yet, so I said, "I will be yours for as long as I exist, Sunshine."

I watched his throat bob, wishing to press my lips against it. His deep green eyes met mine. "And I will be yours until my last breath, and even after."

A star exploded in my chest. For the first time since I died, I truly felt something, not a shadow, not a bare whisper so distant that I questioned it happened. No. This was real. It was... Warmth. The heat spread from my chest to my fingers to the tip of my toes, filling my entire body. I tried to cling to the awareness, but it slipped away. I let it go, not caring. I didn't need it. I didn't need anything besides Fyn. He was my sun.

Chapter 26

ROMANCE UNDER THE STARS.

Caleb

I brushed my fingers over his chest, trailing down his stomach to near his straining cock, then back up again. "Can I see you?"

"Permissions."

Ah, yes. Drakcol needed to talk about everything first. That was fine as long as I got to see my Sunshine at the end. I slid my hand lower once again until it rested right below where I was pretty sure his belly button was. His breathing sped up and his tail thrashed.

"You can come as close as you want. You can touch me whenever you want. I want you, Fyn, and I want everything you have to give me. I will take it all." He couldn't truly touch me. There was basically nothing he could do to me, physically at least.

"Sex?" he asked, voice breaking.

"I want to watch you please yourself," I said, voice husky and rough. Shit. I really did. Imagining him stroking himself off was enough to make me moan. "Do you have anything you need me to know or not to do?"

"No."

I chuckled. "You're not doing well with these permissions, my Sunshine. I think you're supposed to tell me what you like and need, and more importantly, what you don't like."

"I want to give you everything you desire."

That was incredibly romantic, but not healthy. Relationships were a two-way street. "And I need you to be comfortable. What are things you don't want me to do?"

"Well..."

The words he left off practically spoke for him. If I was truly here, Fyn would've had more permissions for me. I couldn't do much to him in my ghostly state. I dragged my fingers up and down his chest, edging nearer to his dick with each pass, making his breath sharpen.

"It's alright," I said. "I understand."

"My apologies."

"Don't. It's the truth. With my limited abilities, what don't you want me to do?"

"The same as I said earlier, you can touch me whenever. I like it, but maybe not anywhere personal unless you wish to start something," he answered. That was more than a fair request. One, I could easily honor. I mean, he didn't want me groping him when I wasn't interested in helping him finish; I got that. However, I believed he underestimated exactly how much and how often I would want to start something.

"Do you like to have sex in public?" I asked, fingers brushing his hips.

"I—" he broke off, taking a heaving breath. "I've never thought about it much."

"Hmm," I said, moving to lean over him. "What if someone came in right now and saw you needy? Saw you utterly desperate for me? They wouldn't see me, but they would see your cock hard and pressed against your pants. What if you were stroking yourself while calling my name?"

Fyn groaned, rubbing his bulge. I flicked at him until he pulled away. From his reaction, it was safe to say he liked the idea, but I needed him to say it out loud. This was something I loved, something I'd always loved—the chance of exposure.

"Would you like that, Sunshine?" I pressed, my fingers dragging up his stomach to circle where I was pretty sure one of his nipples was.

"Yes."

I licked my lips. "I do as well." I'd always been an exhibitionist, and it was perfect that Fyn was into it as well. "Now, can I see you?"

He glanced at the open archway beyond the glowing stones. "Perhaps we should go to my quarters."

So he wasn't ready yet. I was. I loved the thought of someone catching us together, but I wouldn't force Fyn to do anything he wasn't comfortable with. Perhaps one day I would convince him to have sex up here or in the garden. The image of him laying on the mossy ground in the greenhouse while he stroked his erect dick, made me groan.

"Hurry," I said.

Fyn stood and began to extinguish the glowing stones by touching them with a single finger. I glanced at the windows, bouncing on the balls of my feet. One of them looked over the terrace. Fyn could fly down, and I could jump, speeding the process up. I needed him on his back, cock in hand. Now.

When he finished, I said, "Hurry up, Sunshine. I need you." I raced to the window and leaped without any hesitation.

Zoltilvoxfyn

"Caleb!" His name tore from my lips as he vanished over the edge. I dove out the window, wings extending. He glanced at me, mouth open and forehead wrinkled. My hands slid through him when I tried to snatch him out of the air.

The ground rapidly approached, forcing me to open my wings. I shot up and screamed, "Caleb!"

He landed with no issue and gaped up at me. I sped to the ground, scouring him. "Caleb."

"I'm fine, Sunshine," he said, but my soul continued to thrash against my ribs. Caleb's arms went around me, making me shiver. "I'm alright. I'm... a ghost. Remember? I can't die again."

It was true, but the moment I saw him go out the window all of my instincts screamed to grab him. Logic had fled. Caleb had been in danger, and I couldn't live with myself if something happened to him.

"Do not do that again," I snarled, breathing harshly, then added, "Please."

"You're being ridiculous, Sunshine."

"Am I?" I didn't believe so. My instincts demanded I keep Caleb tucked safely against me. He belonged there after all. Caleb belonged beside me, and I belonged next to him.

"Yes." His fingers followed their usual pattern up my spine, over my shoulder blades, and down my sides.

I lowered my head, wanting to taste his lips, but I refrained. "Can I call you mate?"

"I would like that."

"Excellent. Mate."

He beamed. "Now, Sunshine, get in your bedroom because I need to see you naked."

"As you wish, my Mate."

The second I stepped inside, Caleb ran his fingers over my chest, stirring my cock again. It had gone flaccid from Caleb diving off the tower. He groaned when he saw my erection swell.

"Naked," he ordered in a husky voice.

I yanked my shirt off, exposing my chest. His eyes raked down my scales, making my cock harder than ever. Never in my life had I craved someone like this. Merely the heated look was enough to make me explode.

His fingers ran over my exposed scales, circling my pierced nipples. "I'd wondered if you were pierced elsewhere."

My nipples hardened from the cold brushes, and tingles spread from the nubs to my needy cock. "I have another one."

He looked down at my tenting trousers, licking his lips.

"Yes, Mate."

"Show me."

Slowly, I walked backward, a hand out in a silent request for him to follow. Caleb trailed me, licking his lips again. What would it be like to have his mouth on me, tongue meeting mine? To have it locked around me? Kalvoxrencol said that Seth was cooler in temperature than we were, so I imagined Caleb was the same, but my brother had said that Seth's mouth was warm around him. How would Caleb have felt? I swallowed, wishing we'd been able to have the opportunity. Though the chances we would have met while he still lived were minuscule at best.

In the end, it didn't truly matter, I would choose Caleb no matter the circumstance.

I pulled off my boots, then I undid the laces on my trousers and began to peel them off as Caleb stared at me, mouth open. I stepped out of my trousers, standing in front of Caleb naked. He groaned. At the sound, a bead of pre-seed welled on the tip of my cock.

"You're big," he remarked.

I had no idea what human genitalia looked like, but I assumed it wasn't too different. I was average size for a drakcol. My tapered tip was pierced with a gold ring and it was wider than my shaft—the whole of which was covered in small scales. My balls were even and round in my sack.

Caleb trailed his fingers over the shaft of my throbbing cock, the soft touches made a strangled moan come out of my lips. Normally, I would think the cold would dampen my desire, but it didn't.

Every part of me was desperate for Caleb.

"You have no body hair."

My head tilted to the side, my breath uneven. "Only on my head. That's normal."

He chuckled deep within his throat. "Not for humans."

"Truly? Where else do you have hair?"

"I wish I could show you," he answered.

I rutted into him, breaching through his palm. "You are perfect as you are."

He smiled, eyes not leaving my cock as more beads of pre-seed slid down my shaft. "I have hair on my arms, legs, face when I don't shave, above my cock, and all over my balls and ass. I pretty much have hair everywhere, but some is so fine or pale that you can't see it."

I saw hair on the tops of his arms, but I never paid much attention to it. That was clearly a mistake. The urge to run my fingers through the hair on his thin arms, testing it against my scales, flooded me.

"Lie down," he ordered, breaking the silence, and I was more than happy to comply.

Caleb

Fyn grabbed some lube before he lay on the bed, his eyes never deviating from me. My mouth was hanging open as if I was panting, even though I had no lungs. God, I was horny. My spirit was most definitely willing, but my body was unable, or better said, non-existent. Still, I had the instinct to rub my dick, even though nothing was there.

He waited, hand hovering over his dripping cock.

What did he taste like? I ordered, "Touch your tip."

His fingers ran over the tapered head of his cock, making himself whimper. It was more pointed than humans, but it mushroomed out over his shaft. It would've been a stretch to fit him inside of me, but I would've been more than willing to try over and over again until he was fully sheathed in my ass.

When pre-cum glistened on his fingers, I said, "Taste yourself."

He hesitated. I almost asked him what was wrong, but he stuck his fingers in his mouth and sucked.

"What do you taste like?"

"Sweet."

I licked my lips. "I would take your weeping cock into my mouth and run my tongue all over your head, then taste every fucking inch of you."

He moaned, and more liquid escaped, even though he wasn't even touching himself. Drakcol had a lot of pre-cum.

"I would suck you until you were screaming for me before tugging on that piercing with my teeth."

"Caleb."

"Would you like that?"

"Yes." His fingers edged closer to his dick. "Please."

I settled between his legs, so I had a good view of his throbbing dick and heavy balls. "Put some lube on your hand."

Fyn followed the instructions without question; his tail thrashed as his wings spread out over the bed.

"Touch yourself."

He gripped the base of his shaft and pulled upward in one long, smooth motion. His hips arched, and a strangled growl ripped out of his throat. His movements turned frantic, eyes closing, as he shuttled over his dick.

"Sunshine, look at me."

His eyes popped open. "Caleb."

"Slower. Go slower, Sunshine. I want to see you writhe."

With a slight whimper, he slowed down the pace, sliding up and down his thick shaft. The head of his dick was swollen and needy as pre-cum continuously leaked from his slit, mixing with the shiny lube.

"Pull on your ring," I demanded, wiggling. Shit, this was so hot.

One of his fingers slipped into the gold ring, and he tugged on it, then wiggled it back and forth. A loud moan escaped his throat as he arched on the bed. His knees fell open, giving me a decent view of the tight pucker of his ass. It was as beautiful as he was—dark and tight and begging to be licked.

"Touch me, Caleb. Please."

I ran my fingers over his hole, and he groaned. Slightly nervous, I asked, "Like that?"

"Yes, Mate."

While Fyn pumped his shaft, I ran my fingers over his balls and pucker. His moans mixed with rough snarls and my name. His long white hair was like a cloud on the pillow as his head pressed back, the tendons in his neck taut with strain.

He was so gorgeous.

"Caleb," he cried. "My Caleb."

I slid my fingers over his muscular thighs, making him shiver. I whispered against him, "You are so beautiful."

Fyn shouted my name again in a broken voice as his hand slicked up and down his shaft frantically. "I'm close," he warned, eyes barely open and breathing uneven.

I loved seeing him so undone. I moved to his dick, circling the tip and the underside. His mouth opened and his neck muscles tightened. Any moment Fyn was going to explode. My fingers drifted over his dick as he frantically jerked.

"Caleb," he moaned.

"I want to see you come. Please, Sunshine. Show me how much you like me."

He worked even harder until a shudder went through his body moments before his hips arched. Ropes of thick, white cum splattered his stomach. He continued to milk his dick, making more and more cum burst out. Drakcol produced more than humans, and I wasn't mad at it, though I wished to lap it up.

Tremors wracked his body as he panted. His arms started to go around me, but when they slid through me, he jerked as if he'd forgotten I wasn't truly here.

I refused to allow my state to ruin this moment. "Taste yourself."

Two of his shaking fingers ran through the cum on his stomach, and his nose wrinkled. I started to ask what was wrong, but then he shoved them in his mouth. His black tongue cleaned the white liquid off his fingers.

"Fuck, that's beautiful," I said.

"Salty and sweet."

"If I could, I would lick every drop off you."

Fyn swallowed.

I rolled to his side, lying on the bed. One of his wings disappeared into me, but I ignored it. He shifted to his side and draped the other wing over me, enclosing me in his secure embrace.

"Shall we go again?" I had thoroughly enjoyed watching Fyn pleasure himself, and I was more than ready to see him undone and begging again.

"Let me rest first, Mate, but yes." He tucked an arm under his head. "I've never had such a strong release in my life."

I snuggled close. "I liked it."

"Me too."

"Maybe you can get in the shower, and we can see if I can get you to come without any other help."

His eyes darkened with arousal and his dick twitched in obvious interest. "I would enjoy trying that."

"I'm sure you would."

Chapter 27

IT MIGHT BE WORTH THE RISK.

Caleb

Fyn dried his long hair with a towel as he glanced at the door. We'd been in the shower where I'd *planned* to successfully make him come again. Last night, after watching Fyn jerk off, I'd helped him come with my fingers and mouth on his dick as water had cascaded over his black scales in a distracting array. Today, I was going to try again and not have him touch himself, though maybe have him play with his nipple rings, except, this time, we were interrupted by a communication ping.

There was an emergency, and the Cohort, the ruling parliament of Tamkolvanloknol, was called to assemble. While Fyn wasn't a voting member—the whole first phase of adulthood thingamajig—he and his brothers as princes had been summoned. Though, I supposed, Kal had a vote now that he was mated to Seth.

This whole mated-adult thing was odd to me, and I was still trying to get a grasp on it. I always tried to respect other cultures, but come on. Why would being married—or, excuse me, mated make you an adult? It was stupid to me, but whatever.

He glanced at me for the thousandth time, and I said, "Don't worry, Sunshine. I'll make you come later. Nothing else but me on your cock."

"That is not what I'm worried about, Mate."

"No?" I looked down at his half-hard dick, which started to firm up the longer I stared at it.

He ran his fingers over me, making a shiver go down his spine. That adorable divot was between his well-sculpted eyebrows again. I almost moved to smooth the tension away, but I didn't know if my non-existent touch would be enough.

Desire so powerful it was a miracle I didn't combust washed through me. I wondered if it would be worth it to kiss him. To focus as hard as possible and have the slightest resistance of his flesh against my soul. If Fyn knew the cost, his answer would be a decided no, but I hovered in the indecisive gray area. Kissing him might be worth vanishing for a few hours. I needed to experience being with him in some tangible way at least once.

I peeked at my gray fingertips. The transparency was starting to spread up the digits. I kept trying to rationalize that everything was fine... but I didn't know if it was. Kissing Fyn might not be a good idea, but fucking hell, I wanted it so bad.

"Stay here while I'm gone, Little Soul," he said.

"What?"

“I would bring you with me, but my parents will ask, and I will not lie. But I want you here. I don’t know what is happening. Emergency gatherings like this are rarely called.”

“You know I can’t be hurt, right?” News flash, he was worried again. Color me shocked.

“I know, but that doesn’t change my instincts. I have to protect you, Caleb. I need to know where you are. If something is truly wrong and I have to leave, I need to know where you are and how to get you because I will not leave without you.”

“If that did happen and I wasn’t here, you should trust that I can and will take care of myself.”

“Caleb.”

“Zoltilvoxfyn,” I groaned. “Trust me. I have wandered for a long time. I’ve seen all manner of shocking things out there. Trust that I would find you because I would. No matter the distance, no matter the struggle, no matter the circumstance, I would find you. I will never leave you.”

He leaned closer, his lips near mine. “I do trust you, my Caleb, but I must keep you safe.”

I fell headlong into the pressing desire to feel at least resistance. I forced all of my attention onto my mouth. Going up on my toes, I pressed my lips against his and met a tangible force stopping me.

I felt nothing from the contact, but when he gasped, against me, a deep, molten sensation like lava moving beneath the crust of the Earth burned me, and for all of one second, there was the smoothness of his lips and scent of… something earthen or dirt-like, soil maybe, on his scales before it faded. But it *had* been there. I hadn't smelled anything in so long, all memory was gone. I couldn't have made that up.

The resistance faded, and I slid through him.

Fyn brushed my cheek, but his fingers disappeared. "What was that, my Mate?"

"If I focus as hard as possible, I can touch something for a moment." With a surreptitious glance, I saw my hands were vanishing. It wouldn't be too long until I disappeared, which Fyn would not enjoy. God. He was going to freak the fuck out. *Great job, Caleb*. I never think shit through. But, hey, I touched him, even if it was only for a moment.

He pressed his fingers to his lips. "Thank you."

I grinned as brightly as possible and ushered him out of the bedroom. He needed to get the hell out of here before I disappeared. Thankfully, I should reappear before he got back from his meeting.

"Go. You're late."

"I need you to wait here, Caleb. I have to know you're safe," he said, stepping into the living room. "You are the most important thing in my life."

Hands behind my back, I said, "I will be right here. But for some odd reason, if I'm not, don't panic. I will always come back to you."

My Sunshine frowned something deep as he remained rooted in the same spot like a damn tree. "Why would you leave?"

Already my feet and arms were beginning to vanish. It wouldn't take much more for Fyn to notice. "Fine," I said. "I will wait right here. In fact, I will wait in your bed."

"Our bed."

An unstoppable smile spread over my lips. "Our bed. I expect sex when you get back."

His fingers brushed my cheek. "Insatiable."

"Yep."

"Fine, I will leave."

When he turned toward the door, I rushed to the bedroom. I poked my head through the door to watch him leave. At the last moment, Fyn turned around.

"I would do anything for you, Fyn. Anything," I said, and shit, I meant it. I would do whatever needed to be done to stay with him. I would sacrifice my own soul to stay beside Fyn and keep him smiling, even if it was only for one more day.

With one last look, he left.

I slid back into the bedroom, standing on the other side of the door, and lifted my hands, but they were gone. I was disintegrating. I tried to curl my fingers, and for a moment, they wrapped around something soft or maybe smooth or silky, I didn't know, but it vanished so quickly I wasn't certain which it was—this was all new to me.

"Please don't let me be gone long," I begged the universe. "I had to kiss him at least once."

My last thought before the darkness stole me was of my Fyn.

Chapter 28

AN UNINVITED GUEST.

Zoltilvoxfyn

I sat in the amphitheater between Serlotminden and Kalvoxrencol. Seth was on Pest's other side. Even though he didn't have a vote, Seth was allowed to attend because he was Kalvoxrencol's mate, and therefore a prince consort. Father and Mother sat on a pair of thrones, elevated upon a dais, in the center of the arena. Chief Yomqin was on Mother's left and Uncle Jemtonkilsol, Monqilcolnen's father, was on Father's right, as he was Father's advisor. Hallonnixmin and his mate, Gilvaxtin, were seated just off the dais.

"Do you know what this is about?" Serlotminden asked, leaning closer to me, making his stool creak under his weight.

"No," I said, and Kalvoxrencol shook his head.

"Did Caleb come?" Seth asked, clinging to Kalvoxrencol.

"No," I replied. "He's not allowed."

Kalvoxrencol raised an eyebrow, and Serlotminden laughed before jabbing me with his sharp elbow. "Who would know besides you?"

Yes, no one would've known if he came, but I needed to be honest and to follow the laws.

"Seriously, Zoltilvoxfyn," Kalvoxrencol started, "you should have brought him. I wouldn't have left Seth behind."

"Difference, you two are bound, and I'm not as comfortable breaking laws as you are, Pest."

Kalvoxrencol immediately drew back like I'd struck him. Seth wrapped an arm around his waist and glared at me, round cheeks red, and I assumed this blush was caused by anger, not embarrassment. Serlotminden caught my eye, and I easily read the disapproval.

A dark cloud surrounded me as I stared at the floor, swallowing. I hadn't intended to hurt Kalvoxrencol, but Seth and his relationship was different from mine and Caleb's. We would never be recognized as mates by anyone other than my family. I hadn't even told my parents, Hallonnixmin, Dontilvynsan, or Monqilcolnen because I was afraid of how they would react.

A loud bang sounded as Chief Yomqin thumped his wood staff on the ground, calling the Cohort into session. The low conversations around the amphitheater disappeared.

Father stood, pushing his long black hair over his broad shoulders. The severe expression on his face made my soul thrum in worry. Father wasn't a joyous person, but the hardness of his countenance meant the reason this meeting was called wasn't something trivial, not that I'd thought it would be—the full Cohort wasn't called for anything less than an emergency.

"Last night, a ship appeared within our borders. Its make is something that we and the Coalition have never seen before. I sent Captain Dontilvynsan to investigate, but the ship's shields are impenetrable to our sensors. I have reached out to the Coalition, and they are sending reinforcements as well as a team of scientists.

"We do not know why they are here, or what they want, but we must be prepared," he finished.

Everyone was silent for a few moments as we absorbed the information. An older woman with gray scales, whose name I didn't recall, stood. "Do we know where they came from?"

"No," Chief Yomqin replied. "They appear to have slipstream technology, but the energy pattern is not the same as that of the xoi."

"Can we see their ship?" an older warrior with jagged orange scales asked. Gaxbin had retired from the Planetary Navy before joining the Cohort—they'd been one of Dontilvynsan's superior officers for several cycles, so I'd met them socially as well as seen them in Cohort meetings a few times.

Father clicked a few things on his screen before he said, "Captain Dontilvynsan, you are connected with the Cohort."

My second eldest brother appeared. His hulking form was seated on the captain's stool of his ship. He stood, which made him even more enormous. He was the largest of all my brothers in height and frame. His scales were black like mine, though the skin peeking around his scales was green and white. He resembled the rest of us with our mother's green eyes and our father's long nose and wide forehead.

"Emperor Kontolmakqilnen," he said formally, tilting his head to the side and offering his throat. "Empress Vyn. Honorable Cohort."

"Show us the ship," Chief Yomqin ordered.

Dontilvynsan complied, and the ship appeared on the screen on the back of the amphitheater. It was pure white and shaped like a wedge. The metal was perfectly smooth without the slightest seam or bump. The foreign ship was huge, bigger than our warships and similar in size to our long-haul transport ships. Whatever this ship had been built for, I doubted it was for war. It would lack maneuverability. Though perhaps their weapons were advanced enough they weren't concerned about whether they would have to evade attacks or possibly flee.

I leaned toward Kalvoxrencol and whispered, "I don't think that is a warship."

"Are you sure?"

"No, but the size of it." I shook my head. "This might be an accident. They have slipstream technology. It's possible mechanical issues threw them into our space. It has happened before. Remember two cycles ago when that xoi ship was thrown into our space and almost crashed into one of our moons. It hadn't been anything more than a technical malfunction."

Kalvoxrencol stood, wings slipping out of the slits of his shirt before he drew them back in place. The last time he'd spoken to the Cohort was when he was answering for his crime of crashing into a space station; at that time, he'd been on the floor, in the center, and we weren't allowed to do anything more than watch.

"Might this not be an accident?" he asked, voice remaining even, though his tail wiggled with tension.

"Why would you think that, Prince Kalvoxrencol?" Chief Yomqin asked. "Is your creator soul making it hard for you to see the threat that this ship obviously presents?"

I gripped Serlotminden's arm when he tried to stand.

The Cohort never saw Kalvoxrencol; they saw his soul type—the first creator soul in the royal family since it had been established. His mistakes were marks against his honor, but those were nothing compared to his soul type. Kalvoxrencol was the only creator soul in the entire Cohort.

Hallonnixmin stood, and the same anger that burned in me and Serlotminden was reflected in him. His voice was deep as he said, "Tell us what you mean, Kalvoxrencol."

Tail flicking wildly, Kalvoxrencol asked, "Dontilvynsan, have they shown any aggression?"

"No, though they have not responded to our pings."

"The size of the ship suggests this could be a passenger or transport vessel. For all we know this is a simple mistake. Violence should not be our first response," he said.

Most of the Cohort was silent before Chief Yomqin asked, "Then what do you suggest, Prince? If you foolishly think they mean us no harm, then what should we do? Hide in our houses and paint?"

Kalvoxrencol fell silent, and the chief sneered as if he expected as much. I burned to challenge Chief Yomqin for his remarks, but

I would not win, and such actions would upset Kalvoxrencol—he didn't like us protecting him. Though if he challenged the chief, Kalvoxrencol would win, but he wouldn't, not anymore.

Seth stood and asked in a deep voice, visibly shaking, "Haven't you heard of diplomacy, dickwad?"

I blinked at the odd translation, and I wasn't alone. Sudden whispers filled the amphitheater. NAID had to be incorrect. As odd as humans were, they did not have piles of cocks lying around, right? That was simply... not possible. Then again, humans were very interesting beings. I would have to ask Caleb.

"These aliens might not even understand you," Seth snapped, voice breaking, whether in nerves or anger, I didn't know. "Attacking without provocation is idiotic. But you seem like a moron, so I shouldn't be surprised, asshat."

Hats on butts... Humans were indeed odd.

Technically, Seth wasn't allowed to address the Cohort, but he probably didn't know that. I very much doubted that Kalvoxrencol had briefed his mate on the proper protocol. Also insulting the chief wasn't wise, even if I supported it.

Chief Yomqin tilted his head to the side, offering his throat, which made my mouth drop.

Serlotmiden told me, "Seth Harris has the purest warrior soul ever recorded. Much of the Cohort believes he was chosen by the Crystal to make up for Pest's lack of warrior soul."

"Idiots." There was nothing wrong with Kalvoxrencol or his soul type.

"Indeed, but Chief Yomqin is the spearhead of that group, along with the Ranks. They are all quite fond of Seth."

"What do you suggest, Prince Consort Seth Harris?" Chief Yomqin asked.

"Scientists. Diplomats. Try and reach out. Don't attack before we know they mean us harm," Seth said before muttering to Kalvoxrencol, "It's like they've never watched *Star Trek*. Morons."

Kalvoxrencol smiled at him.

Father said, "Kalvoxrencol, you will lead your mate's plan. You will go to Dontilvynsan's ship."

I smacked his leg with my tail, and he glanced at me. I gestured to myself and Serlotminden who was practically bouncing off his stool.

Kalvoxrencol's tail wrapped around mine. "Yes, Father. I would like to request the additions of Serlotminden who is well-versed in diplomacy and Zoltilvoxfyn who is a scholar and well-versed in different cultures."

I sat up straight. Very rarely had I left Tamkolvanloknol and never in a situation like this. No one, besides my brothers, had ever requested my presence, but I knew Kalvoxrencol would at least ask for me if I wanted to come. Whether I was allowed to go or not was another matter entirely.

"You may take Serlotminden," Father said, but he didn't continue, and I fought the sudden wave of worthlessness. Once again, I was being kept on the planet.

Kalvoxrencol opened his mouth, but Seth grabbed his hand, stopping him. Eventually, Kalvoxrencol said, "I understand, Father.

Will the Cohort assemble a team of scientists and diplomats or should I?"

Father glanced at Uncle Jemtonkilsol, then Chief Yomqin before saying, "We shall. Be ready to depart within the hour." He turned to Dontilvynsan. "Prepare for your brothers to arrive."

Dontilvynsan offered his throat again.

Chapter 29

ALL ALONE.

Zoltilvoxfyn

I followed my brothers out of the amphitheater and half-listened to Kalvoxrencol as he ranted against our father. I had very little to offer to the mission, unlike Serlotminden who, in addition to being a shuttle racer, worked as a diplomat. I expected Seth to calm Kalvoxrencol down, but he didn't. He agreed, not as vocally, but he was on my side.

Seth had defended me before, but I hadn't expected this. "Fyn deserves to go as much as anyone," Seth said. "How can your father keep him here?"

When we rounded the corner, I spotted Father and Mother. I crossed my arms, but I didn't say anything. They were trying to protect me. Kalvoxrencol and I were similar in many ways. He acted out, harming himself through idiotic acts. I turned inward, and they feared harm would come to me by my own hand. As such, they kept me here and safe beside them. And unlike Kalvoxrencol, I'd never defied their orders before.

I waited for Kalvoxrencol to lose his temper, but I was surprised once again when Seth, not Pest, stepped forward, forehead furrowed. "Fyn should come with us. He wants to go, and you shouldn't keep him here."

Father asked, "I beg your pardon?"

"He is not weak," Seth practically growled, shaking so violently I feared he would fall, but Kalvoxrencol took a hold of his waist. "I know why you want to keep him here, but if Fyn says he can handle it, he can. Trust him. You have to trust him."

Mother glanced at me. "You told him."

"Yes," I replied. Seth understood in a way no one else in my family did. While he fought his mind in a different way, he recognized the battle.

"We might need him," Seth continued. "For all we know there is a ghost aboard that might help. Not that it matters. He deserves to go as much as his brothers."

Father cupped Seth's cheek, causing Seth to start and turn deathly pale. "Once again, I am pleased by the protectiveness you have shown over my children, but this is mine and Vyn's decision. Zoltilvoxfyn is *our* child and under *our* protection, not yours."

Seth frowned.

"I want to go," I said, moving to Seth's side.

Serlotminden joined me. "I think he should, Father. You never let him leave. You cannot keep him here forever. If he wants to wander the stars, he should be able to. You let the rest of us."

Kalvoxrencol moved to Seth's other side, making a line. He scowled and light gathered under his scales, but he refrained from speaking, which was probably wise because I doubted he would remain calm.

"How can you say no to this, Father?" Hallonnixmin asked from behind us. I peered over my shoulder and he and Monqilcolnen stood behind us. "I'm sending Monqilcolnen to watch them." He threw an arm over mine and Seth's shoulders, which made Seth stiffen. "Besides, we're stronger as a group."

"I agree," Mother said. "Zoltilvoxfyn should go."

Father rubbed his forehead. "Fine, but, Hallonnixmin, you cannot go. I will not send all of my children into an unknown situation."

"Thank you, Father," Kalvoxrencol said.

He pointed at each of us. "I expect all of you to return. Unharmed. Is that understood?"

We all gave him our throats, besides Seth, who wiggled away from Hallonnixmin to press against Kalvoxrencol.

When Father and Mother left, I yanked Seth into a hug, squeezing him. He froze. I almost never initiated physical contact with anyone except my family, but I was so grateful. After a moment, his arms came about my back, and he patted me in halting movements.

"Thank you, Seth."

"Y-you're welcome," he squeaked. I let him go, and Seth backed into Kalvoxrencol, who wrapped his arm around him.

"We need to go," Monqilcolnen said.

Hallonnixmin took Monqilcolnen's tail with his own. "You will take care of them, right?"

"Certainly."

Looking at each of us, Hallonnixmin paused on Kalvoxrencol and ordered, "Behave."

Kalvoxrencol rolled his eyes and pulled Seth down the hall. I dashed after them, heading to me and mine's quarters. I needed to get Caleb. I refused to enter this unknown situation without him beside me.

I stepped into the shared space and didn't see Caleb, but I wasn't surprised. He promised to wait in bed for me. My cock stirred at the thought. I wished we had time to fuck, but we were expected on the shuttle shortly.

"Mate," I said, opening the door, "we need to leave, but once this issue is resolved, I promise we can fuck as long as you like." I paused. The bedroom was empty. My soul began to race. "Caleb?"

Silence was my answer.

"Caleb?" I called, racing around our quarters. He was nowhere in sight. Where was he? What happened? Did he vanish? Panic mixed with agony ripped through me. I gripped my hair. Where was my mate?

I forced myself to take a deep breath. Caleb had probably grown bored and gone to the greenhouse. I leaped out of the window and glided over to the glass structure. There was no one inside. As I wandered around the garden, calling his name, I didn't find him.

With every moment that passed, the more tense I became. My mate was gone. I'd asked him to stay here, to wait for me. Caleb's words came back to me. He'd asked me to trust him, but I didn't know how to do that.

Every instinct in my body demanded I find Caleb and keep him right by my side. He was mine. I could not live without him beside me. I needed him. I returned to our quarters on the off chance he'd come back in the time I was gone.

Our quarters were empty.

"Caleb," I called, chest heaving.

The chime came from the door, and I ignored it. Caleb might have gone to see Tinlorray for some reason. Why he had to do it *right* now, I could not say. Another ring came followed by Kalvoxrencol yelling, "Zoltilvoxfyn, open the door."

I let him and Seth inside.

"Are you and Caleb ready?" Kalvoxrencol asked.

"He's not here," I said, throat tight.

"What?" Seth looked around, even though he couldn't see Caleb.

"I asked him to wait, and he's not here."

Seth asked, "Did Caleb say anything?"

"He asked me to trust him if he was gone."

"Then you should."

Kalvoxrencol's tail wrapped around mine. "Come on. Caleb will be safe, and he'll be here waiting for you when you get back."

"Would you leave Seth?" I asked.

Seth laughed, shaking his head. "No. He wouldn't. Shit, he'd rip the palace apart to find me."

Kalvoxrencol frowned at his mate, but he didn't say otherwise, because it was the truth. He would never leave his mate behind. I glanced around our quarters as my soul thrummed at a rapid pace. Caleb was gone. *What if he passed on?* The thought was like a claw to the gut—it ripped me open. I should want that because it would be the best thing for Caleb, but selfishly, I desired him to remain with me for forever.

Seth grabbed my hand. "Trust him, Fyn. Come on."

I tightened my fingers around Seth's much cooler ones and allowed him to pull me from me and mine's quarters.

I stood in Command of Dontilvynsan's ship. The scientists had sent out a greeting in every language we had access to, trying to find a way to communicate with the foreign ship. For all we knew, the vessel was empty, though that wasn't likely from the sheer size of it. The ship was far too large to be a probe or unmanned shuttle.

No matter what we did to alter our sensors, the shield was impervious, so we had no way to know if the ship was experiencing mechanical issues or not. The sole thing our sensors perceived was the shield.

Dontilvynsan refused to fire on them first, unless ordered to do otherwise. Firstly because a shot would end any hope of this resolving peacefully, and secondly, because he didn't know what type of weapons the ship possessed. But from their technology, it was safe to say their weapons would be powerful—more powerful than ours.

Seth and Dontilvynsan, who glanced at me frequently, chatted while Kalvoxrencol and Serlotminden added in occasionally. Each had ideas, as did the scientists and the one diplomat—a Fynlincoxmin—but I was unable to focus on anything besides the fact that Caleb was gone. My soul felt carved out. I was empty without him.

What if I'd done something wrong and he left? What if he'd moved on? What if I never saw him again?

"No," Fynlincoxmin cried, waving his arms around dramatically. "That could upset them."

"We don't know who they are," Kalvoxrencol snapped, "so how would it upset them?"

"Still that message is unnecessarily aggressive," he continued in a loud voice. "Why have me, a skilled diplomat and a seeker soul who holds a prominent position in the Council of Seekers, if you are not going to listen to me?" he demanded, silver eyes flashing. The drakcol had dark gray scales with pink and gold glimpses of his skin. He was easily in his fifth decade, but his appearance suggested he was cycles younger. However, his delicate features and flamboyant aspect tickled some recognition deep within me.

I tried to focus on where I'd seen him instead of the all-consuming darkness within me. His name was somewhat familiar. He was obviously part of the peerage from his long name. Perhaps a *very* distant cousin. I wasn't sure.

It hit me. Talvax. I had seen him with Talvax and Doctor Qinlin at some party. Why or how they knew this man escaped me, not that it mattered. I didn't truly care. I didn't care about any of this. I had been so desperate to leave the planet, and I stood here pointlessly.

A void of numbness consumed me, and everything around me had lost its importance. Why was I even here? I had nothing to offer like my brothers did. I never met with other species or represented my people. I was nothing. I should have remained on Tamkolvanloknol.

A voice yelled right before something crashed through me, making me shiver. The cold was so severe that it burned.

Caleb stood right in front of me.

"Caleb," I gasped.

Kalvoxrencol whipped in my direction. "Caleb? He's here?"

Dontilvynsan peered at me, and I tried to empty my mind so he wouldn't hear me; though, it most likely didn't matter. Dontilvynsan had probably already intercepted my bleak thoughts earlier.

Powerful joy swept through my body at the sight of Caleb standing in front of me. His brown curls, blue eyes, and strange clothes had never looked better. My mate was here. He was back.

"Caleb," I said softly.

Caleb shivered. "Where are we, Sunshine?"

"Caleb."

Everyone on Command was staring at me, and I didn't care. My Caleb was here.

"Zoltilvoxfyn," Dontilvynsan said, drawing my attention away from my mate. He stared at me, and I crossed my arms. He no doubt heard my thoughts and sensed my sweeping emotions, but I refused to be embarrassed. "Why don't you take your mate outside for a moment to collect yourself."

"He knows," Seth whispered.

"I read thoughts, Seth Harris," Dontilvynsan replied, and Seth blanched.

"You're not mad?" I asked.

"At you?" he asked. "No. Pest and Speedy? Yes."

"Why are you mad at us?" Kalvoxrencol demanded.

"No secrets, Pest. You or Serlotminden should have told me."

"Now, Hallonnixmin is the only one who doesn't know," Monqilcolnen said, arms crossed and tail flicking in agitation.

I ignored them and focused on Caleb. How had he even gotten here? He had been on Tamkolvanloknol. Could he fly? I shook my head at the ridiculous thought. He couldn't have left the atmosphere, let alone found me in space.

"Come, Mate."

People watched as we, or rather I, left Command. I slammed my hand on the closest door, Dontilvynsan's office, and directed Caleb inside. I pressed against him, then hissed. His soul was freezing, like ice. "What happened?"

"I don't know."

"Caleb." I brushed his cheek, ignoring the sting. "What do you remember?"

"What?" His pupils were blown wide.

"Talk to me."

Shivers wracked his body. "I kissed you and vanished. I don't remember anything else."

My soul dropped to the soles of my feet. "What?"

"I don't remember."

"No, Caleb. You vanished?"

Eyes unfocused, he answered, "I extended myself too far. When I focus to the extent I can touch something, it stresses my soul."

"You shouldn't have kissed me. Why would you do that?"

Caleb, my Caleb, finally looked at me, seeming like himself. "Because I wanted to, at least once. I deserve to kiss you, Fyn. I want you so bad. It kills me. I needed to be with you, even for a moment," he snapped, hand on his chest. "I want this, even if I can't actually have it."

His words gutted me. I longed to touch him too, but I couldn't risk him for that, for anything.

Caleb glanced around. "Where are we?"

"Dontilvynsan's ship."

"Space? I'm in space. How did I get here?"

I had no answer to give him because I was as confused as he was. Reaching out, I touched him and yanked back. "Why are you so cold?"

He shrugged. "Who knows, but it hurts."

"What?" Spirits did not experience pain. They didn't experience physical sensations whatsoever, according to Caleb.

He didn't answer, and tremors continued to shake him. The edges of his soul were more blurred than usual, which allowed me to see through him. Normally, Caleb appeared solid, but now, his aspect was wispy. And gray. His fingers, ankles, and shoes were gray, and I saw the blue moss floor through him.

I shifted closer, ignoring the burn of the intense cold. "Put your hands on me, Mate."

Caleb snuggled close, almost disappearing inside of me, and I swallowed a hiss. For once, I wished I had Kalvoxrencol's inner fire. He could banish the cold plaguing Caleb with ease. Even Serlotminden with his ability to craft fire would be helpful, though the fire suppression systems would be triggered.

My mate stayed against me, and the chill slowly dimmed until he reached his normal frigid temperature. I kissed the top of his head, relishing the tingling. It was perfect. He was perfect.

"Don't leave me."

"I won't. I didn't mean to. I came back. I will always come back. I promise, Sunshine."

I looked down and swallowed. The edges of his hair were going gray. It was like the color or life was bleeding out of him. Caleb was coming apart. I wrapped my wings around him. I would not let him go. We would figure something out. We had to.

Chapter 30

AN UNFORTUNATE PLAN.

Caleb

Pain. Actual pain. God. This was new. Years had passed since the last time I'd experienced this. I hated and loved the sensation. Feeling anything was a miracle, but why did it have to be pain? From the tip of my toes to the top of my head, everything ached and I was oddly heavy. Like this non-existent body had actual weight.

Fyn kept his wings around me as he huddled close. I slid my hands over his chest and froze, then moved to his back in my usual pattern. I felt warmth. A true, real heat. No second-guessing, no wondering. I felt Sunshine, and the sensation didn't disappear after the barest moment.

"You're warm." I shifted nearer, to the point I started to slip inside of him, but I didn't care. He was *so* damn warm.

"Can you perceive my body?"

"Distantly, but it's there, Sunshine. You're there. You're here. I'm here," I answered. His hands slid up my back, and a tremor went through me. "Don't stop."

Without a word, he continued to stroke my back until I was groaning. I felt him. It was faint like a breeze, but dammit, it was there. It was miraculous. Every stroke was perfect and made me fight back sobs and groans at the same time.

"Fyn," I moaned. I tilted toward him, wanting another kiss, but he stayed well out of reach, not that I would have focused to the point of resistance. "Sunshine? What's wrong?" His glassy eyes turned to the ceiling, and my pleasure vanished. "What's going on? Are you hurt? Did something happen? Is it Seth?" When he didn't say anything, I snapped, "Zoltilvoxfyn, what is wrong? I need you to talk to me."

"Nothing is wrong, my Caleb."

"Why are you lying? Are you upset I can feel you?"

"No."

"Then what's going on?"

He cleared his throat, tail lashing behind him. "You're going gray."

"Oh." He finally noticed. That wasn't ideal. With a surreptitious glance, I saw more gray spreading, my shoes, my calves, my hands. If I was becoming more ghostly, that probably meant I was fading. Maybe physical sensations were a final blessing before I was ripped apart.

"You have to go, Caleb."

"No."

"Caleb."

"No," I snapped. I went on my toes and caught his gaze. "I choose you, Zoltilvoxfyn. I will always choose you. I never thought there was anything after death, and I'm willing to risk my soul to stay with you, even if it's only a few more days. We belong together."

"I can't lose you. If you move on, perhaps I will get to see you again one day."

"I am not leaving you. You said I was yours, and that you were mine, so I get to stay with you." I couldn't leave him. Something deep within me refused to even accept such a possibility. I was meant to be here, with him. We were made for each other, and nothing would ever convince me otherwise.

"Mate," he started, and I crossed my arms, making him fall silent.

This conversation was not even close to being resolved, but it would have to continue later after we'd both had a moment to breathe and could discuss it calmly. Or as calmly as possible because I doubted Fyn would ever be calm about this situation. He was my worrywart after all, and I would never want him to change.

"Why are we in space?" I asked, changing the topic.

"There is an unknown vessel not far from Tamkolvanloknol, which is why there was an emergency Cohort meeting. The craft is not answering pings or responding."

"What do they want?"

"We don't know."

I slid my fingers over his back and was instantly distracted by the feel. I couldn't perceive the texture of his clothes, but god, there was a slight resistance and heat. If I could, I would rub myself all over him. If I did, I imagined Sunshine would want sex. Mmmhh. Sex. Now that might be fun. How much would I feel?

I peeked around the office for a soft surface, but all I spotted was a desk with a stool and some plants. Maybe Fyn could sit on the desk while he jerked off and I helped him? The floor didn't look too bad, either. It was mossy, so probably soft enough for his back. Of course, he could remain standing too. I was good with that. I was good with *all* of the possibilities.

"Caleb, focus."

My gaze shot to his face. "What?"

"You're touching my cock."

I glanced down, and yep, my hand was on his hard cock, rubbing. I licked my lips. Could I taste him? Oh god, I wanted that.

"We cannot fuck in my older brother's office," he said, ruining the moment.

"A *quickie*, maybe?"

"A what?"

Damnit, I didn't know the Drakconese word for a quickie or blowjob. Unfortunately, my sex terminology was lacking. I should've haunted more couples like a creepy perv. "You stay basically dressed and I play with your cock until you come."

He swallowed, and I tracked the bob in his throat. "While that sounds pleasant, not in my brother's office."

"So where's your quarters? Nearby? Maybe we could stop there for a few minutes. I'd make it worth your while. It'd be fun. So fun."

"Focus, Little Soul. There is a possibly dangerous vessel within range. There is no time for sex."

"Sorry," I said, ripping my gaze from the bulge in his pants. Being a ghost had killed my sense of urgency, but clearly not my horniness. "Yes. Bad ship. What can I do?"

Fyn smiled softly, which caused an odd vibration to start in my chest. Fuck. It was my heart; my pulse was racing. He touched my cheek, and I wanted to press into it, but I stayed still.

"Hands away from my cock so I can pay attention, please."

I licked my lips. "I can do that. For now. But only for now. I will have to get my hands on you later. I need it."

"Stay beside me," Fyn said, ignoring my rambling. "I can't lose you."

"You won't."

He smiled again, but it was laced with sadness.

Zoltilvoxfyn

Me and mine returned to Command, but this time, I was in a much better mood. Worry for my mate still plagued me, though. He was beside me, safe. For now. Caleb was ripping apart; I was sure of it. He would be torn from this plane and my arms sooner than I'd ever thought possible. He needed to move on, and yet, I didn't want him to, and neither did he.

Dontilvynsan glanced at us when we entered, and no doubt my thoughts skittered through his mind. He tried not to hear, but he couldn't help it. Reading minds was his inner fire, and there was no way for him to silence the gift, no matter how much he wished there was. He did form a shield—I supposed was the best way to phrase it—around his thoughts, but it wasn't perfect, especially regarding those he was closest to both physically and emotionally.

"Greetings, Caleb," he said. "I shall like to formally meet you after this issue is resolved."

Caleb bounced at my side. "Me too."

As usual, I related his words, though, with Dontilvynsan, I probably didn't need to, because he would hear my thoughts about Caleb.

My brother turned toward the screen, and people began talking again. Kalvoxrencol held Seth securely, and they remained quiet as Serlotminden and Fynlincoxmin suggested different greetings that they'd encountered in their travels and diplomacy work.

Nothing had occurred while Caleb and I were gone. The vessel hadn't moved or threatened us. The white craft floated in space without any hint of life.

"Has the Coalition sent an update?" I asked.

"No," Dontilvynsan answered, looking up from his screen, though his fingers kept moving with ease. "But the Vveekian Authority is sending a science vessel to investigate as well as a warship in case we need assistance, though this close to Tamkolvanloknol, we are hardly likely to need it. Still, the ships are twenty hours from us."

Not a horrible amount of time, though much could happen in twenty hours, especially depending on the strength of the technology of this vessel.

"So you guys don't have..." Caleb trailed off for a moment. "Something to prod the ship?"

"Sensors," I said, supplying the word. "We do, but they cannot penetrate the shields."

"Ah." His head bobbed while his lips pursed. Suddenly, his eyes widened. "I have an idea, but you won't like it."

My tail twitched and wings rustled on my back. "You are not doing anything dangerous."

"I'll be fine," Caleb protested, patting my arm, which made his fingers disappear inside me and sent tingles up the limb.

Even without hearing his idea, I didn't want him to do it, because it would take him from my side. Caleb needed to stay right here, out of danger, and within sight.

Dontilvynsan spoke as he stood. "Will my brothers, their mates, and Monqilcolnen join me in my office to discuss Caleb's idea in private."

"Caleb has an idea?" Seth asked.

Serlotminden answered, "Dontilvynsan must have overheard Zoltilvoxfyn's thoughts about it."

"Oh," he said.

"Come on, Husband," Kalvoxrencol said, directing Seth out of Command. Serlotmiden and Monqilcolnen followed them, but Dontilvynsan waited for me with his eyebrows raised, silently challenging me. If I fled, he would chase me. I couldn't hide from him. Even if I did wish to fight him, which I didn't, I would not beat him. After Kalvoxrencol, Dontilvynsan was the next best fighter.

I offered him my throat in concession, and Dontilvynsan patted my cheek. "Come, Bloom. Let us hear what your mate has to say."

When we stepped inside Dontilvynsan's office, he went behind the desk, and Caleb and I found a spot near the wall.

"It's probably a good thing we didn't fuck in here. Everyone would have smelled it," Caleb said, and I laughed.

Everyone turned toward me—I rarely laughed. I didn't relate what my mate said, because it would bring up a round of unnecessary questions. Unable to stop it, the memory of us in our bed with Caleb ordering me to pleasure myself invaded my thoughts and heated my blood.

Dontilvynsan cleared his throat, and I jolted, immediately regretting my thoughts.

"Please don't have sex in my office," Dontilvynsan said in his usual monotone voice.

"What?" Kalvoxrencol demanded, while Serlotminden laughed uproariously.

"I like your Caleb," Serlotminden said. "Anyone willing to fuck in here is worth being with."

"How do you..." Kalvoxrencol started to ask, but Seth elbowed him, bright red.

"We should get back to the matter of the strange vessel," Monqilcolnen said, and I had the odd impulse to hug him for the redirection.

"Indeed," Dontilvynsan said. "Caleb, what's your plan?"

"You'll take me in a shuttle beneath the vessel and I will go inside," he suggested, like he was planning a walk in a garden.

Ice clogged my veins. “No,” I snarled, turning toward him, not even bothering to relate his plans to the others because it didn’t matter. Caleb would never do this. I refused to let him.

“Interesting,” Dontilvynsan said before telling everyone Caleb’s reckless idea. “That might work.”

“No,” I growled, standing in front of my mate to shield him from my brothers.

“Zoltilvoxfyn,” Kalvoxrencol started, but I cut him off with a sharp wave.

“My mate is not doing this. We have no idea what’s inside the vessel, let alone knowing what the vacuum of space will do to him. Caleb is remaining here.”

Cold fingers trailed over my back, stronger than ever. His touch was growing stronger while his spirit was growing weaker. Eyes closed, I savored it. I didn’t know how much longer I would have this, and I would never recover from losing Caleb.

“It’s my choice, Sunshine,” Caleb said.

I turned around. “Please do not do this, Caleb.”

Caleb cupped my cheeks before immediately groaning, which made me swallow. His reactions were hard for me not to respond to. “Sorry,” he whispered, biting his lip. “Still not used to feeling you.”

“Stay.”

His thumb slid over my cheekbone. “I want to help.”

“You don’t know what this will do to you.”

“I do,” he replied. “I have gone into space before. I’ve done it, more than once. I’ve jumped from ship to ship before. I can do this.”

“Caleb, you’re weakening. I cannot lose you.”

Going on his toes, he said, "Trust me. I have no intention of ever leaving you."

Intentions or not, Caleb could be taken from me. "Mate," I began, planning on forcing him to stay, but he placed his fingers on my lips, sending a shiver down my spine.

"My choice. I am not helpless. I can do this, Sunshine."

I had lost this fight. Caleb would do it with or without me, but he would have an easier, not to mention safer, time with me present. "Fine."

He pushed his forehead into my shoulder, rubbing, though he disappeared into my scales. Without a body, Caleb couldn't properly scent mark me, not that humans did that, but I loved it nonetheless.

I faced my brothers and Monqilcolnen, who all watched me. They'd only heard my side of it, except Dontilvynsan.

"Caleb will do this," I said.

Dontilvynsan replied, tail touching mine for the barest moment before flicking away, "I will do all I can to keep him safe."

"I'll fly the shuttle," Serlotminden instantly offered.

"No," Dontilvynsan said. "You, Kalvoxrencol, and Seth will stay here, under my protection. Monqilcolnen will fly the shuttle with Zoltilvoxfyn and his Caleb." Serlotmiden opened his mouth to complain, but our older brother silenced him. "This is my ship, and I give the orders. Monqilcolnen is in the navy. You are a shuttle racer."

He scowled. "I can do this."

"Worry not," Monqilcolnen said, tugging Serlotminden against his side. "I might not be as good as you, but Zoltilvoxfyn and his mate will be fine."

Serlotminden wasn't the only one upset. Kalvoxrencol was snarling under his breath, but Seth had his arms wrapped around him, keeping him calm. No doubt, Pest wanted to go himself.

"Thank you, Caleb," Dontilvynsan said, looking unerringly at where Caleb stood at my side.

Caleb stuck his straightened hand to his forehead, then shot it out in an oddly stiff move at Dontilvynsan, bouncing on the balls of his feet. "Not a problem, oh Captain my Captain. I'm excited. It'll be fun. A little bit of adventure. I haven't had one in a while."

My mate might be excited, but dread curled in my soul.

Chapter 31

A WALK IN SPACE.

Caleb

I skipped from one end of the shuttle to the other. Zoltilvoxfyn tracked my movements from his seat near the wall. I'd tried to sit next to him, but I was too excited. It had been way too long since my sense of adventure had been tickled. I loved the little thrill of what could happen or what I would or would not see. God, what was happening on the cheese-shaped ship? I had to know.

"You're happy," Zoltilvoxfyn said.

"Hmm?"

"You like this."

"It's the unknown. What's on the ship? Who is on the ship? What if it's empty? What if it's not empty? I can't wait to find out."

His shoulders relaxed and his writhing tail settled. "Your tether."

"What?"

"You must be a seeker soul. Your tether is the unknown. It's why you wandered the universe, Caleb."

My head cocked to the side. Possibly. I did love to explore, but something about his words rang false deep within me. I instinctively knew that wasn't my tether.

Shaking my head, I said, "That's not it."

"No?"

"I don't know how, but I know that's not right."

"Well, I still love watching you excited, even though I wish you wouldn't do this."

"I'll be fine," I said, finally taking a seat next to him. "I promise. I will come back, and I will remain right here beside you. Mostly."

"Mostly?"

"I have to explore your planet." I bounced in my seat. "Maybe we can go on another date in the city. I want to see the shops. And the forests. And oh, that canyon we flew over might be interesting, but going back to the beach would be great too. Or the mountains in the distance. I want to see those too. Do you have plants that eat people? Cause that would be fun."

"As long as you return to me, you can have whatever you desire, Mate."

I licked my lips. "Anything?"

"You are insatiable."

"Yep, and I want to see how much I can feel."

"You will not strain yourself again, Caleb."

This was a conversation we needed to have later when I had a chance to argue my stance. I was going to touch him, as long as he allowed me to, but I wasn't going to focus until I met resistance again. The risk was too great. Continuing what we'd been doing should be perfectly safe.

"We are right below the vessel," Monty said from near the front of the shuttle. He'd probably heard everything Fyn said, not that it mattered. I wasn't shy, and he was Sunshine's family. Still, I appreciated the interruption.

"Mwah," I said as I pressed a non-existent kiss on Fyn's cheek. "I will be right back, Sunshine."

When I stepped away, he reached for me, and I paused. "Please," he said, "come back, my Mate."

"I will. Wait for me."

"I'm not going anywhere."

I stretched like a fighter going to the mat. "Here we go."

I began to slide through the floor, and he tensed. Right before I disappeared, I said, "Don't worry, Sunshine, you're not getting rid of me that easily."

His expression didn't change, and he vanished from my sight and was replaced by the inner workings of the underside of the shuttle, then nothing but space. Stars stretched out in the distance with nothing to mar them.

Spacewalking was an art that I had not mastered. Sure, I'd left the protection of a ship twice in my afterlife. The first time had been an accident, and I spent the entire time screaming bloody murder, not that anyone heard it. Not a pleasant memory. The second time had been a necessity. The ship I'd been on blew up, and I needed to hitch a ride on a passing shuttle.

None of this I told Fyn because he wouldn't have let me do this, not that he could stop me. But he would've worried more than he already did, and I didn't want that.

I curled into a ball and rolled, so my head pointed at the foreign ship. The trick was convincing my soul to move. Physics did not apply to me. I didn't need to push off anything; I could move at will. Like everything, I merely had to believe it was possible.

"Let's go."

Painfully slow, I lifted toward the ship. Now came the scary part. Would the shield keep me out or burn my soul? I had no way to know, so fun times. As always life—rather death was an adventure.

My eyes scrunched closed when I approached the white wedge-shaped ship. This was the moment. I would either crash and burn or be totally fine. Hand out, I waited and waited *and waited.* Nothing happened. More time passed, and still nothing. I cracked one eye open, and I was right next to the ship, alive—or as alive as I got. I pushed through the hull, legs wiggling, and I slid inside.

Aliens, here I come.

Zoltilvoxfyn

I watched Caleb disappear through the floor and my soul fled my body. My instincts roared that I draw him back into my arms, but he'd asked me to trust him, and I would try.

"Monqilcolnen, show me the underside of the shuttle."

"Will you be able to see him? Dontilvynsan's inner fire doesn't work over screen."

"I have no idea," I snapped. "I haven't had many opportunities to ask spirits to enter the void of space and check if I can see them."

He lifted a single eyebrow at my harsh tone.

"Show me," I demanded, desperate to see Caleb.

Monqilcolnen pressed a few buttons on the console, and the underside of the ship came into view on the screen spanning the front of the shuttle. My breath stopped as I scanned space, begging the Crystal for any glimpse of my mate.

"Anything?" he asked.

I shook my head as the backs of my eyes burned. He was lost to me, and I didn't know what to do with that. Something flickered, and I turned, then paused. Caleb. He was curled into a ball.

"Something's wrong."

"What?" Monqilcolnen asked.

"I see Caleb, and he's not moving. Move the ship, so he'll be inside."

"Maybe he needs a moment?"

"Or he is being ripped apart. Move. Now." When Monqilcolnen didn't shift, I growled. I couldn't pilot a shuttle; I'd never learned.

"One moment, Zoltilvoxfyn. Give him a chance."

"I can't." Every fiber of my being was screaming to protect Caleb.

"Breathe," he said, tail wrapping around my forearm.

I took a shuddering breath, and before I finished, Caleb rolled and stretched out. "He's moving."

"Good."

Caleb appeared incredibly peaceful as he drifted to the ship, as if he'd done this frequently. As much as I knew about my mate, he hadn't spoken of his wanderings, and I didn't know why. Now, I was determined to ask him. I wanted to know everything about him.

He paused right outside the ship, hovering in place, completely at ease. Caleb had never looked more beautiful, but he was so far away, untouchable. My soul clenched at the thought.

Finally, Caleb slid through the shield and into the ship without a hint of trouble. When he disappeared from sight, I said, "He's inside."

Powering up the engines, Monqilcolnen said, "Time to head back."

"What? What about Caleb?"

"You can see him on the screens. When he exits the ship, we'll come get him."

"No," I said. "I will wait here for him."

"Dontilvynsan ordered me to come back if you could see Caleb from a distance."

Anger rumbled in my chest. I would not abandon my mate. Not ever.

His tail wrapped around my forearm again. "I don't say this to injure you, but Caleb is dead. You are not. I have to protect you. We are going back to the ship, and you can watch for him there. I swear by the Crystal's light, the second you see him, I will take you to get him regardless of the danger."

My hands fisted as I stared at where my mate had vanished. "I will hold you to your word."

"Don't fret. My instincts tell me this all works out."

"What?"

He said, "I sense things."

"Precognition?" I asked, shocked. If there was a gift rarer than mine, precognition was it.

"Not quite," Monqilcolnen said as he directed the shuttle away from my mate. "I do not get visions. Sometimes I know things. It's not true precognition, but I do have a sense that this will work out."

Part of me wanted to snarl at Monqilcolnen. He expected us to be honest with him, and yet, he rarely told us anything. While inner fires didn't have to be disclosed, nor was it odd for someone to keep it to themselves, it irked me that Monqilcolnen had never told us, though he might have told Hallonnixmin and Dontilvynsan because they were all the best of friends.

I wished when I was a child that I had kept my inner fire secret, as apparently Monqilcolnen had. It would've spared me a considerable amount of trouble.

Pushing my anger aside, I glanced out the front screen to see the ship that held my soul. "I hope you are right."

Chapter 32

INTO THE SPACE CHEESE.

Caleb

My first impression of the ship was: *God, this is boring.* There was nothing besides endless dull white corridors. No windows. No doors. No people. Nothing. I saw absolutely positively nothing. I poked my head around a curve, and more nothing. Damn, this ship wasn't worth the freak-out it brought about.

Over the years, I'd seen numerous ships and vessels, but this was by far the most uninteresting one. It was a hunk of white cheese floating around space scaring the shit out of people.

Well, if the ship was empty and non-threatening, then I could leave. Fyn would like that. A heat bloomed in my gut at the thought of getting him naked, and arousal filtered through my mind. I reveled in the feeling that pulsed dimly in my soul. I shook my thoughts off. I needed to thoroughly search the ship before Sunshine and I could have fun. But then we would have lots and *lots* of fun. He would not leave the bed for days if I had my way.

I skipped down the hall, whistling a lively tune, and searched for any signs of life. The longer I wandered, the more relaxed I became until I was as calm as a Sunday drive.

Smiling, I rounded a corner and skidded to a stop. An alien who came to my waist appeared before me. The alien's four pupilless eyes widened, and their coral pink skin turned to a sickly pus yellow. An ear-piercing shriek ripped out of them, revealing their two forked tongues and square teeth.

I pointlessly covered my ears to try and block the sound.

Like magic, doors appeared on the smooth walls and aliens poured into the hallway. As one, they turned toward me and began screaming as they ran around. Some crashed into the walls, and their jello-like bodies bounced off and sent them to the floor, where they continued to shriek at a mind-numbing decibel.

"You can see me," I shouted over the racket, which made another round of screaming start.

Something pulled me to the left, and I looked down to see an alien had come up behind me. One of their tentacles, I guessed, or jelly-like appendages curled around my forearm. They were touching me. They were touching me! I yelled in pure fucking joy. These aliens could touch me.

The alien turned frightfully white and shrieked back at me. All the other aliens screamed and raced around the hall. One bumped into me, and I released another cry, and seized them around their middle, squeezing as hard as possible.

I could touch them. I didn't have to focus. I didn't have to struggle. I squeezed even harder, rocking the alien back and forth like a big, jiggly, jello baby. Probably a bad decision on my part, but I was so excited to touch something, even if it was an alien.

The alien trapped in my embrace released such a racket that the others desperately tried to get away from us, but they rammed into each other and the walls, landing on the floor in heaps. I released the alien from my grasp, and they turned into a gelatinous puddle at my feet.

"You can see me," I shouted, pumping my fist in the air. "Booyah!"

More shrieks came from the aliens.

Aliens came down the hall in a line carrying bubble-shaped squirt guns that were bright green with pulsing lights. One raised their weapon at me, and a red beam whizzed past my shoulder, burning me. Not squirt guns. Definitely not squirt guns. Whoever these aliens were, they not only saw me, they could injure me.

I clutched my throbbing shoulder. My shirt and skin were fine, but whatever they did burned. I bolted around the corner. So the aliens weren't friendly (good to know), but some scared easily. I pressed against the wall, but there was nothing but empty hallways, screaming aliens in the distance, and other aliens bent on destroying me.

Time to abandon ship. I relaxed, as hard as it was, and began to slide through the floor. The armed aliens came around the corner, and I willed myself to go faster. The aliens paused, guns lowering.

"Please don't shoot me," I said on the off chance they understood. "I didn't mean any harm. I was shocked you saw me."

One of the aliens raised a shapeless appendage. "Peace, Spirit. We will not harm you."

I froze, half in and out of the floor. What a sight I must be on the next level. I fought a chuckle at the thought of blob aliens screaming from a pair of floating legs. Swallowing the inappropriate reaction, I asked, "You won't?"

"No. We thought you were an intruder coming to harm us, not a lost soul," the alien answered in a warbly voice.

I rose out of the floor. "Well, I kind of am an intruder, but I have no plans to attack you."

All of the blobs moved in unison; they tilted to the side. Maybe it was the equivalent of cocking their head. They didn't really have heads. Or necks. Or bodies. They were like pink blobs of ooze.

"Why are you here?" the lead alien asked, extending their gun again.

"No, no. I mean no harm. I swear," I said in a rush, lifting my hands, then lowered them, afraid they would perceive it as a threat. I didn't know. I wasn't an anthropologist. "I'm with the other ship. The drakcol want to make sure you're not here to hurt them."

"Why would we harm them?"

"Why would I harm you?" I asked, and they did the tilt thing again. "I'm new, scary, and you have no idea of my intentions. You are the same to them."

"Boobaas never threaten. We are peaceful."

I stifled a laugh. Boobaas. God. I'd never wanted to laugh so hard at a name, but I swallowed it. I wasn't twelve anymore. "Excellent,"

I said, unable to stop bouncing. "So are the drakcol. We can be friends."

A literal ripple went through the aliens. "They wish to be friends?"

I hoped friends meant the same thing. "They wish to know you and for peace between your two species." At least, I thought they did. I really didn't want this to dissolve into a fight. I had a bad feeling these pink blobs, boobaas—what a name—would win.

"Friends," the blobs said as one.

Were they a hive mind? That might explain the screaming. One had started panicking and so did the rest. When the lead blob spoke, the others followed.

"Yep, friends," I said. They bobbed up and down, and I frowned until I realized they were copying me. I bounced harder, and they copied, jiggling like jello. "Do all of you see ghosts like me?"

"Yes, Spirit. We exist between the planes. Both are seen and touched by boobaas."

"Awesome."

"Awesome," they parroted.

"Can we be friends?" I asked.

The lead alien said, "That is up to Tatas."

I snorted. First boobaas, and now Tatas. What was a guy supposed to do?

"Tatas will decide if we shall be friends or we shall disintegrate you."

"Right." Well, that wasn't terrifying or anything.

Chapter 33

THE GREAT AND POWERFUL TATAS.

Zoltilvoxfyn

I paced Command, tail thrashing. I scoured the screens for even the slightest glimpse of Caleb, anything to prove that all was well. Several hours had passed and nothing. Serlotminden had tried to comfort me by saying it would take hours, days even, to search a ship of that size. His words didn't help. Pest had kept an arm around me until I pushed him away. Dontilvynsan and Monqilcolnen had held their peace, but they both watched me. I ignored them all and everyone else in Command. All that mattered was Caleb, and I didn't see him.

A console beeped, and I froze.

Commander Bimwoxcol, Dontilvynsan's second in command, said in a light voice, "Captain, we are receiving a ping from the ship."

"Put it on the screen."

A pink blob with swirls of green and purple appeared, and more importantly, Caleb was right beside them.

I rushed forward, ignoring protocol. "Caleb."

"Sunshine," he called back, waving.

"Caleb," Seth whispered.

"He's there," I said.

Seth came to my side, mouth open. He pointed. "Caleb, I can see you."

Caleb beamed. "I know, like the drakcol can understand me in English. It's the boobaas's technology."

A sort of strangled sound came out of Seth that made Caleb wiggle his eyebrows.

"It's good to see you, man," Seth said. "You're wearing an Einstein shirt."

"I'm kind of a geek. *Star Trek* fan and all that."

"*Star Trek*?" Kalvoxrencol asked, coming to his mate's side. "I love *Star Trek*."

"You do?" Caleb asked.

"Are you short or are they tall?" Serlotminden asked before Kalvoxrencol could reply.

"Short," Caleb replied. "I'm five-two."

I had no idea what that meant, but Caleb was short. I wasn't alone in my confusion. Kalvoxrencol stared at Seth, who held up a hand to demonstrate Caleb's height, I assumed. I readjusted his position because I was intimately familiar with Caleb.

Serlotminden blinked. "You *are* short."

"Yep."

"As much as I like seeing you, mate of my brother, I would like to address the foreign ship in our territory," Dontilvinsan said in an even voice.

"Ah, yes. Sorry. I was super excited to see everyone. Actually, I was more excited for everyone to see me! I mean, now you all know what I look like, and we can talk. It's so nice."

"Caleb," Dontilvynsan interrupted, and I fought a laugh. My mate liked to talk.

"Right. Sorry," Caleb said before turning to the pink alien with different swirling colors in their depths. "This is Tatas of the Boobaas."

Seth repeated in a tight voice, "Tatas of the Boobaas."

Caleb smirked. "Dude, I had the same thought. Like literally the exact same thought."

The humans chuckled, and the rest of us stared at them, except Dontilvynsan. "Children," he muttered before facing Tatas. "I am Captain Dontilvynsan of the Drakcol. I am also the second prince of Emperor Kontolmakqilnen and Empress Vyn."

"Are you the one who claims this spirit?" Tatas asked.

"He is my younger brother's mate," Dontilvynsan gestured to me, and I stepped forward.

"I am Prince Zoltilvoxfyn. Caleb is mine."

Tatas rippled. "Caleb has offered friendship between the boobaas and the drakcol. I am inclined to accept, for he is a soul without guile."

Dontilvynsan stood. "We do not wish to fight, but what would friendship entail?"

"The exchange of cultural information to start. We are unwilling to have a deeper relationship until more is known about you." Tatas patted Caleb's head, and I fought a surge of possessive anger. This being could touch what was *mine*, and yet I could not. Tatas continued, "This spirit is honorable and true, but we do not know if you are."

"What about this technology that allows us to see Caleb?" Dontilvynsan asked, and I could have hugged him. My Caleb deserved to be seen and heard whenever he wished.

"We do not share technology."

I opened my mouth to argue, but Dontilvynsan stopped me with a flick of his tail, no doubt hearing my intentions. He offered Tatas his throat. "An understandable rule. We have much the same, though we are a part of the Coalition of Planets."

Tatas leaned to the side. "What is this Coalition?"

"It is a group of individual planets that have joined together to share resources, technology, and abide by some universal laws, though each planet has its own government and laws."

"Boobaas have no such interest or need."

"The offer to join will always be open." Dontilvynsan glanced at Kalvoxrencol, and I frowned. Was he having an odd idea to help Caleb and me? Kalvoxrencol lifted his palms, and Dontilvynsan gestured to the screen.

Kalvoxrencol was the only recognized adult here and a voting Cohort member, even though he was the youngest of us all.

"I am Prince Kalvoxrencol," he said, stepping forward. "This is my mate and husband, Seth Harris." Seth clung to Kalvoxrencol.

"As a representative of the Drakcol Empire, I would like to extend an offer of friendship."

Tatas stared at Seth. "You are not a spirit."

"No," he replied, starting.

"You are the same species as Caleb."

"Yes," Seth said.

The alien jiggled. "We shall take you as well."

A roar ripped out of Kalvoxrencol, and he shoved Seth behind him. "You are not taking my mate anywhere."

"He does not belong here, and we shall return him."

Kalvoxrencol snarled something unintelligible. Dontilvynsan, Monqilcolnen, and Serlotminden moved to his side, and I was a moment behind them. Seth was one of us. No one was taking him. Also, Kalvoxrencol and Seth were genetically linked; they couldn't go too far from each other without suffering fatal consequences.

Seth pushed out from behind Kalvoxrencol, ignoring his grasping hands. Staring straight at Tatas, Seth said, "I do belong. I'm mated to Kal and he is mine. I have no interest in leaving."

"I suppose you can make up your own mind, but I believe your hive shall miss you," Tatas said.

"Hive?" Seth asked.

Caleb turned to Tatas. "We don't have hives like boobaas. We have families."

They tilted. "I do not understand that word."

"We are born to a group of people who care for us until we reach maturity," Seth said. "I'm grown. Kal is my family. My hive, I guess."

Tatas tilted again. "You are an odd species."

Kalvoxrencol's low growl was drowned out by mine. Humans were perfectly fine. My Caleb wasn't odd. Well, not that odd... Alright humans were odd, but I wouldn't allow anyone to insult them.

Seth covered Kalvoxrencol's mouth and asked, "Are you going to accept the drakcol's offer of friendship?"

"Perhaps."

"Tatas, you said you wanted to be friends," Caleb said.

"The drakcol are a more aggressive people than I thought. Boobaas are not violent."

"Neither are we," Kalvoxrencol said. "But you threatened what is ours. Seth is my husband and mate, and you tried to take him away."

Tatas's colors swirled. "What are these words?"

Caleb pointed at them. "They fuck."

Seth turned bright red, while a snicker came out of my lips at his direct response.

"Copulation?" Tatas asked.

"Yep," Caleb said.

"Hmm. Drakcol and humans are odd. Perhaps you do belong here, Seth. Boobaas do not copulate. We split. The resulting puddle is mixed with the Great Ooze to forge a new hive member."

Arms around Seth, Kalvoxrencol said, "We copulate and are very protective of our mates."

"How interesting. Boobaas do not interact with many species. Our planet is not in phase with yours. It was quite a mistake that landed us here and our ship is damaged. Perhaps friendship is not possible."

"The offer will stand," Kalvoxrencol said. "If you mean us no harm, you and your kind may remain in Drakcon space and fix your ship."

Tatas replied, "We shall accept your offer to fix our ship. Once repairs are complete, we shall leave."

"Caleb," I said, "come back now." I was done having him away from my side. Every instinct in my body demanded he return to where I could see him. Caleb was mine, and I needed him here.

"Aye aye, Sunshine," he said, lifting his hand to his forehead and performing that gesture I didn't understand again. "Well, Tatas, it was nice to meet you." He started to slide through the floor. "Hate to peep and run, but home is calling."

I signaled Monqilcolnen to come with me, but Tatas spoke, stopping me. "No." They grabbed Caleb around the wrist and dragged him up. His face scrunched as he fought their hold.

"Release my mate," I demanded.

"This lost spirit needs to leave this phase, and we shall take him. He will be safer with us, and we may one day return him to where he belongs so he can join the Great Ooze of Beyond."

Caleb tried to yank out of their grasp. "I'm going to stay with Zoltilvoxfyn."

"Let him go," I demanded. "Caleb!"

"Sunshine," he called, trying to wiggle free.

"We cannot release him. As soon as our ship is ready, we shall depart," Tatas said, and the screen went blank.

Caleb

I fought to escape Tatas's clutch. Sunshine must be frantic. I had to get back to him. "Let me go," I screamed, kicking them. My foot bounced back at me while their blob-like body rippled.

"Spirit, you are coming apart at your very molecules. If we leave you be, you shall dissipate. We must preserve you by taking you to our home, then eventually to yours," Tatas replied, not loosening their solid grip.

"I'm coming apart?" I asked, stilling. I'd suspected it, but to have it confirmed was... My poor Sunshine.

"You are losing your vitality and solidity. You must pass on. Relinquish your hold on this plane."

"My tether." I swore my heart pounded, though it was softer than I remembered. "Zoltilvoxfyn." It was like the sun had broken through the clouds on a rainy day. He was my tether. He held me here.

"Your mate."

"He wasn't my mate when I died. That was years ago. I don't even know if he was born when I died. He can't be my tether."

"Your soul knew he was out there, so you went searching."

After I died, I had an inexplicable need to wander. The urge had never disappeared until I saw Fyn. The second I saw him, something had changed. He was the center of my existence. The vibration in my chest grew louder and my fingers curled around something as whispers tickled my ears.

He was my tether. If I let Fyn go, I would pass on.

No. I'd promised to never leave him, and I wouldn't. I was willing to vanish. I was willing to cease to exist. Fyn needed me, but more than that, I needed him. I refused to live without him.

"No," I said.

"He *is* your tie to this plane. You cannot dispute it."

"He is, but I'm not leaving him."

"Your time is short. You must go."

"No," I said, yanking on my arm. "I am Zoltilvoxfyn's."

"To allow a mind to cease to exist is a great crime among my kind. You must rejoin your hive or ours, so the next generations might be blessed with parts of you."

I didn't know what they were smoking or how death worked for them, but I wasn't about to let anyone keep me from Fyn. I scratched my forehead to hide that I was focusing as hard as possible so I would disappear. When I came back, I should reappear at my Sunshine's side—like last time.

"Stop," Tatas ordered, pulling me to the door.

I dug my feet in, and I concentrated. The solidity of their tentacle grew by the second, and my fingertips began to turn transparent. It wouldn't be long now.

Tatas tried to tighten their clutch, but their tentacle slid through my arm. "You must come with us boobaas."

"I won't leave him. I will *never* leave him."

Darkness crashed over me like a wave, and right before I lost all sense of self, I heard a voice cry, "Come back to me, please."

Chapter 34

SO I'M LOOKING A BIT SEE-THROUGH.

Zoltilvoxfyn

Caleb. Caleb. *Caleb.* His name circled my mind as I stared at the blank screen. I couldn't think; I couldn't breathe; I couldn't move.

The door to Command slid open, and an irked voice asked, "What was the great emergency? I was attempting to sleep for but a moment to gather my thoughts and I was interrupted." Fynlincoxmin tightened the pink silky robe around him.

Commander Bimwoxcol replied, "The leader of the boobas, or perhaps just this ship, contacted us."

His mouth fell open. "Seriously? Seriously?" He crowded closer to her. "Tell me everything. Better yet, did anyone think to record it? Viable information can be learned from the slightest tic. Show me now."

As Bimwoxcol pulled up the recorded feed and Fynlincoxmin babbled about how he should have never attempted to rest,

Dontilvynsan curled his tail around mine and motioned for the rest of our brothers to follow as he led me out of Command. He moved to his office and everyone slid in behind me.

I was frozen against the wall, panting. Words swirled around me with little meaning. Monqilcolnen was saying something about the shields and our weapons, but I couldn't focus.

All I heard was Caleb's panicked cry. He didn't want to leave me, any more than I desired to be apart from him, but the boobaas were going to take him away, and there was nothing I could do.

Perhaps Caleb would escape from Tatas's clutch and slide out of the ship.

My head jerked up. "I need to see a monitor of the space surrounding the boobaas's ship."

Serlotmiden paused in the middle of his sentence, then asked, "What?"

"Do you think Caleb will get away?" Seth asked.

"He might. I need to see. Now." I said, racing to Dontilvynsan's desk and poking at his screen. He pushed me away and pulled up the exterior sensors with a few taps of his fingers. I studied his screen as images of the boobaas's ship appeared before me. I didn't see anything.

"Caleb," I whispered. "Where are you?"

"I do not wish to sleep."

Kalvoxrencol stood in front of me, arms crossed. All of my brothers had tried to pull me away from the monitors displaying the boobaas's ship, but I refused to shift.

Caleb was somewhere within that vessel.

Dontilvynsan had tried to ping the boobaas multiple times, but they refused to respond. The Coalition's support ships were still hours away. The boobaas might leave before the Coalition even arrived to assist if they finished repairing their ship.

Seth popped out from behind Kalvoxrencol and grabbed my wrist. He stared at me with his deep brown eyes, his odd, round pupils so like Caleb's. "Come on, Fyn. You need to sleep, even if it's for a few minutes. Caleb will find you."

I twisted in his grasp and held his hand while my eyes flicked to Kalvoxrencol. I practically saw the stress in his shoulders and in the way his tail thrashed. Being as close as we were, sometimes the pain of one of us became the pain of both of us.

"I will rest."

His shoulders relaxed, and he wound his tail around mine. "Thank you."

I squeezed his tail before shaking Kalvoxrencol and Seth off. I left Command without a backward glance and went straight to the quarters I was staying in. Once inside, I sank to the couch to grab my screen and pulled up the sensor feeds. I might have abandoned Command, but I wasn't going to stop searching for my mate. Sleep was impossible when I knew he was in danger, and they were foolish to believe otherwise.

My gaze never deviated from the shifting images as I scoured every frame for Caleb. He had to be somewhere. I couldn't live with the alternative of the boobaas leaving with him. He was mine, and he belonged here with me. We belonged together.

A shiver went down my spine. The shared space had turned frightfully cold. Something must be wrong with the environmental controls. I let it go and studied the sensor images, determined to catch sight of my mate, somewhere.

When another tremor went up my spine, I paused, breath turning harsh. My head snapped up. Caleb stood in the middle of the room, shivering violently.

"Caleb," I breathed, something relaxing deep within me. He didn't react to my voice, though. I rushed toward him, brushing his spirit, and I yanked back, hissing. Caleb was so cold, he froze my very scales. I clenched my fingers into a tight fist in an attempt to warm them.

"Caleb," I said again, and he stared blankly back. "Mate, please speak to me." His body trembled. I tried to touch him, but the cold emanating from him was too extreme.

An idea formed in the back of my mind, and I shoved my hand into my pocket. "Kalvoxrencol," I said into the glowing blue touchstone.

"Zoltilvoxfyn, what's going on?" he asked moments later.

"Come to my quarters. Now." I disconnected and raised the temperature in the shared space. It wouldn't help Caleb like direct heat, but it was better than nothing. I then forced myself to press against him. "Mate, I'm right here."

I kept whispering reassuring words to Caleb as I traced my fingers over him, but he didn't react. "Caleb," I said, unable to keep the broken tone from my voice. The gray had spread to the whole of his body. My Caleb was steadily ripping apart.

"Oh, Mate, I'm sorry," I told him. I shouldn't have started courting him or allowed him to remain. I'd failed him. Completely and utterly failed him.

The door opened without permission, and Kalvoxrencol strode inside alone. "Zoltilvoxfyn?"

"Caleb is here and freezing cold. I need you to unleash your inner fire."

"Where is he?"

I directed Kalvoxrencol to stand behind Caleb, and light pooled under his scales. Heat poured off him in waves, and Caleb didn't react. I traced my fingers down his arm. He twitched. Placing my mouth near his ear, I whispered, "Caleb."

He jolted.

I brushed the tip of my nose over his frozen spirit, ignoring the cold that burned my scales. "My Caleb."

"It hurts," he whimpered.

My soul clenched. "What? Pest's light or the cold?"

"Cold. So cold."

"Am I hurting him?" Kalvoxrencol asked as the burning light dimmed.

"No," I ordered. "Don't stop, Pest."

Sometimes I had a hard time remembering that everyone didn't see or hear Caleb as I did. From his perspective, he stood a small distance in front of me while I spoke to no one. Though he had to feel the cold coming off Caleb.

"Place your hands on me, Mate," I said.

Caleb shifted as close as he could without disappearing inside of me. I traced my fingers up and down Caleb's back as Kalvoxrencol let off a steady heat and light. My chest was frozen by Caleb, but my fingers and face were burning from Kalvoxrencol's inner fire, both equally uncomfortable, but I remained quiet.

My wings slid out to envelop Caleb and Kalvoxrencol in my embrace. The light burned the delicate membrane of my wings, but I gritted my teeth, ignoring it. Kalvoxrencol glanced at me, and the light dimmed.

I growled at him.

"I'm hurting you," Kalvoxrencol whispered.

"Caleb needs it."

Kalvoxrencol's wings escaped from his shirt and rested under mine, trapping more of the heat with Caleb in the center. My breath turned harsh, though Kalvoxrencol did not react. His own inner fire didn't bother him, no matter how hot he burned.

After a bit, Caleb stopped shivering and relaxed against me. When touching his soul didn't freeze me, I said, "He's fine now, Kalvoxrencol."

The light vanished, and his wings retreated under his shirt. He slipped out of my quarters without a word to give me and Caleb privacy and to, no doubt, tell our brothers of his return.

My fingers continued to move over his back, brushing through the outline of his soul. Whether he perceived my touch or not, I couldn't stop myself. I needed reassurance of Caleb's presence. He was here. He was safe.

My eyes flicked down to his slight form, and my soul clenched. Caleb was transparent. He'd always been fuzzy on the edges, but this was different. More extreme. I easily saw the floor through his soul; Caleb was barely here.

"Mate, can you tell me what happened?"

He didn't respond and continued to huddle against me, almost as if intended to crawl inside of me.

Not speaking, I continued to keep my arms around my mate and pretended to hold him within my embrace, like I could keep him here by sheer force of will.

Caleb

Everything hurt. I recognized the pain was rather faint, but years had passed since the last time I truly experienced pain, barring that short stint after the last time I'd vanished, and I didn't know what to do with it or how to cope. My Sunshine kept speaking to me, but his words floated in one ear and out the other. While I didn't understand what he said, the even timbre of his voice soothed me. Like sunlight, his fingers trailed over my back, and I adored the slight pressure.

Each time I vanished and reappeared since meeting Fyn, my physical awareness had grown exponentially. Though, I doubted it was wise to keep disappearing. Perversely, that was exactly what I wanted to do. I wanted to scrape Sunshine's scales across my nonexistent skin. I wanted to kiss his lips. I wanted to feel him. All of him.

What I truly wanted was to be alive. But that ship had gone and sailed. On the other hand, if I hadn't died all those years ago, I wouldn't be here with Fyn right now. There was no choice between the two. I would pick Sunshine over life, over physical sensations, over existence itself.

My gaze moved upward, and Fyn was already looking at me. "Told you I would come back," I said.

"Yes, you did."

I went up on my toes. "Hello, Sunshine."

"Greetings, Little Soul."

Sliding out of his arms, I peered down at my body. I finally looked like the ghost I was. I could see through my arm to the wall and I'd turned mostly gray.

"Well, fuck."

Fyn brushed my cheek and asked, voice grave, "How did you escape?"

"You know how."

"You made yourself vanish."

"I focused as hard as possible to come back to you." My tether. How he was my tether before I'd even known he existed seemed implausible. But for better or worse, my soul was tied to Zoltilvoxfyn, and to move on meant I had to let go of him, which would never happen.

Chapter 35

MY CHOICE.

Caleb

The longer Fyn touched me, the more I fought the urge to yank his clothes off and test how much I could actually feel. Maybe I could convince him to relax for a short time or a long time. I mean, this was his brother's ship—he wasn't going to kick us off if we holed up for a couple of days.

I moved downward until I brushed the outline of his cock in his pants. I chewed on my bottom lip, running my fingers over the growing bulge.

"Caleb," he breathed, sounding heartbroken, not aroused.

I stalled in stroking him. "What?"

His eyes turned glassy.

"What's wrong?"

Fyn straightened and shoved his hand into his pocket. "Yes, Dontilvynsan," he said into the glowing touchstone. I didn't hear the other end of the conversation, but I didn't expect to. "I understand. We'll be right there."

"What's going on?"

"Tatas is demanding your return."

I was afraid of that.

"My brothers need us in Command," he said. His tail flicked at me, and I followed him.

Command was alive with activity. Dontilvynsan was sitting on his stool with all of Fyn's brothers and Monqilcolnen standing beside him. Dontilvynsan's commander, whose name I hadn't caught but she was rocking short black hair and dusty red scales, frantically moved her fingers over the console, and she wasn't alone. Most of the crew was racing around or slapping their consoles.

"What is happening, Dontilvynsan?" Fyn asked.

"Tatas's ship has powered their weapons. They are demanding Caleb's return."

"Caleb is not going anywhere," Fyn growled.

Kal said, "We already know that, Bloom. He's one of us."

A warmth started in my chest, followed by the slow pound of my heart. Growing up, I'd had a close family, always surrounded by siblings and cousins. Now, I had another family. They couldn't see me, and yet they accepted me, protected me.

It was fucking amazing.

I looked at each and every one of them, landing last on Fyn. I loved them, I loved him, and now it was my turn to protect them.

Stepping forward, I said, "I need to speak to Tatas." When Fyn didn't share my words, I peeked over my shoulder at him. His arms were crossed, and his expression was hard. He was afraid to lose me.

"Sunshine, I need to do this."

He remained quiet, lips clamped.

"I heard your request, Caleb," Dontilvynsan said, glancing at Fyn with a stern glare. "Commander Bimwoxcol, ping Tatas."

"No," Fyn protested.

Dontilvynsan didn't even look at his little brother. "Your mate requested to speak to Tatas, and I will not silence him."

"Thank you, Don," I said, knowing he would hear my words echoed in Fyn's mind. I glanced at my Fyn. "Trust me."

"I do," he said, "but I cannot lose you."

"You won't."

We didn't have another chance to speak, because Tatas appeared on the front monitor. Their jello form wiggled and swirled with color. While I didn't know exactly what it meant, I guessed it was because they were upset.

"Caleb, you must return," Tatas said.

"You can see me?" I asked.

They bobbed. "Yes. You must return. It is our duty to take you to the beyond. Your mind cannot be lost to the hive and future generations. You must return to the quagmire that will become the future."

"No, I belong to Zoltilvoxfyn. This is my choice."

"You are going to rip apart."

Fyn's breath caught and his arms moved around me. I hadn't even heard him come up behind me.

"Yes," I answered because what they said was the truth. I couldn't deny it. Well, I could, but what would be the point? Tatas would know I was lying. Sunshine would know I was lying. Hell, the whole ship would know I was lying if they could see me. I was vanishing by the second. "I don't care."

Their form leaned to the side. "You do not care?"

"No. I never believed in the afterlife, so I'm not afraid to cease to exist. I choose to stay with my mate."

"Your tie to reality."

Fyn's breath sharpened, and from the corner of my eye, I spied his tail thrashing.

"My tether."

Tatas stared at me and the silence in Command swelled with tension. This was my choice, but in the end, if they threatened to destroy the ship, I didn't know what I would do. Leaving Fyn would... I couldn't even formulate the words, but I couldn't allow him or the others to be killed.

They bobbed. "Your choice, but we fear you will regret it. You will be nothing, Caleb. You might wish to change your mind in the last moments, but when you become too weak for even your mate to see, it will be too late for you to move on."

"I won't regret it," I said with complete confidence. Any day with Fyn was worth the price to be paid.

"You are out of our grasp." They shifted to Kal. "We retract any offer of friendship. As soon as our ship is repaired, we shall return to our plane."

"Understood. Should you change your mind, send a note." Kal barely tilted his head to the side, acknowledging Tatas.

Without another word, Tatas disconnected.

Everyone in Command stared at Fyn, who had his arms wrapped around me. Of course, from their perspective, he was clinging to nothing but air. Kal, with Seth at his side, moved toward us, but Fyn stopped them. "I need to speak to my mate."

"Take all the time you need," Don said. "I shall have to remain here until the boobaas leave, but a shuttle can take you home as soon as you're ready."

"We'll stay with you," Kal said, and Seth nodded.

Mindy piped up. "I'll stay here too."

"I can take you and Caleb home," Monty said.

"Thank you." Fyn headed out of Command, and I trailed silently behind him to the shuttle, wishing Tatas hadn't said anything.

Zoltilvoxfyn

The entire flight back to Tamkolvanloknol I remained silent. Caleb tried to initiate a conversation, but not a single word came out of my tight throat. I was the reason he was here. I'd guessed it, but I didn't know I was his tether—the one thing tying him to the mortal plane. He was being ripped apart, and he still chose to remain by my side.

Wave after wave of self-loathing crashed over me, making it hard for me to breathe. It was as if I was drowning. With every moment that passed, the cloud over me grew until I couldn't see around me. A strangling pressure squeezed my chest and a ringing numbness filled every cell of my body.

I was causing my mate, my other half, to destroy himself.

I certainly wasn't worthy of his loyalty or love. Caleb deserved to move on, but I desperately needed him to stay. Selfish, I knew, but the thought of continuing without Caleb bouncing by my side was too much. Yet that was to be my fate. Time would rip him from me, and I would never see him again.

If he moved on, I might see him someday or I might not. I had no way of knowing.

I leaned back against the bulkhead of the shuttle. What should I do? I knew the answer, but I did not like it. Caleb was mine and he belonged beside me, but he *was* mine. It was my responsibility to protect him, and how could I cause him harm? I was meant to shield him with every fiber of my being, yet I was the one hurting him. I had to let him go. He needed to move on, no matter how much it destroyed me.

When we landed on the palace shuttle port, I stepped outside into the bright light of Tamkolvanloknol, leaning into the ever-present wind. Caleb walked right beside me, without even a slight bounce in his step.

"Come, Mate."

He bobbed his head.

I led him to our quarters; I didn't want to have an audience for this conversation. I faced Caleb, and he shook his head. "What?" I asked.

"No."

"I did not say anything."

"You don't think I know you, Sunshine?" he asked. "I am not leaving."

My lips parted.

"I am not letting you go."

"You have to. I cannot be the cause of your suffering."

"You're not," he said, coming to stand in front of me, his hands on my chest. The chill made longing spike in my gut. I craved his fingers stroking me as he told me exactly what he desired. But I wanted my mate to be safe more.

"I am," I insisted. "I'm your tether."

He smiled, going up on his toes. "I searched the universe, looking for something I didn't understand, but it was you. I was always yours. You're the sun of my existence, Zoltilvoxfyn. I cannot live without you."

I swallowed, pain blooming in my soul. "I am not worth that devotion."

"You are," Caleb said firmly, cupping my cheeks. "You are worth everything."

"You are mine, Caleb. That is why you need to leave, so someday I might see you again."

"I am not leaving."

"Mate."

"No," he snapped. "This is my choice. You cannot make me leave. I'm staying with you."

"Please."

"No," he repeated.

I snarled, my anger finally surfacing. "I am failing you, Caleb! I am the one harming you. How can I live with myself when I am the one hurting you? I can't. You must leave. It's what's best. I do not deserve you nor am I worth your suffering."

He threw his hands into the air. "Did it ever occur to you that I'm being the selfish one? That, knowing it's hurting you, I'm staying anyway? That I'm being so incredibly selfish by staying?"

My jaw worked side to side, tears threatening to escape.

"I am not as selfless as you are portraying me to be, and you are not worthless, Zoltilvoxfyn. I am staying for me. I cannot bear the thought of even a moment away from you. I would rather cease to exist than have eternity without you by my side. Do you understand that? I care about you so much it hurts, like *actually* hurts. You are my reason. I am going to stay here, no matter the cost, because I am that selfish."

He held my face once again, and I leaned into him, even though his fingers would disappear beneath my scales.

"I love you," Caleb said. "I love you, Zoltilvoxfyn."

Tears slid down my cheeks. "I love you, Caleb."

He smiled, but the joyous expression was like a knife stabbing my soul.

"I love you," he repeated, over and over again.

Every time he said the words, something inside me grew—a helplessness. I loved him, desperately. He was my one and only mate. There would be no others after Caleb; my soul wouldn't allow it. But he was being ripped from me, suffering because of me, and I didn't know what to do.

Chapter 36

WHO NEEDS SLEEP? NOT ME.

Zoltilvoxfyn

The water sluiced over my scales as I attempted to wash away the stress. I'd met with my parents about the boobaas, but I barely recalled any of it. Monqilcolnen had to do most of the talking, though he'd glanced at me periodically. Caleb had remained by my side, not speaking, but he refused to budge on his stance, even though he was so transparent and gray that I struggled to see him clearly.

Cold wisps bloomed on my side, sliding up before forming the usual pattern on my back. Caleb slid in front of me and lowered to his knees. My stomach swooped as a pulse of want throbbed inside of me. I craved his touch, but more than that, I needed intimacy with my mate.

His fingers stroked my limp cock. Steadily, it swelled. My body was attuned to him—he fueled my desire with no effort whatsoever.

"Let me love you, Sunshine. We both need it."

Any protest died on my lips when he stroked up and down my shaft. With my hands braced on the wall, I groaned. His fingers ghosted over my cock. Stars, his touch was slight, but every shift made me shiver.

Cold enveloped the head of my cock, and I looked down. Caleb had his lips wrapped around me. There wasn't any pressure, but I saw the tip through the top of his head. A moan at the sight ripped out of me.

His fingers traced over my balls and hole as he slid up and down my cock, doing his best to maintain the image of sucking me. Unable to stop it, my hips canted forward. With his steady touches, I soon lost myself to the pleasure growing with every passing moment.

My fingers slid down to my shaft. Caleb wrapped his hand around mine as I pumped. "Caleb," I cried, my balls drawing up tight.

"I want to see you come, Sunshine. I need it."

With a strangled yell, I came, white ropes splattering the shower wall.

Caleb pressed against me, forehead rubbing my hip. "I love you."

I stared at my mate, soul shattering with every passing moment. "I love you more than the sun in the sky or the earth beneath my feet or the wind in my wings. You are my very soul."

Caleb

Fyn had tried to fight sleep, for hours, but eventually, it came for him. I wished I could give him physical reassurance, but I couldn't.

There wasn't even anything I could say to calm him. I was fading, dying again. My days were almost over.

I'd died once already, and it hadn't been so bad, but somehow I didn't think this would hold true the second time.

I bit my lip when a dull ache throbbed in my legs, and the thud of a heartbeat whispered in my ears. The longer I stayed, the worse it got.

Focusing on my Sunshine, I pushed the pain away. He was what mattered. Another day, another hour, another second. Even if I only had minutes left, I would spend them with Fyn.

But soon I would be gone, and he would be left alone. Drakcol mated once, but I hoped, because we hadn't been together physically, he would one day move on. Fyn had said I was his only, but maybe I wasn't. It might be possible. How many people fell in love with ghosts? Not many, I assumed.

I wished I could write him a note or leave him a message, but Drakcon technology didn't perceive me. Though... Wyn had been working. The hour was late. It would be impossibly rude to bug him, and he couldn't even hear me.

One glance at Fyn was enough to convince me. Sleep was unnecessary, right?

I pressed my lips against Fyn's forehead, and there was something—maybe a scraping? It had been too long for me to truly identify the sensation. "I'll be back, Sunshine. I promise."

I went downstairs to Wyn's quarters. Thankfully Seth had paid a visit before, and I'd been able to see it. I stepped inside the nearly empty one-room apartment.

Wyn was sprawled on the bed. His bubblegum pink hair tickled his forehead while the sheets clung around his legs, leaving his round ass and thin back bare. I'd never seen his lavender wings, and now, I guessed why. One was long and stretched over the bed, the other was oddly shaped and the talon curled inward, against the membrane. The wing was small and malformed like he had a congenital disorder. There was no way Wyn could fly.

My thoughts went to all the staircases with channels for flying and the streets without lights or decoration. This was not a world built for those who didn't fly. And Wyn wasn't alone. Tinlorray couldn't fly. I imagined there were others, whether from age, injury, or congenital disabilities.

Drakcol were a warrior species, and I imagined that had played a part in how they viewed people with disabilities, but I didn't know for certain.

None of that mattered at the moment, and I doubted Wyn wanted me to wake him up in the middle of the night to discuss accessibility. Right now, I needed Wyn's help, and he didn't need me staring at him. I poked him, sliding my fingers down his spine. "Sorry, Dude. Not trying to invade your privacy like a creep, but I need to talk to you." I glanced at his tail. Fyn's was sensitive, so it stood to reason Wyn's was as well.

"Sorry," I said before dragging my fingers down the appendage. A shiver went up his spine. He rolled over, and I slapped a hand over my eyes. "Please cover yourself. This is creepy enough without your junk flapping in the wind."

"What's going on?" Wyn thankfully dragged the sheet up.

I patted his chest over and over again, trying to make him cold.

"Are the environmental controls acting up?"

"Yes," I said, "grab your screen. See the phase variance." I poked his head. His tail flicked. He rolled over, yanking the covers over his head. That was not a barrier for me. I shoved through the blanket and dragged my fingers over his chest.

He shot up. Naked, he strode over to the monitor on the wall. I kept my gaze on the ceiling. Wyn's claws clacked on the glass for a few moments before he said, "There's a phase variance." He whipped around, seizing the sheet and winding it around his narrow waist. "Caleb, if you are in here, this is a *huge* violation, and I will be speaking to Prince Zoltilvoxfyn about it."

"I know, I know. Don't get your tail in a knot," I said, "but I need something." He couldn't hear me, so I poked him in the chest again.

Wyn shivered and rubbed the cold spot. "Yes, you're here." He froze. "Is something wrong with Prince Zoltilvoxfyn?"

"No."

"NAID," he shouted.

She popped into the monitor. "Hello, Wyn."

"Scan Prince Zoltilvoxfyn's quarters."

"Why?"

"Caleb is here."

She blinked. "Prince Zoltilvoxfyn is perfectly fine according to my readings."

"Then why is he here?"

"Are you certain he is?" she asked, disembodied head tilting to the side.

I stabbed Wyn in the chest.

He rubbed the same spot. "Yes."

"Perhaps he needs something from us."

"What can we do when Prince alone hears and sees him?" Wyn asked in a grumble and sank to the bed, the sheet bunching around his legs. "It's the middle of the night."

NAID's head tilted to the side again, and I couldn't help but stare at her. If there was anyone in the universe that I wished to see, it was Nana. I missed her so much.

"I will attempt to apply the algorithm we have been working on," she said.

"I suppose now is as good a time as any to test it," Wyn said, scrubbing his hair before snagging his screen.

"Hey," I yelled, jumping, to get their attention.

"Anything?" Wyn asked.

"There is some movement in the variance."

Wyn dragged a hand over his face. "It's going to be a long night. Let me get dressed. Caleb, turn around or float through the door."

I complied.

When Wyn called my name, he was dressed in soft black pants and a loose white tank top, the collar stiff and almost brushing his jaw. This was a much better look for him than the uniform. He seemed more approachable. Though uniforms weren't really supposed to make someone appear more friendly.

While Wyn and NAID made adjustment after adjustment, I talked and talked, trying to get them to hear me. I needed to leave something for Fyn behind to remember me by.

As the sun crested the mountains in the distance, I spoke again for the millionth time. I needed to get back to Fyn before he woke up.

"Come on!" I begged. I wasn't sure if I was talking to Wyn, NAID, the magical Crystal, or the whole fucking universe at this point. I would plead my case to anyone and everyone if it meant sparing Fyn even a dash of pain when I was torn from him.

NAID said, "I heard him."

"You did?" I asked at the same time Wyn did.

Her head bobbed up and down as a huge smile spread over her face, making her eyes disappear into her baggy skin. "I did. Caleb, it's lovely to speak with you."

"Thank god. I didn't think this would work. Don't get me wrong, I wanted it to. To like the extreme. I need it, but I figured I was waking up Wyn for no reason. I mean, his ass is nice, but he's not Fyn and it's not a reason to wake someone up."

"What's he saying?" Wyn asked.

NAID blinked. "A lot. He likes to talk."

"Well, so would you if basically no one heard you," I remarked.

She ignored me and asked, "What do you need?"

I glanced at Wyn. I wanted this to be private. "Can we speak in my room?"

"That is easy enough." NAID translated what I said to Wyn.

"Perfect. I stayed up all night, and get to miss everything exciting," he said.

"Thank you, Wyn." I wrapped my arms around him, and he shivered.

"You're welcome," he replied when NAID told him what I said. "There is more work to do, but now, we should be able to talk more. Seth will enjoy conversing with you. I think being the lone human here is harder for him than he or Prince Kalvoxrencol anticipated."

"Yep, lots of talking." I was such a liar.

Leaving Wyn behind, I went back upstairs and poked my head into mine and Fyn's bedroom. He was stretched out on the bed asleep. Returning to the couch, I said, "NAID."

"Yes, Caleb."

"I need you to do something for me."

"Anything," she said.

"I know you have access to a huge amount of data from Earth. Do you happen to have any pictures or recordings of me? My name's Caleb Smith."

"There were many Caleb Smith's in your history. I will need more information to narrow the search parameters. As I cannot see you, I cannot search for your likeness among the billions of your planet."

NAID needed more information? Well this should narrow it down very easily for her. "You're wearing my grandmother's face."

Her mouth fell open. NAID stared at me for several moments before she asked, "You're Edith's grandson who died?"

I nodded, then realized she couldn't see me. "Yes."

Shuttering, the image of my grandmother disappeared and was replaced by a bland silhouette of a drakcol, like the non-sentient NAID wore. "I'm so sorry."

"Don't apologize. I loved being able to see and hear her, and I honestly think she'd be honored. My grandmother's a huge advocate for people to live authentically and beautifully as themselves."

NAID's form didn't change. "What can I do for you?"

"I would like you to gather every picture or recording of me you have. I can't imagine there's much, if anything at all."

"That is incorrect. Your parents, siblings, cousins, aunts and uncles, as well as your grandmother uploaded everything onto the internet. They never forgot you, Caleb. It was obvious in every post and video where they talked of you."

"Can you move all of it to a database?"

"Yes, but why?"

I glanced at the closed door. "For Zoltilvoxfyn."

"I understand." A moment passed before she said, "Done. Everything is arranged in chronological order for Prince."

"Can you show me the most recent picture of myself?" I asked.

"Certainly. But why?"

"I don't remember my own face," I replied. It had been too long, and nothing reflected me in the universe, so my appearance had faded. I hadn't remembered what Nana looked like until NAID appeared in front of me, reminding me, but I couldn't recall any of my other family perfectly. I remembered bits and pieces of them. Like my mom's blue eyes, or my dad's booming laugh, or my brother Matt's sharp elbows as he jabbed me.

An image appeared, and my pulse picked up for a few seconds before fading. The young man in front of me had brown curls, brushing his narrow shoulders, a blindingly bright smile, blue eyes like my mother's, and rather large ears.

Me. This was me. I sort of remembered myself, and not at the same time. The Caleb in the picture was alive and vibrant. It was like looking at a stranger.

"Thank you, NAID," I said.

"Did you want to see a picture of your entire family?"

"No," I said instantly. I didn't want to miss them even more. I didn't want them to be strangers, like I was to myself. "No," I repeated, calmer this time.

"Alright."

"Can you record a message for me that he will be able to hear?"

"I believe so."

I cleared my throat as I tried to organize my thoughts, putting my family out of my mind. What did he need to hear?

The truth.

"Hey, Sunshine. I imagine if NAID is letting you hear this, I'm gone. I hope a long time has passed since I recorded this, but I can't take that chance. I need to tell you one thing: I love you. I think I lived my entire life waiting for you. I didn't know it, but I was waiting for you, and when I died, I went searching.

"I know you're upset, or at least I hope you are, even a little, because that means I meant something to you. So it sucks. Grief is rough, but you can survive this. You have to. Don't push your brothers or parents away. Garden. Breathe. Live. One day, I hope you meet someone else who makes you happy.

"Anyway, I love you. I don't regret anything. You are my everything, Zoltilvoxfyn, and you are completely worth it."

"Are you finished?" NAID asked when I stayed quiet for a few minutes.

"Yeah." I stared at the silhouette. "You really should go back to your previous appearance."

"I don't want to offend you."

"You're not," I replied. "Trust me. She would love it that she helped you become more comfortable with yourself. Like she says, 'In the end—"

"'You only have yourself, so make sure to love yourself,'" she finished. NAID's form shifted back to my grandmother's likeness.

"Much better," I said.

Her eyes flicked to the side. "I picked a name, but now, I don't know."

"You want to be called Edith."

"I'm sorry."

"She would love that, Edith."

Edith's face scrunched with emotion. "Thank you."

"When you were orbiting Earth, was she..." I trailed off, unable to ask if she was still alive or not.

"Your grandmother was still alive, but she was not doing well."

Grief pierced me like a rusty knife. I'd died years ago, leaving my family behind. Why should I grieve now for what I'd lost so long ago? An odd burn gathered behind my eyes, and I touched my face, expecting tears, but there was nothing.

"Are you truly disappearing?" Edith asked.

I stared at the light from the rising sun shining through my transparent gray skin. I was fading faster and faster. "I don't think I have much time left. A few hours. A day maybe. Don't tell Fyn," I said, glancing at her. "He'll worry."

"Too late," Fyn said from the doorway of the bedroom.

Shit.

Chapter 37

RECKLESS ACTIONS ARE USUALLY A BAD IDEA.

Caleb

"Sunshine," I said, forcing a smile to my lips. "You're awake? You should eat. You didn't have dinner last night. Eating is super important. Maybe some water too. Or a shower. Did you want to take another shower? I'll make it worth your time."

"You're fading, and you weren't going to say anything to me?" he asked.

Yeah, he was not going to be distracted. "I wanted to spend as much time as I can by your side without tainting it."

He crossed the space between us, breathing hard and tail lashing. "I cannot and will not live without you."

"You don't have a choice." Even if I let go of him and passed on, Fyn was going to have to live his life without me. My time, no matter what I did, was finite—like anyone.

"I do." He strode to the door in nothing but his loose trousers. "Caleb, come on."

I followed, sparing a glance at Edith. "Where's Kal and Mindy?"

"In space. Hallonixmin and Gilvaxtin are with their royal majesties meeting the Coalition representatives."

There was no one.

I chased after Fyn as he raced down the hall. "Stop! Where are you going?"

"Come on, Mate," he ordered.

We wound through the palace, not seeing anyone. When he stepped outside, barefoot, he turned to the glass building I'd entered when I first came.

"Where are you going?"

Fyn didn't respond and charged toward the towering structure.

A hulking form appeared in front of him. Monty's hair was ruffled and his clothes were haphazardly yanked on. He was the one family member who was here and available. Edith must have gotten him.

Monty planted a palm in the middle of Fyn's chest. "I know what you're intending. Don't do this. It will cause you great agony. I know this, Bloom."

"Well, I don't know what he's planning," I shouted uselessly.

"Caleb is my mate. I will not spend my life and afterlife without him," Fyn yelled, slapping Monty away. He stalked to the glass wall, which opened seamlessly, and strode in, leaving me to follow him.

The early morning sunlight streamed through the cathedral ceilings. Plants covered every inch of the building, but the glowing Crystal in the center pulled all my focus.

Monty swiveled in front of Fyn. "You need to stop. Please. I beg you."

"He is my mate. I will be bound in life and death to him."

"Who defiles the Grand Sanctuary?" a resounding voice demanded.

Monty shifted to the older drakcol. Fyn did not waste a single moment and dashed to the throbbing Crystal. When I was here before the rock appeared harmless, but I was getting some seriously bad vibes from the thing. Like a supervillain, destroy the world vibes.

"Sunshine, I don't know if we should do this," I said. Whatever this was.

He placed his hand on the Crystal; it began to throb faster and faster. The priestess and Monty gaped at him.

"Prince Zoltilvoxfyn, step away. Now," she ordered.

"Please," Monty begged. "You don't understand, Bloom. Do not do this."

"Caleb, do it now."

I slowly approached, glancing at Monty, who kept pleading for Fyn to step away. "We shouldn't do this."

"Touch the Crystal," he shouted, his voice breaking. "I can't lose you. I won't."

"Fyn." I glanced at the throbbing Crystal, then Monty and the priestess who ordered him to move away. "This isn't right."

"Touch it. Now," he snapped, eyes glassy. "The Crystal shall connect us as mates, binding us together forever."

"Don't, Caleb," Monty said, not looking even close to where I stood. "Don't touch the Crystal."

"I already tried this, Sunshine," I said. "I touched it when I first came. Nothing happened."

He shook his head. "Please. I need you to try. I need you."

"Nothing will happen. You need to accept that I'm going to disappear."

"No. No!"

I placed a hand on the Crystal to prove my point, and it vibrated beneath my palm, alive and angry. My eyes fluttered closed of their own volition. Hundreds of voices reverberated in my mind. *Why do you try to reaffirm what has not been forged? We sent you on the path, Caleb, seeker, wanderer, most faithful soul. Yet you chose to not forge what we set in motion?*

A scream ripped through the air, and my eyes shot open in time to see Fyn crash to the ground some distance away. He grunted, trying to move.

"Sunshine!" I tried to run to his side, but I remained frozen to the Crystal. I yanked, but it was like my fingers were glued to the smooth surface. A burning began and grew stronger and stronger.

"Ah," I yelped, tugging on my arm. "I'm stuck."

"Caleb," Fyn called.

If you will not tread the path we have set you upon, we shall force you to the conclusion.

I was on fire. Every nerve ending that I'd lost when I died screamed in agony. I thought I knew pain from the weak throbs of my soul, but this was nothing compared to that. A shriek tore out of my throat. I tried to escape but the Crystal would not let me go. Light flooded my soul as I expanded outward.

"Caleb," Fyn shouted, crawling toward me.

Agony of the like I'd never thought possible consumed me before blessed oblivion took its place.

Zoltilvoxfyn

Caleb's agonized cry rang in my ears as light blinded me. "Caleb!" I dragged myself over the mossy ground. I needed to be near him. "Please," I begged the Crystal. "Don't take him."

His pain-filled eyes met mine before the light swelled and his scream vanished, along with my Caleb.

My soul froze. "Caleb!" He was gone. He was gone, and it was my fault.

"No!" I fisted my hair and called his name over and over again. I tried to claw over to where Caleb had once stood, but Monqilcolnen's arms surrounded me, holding me back.

My very cells fought against what I'd seen. Caleb couldn't be gone. No. No. No. He had to be there. He had to be. No. No. Please. Please, no.

"Caleb, please," I cried, but no matter how much I called, he did not answer.

Chapter 38

WHAT COMES AFTER.

Zoltilvoxfyn

Caleb was gone. There was nothing else to say. I lay in our bed watching the images and videos of him go by on my screen while his message played over and over again on a loop. I'd failed him. Plain and simple. It was my responsibility as a medium to help him move on, and yet I'd kept him here with me because I loved him. I'd failed to protect him as his mate by forcing him to touch the Crystal because I'd been afraid to lose him.

My perfect Caleb had deserved more.

Kalvoxrencol ran a comb through my long hair. I didn't react. What was the point? When he finished, he settled behind me, arms wrapping around my waist. He nuzzled my back, scent marking, and I didn't bother to protest, even though I hadn't allowed anyone to do so since I was a child. Kalvoxrencol was doing it to soothe himself, as he feared losing me.

He and the rest of my family hadn't left me alone since... since everything.

The one person whose presence I couldn't bear was Seth. The first time he entered my bedroom, I'd screamed at him to leave before breaking down into a shivering heap. He was what my Caleb should've been—human and alive.

Seth had simply left. I'd expected Kalvoxrencol to snap at me, but he let it go.

The door opened, and Hallonnixmin flopped onto the bed in front of me, jostling my screen. I growled at him. Ignoring my protest, Hallonnixmin brushed his claws through my greasy hair and said, "Perhaps you can clean yourself or leave your quarters. The garden is lovely today."

I didn't answer.

Yesterday Mother had asked the same thing, and Father the day before. They'd even asked Dontilvynsan to steal my grief for a moment, to give me a chance to breathe without the suffocating emotions, but he couldn't get close enough to me without it causing him harm; my agony was too much for my elder brother.

All of them, even NAID and Urgg, had tried to get me to leave my quarters, but I didn't want to. Caleb wasn't there, so what was the point?

Caleb

I groaned, voice deeper than I remembered, trying to move. Everything hurt. No, that was an understatement. Agony, clear and simple, wracked me. Still, I struggled to move, twitch, anything. My eyelids were so heavy, though. Eyelids?

Voices spoke in the distance, but they were warbled murmurs like they came from underwater. I wanted to cry. I wanted to scream. But nothing happened. I was frozen.

Sunshine. Fyn. Zoltilvoxfyn. My mate.

Wait for me. I'll find you.

Zoltilvoxfyn

"Give it back," I roared, wings extended and tail thrashing.

"No," Kalvoxrencol snapped back, keeping my captive screen with Caleb's message and images on it aloft.

All of my brothers—except Dontilvynsan—Monqilcolnen, my mate-sister Gilvaxtin, and my parents filled the shared space of my quarters. It had been a month since Caleb had been ripped from me, and I couldn't function. I hadn't begun to waste away yet, as many drakcol did when their mates died, and my family feared it would start soon, but I welcomed it. I refused to live without Caleb.

He was my reason—for everything.

"You're not taking care of yourself," Hallonnixmin said while Gilvaxtin agreed.

"You're not living," my mother said.

"Caleb is gone," I said. How was I supposed to live without his rambling commentary about everything and his bouncing presence beside me?

"You have to live," Father said. "There is no choice."

Yes, there was. I could die.

My father continued, "We would like you to speak to Doctor Jalnin."

"I don't need him. I *need* Pest to return my screen before I gut him," I said, voice dropping. Kalvoxrencol waved me forward, not scared in the slightest by my threat.

Serlotminden stepped closer. "Please, try. For us. You barely eat. You won't shower. You don't do anything except look at images of Caleb. You haven't even stepped outside or visited your greenhouse. Please, Bloom."

My plants were dead. What did it matter anymore?

I turned away from my family and to me and mine's bedroom. I would have NAID—Edith—download Caleb's message and images to another device. My wings fell limp and my tail dragged on the ground.

My family called for me, but I didn't stop. My limbs were heavy like I slogged through mud, and each breath wasn't enough. I was slowly suffocating every moment of every day that passed because Caleb was gone. There was no point anymore.

The bedroom door opened, and Kalvoxrencol appeared before me, wings out and light pooling under his scales. I tried to step around him, but he blocked me.

Kalvoxrencol started Caleb's message. I'd heard it hundreds, if not thousands, of times. *I know you're upset, or at least I hope you are, even a little, because that means I meant something to you. So it sucks. Grief is rough, but you can survive this. You have to. Don't push your brothers or parents away. Garden. Breathe. Live.*

"He loved you, Zoltilvoxfyn. More than anything. Even life. He would not have wanted this for you." Kalvoxrencol threw the screen on the bed. "Grieving is fine. Grieve for as long as you need. There is no timeframe. But don't stop living. You're still here, and you have people who love you. Let us hold you together like you promised." He gave me one last look before he left.

I fell on the bed, listening to Caleb's voice as I stared at an image of him grinning. I curled into a ball, my tail wrapping around my calf while my wings hugged my shoulders.

"Caleb, please," I begged, not knowing what I was asking, but I couldn't stop the words. I would give anything for him to be next to me again. I would do better, be better, anything; I would do anything to have him back. "Caleb," I cried, knowing it wasn't possible.

Caleb

Zoltilvoxfyn, I repeated like a mantra. I was somewhere dark, unable to move. A heavy weight kept me in one place as distant noise floated in and out of my ears. Pain lived inside my soul and was my closest companion. I was never free of it.

I slipped in and out of awareness, but Zoltilvoxfyn was always in my thoughts. I knew he had to be upset, scared, angry—I didn't even know, but I needed to see him. A longing existed deep within me, demanding I see him, claim him, and never let him go.

I'm coming, I promised. My fingers wiggled over something smooth. *I'm coming, my Sunshine.*

Zoltilvoxfyn

Doctor Jalnin sat on a stool across from me in my quarters. His pink hair was perfectly styled, falling into gentle waves to his shoulders. His black clothes were crisp and clean against his gray scales. Unlike me. I was a mess. Physically I was clean, but mentally I was shattered.

We hadn't spoken much all session. This one or the last. My gaze went to the open window, leaves blowing in the wind. The plants in me and mine's quarters hadn't survived. Kalvoxrencol had taken them away. I assumed the same happened to my greenhouse; I hadn't gone outside to check, though.

Six weeks. The days had blurred together in one giant mass without meaning.

"Have you wept yet?" Doctor Jalnin asked.

"No." Not a single tear had fallen since I'd been dragged from the sanctuary. The love of my life was gone, ripped apart, and I couldn't muster a single tear. What was wrong with me? I should have been sobbing and screaming, yet I couldn't shed one tear.

"I see you bathed."

"Yes." I couldn't manage to say more than a single word, and Doctor Jalnin didn't press. Often he sat with me in silence, giving my family a break.

"Have you seen Seth Harris?"

My jaw clenched, and I wrapped my tail around my leg. "No."

I couldn't. He was human. He reminded me of my Caleb. I glanced at the screen that never left my side. Edith had assured me, multiple times, that she had all of the information backed up, but a part of me worried somehow I would lose it and never hear his voice again.

"Prince Kalvoxrencol has expressed Seth's interest in seeing you."

I kept my gaze on the leaves dancing in the wind.

"I'm afraid you're not dealing with your grief, Prince."

"My mate is gone. How can I move on? I have no future." Drakcol mated once. Most mates didn't outlive each other long. My soul beat for him, and now that he was gone. I had no purpose.

"He is, but you still have things to live for. You are here, Prince Zoltilvoxfyn. You have to find a way to live for yourself."

That was impossible.

"There are drakcol who survive their mate's loss. It is not easy, but you can survive this, Prince. You have to choose to, though."

The session went to its allotted time, and Doctor Jalnin left and Kalvoxrencol returned. My family still didn't leave me alone at any time, though they were less afraid I would do something regrettable. I wouldn't harm myself. Caleb would've hated the thought of me taking my own life, and my family did need me, even if it was to watch me wither.

My eyes followed the wind in the leaves. I should've had the desire to go outside, but I felt nothing. Kalvoxrencol's tail wrapped around my wrist, and I didn't even glance at him. He was the one who spent the most time here with me. I should apologize for taking him from his new mate, but I couldn't muster the words.

He tugged on me. "Let's go outside. Please."

I finally looked at my youngest brother. His expression was pinched, his purple eyes tired, and his shoulders slumped. Not managing a response, I got to my feet and allowed Kalvoxrencol to pull me outside.

The balmy sun brushed my scales as the wind ruffled my hair. The fresh air, the vibrant aromas of the flowers, and the loamy soil. Crystal, it had never smelled so good.

Kalvoxrencol's tail wrapped around mine and we wandered the jungle terrace. My fingers trailed over the rough bark and the smooth flowers, waiting for the normal peace to descend, but it didn't. I was still numb.

He brought me to my greenhouse, and I balked; everything would be dead inside. I scoffed. So was I. What did it matter?

The door opened, and I froze.

Bright colors and deep greens greeted me. Not a single plant was dead, let alone struggling.

Seth pointed a finger at my grappling fern. "Now see here, Susan, you do not get to eat me. I fed you several bugs." Scrapes marred his hands from the carnivorous plant. "You're a monster, Susan. I will give you a damn bug if you leave me alone."

He lifted a wiggling bug with a pair of tongs. The fern snapped out and grabbed his fingers wrapped around the metal. Seth yelped.

Glaring at the fern and holding his injured fingers to his chest, he said, "You bitch."

"It can't understand you."

Seth whipped toward me, his brown eyes with their round pupils that were so wide and expressive, like my… The sight of Caleb burned in me as tears threatened to spill. I couldn't say why right now was the time my body decided to release the numbness, but it did. Grief crashed over me in waves, making liquid spill down my cheeks.

Arms wrapping around me, Seth said, "Let it out."

With heaving sobs, I fell to the ground, dragging Seth with me. He gathered me close.

"I've got you," Seth said. "I have you. I promise I have you, Fyn."

Chapter 39

SO THIS IS WEIRD.

Caleb

The voices around me were growing more insistent with each passing moment. I tried to force my heavy limbs to move, but they didn't, like someone had tied them down. Focusing, I tried again to move, to wiggle, to do something, but I was stuck. I couldn't be, though. Fyn needed me. I knew he did.

Still, no matter what I did, I was frozen in place.

Something smooth lay beneath me. Like I actually felt the texture. Whatever it was had a squish. I swallowed at the sensation, the true sensation, then flinched at the muscles in my throat contracting. What the fuck? I didn't have a throat. I did it again, and my breathing increased. Fuck, I was breathing. It was weird and disconcerting; I hated it. Pain infected every fiber of my existence, and there was no escape from the constant stabbing ache.

If this was oblivion, it sucked more than I thought it would.

"Open your eyes," someone ordered. "I know you can do this. Open your eyes."

Zoltilvoxfyn. It didn't sound like him, much higher pitched, but nothing was right in this... whatever this existence was, so maybe his voice was different too? There was too much happening inside of me. The pain. The smoothness of whatever was beneath me. The way my muscles clenched and loosened. My lungs expanding with each breath. There was way too much.

But Sunshine needed me; I'd promised I would never leave him, and I wouldn't. Slowly, one eye cracked open, then the second one followed, but it wasn't Fyn above me.

"Tinlorray," I croaked in a deep voice unlike my own that made me cringe. What the actual fuck was that?

"Yolkeltod," she cried, falling onto me.

My nose burned from a different sharp odor surrounding me, and twitched at the soft fragrance coming off of her. I tried to get away from both, but I couldn't; her solid weight pressed me down, trapping me.

"Yolkeltod?" I asked as a tremor started. God, I was vibrating. I was fucking shaking, making whatever was under me move. What the fuck? A thrumming sped up, filling my ears. "You can hear me. You can touch me. I can touch you. What is happening?"

Tinlorray didn't answer. I lifted my hand, and the world swirled around me. My fingers were covered in dove-gray scales and tipped with black claws. What the actual fucking hell was happening?

"Yolkeltod," Tinlorray said, squeezing me.

Pain. Pressure. Touch. A harsh, burning smell. A soft, light fragrance. My heart raced in my chest, thrumming in an odd beat, while beeps grew louder and louder, stabbing my brain.

It hit me like a freight train. I was in Yolkeltod's body, and I was alive.

Holy fucking hell. This was bad. This was wrong.

She touched me, and I yanked away. My tail thrashed. I had a tail. A tail. It kept moving and writhing. Every single flick caused shards of pain to dash up my spine. Wings pushed against my back. Wings. Tail. Claws. Oh my god. The wind blew in from the window and stirred my hair, making me yelp from the tickling brush.

Stop. God. Please stop. There was way too much happening.

"Don't touch me," I snapped. A deep pull in my gut urged me to run, to go somewhere else. Somewhere else was safe.

"Yolkeltod?" Tinlorray asked.

"No." My head whipped back and forth; the beeping was so fucking loud. The texture of the sheets rubbed against me. The squish of the mattress. The rush of wind. The sharp sting invaded my brain with every inhale. What was happening? My heart throbbed, thrumming, vibrating.

"Sunshine," I screamed. I needed him. Everything would be fine if he was here. "Zoltilvoxfyn."

"Dr. Maklownil, something is wrong."

"Yolkeltod," an older drakcol with rough pink scales said. "I'm going to give you something to calm you."

"No." I threw myself off the bed, landing on my stomach. I grunted, body absorbing the hit, though it reverberated through my spine, sending electricity through my veins. Something crashed in the distance, and there was a tug somewhere in my gut. Tears slid down my cheeks, and I tried to yank away from the liquid sliding over my skin—scales. The cold floor burned me. It was too much. I couldn't breathe, though, even as I thought that, my lungs expanded, adding to the cacophony in my mind.

I had to get away.

My arms trembled when I tried to lift myself up and my legs shook. I couldn't stand. This borrowed body wouldn't work. "I need Zoltilvoxfyn."

"What is happening?" Tinlorray asked.

"I don't know," the doctor said.

I tried to claw my way out of the room, but the cool flooring scraping against my scales made me shiver. The wind rushed over my bare backside, and I yelped, hating how my throat moved. My tail thrashed, sending knives up my spine, and my wings flared, catching on the bed.

It was too much. I couldn't do this. I *couldn't* fucking do this. People kept talking, aromas wafted in through the window, my muscles burned, and I could barely think. The intense need to see Zoltilvoxfyn overwhelmed me.

I gripped my head, claws pricking and sending blood dripping down my cheeks. "Make it stop!" I screamed, writhing on the floor. "Make it stop!" This voice wasn't my own. I hated it. I hated it all. I screamed a wordless shriek.

Something pricked my arm and everything dimmed to a distant murmur that was more manageable. Tinlorray leaned over me, her long hair brushing my cheek, which made me flinch.

“Please,” I begged. “I need Zoltilvoxfyn. Please.”

Her brow furrowed. “It’ll be alright, Yolkeltod.”

“I’m not Yolkeltod. My name is Caleb. Caleb Smith.” My name was a garbled growl that the drakcol vocal cords struggled to make.

Tinlorray’s eyes went wide.

“Please. Tell Zoltilvoxfyn I’m here. I didn’t fade. I’m here.” Darkness started to crowd my vision. “Sunshine,” I breathed before everything vanished.

“You have to understand,” I said for the millionth time, “I’m not Yolkeltod. My name is Caleb Smith. I was a ghost from Earth, and somehow got stuck in this body.”

Doctors Maklownil and Dak sat in front of me on metal stools. It had been... I didn’t even know how long. Keeping track of the time was difficult, but I thought it had been a couple of weeks since I’d woken up. I’d been moved from the airy room I’d first woken up in to a locked ward almost instantly. I was getting treatments for the atrophied muscles to stimulate growth in this borrowed body. The wings and the tail, I had no idea what to do with. Also, I wasn’t used to being so tall or broad. Yolkeltod’s body towered over people compared to my old one.

"Yolkeltod, we understand this has been a trying time, but clearly, you're not a human spirit," Dr. Dak said, pushing her chin-length hair behind her tapered ear adorned with several bronze studs. She was new. A therapist.

Maklownil, Yolkeltod's original medical doctor, watched me, a bony hand on his chin. He was more pensive than usual. "You say you spent time with Prince Zoltilvoxfyn?"

Dak glared at him, grass-green tail flicking. She hated him indulging me.

"Yes," I snapped, then flinched from my voice. It was so deep. I wasn't used to it, and every time I spoke I cringed. This wasn't *my* voice; it belonged to a stranger. "Tell him I'm here. He'll come for me. Zoltilvoxfyn will always come for me."

He gave me a kind smile, but I knew what lay behind that look—disbelief. No one would tell Fyn I was here. I'd begged Tinlorray, multiple times, to help me. She always said she was. She didn't believe I wasn't her brother, though I didn't act the same as Yolkeltod had nor could I answer her questions about his life.

Deep within me was an intense longing. I had no words for it. The need to see Fyn was overwhelming. At times, I thought I would go mad from the itch that never vanished.

I had to get out. I had to see him. He was *mine*. All *mine*.

I blinked at the claiming thought. I'd become more aggressive, and odd instincts, like to growl or spread my wings, reared up at the weirdest times. I had no idea what to do with them, besides hope they'd disappear. But this need for Zoltilvoxfyn wouldn't fade. He was mine, and I wouldn't let anyone separate us.

My wings flared, spanning the cell, and my tail lashed. Both of the doctors pulled back. My wings refused to curl up, and my tail wouldn't stop slashing; all the while, a rumble started to form in my chest that refused to be silenced. I couldn't get this damn body to respond.

How the hell did drakcol do this?

"I *need* him," I snarled. "He's mine!"

"You touched the Crystal in your dream, correct?" Dak asked, smoothing her black pants while her tail wiggled rapidly.

I'd told her this, both of them this, hundreds of times. "Yes."

"Perhaps you believe in your addled state that you are Prince Zoltilvoxfyn's mate."

"I am his mate," I yelled, standing, though my knees threatened to give out. My tail slapped the bed's leg, and I hissed from the sting. The damn thing was beyond sensitive, and every time it moved, it sent fire up my spine. "No one will take him from me."

Her claws clicked on the tablet as she made more notes.

Maklownil tapped his finger on his chin.

Neither of them said anything of value for the rest of the session; all they did was ask the same damn questions while my all-consuming desire for Zoltilvoxfyn raged inside of me. Alongside it was worry. Fyn had to be freaking out. I had to get back to him. Now.

Chapter 40

PLEASE BELIEVE ME.

Caleb

Footsteps slapped on the gleaming and recently cleaned floor. How did I know it was cleaned? Because a cleaning bot had slowly worked back and forth over the floor before disappearing from sight. That had been the sole moving thing I'd seen in two days. Tinlorray hadn't shown up, and none of my doctors had seen me, even for treatment on my muscles. I was left alone in a tiny cell with a bed, toilet, and TV the size of my thumb that displayed a view of a forest. A cubby in the wall would generate food and water twice a day.

The wall facing the hallway was a force field, keeping me locked in. I had no idea how long I'd been here or how long since I'd last seen Fyn. No one would tell me any information about him. Of course, they might not know. He was a prince, and I wasn't sure how much information the palace shared about the royals' daily lives.

I'd wandered the universe for years, never staying in one place, driven by a need to see everything. But none of that knowledge helped me right now. I was trapped—trapped like a bug under a glass.

I plopped on the bed, then jerked upright because needles shot up my spine, only to groan from the sudden movement as my breath turned harsh. The shuttle accident had done severe damage to Yolkeltod's body. I couldn't make any sudden movements without triggering pain of some kind.

I'd never known there were so many varieties of agony until now.

I couldn't walk for long distances, my wings didn't work, not that I knew what to do with them. My tail had also been damaged, making it even more sensitive. My head always ached, edging on a migraine no matter what anyone did.

Basically, I was a ball of pain that barely moved.

Clearing my throat, I tried to force the drakcol vocal cords to correctly pronounce English. All of the words sounded grumbled and harsh, but I refused to forget my first language. "I am Caleb Smith," I said, repeating what I did every day. "I am human. I am from Earth. My parents are John and Eden. I have three brothers. I died falling down the stairs. I wandered the universe. I met Zoltilvoxfyn. I fell in love with Fyn, and he fell in love with me. He is my mate. I am Caleb Smith, not Yolkeltod."

No matter what the doctors told me, I wouldn't believe differently.

"Are you really not Yolkeltod?" Tinlorray asked from behind me. Stiffly and with a deep grimace, I turned. Tinlorray stared at me with glassy eyes, tail coiled around her ankle.

"I'm not Yolkeltod. I met him, briefly, when I was wandering your planet. You were his tether. What tied him to this plane," I explained. "He asked me to take care of you before he moved on." I'd told her as much before, but she hadn't believed me. Maybe she would this time. I hoped to god she would believe me this time. I needed someone, anyone to believe me. "I was the one in your house. I was the one who tried to comfort you. I'm sorry."

"Then why are you in this body and not him?" she demanded, tail thrashing.

"I don't know," I answered honestly. I had no clue. None. "I touched the Crystal, and here I am. I have no idea why Yolkeltod left, and I'm in his body. I don't have any answers, Tinlorray. I wished I did."

She stared at me. "You have to be Yolkeltod."

"I'm not, Tinlorray," I said, my voice turning pleading. "I know he was everything to you, but I'm not him and I never will be, no matter how long you keep me here that will not change. I will always be Caleb Smith."

"I must be insane to even contemplate this."

"You're not. As odd as it is, this is happening. Honestly, I would have guessed such things were common for a species as advanced as yours. Weird stuff has to happen all the time, right?"

Tinlorray scoffed. "A human soul being trapped in my little brother's body normal? No."

Forcing Yolkeltod's body to stand, I shuffled to the force field and placed my hand on it. The invisible wall vibrated slightly under me. It was so faint, I wasn't sure if I'd still been in a human body that

I would've felt it—not that I remembered what being in a human body was like anymore.

"I wish I could bring him back, but I can't," I said, pulse racing. I hated it. I hated it all. I would give Yolkeltod his body back and return to my previous ghostly state if I could. "You were everything to him. He loved you. That's why he asked some random spirit to watch over you."

She swallowed, and tears slid down her scaled cheeks.

"He loved you, Tinlorray," I repeated, slower, "but Yolkeltod is gone."

Tinlorray swiped the tears away. "I don't know why, but I believe you. You don't feel like my brother. I see you in front of me, but here," she rested a hand over the center of her chest, "I know you're not him. It's like I'm looking at a stranger, and stars, it hurts. It hurts so bad."

"I'm sorry, but I *am* Caleb."

"Caleb," she said, voice breaking into a sob. "Greetings. I'm Tinlorray."

"Hello, Tinlorray."

She broke down, tears streaming down her cheeks. Her arms wound around her waist while her tail curled about her calf. She crouched, sobbing, shoulders shaking.

Once again, I was a voyeur to her grief. I shouldn't be here, watching this, but I literally couldn't go anywhere else.

When Tinlorray's cries subsided to quiet tears and heaving breaths, I said, "I need out."

"They're not going to let you out," she replied, getting to her feet. "The doctors are afraid you will harm yourself or attempt to harm Prince Zoltilvoxfyn. Our appointed guardian agrees with them."

"I won't, I swear," I said. "I would *never* hurt him. Never. Nothing in this universe would make me hurt him. I love him."

She lifted her palms up—the drakcol version of a shrug. "That may be true, but they will not believe you."

"Then I need you to get a message to him. You have to tell him I'm here. My Sunshine will not abandon me."

Laughter slipped out of her lips. "And how would I speak to a prince?"

"Right." Fucking nobility. Legs trembling, I hobbled to the bed to sit down. With a grimace, I rearranged, wings sprawled and tail wiggling. God, I hated the extras. I had no idea how to use them, and with each movement, they brought new sensations that seared my brain.

"Perhaps you could reach out to Seth Harris?"

Her brow furrowed. "The human?"

"Yes."

"He'll be even harder to contact. The royal family has closed wings around him. No one is allowed to see or talk to him."

"Why?" Kal was ridiculously overprotective of Seth, but there was no reason for him to be completely isolated, not that he would mind.

"I don't know for certain, but the rumor is it's about his soul. He has the darkest warrior soul ever recorded in our written history. I imagine the Ranks are requesting to study him, and Prince

Kalvoxrencol has probably refused. If Prince did refuse, the Ranks might appeal to the Cohort for access to the human, but I truly don't know. The palace hasn't released any information about him besides his soul testing."

Poor Seth. My dude was introverted to an extreme, not even mentioning his anxiety. Being studied wouldn't be something he was interested in, especially not for this soul crap.

"So not Seth," I said, thinking. "Maybe Wyn?"

"Who?" she asked.

"Ensign Wyn. He works for Seth on NAID's—I mean Edith's independence."

"It will take some hunting, but he's a more likely candidate to be able to speak to. I would have to find him among, what I imagine to be several Wyns in connection to the palace. It will take time." She crossed her arms. "You stole my brother's body, and now, I have to help you."

"Not intentionally," I said. "I didn't mean to take him. Not that it actually makes a difference. I did steal his body, and I am so sorry. I didn't have a choice in the matter. The Crystal shoved me in here." And I didn't think I wanted to be in this body or any body for that matter, not that I would tell her that.

She didn't reply, nor did she meet my gaze.

Man, I wished I didn't need her help. I felt guilty for taking her brother and now using her, but I didn't have a choice. I sucked for even using that excuse, but it was the truth. I needed her to get back to Fyn. Somehow, someway, I would find a way to repay her.

Tinlorray took a deep breath. "I know exactly what Yolkeltod would say if he was here."

"What?"

"'Tinlorray,'" she said in a whiny voice, "'he needs help. You can't abandon him. I'm dead, but he's not.'" She shook her head, tears sliding down her cheeks again. "He was a warrior soul, but I'd never met someone so kind. He helped everyone and everything in trouble. I cannot tell you how many injured animals he brought home over the cycles to patch up. He saw his soul as a mark to protect anyone who needed it, and stars, he did." More tears coursed down her cheeks in a never-ending river.

"I think we would've gotten along."

"Everyone liked him."

Chewing on my bottom lip, I debated about asking her for yet another favor, but in the end, needs must. "Perhaps I could see the Crystal. If Zoltilvoxfyn is acknowledged as my soulmate, I can see him, right?"

"Getting access to the Crystal is not easy. For royalty? Yes. Us? No. We have to apply to the Ranks for access. If they allow it, we have to wait for the appeal date. The Ranks have three days a cycle where all the petitioners come to the Grand Sanctuary. And for you, it would be harder to become a petitioner."

"Why?"

"You're in the first phase of adulthood. Our guardian would have to approve, and there is no way she will with the current questions regarding your sanity."

That was right. Drakcol only recognized mated people as full-fledged adults. My mouth opened. “Monqilcolnen.”

“What?”

“Commander Monqilcolnen. He could help.”

“Cousin to the royal family and part of the peerage? I’m sure he could, but he will not be easy to contact.”

I slammed my fist onto the bed and swallowed a groan.

“I shall seek this Ensign Wyn, but the doctors are not going to release you.”

“One thing at a time.” Just one thing at a time. But if I didn’t see Fyn soon, I worried I was going to lose my mind, and worse, I feared how he was coping with my loss. I needed to see him; there wasn’t a choice.

Chapter 41

zoltilvoxfyn

My fingers plucked the wilted blooms off the plant with mechanical precision. Eight weeks and three days had passed since my Caleb had vanished. I was still meeting with Doctor Jalnin almost daily, and my family didn't leave me alone yet either. Now, though, I spent a good amount of time with Seth in my greenhouse. He was an easy companion. He didn't pester me with questions or try to get me to talk about Caleb or what I felt—we simply existed.

I also provided a shield for him. The Ranks had been increasingly pressing Kalvoxrencol, Father, and Mother to see him. Seth didn't want to, and Kalvoxrencol was bristling about anyone coming near his mate. Seth wasn't to be left unguarded, and Kalvoxrencol trusted me to protect Seth when he could not, and I would. Nothing would harm him physically or otherwise while I was present.

He stared out the glass windows, sweat coating his red face, as he fiddled with his touchstone. Kalvoxrencol was currently speaking to the Cohort to relate Seth's desire to be left alone. The two of them hadn't been spending much time together, because of me and this new issue, but it was mainly my fault.

A sudden wave of darkness crashed over me, pulling me under. I was so pathetic. I dragged everyone down with me. No one was safe from my gravitational pull. Even Caleb. Especially Caleb. I'd hurt him most of all. Everything was my fault. My poor mate. He'd deserved far better than me.

Tears burned the backs of my eyes, and I lowered my head, allowing my hair to form a curtain around me. I ripped a withered bloom off the bush so hard that the leaves rustled and the branch cracked, threatening to break. I was a pathetic excuse for a warrior soul. I couldn't keep anyone around me safe. I couldn't keep my mate safe. My mate. Oh, my Caleb.

"Stop."

I jolted.

Seth stared at me. "Stop."

"What?"

"Hating yourself. I recognize the expression."

"I must apologize that you and Kalvoxrencol cannot spend as much time together."

"That's not your fault," he said.

"It is."

"No," he repeated, "it's not. None of this is."

My mate-brother was wrong. "Caleb is. All of this is."

A long rush of air came out of Seth. "I'm going to say something mean, but I'm not trying to hurt you."

"What?" "

"Not everything is about you, so stop acting like the weight of the world is on your shoulders or that everything bad is your fault."

A tear slid down my cheek.

"I know your brain is fighting you, Fyn, making you feel less than, but it's lying," Seth said. "Blaming yourself and saying everything is your fault is belittling and undermines other people's choices. Kal and I are here with you because we love you. We choose to spend time with you.

"Caleb chose to stay. He loved you, and you blaming yourself is making Caleb's fading about yourself. He knew the risk, he knew the cost, and he chose to stay. He chose to stay because he loved you. Not because you loved him or needed him, but because he chose to be here with you. Not your fault."

He grabbed my arm. "All the problems in the universe are not your fault."

I looked away, tears streaming down my cheeks.

"I know what it's like to fight your mind every day of your life, but you need to remember something."

"What?" I asked, voice thick with emotion.

"We love you, Fyn, and we want you in our lives. You're not a burden. You are not unwanted."

I shut my eyes.

"Now, I am going to make us both uncomfortable and hug you." True to his word, Seth stiffly pulled me into a hug. I clung to him tightly as tears poured down my cheeks.

"I miss him."

With every day that passed, the longing to see him grew. Deep in my gut, I still perceived the connection to Caleb. I needed him, but he wasn't anywhere to be found. Would this longing ache ever fade? Did I even want it to?

Caleb

Dr. Maklownil stood on the other side of the force field next to an old woman with wispy green hair, rough brown scales, and milky gray eyes. She held a piece of glowing glass in her bony fingers.

"What exactly is happening?" I asked.

Maklownil replied, "Priestess Hok is going to test your soul type."

"Why?" I wasn't sure if I even believed in soul types or not, so what was the point?

"If you are indeed who you say you are, your soul type will be different than Yolkeltod's recorded one," he said with a smug smirk, as if he'd found a way to prove I wasn't who I thought I was.

"And if I'm a warrior?"

"The shade will still be different."

"Fine." I knew who I was.

I peeked at Tinlorray. I was hoping she would find a way to speak to Wyn, though she hadn't yet. When she did, Wyn, who would hopefully believe her, would talk to Seth, who would get me the hell out of here and back to Zoltilvoxfyn where I belonged. He would help me figure out this whole new body thing. Everything would be manageable with him by my side.

Maklownil released the force field, eyeing me. While older and smaller than me, I had no doubt he would win in a confrontation. I was shaky and weak. Treatments to stimulate muscle growth were not going well when they actually did the appointments, and they didn't let me out to walk very often.

The old priestess said in a ceremonial voice, "All soul types have value and are treasured."

Tinlorray scoffed.

"You disagree?" Priestess Hok asked, lips pursing, probably at the interruption.

"Warriors are venerated because of our violent past. Spiritual souls are treasured because of their connection to the Crystal. Seekers are now important because of the technology they bring. Creators are cast aside. Drakcol do not value art," she replied.

Hok huffed. "Red is warrior. White is spiritual. Blue is seeker. Green is creator."

She extended the piece of glass that glowed bright white. Without ceremony, I touched it. The light swirled around my fingers, caressing me. The white light changed colors to a grayish-blue. Maklownil's mouth fell open, and even the priestess gaped at me like a caught fish. Though Tinlorray appeared nonplussed. Not much could shake her after accepting that her little brother's body no longer housed his soul.

I wasn't a warrior soul. I was a seeker. A mix apparently, edging on the spiritual side, if the gray meant what I thought it did.

"I think this proves I am who I say I am," I said, crossing my arms. "I am Caleb Smith. Zoltilvoxfyn is my mate. Give me access to the

Crystal, and I will prove he is mine, no one else's." I couldn't help the growl that rumbled in my chest. I needed Fyn, and he needed me. And with every day that passed, the longing got worse.

Both of them continued to stare at me and the glass until it faded into a soft glowing white. Eventually, the priestess said, "I need to speak to my superior."

The doctor didn't respond, but he secured the force field and left.

So my specialists were consulting more special specialists. Lovely. That was an excellent sign, I was sure.

Tinlorray followed them without a word.

"You should not be here, Seth. Pest will challenge and kill me when he finds out about this, and I am not teasing," an even voice I recognized said.

I leaped up from the bed, ignoring the fiery knives raking over me, and slammed into the force field with a thud, trying to see. No one was in sight, but I heard Seth respond, "As you've said over and over again, Monty, and I don't want to be here, believe me, but I have to know for sure. Besides, I doubt he'll kill you."

"He will. Of this, I have no doubt."

"Maybe. But do you think he would've been alright if I came alone?"

"Seth, Kalvoxrencol would not want you to come at all."

"I don't care. I *have* to know."

"You shouldn't have told him," Monty said, but I didn't know who he was talking to.

As they stepped into view, Wyn replied, voice quiet and head down, "Seth is my closest friend, Commander. When Tinlorray found me, she didn't give me a choice but to believe her, and once I did, I had to tell him."

Tinlorray stood next to Wyn, and Seth was in between Wyn and Monty. I placed my hand flat on the force field. My tail wrapped around my calf and my wings hung lifeless against my back, but they twitched and fluttered.

"Seth," I warbled.

He started to step toward me, but Wyn and Monty held him back.

"He can't get out," Tinlorray said. She sidled up to the force field and punched it, then shook her hand out. "It's unbreakable. Only his doctor and security can release it."

"You got them," I told her, tears spilling over my cheeks. "Thank you. Thank you so much."

She gave me a forced smile but didn't say anything.

Seth knocked Monty and Wyn's hands off and approached the force field. His round face was red, and sweat gathered on his temples. He must be nervous because I saw the vein in his neck throbbing. "What is your name?"

"Caleb Smith."

"How am I supposed to believe you're him?" he asked. "I'm not trying to be mean, but anyone can say that. If you or Tinlorray," he said, glancing at her and blushing, "were in the palace you might have heard Fyn say that name."

"Ask me anything," I said in garbled English. "Anything about Earth. I can name presidents, weird events, or food. I can tell you what we talked about when we first met. I can tell you about the paintings in your room, the plants in Sunshine's greenhouse, or anything." Tears coursed down my cheeks. "Please believe me, Seth. Please get me the fuck out of here."

A smile tugged on his lips. "Hey, Caleb."

I bawled, sinking to the ground. He followed, pressing against the force field. I couldn't stop the heaving sobs. I wanted to, but I couldn't. Every emotion was stronger. Every touch, sight, smell, or sound was potent as hell. I'd been a ghost for so long, and now I wasn't. I had no idea what to do with any of it.

"Sunshine," I said, hitting the force field with the flat of my palm. The sharp sting reverberating up my arm made me whimper. "How is he?"

Seth started to say something, but Monty growled. "I will not allow you to speak about Zoltilvoxfyn. I do not accept this drakcol is Caleb."

Wyn glared at him, but his tail wiggled and his shoulders hunched as he said, "Do not threaten Seth again, or you and I may have an issue, Commander."

Monty looked at him, but Wyn would not meet his eye, tilting his head to the side to offer his throat.

Wyn had never struck me as protective, and he always wilted under Monty's gaze, but he was ready to throw hands at the perceived threat to Seth. "Still not quite over the puking incident yet, but you're getting better."

Wyn gaped at me, but Monty was the one who asked, "What did you say?"

I pointed to Wyn. "He puked on you on the Admiral Ven. I was there."

He crossed his muscular arms. "That incident is well known."

"Yolkeltod has been in a coma since before you returned, Commander," Tinlorray said. "Caleb here hasn't had access to any technology. How would he know? He doesn't have visitors, except me and his doctors. Or do you fear he and I are trying to trick you? For what gain? I had not even heard of Caleb before he introduced himself. How would I have?"

Monty did not respond.

"I believe you," Seth said.

"Seth, I need out. Please. I need Fyn. I can't take it. How is he?"

"Fyn is... existing. I will try to find some way to get you out of here."

"Did you hear about my soul testing?"

"What?" Seth asked.

Tinlorray replied, "His soul type was tested again. Yolkeltod was a warrior. Caleb is a seeker."

"His soul changed color?" Monty asked.

"Yes," Tinlorray said.

Seth commented, "You seem like a seeker."

I didn't care about any of that. I wanted out. I wanted Zoltilvoxfyn. "I need him," I repeated, breath growing harsher by the second.

"I know."

I gripped my stomach. "You don't understand. I *need* him. I don't know what's wrong, but it's like I'm dying. No, it's worse than that. I have to be with him. I'm losing my mind."

"You touched the Crystal," Monty said, "before you faded."

I chose not to rub it in that he was starting to believe me. "Yeah. So?"

Seth laughed. "It forged a link. The damn Crystal linked the two of you. You have to answer the soulmate-call-thing."

"They will have to let you go," Monty said, arms crossed. "We do not keep people from answering the longing for their mate."

My heart thrummed. It sounded different than my human one had, but I was grateful for it… and hated it at the same time. God, I was so confused. "I will get to see him?"

"After you're proven to have a call placed on you. The Ranks have means to see and track who your mate is."

I lifted a skeptical eyebrow.

"It's real," Seth said. "They found me across the universe."

"True." My tail squeezed my calf as my wings hugged my shoulders. I chewed on my lip, hating the cold, smooth floor while also wanting to roll on it. I scratched my arm, then stopped, hand fisting. "How soon?" I asked, rocking. I needed Zoltilvoxfyn. He would fix everything.

"Soon," Seth promised.

I looked at Monty, who said, "I will speak to the Ranks."

"Thanks."

"We need to leave before Kalvoxrencol realizes you're missing," Monty said. "Pest will not handle your absence well."

Seth started to stand, and I tried to grab him, but the force field stopped me. “Don’t go,” I pleaded. “Please, don’t go.”

He wavered. “I have to, but I’ll be back.”

I nodded, tears gathering again. “Hurry.”

“I will.”

Chapter 42

ANSWERING THE LONGING.

Caleb

"You expect me to believe that *he* is Caleb," Kal whispered loudly to Seth, gesturing to me from the corner of their apartment.

"He is, and even if he's not, he's Fyn's soulmate."

Kal scrubbed a hand through his long hair. "I cannot believe you kept this from me. How could you?"

"I had to. You wouldn't have let me go, Kal. You barely let me out of your sight right now," Seth snapped. "I had to know if he was Caleb. He's human, and I have to protect him. Not to mention Fyn needs him."

They were about to have an *epic* fight, but I wished they would wait until after I was with Fyn, then they could fight to their heart's content. All I wanted—needed was Zoltilvoxfyn.

Earlier today, Seth had shown up at the hospital with Tinlorray, Wyn, and Monty. The Ranks had proof I sought the Crystal and needed to answer the longing it instilled. Interestingly enough, the record of me touching the Crystal was my first day here, not the day I faded, which explained why I had the weird urge to explore the terrace, toward my mate.

Their technology had shown Zoltilvoxfyn was my mate (originally they'd thought their technology was malfunctioning when Fyn randomly appeared on the screens weeks ago. Now they knew it was me), and with that, I'd been released… well, after Seth took responsibility for me and Yolkeltod's guardian approved.

We'd returned to the palace immediately. I'd tried to run off and find Fyn, but Seth and Monty wouldn't let me. They'd kept everything from the family. Now Monty was telling the emperor and empress as well as Fyn's brothers, and Seth was telling Kal before he took me to Fyn.

Clean, and in new clothes, I was ready to see Fyn. My mate. Tremors wracked my body and my tail strangled my calf, and I had no idea why. I needed my Sunshine, and I *knew* he needed me. Everything would work out. It would be fine. I had to believe that. I had to.

Kal and Seth continued their whisper fight from near the table while I remained on the couch. Lucy sat in the doorway to the bedroom, tail twitching. My wings squeezed my shoulders from the intense golden stare. The chubby black cat would not look away, even as the argument grew louder. I swore she knew I was the same soul who'd teased her.

I wiggled my fingers, and she continued to stare at me.

Seth popped in front of me, and I jerked back, practically falling off the back of the couch as my wings automatically sprawled and I snarled. Kal yanked Seth behind him, his wings sliding out.

"Kal," Seth snapped, but Kal did not release his mate. Light started to pool under Kal's scales, and my breath sharpened. A sculpture lifted into the air of its own accord, as something yanked in my stomach, and crashed to the ground.

We gaped at it. Another one rose before falling and shattering. I was shaking so badly that I could barely focus on Kal and Seth. My wings curled around me and my tail squeezed my leg hard enough to hurt.

Kal finally let Seth go and took a deep breath. The light dimmed, and his wings slid back into his shirt. "You're doing this. You're breaking the sculptures."

"What?" I was panting. I couldn't stop it. It was like something was in my stomach, clawing to get out.

He lifted his hands and slowly laid them on my knees as he crouched in front of me. "You must have telekinesis. It's one of the more common inner fires."

I couldn't be the one doing this. It wasn't possible. Books flew off the shelf, landing on the other side of the room.

"You need to calm yourself," Kal said.

Seth sat beside me. I yanked away from him and knocked Kal off. The pressure was too much. "I need Zoltilvoxfyn."

"I can see that." Kal glanced at Seth. "I don't know if Fyn's ready for this."

"Caleb needs him, and Fyn needs Caleb."

Kal and Seth stared at each other like they were having a silent conversation. Eventually, Kal said, "Alright, Husband. Let's take him to Zoltilvoxfyn."

Zoltilvoxfyn

I moved an empty pot to the workbench before placing a layer of rocks on the bottom, followed by loamy soil. Near the top, I placed a hybrid seed in the dirt before covering it. I'd continued to produce a rose hybrid for Seth and... Caleb.

My eyes shut of their own accord. The mere thought of my mate was enough to send waves of despair crashing over me. I tightened my grip on the clay plot, claws scraping the glaze, and forced myself to take a shuddering breath.

When the icy grief receded to a dull ache, I continued my work. I had nothing else. Plants were my solace and the sole reason I was alive.

For the first time in weeks, I was alone. Normally, I enjoyed solitude, but today my thoughts were loud and I needed distraction from them. The longing in my gut swelled. I missed Caleb. It felt as if he was right out of reach, and if I followed this longing, I would see him and be able to hold him.

"Zoltilvoxfyn," Kalvoxrencol said from behind me.

"Did you sort out whatever Seth needed?" I asked. Kalvoxrencol had been spending the afternoon with me because Seth was busy, probably with Wyn or Urgg. But when he'd summoned

Kalvoxrencol, my brother had gone after his mate, though he extracted a promise that I would be here when he returned.

"Yes."

I didn't bother to respond, let alone turn around.

"I need you to look at me, Bloom."

I frowned at his careful tone, facing him. His arms were crossed and his tail twitched something fierce. I asked, "What's going on, Pest?"

"There is someone you need to see, and you must remain calm." Kalvoxrencol gripped my tail with his.

"I'm in no mood to meet someone. Tell them to leave."

"I cannot. You have to, and I believe you'll want to."

"What is going…" The words died on my tongue as Seth moved into my line of sight. He wasn't alone. A tall drakcol male stood beside him. His scales were light gray with glimpses of gold and emerald green. His jewel blue eyes were fixed on me, and his rich brown hair was shaved on one side with a long scar on his scalp, revealing his mottled skin where the scales hadn't grown back.

Something lurched in my gut as I stared at him. My soul throbbed. *Mine*. This drakcol was mine. Anger, potent and hot, swept through my veins like wildfire. How *dare* the Crystal reject Caleb and yet give me another? Caleb was my everything, and I would accept no other. He was my mate.

My wings sprawled. "I don't want you."

"Fyn," Seth admonished.

I slashed a hand through the air, and Seth flinched. Kalvoxrencol growled in warning, which I ignored. I couldn't take my eyes off the intruder. Caleb was my mate, not this drakcol. I did not care what the Crystal said. I would die before I accepted another soul.

The gray-scaled drakcol grinned at me, bobbing on the heels of his feet before stopping with a grimace. "Hey, Sunshine."

My breath harshened. "You do not call me that."

"Yes, I do." He wiped a hand down his chest, straightening the red tunic. "I know the... container is different, but I'm still me."

"What?"

He stiffly limped toward me, and my wings spread to their full width. I would not be disloyal to my mate.

"I know this is not what you're used to," the drakcol said. "Fuck, I'm not used to it. I'm taller than you now, which is... unbelievable. I mean, you know how short I was better than anyone, and I was tiny. Now I'm ginormous. How do people deal with being so big? It's weird, and I don't like it." He sucked in a breath. "It was easier to ramble when I was a ghost. I didn't need to breathe. Anyway, I am still *your* Caleb."

"Liar," I hissed. I moved to shove him, but the instant I came in contact with his scales, I froze. Unable to stop it, my fingers curled around his tunic and hauled him closer, the warmth of him sinking into me. I desired the bite of tingly cold, not this.

"I'm not lying, and you know it," the man said. "That's why you're holding me. You know I am yours. Fyn, you know I belong with you and you belong with me."

"No." I forced myself to let him go. "Pest and Seth must have shared things or you somehow found out." No one truly knew much about Caleb, and all of the information on humans was currently restricted; I didn't even have access to it. "My Caleb is gone."

"I'm still here, Sunshine. I never left you. I promised I would always come back to you. Now and forever. You are mine, and I am yours. I can tell you anything you want from the first time we had sex to the random things you said. Whatever you need to prove who I am. But I am Caleb, your Caleb, and you are *my* Sunshine."

I shook my head, staring up into the blue eyes, such a different shade than what I was used to.

"I am," he yelled; his voice was deep and not the one I knew. "I am your Caleb. The Crystal marked us as mates."

"I'm refusing you. I will be loyal to my mate."

"I am your mate, Zoltilvoxfyn. I did not spend weeks fighting with doctors about who I am to debate it with you. I am Caleb. I am your mate. I love you, and I know you love me."

"I love Caleb," I shouted.

"Fuck everything," he said. "Fine, you don't have to believe me, but I am who I say I am. And guess what, you still have to bond with me before the Crystal will allow us to break apart. You want to reject me? Go ahead. Either way, we have to become mates first before you can reject the bond in front of the Crystal. So one way or another you will be mine. If you still don't want me after that? Fine. I will spend the rest of my life chasing you. I was willing to risk oblivion for you, so why wouldn't I be willing to spend my life fighting for you?"

My instincts demanded I draw him close, claim him, protect him, and never let him go. But my mind warred with my soul. This wasn't Caleb, but my soul demanded he was mine.

The man grabbed me, yanking me against him. "You are worth it, Zoltilvoxfyn. You are worth everything. I will always stay with you."

I crashed into him and knocked him to the ground. The drakcol yelped. I seized the front of his tunic, shaking him. "You are not Caleb!"

"Zoltilvoxfyn, release him," Kalvoxrencol ordered.

"Caleb," Seth cried.

I ignored them both.

Arching, he pressed a light kiss to the corner of my lips, sending sparks through me. "Sunshine," he whispered. His fingers slid up and down my back, the pressure hard, hard enough to be unpleasant, but that wasn't what bothered me. The movements were achingly familiar. The pattern—up my spine, across my shoulders, and down my sides. I knew this. This was not something I'd told anyone, nor had Caleb. No one but us knew.

"Caleb?" I asked, barely believing it.

A bright smile pulled on his lips. "Sunshine."

Something snapped in my mind and sent me reeling like I'd been punched. This was Caleb. My Caleb. He was nothing like I remembered or expected, but all the same, he was mine. He'd crossed the universe for me. He fought off oblivion for me. He, against all odds, found life again for me. All for me.

I gripped his cheeks and pressed my lips against his. He moaned, and I swallowed the sound, feasting on it. I swiped my tongue against his. Thrusting in and out, I claimed his mouth. I went to the hem of his tunic and tried to yank it off, but his wings were out, blocking my efforts. Frustrated, I shredded the fabric with my claws; it came apart with ease.

Caleb clutched my back, hard enough to the point of pain. He probably didn't know how to regulate his strength. That was something we would worry about later. I needed Caleb, and I needed him right now. I did not care if Seth and Kalvoxrencol were still there. I did not care that we were in the garden for anyone to see. Caleb was mine. I'd thought he was gone, but in truth, he'd been fighting to come back to me. I would never deserve the loyalty and love he had for me.

He trembled beneath me, and his hard cock pressed against mine through his trousers. I rutted into him, and he gasped. My lips wandered over his face and down the wide column of his neck. I pushed his head to the side to nibble on the tight tendons.

"Permissions," I demanded.

"What?"

"Your permissions. I need them now before I take you."

He did not answer me, so I pulled back. His eyes were wide, pupils blown. Tremors wracked his body, and his wings hugged his sides. I glanced down, and his tail was hugging his leg. Caleb was afraid. Why? He didn't fear me. Or did he?

His hips bucked into mine. "Why did you stop?"

"You wish for me to continue?"

"Of course." His shaking hands pulled me closer.

Suddenly, I understood. Caleb had no idea what his own body was telling him. It had been over twenty cycles since he'd had one, and he'd never been a drakcol. He didn't understand the signs.

I gently kissed him, keeping the pressure soft and the tempo slow. I traced his lips with my tongue, tasting him, then nipped the bottom one, drawing it into my mouth and sucking. Caleb moaned beneath me, hips canting against mine, but the tension in his body didn't leave no matter what I did.

"Let's go to our quarters," I said against his ear, and Caleb shivered, drawing away. I stood, my erection tenting the front of my trousers. As much as I burned for Caleb, I wanted him to be comfortable more. He was far more important than the flash of lust raging through me.

Besides, as I glanced at him, then quickly away, I still had a hard time accepting the drakcol in front of me as Caleb. He wasn't my Caleb. I should be grateful, and I was, yet I longed for a smiling face with bright blue eyes and creamy skin.

Hooking my arms beneath him, I helped him up. He grimaced, making my soul scream in terror. "Did I injure you?" If I'd hurt him, I would never forgive myself.

"No. I—Yolkeltod's body was in an accident. It's still recovering."

I traced the scar on the side of his head, and he shivered. "This is Yolkeltod?"

"Yep."

"How?"

He lifted and lowered his shoulders. "The Crystal. I guess."

That was as good an answer as any. I wrapped my tail around his, and he shied away, yelping. A needle stabbed me at the rejection.

"Sorry," he whispered. "The tail is even more sensitive."

"Ah."

"Yolkeltod has spinal damage."

That explained the stiff way he moved. Worry plucked at me, dousing my lust. "Are you well?"

"I guess."

A trip to the doctor was in order, though not today. I grabbed his hand. I'd seen Kalvoxrencol and Seth holding hands—a human thing, I supposed. Caleb's fingers intertwined with mine, our palms pressed together. I couldn't help but wonder what Caleb's human hand would have felt like. Would he have been as soft as Seth? How would his small hand have fit within my much larger grasp?

When we stepped into our quarters, Caleb glanced around. "Where are the plants?"

Shame crept up my spine, settling into a cold ball in my gut, and I kept my gaze averted. "They died. After you…" I couldn't finish that sentence. "I didn't care for them."

"We'll plant more," he said easily, like it was nothing, and my muscles unclenched.

Caleb shifted in front of me, and I cupped his hips, tail coiling about his ankle. His hands ran down my chest, hooking on the edge of my tunic and tugging it off. I stared up at him and wanted to laugh, but I couldn't force the sound out. Caleb was taller than I was now. His shoulders were broad, though he was underweight. He was attractive with his long face and strong nose. Still, he was a stranger. I didn't recognize him, and yet he was mine.

He brushed my pierced nipples, playing with the gold rings, and I moaned. My cock started to firm up. While my mind was struggling to recognize Caleb, my body had no such issues. It craved him, desperately.

I glanced at his wings that hugged his sides and his tail that clung to his leg. Caleb was still stressed, but I doubted he knew that.

"Come on," I said.

I led him to the bedroom. Caleb didn't fight and his cock was hard and ready. *He* wasn't, though. I divested him of clothes, having to rip the rest of his shirt off. Scars marred his left side where scales hadn't grown back to cover his mottled skin beneath. I would have to make sure he took care of his exposed skin. It would be sensitive to extreme temperatures or drying out.

He watched as I stripped off my clothes, leaving us both bare.

"Lay down," I told him. Caleb did. As he lay on his back, he shook. While his cock dripped pre-seed, the rest of him radiated unease. I settled next to his side and rolled him until he faced me. Arms around him, I draped my wings over him before throwing a leg over his hip and securing my tail around his leg.

"Sunshine?"

I heard the question in his voice. I nuzzled his forehead, breathing in the floral perfume that was my mate. Had Caleb smelled like this before? I had no idea. Did it matter? This was my mate's scent now. Still, I wondered.

"Wrap your tail around my leg, Mate."

"I-I can't c-control it," he said, voice breaking.

"You can. Breathe. Hold me tight. It will be alright."

His arms enfolded me, pressing us against each other. His cock had softened. Maybe his mind was finally grasping the strain his body was exuding. Several moments passed before his tail wrapped firmly around my leg.

Stroking his back, I told him, "I must apologize."

"For what?"

"Pushing you. My relief and desire outweighed my sight of you."

"No." He tried to wiggle back, but I didn't allow him to. "I want you."

He did, but he didn't at the moment. I kept rubbing his back in long, smooth movements. A hiccup came from Caleb moments before tears dripped onto my chest. "Why am I crying?"

"You're scared."

"No, I'm not. Why would I be? I want you. I promise."

Yes, he did. How long had he been struggling to get to me and ignoring everything his body was screaming at him? "I'm here. I'm right here."

Another sob escaped him. I continued to stroke Caleb as he wept. I would be here with him, and we would sort everything out. Nothing would keep us apart, not even my unease as my brain struggled to catch up with this new reality. I would keep him safe this time. I would. Never would I fail my mate again.

Chapter 43

WHO IS THAT?

Caleb

I stared at Fyn's reflection in the mirror, embarrassed. He was in the shower, eyes flicking in my direction every few moments. It hadn't taken much to get my Sunshine to see me beneath the new package, and we'd started to get intimate, but then we stopped. I didn't know why. I also didn't know why I'd started crying moments later.

Part of me feared Fyn wasn't as *fine* as he was acting. I didn't look, sound, or even act like myself. It was as if everything I'd been was ripped apart and was somehow remade into a completely new being. I knew logically that was false—I was still me—but it didn't stop the intrusive thought.

I looked in the mirror and froze. A bubbling panic surged from deep within my gut. A face I didn't know stared back at me. Yes, I hadn't remembered my human face until Edith had shown me, but this... the person who stared at me was not me. The long face, the thinner top lip and plump bottom one, the wide forehead, and the glittering blue eyes.

Forcing myself to look downward, I turned the water on, swallowing at the sight of the scales covering me. Washing my hands, I shied away moments later. The water sluicing over my scales made a panicked tattoo start in my chest. The sound was so loud in my brain, thudding in my ears, and I wanted to flee from it.

Arms wrapped around my waist as a wet body pressed against my back. I swallowed at the slickness, my tail wrapping around my calf despite the prickles shooting up my spine from the movement. My dick immediately reacted, though, as the soothing tang of wet dirt filled my nose.

Zoltilvoxfyn.

I hadn't even known what he smelled like previously, but something primal within me loved his scent. I was desperate to rub all over him, rolling around in the fragrance while covering him with my scent, and I had no idea why. At the same time, I wanted to claw the smell out of my nose.

How had I lived like this before? The humid air. The smell of soap. The cold stone floor beneath my feet. Fyn. Every sight, smell, sound, and touch was overwhelming. I was in a state of constant terror, filling me with the urge to flee as fast as this body could, which wasn't fast.

Of course, when I was alive, all these *senses* had been the norm for me. I'd always experienced as much. But now, after being a ghost for over twenty years and then plopped into a different body, I found it all horribly overwhelming.

I was grateful to be alive, for having a second chance, for every sensation, and yet part of me wished to go back because being a ghost was what I was used to.

My wings flared and smacked into Fyn. "Sorry," I immediately said. Had I cut him? The talons on my wings were sharp.

He kissed my bare shoulder, making me shiver. "It's fine, Mate. Here. Let me help you." Carefully, he curled my wings up and settled them against my back.

Tears burned the backs of my eyes *again*, and I had no idea why. I'd never been a crier before. Was Yolkeltod weepy (did it even work like that)? Maybe. I had no idea, but every other second I was sobbing. I hated it. I was turning into a fucking crybaby.

Fyn pushed my hair over my shoulder, eliciting a flinch, before rubbing his nose along the nape of my neck. "I shall teach you how to control them."

The first tear slid down my cheek, and Yolkeltod's tail hugged my calf.

"It's alright," he said. "Everything is fine. I am here, my Caleb."

I started to brush the tears away and froze as my claws came ridiculously close to my eye. My wings flapped out, squishing against my shoulders. I opened my mouth to apologize, but Sunshine settled them against my back. He placed a kiss between my wings, and I shuddered at the tingles that went down my spine, dick throbbing in need.

God. He only had to look at me for my body to react. He didn't press for more as he kept his arms about my waist and trailed gentle kisses along my neck.

More tears slid down my cheeks. "Why am I crying?" I warbled. "I swear I never cried like this before. I don't understand." My words broke off into heaving sobs.

"You're stressed."

I was alive. I should be overjoyed. The thrumming, so different from the heartbeat I remembered, sounded in my ears. My tail strangled my calf, making me grimace.

Zoltilvoxfyn's hand rested on my sternum as he kissed my neck and rubbed his forehead on me. "Wrap your tail around my leg."

"I can't." I didn't know how to control the damn thing. It did whatever it wanted, along with my wings.

"You can. It's yours."

But it wasn't. This was Yolkeltod's body. His tail. His wings. I'd stolen it. Unintentionally. But still, I was a fucking thief. How did I live with that? How would Tinlorray ever forgive me? She could barely look at me, and I didn't blame her. This wasn't my body. This was Yolkeltod's.

God, I wanted to claw my skin, or scales, off. I hated this body. I hated myself. I couldn't even see my reflection in the damn mirror without cringing.

"Calm down," Fyn said in a low voice. "Follow my breathing."

He took a deep breath in, and I followed him—my every breath matching his. The longer we stood in the bathroom, breathing in the humid air, the more I calmed until the tears stopped.

Focusing on Zoltilvoxfyn, I continued to take measured breaths in an attempt to calm the storm raging inside of me. All I allowed myself to think about was him. The pressure from his lips, the strength of his embrace, the way his pierced nipples scraped against my scales, the sureness of his arms, and the way his hips cradled me. As I relaxed, my tail unspooled from my calf and wrapped around his ankle.

"There," he whispered. "Better, right?"

I nodded.

"I will be right here," Fyn said. "It will take time, but I promise it will be alright."

I wanted to believe him, but I didn't, not yet.

Chapter 44

A FAMILY VISIT, AND I'M CRYING. AGAIN.

Caleb

I stared at the tablet, but my message to Tinlorray had gone unanswered. I'd sent her four messages since I'd returned to the palace. She'd ignored each one. When I'd tried to call her with Fyn's touchstone, Tinlorray hadn't answered. I was hurting her—my literal existence was hurting her.

This was worse than grief. Her brother's body was alive, but Yolkeltod was gone. I hadn't had any more choice in this than her, but my heart ached for Tinlorray. I knew she was grieving, and I couldn't do anything to help. I couldn't watch over her like Yolkeltod had asked me to.

Someone sat behind me, and my wings flared out. Fyn grunted, and I immediately cringed. "I'm sorry, Sunshine."

"It's alright," he said, helping my wings curl up, which sent shards down my spine. Fyn kissed the back of my neck before nuzzling me.

It wasn't, none of this was. I tried to breathe through it, but the curling emotion remained deep in my gut. Fyn rubbed his forehead on the nape of my neck. The scent of him grew stronger and stronger by the second. I gripped one of his arms, focusing on how securely he held me.

"Softer, Mate," he said.

I jerked away. "I'm sorry. I didn't mean to, Sunshine. I'm so big now. I don't know what to do. I keep messing up."

He nipped my neck, and I groaned in pleasure while part of me recoiled from the pressure of his teeth and the wetness of his mouth.

"You are not messing up, Caleb. You are learning."

At one point in my life, actually all of my life and afterlife, I'd loved learning, but now entering my second life, I couldn't say I enjoyed it. I would rather have everything go back to how it was. I didn't want to struggle, but that was the price of being alive.

Fyn didn't say anything more as he cuddled me. I looked down at my tablet, or more accurately Fyn's tablet—I hadn't been added to the Drakcon system yet. My sudden appropriation of Yolkeltod's body had caused a slight uproar. It had been four days since I came to the palace, but word about me had spread. The Ranks had shared my new soul testing as proof as well as the fact I was Zoltilvoxfyn's soulmate.

The Council of Seekers had already appealed to study me as well as Fyn. They were curious if what happened to me could be replicated. The Ranks were curious as to why the Crystal had drawn me all the way from Earth to here. There was also a small subset of people who were angry. A drakcol prince had gotten his dead soulmate, but Yolkeltod hadn't been returned to his body. Yolkeltod had been as popular as Tinlorray had hinted, and his friends were less than pleased.

I hadn't told anyone about me speaking to Yolkeltod, and neither had Fyn or Tinlorray, as far as I was aware, which was probably for the best. If the general populace knew Yolkeltod had hung around after his accident, they would demand to know why the Crystal hadn't returned him to his body.

I wanted to know that as well. Why me? It was the same question I'd asked when I died, and I had no more answer now than I did then. I was alive and Yolkeltod wasn't. It wasn't fair; it wasn't right.

For now, the emperor and empress had asked Fyn and I to remain on the palace grounds. They were afraid someone might harm us or that we might further enrage the public about me—a human, inside Yolkeltod's body. Fyn was fine with their request... and I felt a little like a caged bird.

The bell rang, and Fyn stood, tail brushing my arm; I followed suit, heart rate picking up. Seth and Kal were on the other side, and Fyn waved them in; whereas, I stayed back, tail around my leg and wings hugging my shoulders. I was barefoot, unable to tolerate shoes, preferring the chill of the floor in comparison. The wind wafted in from the open windows and ruffled my hair, making me flinch. I might have to cut off the long locks, though that felt disrespectful. Yolkeltod had long hair. Clearly, he'd liked it. This was his body. How could I cut his hair?

I wrapped my arms around my waist, swallowing more tears. I refused to cry again.

"How are you?" Seth asked, startling me. He'd moved in front of me without me noticing.

I shrugged, then winced. Shit. Yolkeltod's body twinged at the slightest movements.

He patted my shoulder, stretching to reach it. I was tall, like humongous. I was taller than Seth, taller than Kal, and even taller than Fyn. I'd always been the shortest person around, and now I was the tallest.

"I'm glad you're back," he said. "I'm not the only human anymore."

A vicious knife plunged into my gut, making my wings sprawl. I wasn't human. Not anymore.

Kal was at Seth's side in an instant. He drew his mate behind him, lips curling. I shied back. Why was Kal mad? Fyn slid in front of me and growled at Kal. What the fuck was happening? The first tear slid out as I trembled. One of the new planters with a seedling rattled before crashing to the floor, making me leap, which, in turn, forced a yelp out of my lips.

"Stop," Seth ordered, moving to Kal's side. "Everything's fine. Caleb is not threatening me."

Why would I threaten Seth?

I huddled behind Fyn, tears sliding down my cheeks. What was going on with me? I hardly ever cried, but now, I was bawling at the drop of the hat. I hated it, but I didn't know how to stop it or the tension radiating through me.

The thought that this wasn't my body and it didn't belong to me kept circling my thoughts. I needed out, but that was ungrateful.

Yolkeltod hadn't had a second chance, and here I was in his body, squandering it.

A few breaths passed before Kal relaxed, and once he did, Fyn did. My Sunshine waved to the couch. Seth plopped down, pulling Kal with him, while Fyn and I settled on the rug. Legs crossed, I pressed against his side and seized his hand. He wiggled in my grasp, and I loosened my hold.

I kept hurting him.

Seth glanced at Kal, biting his lip. Seth didn't do well in the quiet or with new people. Was I a new person? We'd spoken through Sunshine a few times. But now I was in a new body. Oh my god, I was a new person. He probably didn't like me anymore. All I'd wanted since I saw him for the first time was to be his friend, and now, we had to start over.

"Breathe, Mate."

I took a heaving gasp, lungs burning. How the fuck did I keep forgetting to breathe?

Kal crossed his arms, and I blinked. Maybe Seth wasn't nervous about me, but rather, they were having a silent conversation again. They did that often, though I didn't know how much they could communicate like that. No one had properly explained it yet.

Eventually, Kal said, "Seth and I would like to invite you and Zoltilvoxfyn to the beach for an outing."

This plan was definitely Seth's idea, and I wasn't sure why Kal was so resistant to me. He'd liked me before. I squished against Fyn, tail curling around his leg. It hurt the sensitive appendage, but I liked it better than wrapping around my own leg. Something about it calmed me.

"Today?" Fyn asked. "You know Father and Mother told us not to leave."

"I cleared it with them, but no, not today. I was thinking about next week. We'll go somewhere private; it should be fine," Kal answered. "Serlotminden is willing to take us, or we can take a different shuttle, so everyone can go."

A family outing. Part of me bounced to say yes. I liked spending time with people, but the thought of the ocean with its constant breezes, the sand, the noise, and everything else was too much. Unbidden, I tightened my tail around Fyn's calf, somehow terrified I would lose him all over again. What if a wave took him? Or some kind of creature I didn't know anything about?

An urge to rub all over him struck me again, and I couldn't control it. I nuzzled his shoulder, and my floral fragrance grew. I couldn't remember what I smelled like when I was human, and I didn't hate how I smelled now... but it was new.

He brushed my cheek, and I shivered. Looking at Kal and Seth, he said, "Caleb has to see the doctor first."

Seth asked, "Are you alright?"

"Yolkeltod was in a shuttle accident."

His eyes flicked to the wicked scar on the side of my head. My fingers twitched as I resisted the urge to cover it. Yolkeltod's hair and scales hadn't grown back, much like spots on his side.

Fyn drew me closer, arm around my waist. A flash of longing went through me. What would this have been like if I was still human? As

Yolkeltod, I was broader and taller than Sunshine. As a human, I'd been much smaller. Would he have been warm or cold against my skin? How would his scales have felt?

As a drakcol, I liked how he felt (when I wasn't freaking out). He was the same temperature as me, our scales would scrape delightfully, and the solidness of him against me was wonderful. My dick perked up, and I stared down in horror as the front of my trousers tented. I shifted to hide the obvious bulge. A glance at Seth's red face assured me I hadn't acted fast enough.

Kal and Fyn didn't visibly react, but Sunshine did rub his fingers over my spine, sending electric shocks to my dick. I swallowed, fighting the instinct to tackle him and rub all over him, taste him, and hear him call my name, though, at the same time, I recoiled from such touches—so new and strong.

My head was a confusing place to be.

"Next week, though?" Kal asked. "It would be nice to do something as a family." His gaze lingered on me. "The whole family."

I grinned, bouncing my knees, then hissed from the sharp sting.

"Are you well, Mate?" Fyn asked, voice turning sharp as he whipped toward me.

I nodded, but the worry in his expression didn't fade.

"When are you two making it official?" Seth asked.

That's right. We had to be bound, and then reaffirm the bond in front of the Crystal. "I don't know."

Fyn's arm tightened around me. "Not yet."

I blinked back tears. Was he going to break up with me? Had I scared him off? I couldn't handle that. Everything was too much, and Zoltilvoxfyn was the glue keeping me together. If he wasn't here, I would shatter.

Kal laughed. "You hate the thought of being separated from the time you agree to bond and when the ceremony actually takes place."

"If I don't outright agree, then we can stay together," he said.

The hurt vanished in an instant. "What?"

Seth explained, "You're not allowed to see each other in between. I don't know why."

"It's a leftover tradition from when we were warring clans. It was so the fated mate wouldn't run away when they saw who the Crystal had chosen. It's the same reason why the genetic link exists and doesn't allow us to travel too far apart from each other. Though the distance has increased from what it used to be," Fyn commented. "But I shall stay right here, beside you, for the foreseeable future."

Something feral roiled inside of me, and without thought, I grabbed his cheeks to haul him closer to me, kissing him. Fyn started, but he didn't pull away. Our lips molded together as a gentle symphony started in my chest, growing louder and louder, drowning everything else out.

I forced my tongue into his mouth, swiping his, and he groaned into me. Fuck. Nothing was better than that sound. My movements grew more frantic, desperate. He tasted so damn sweet. His scaled tongue curled around mine as he slid a hand beneath my shirt, tracing the line of my back all the way from the top of my tail to my wings, which made me moan.

Someone cleared their throat, and I jerked back, breath jagged.

Seth was cherry-red, and Kal was shaking his head, but he was grinning.

I wiggled, embarrassed. "Sorry."

"Instinct," Kal said, sliding his fingers over Seth's neck. "You can't help but desire your mate."

"I suppose," I replied, and Fyn raised his eyebrows. "Yes," I begrudgingly added, crossing my arms.

He pressed a kiss to my cheek before tugging me into his arms. I settled partly on his lap and marveled at how large I was. I didn't suffer from issues with my center of gravity. Yolkeltod's body was used to this size. I wasn't. I expected things and people to be taller and I smaller. My different size was throwing me off.

A strong panic seeped into me. I tried to breathe through it. I didn't understand the fear or the urge to move away, even though I liked Fyn touching me. How did I want to be touched and not touched at the same time?

Tail flicking, I smothered a growl growing in my chest. I growled now. God, everything was so different. My wings started to slide through the slits in the back of my sleeveless tunic, but one got caught on the light fabric, succeeding in dragging a snarl from my lips as I turned around pointlessly.

Calm hands rested on my shoulders, and I stilled. Fyn's earthy scent enveloped me, soothing the tension. "It's alright," he said. Carefully, he directed my wing out of the slit. Immediately, I hugged myself.

Shame burned me as I glanced at Seth and Kal who watched me. The first tear escaped, and I scoffed. I was fucking crying again, like a giant, pathetic baby. I needed to get a hold of myself.

"Maybe we should go?" Seth offered.

"We'll see you both later," Fyn said.

The moment the door closed behind them, Sunshine helped me lay down on the rug before rolling me onto my side. His arms came about me as he hooked a leg over my hip and curled his tail up my calf. The instant I was surrounded by him, I felt better.

Breathing in his perfect fragrance, I nuzzled his neck. The tears wouldn't stop falling, and I had no idea why. I wrapped my tail around Fyn while I continued to nuzzle him, almost frantically.

Chapter 45

GRIEF IS WEIRD.

Zoltilvoxfyn

Caleb sat in the center of the medbay. The palace's was fairly large with several beds and monitors, and it was fully staffed as well as equipped for our basic needs. Doctors and technicians bustled around him while he remained as still as the mountain, which was odd.

In the short time since Caleb had returned to me, he did not shout or bounce around as he once did. Pain was probably the reason, and it destroyed my soul that he was hurting so badly. But at the same time, his stillness separated this Caleb before me from my Caleb. I didn't want such a distinction, and yet, it existed.

I caught a glimpse of Edith popping in on a monitor behind him, and I started. Apparently, she was expanding from Kalvoxrencol's system. Seth had probably asked her to check on Caleb, or she was being nosy. It was hard to tell with Edith. She was an interesting person.

I wanted to wrap my arms around Caleb and ease the tension in his body, but I would get in the way of the technicians or the doctor if I did. We needed to know exactly what was going on with him so I could better take care of him. Nothing would happen to my mate *ever* again.

The doctor pressed a vial against Caleb's neck, and he jumped, making me snarl. The woman offered her throat but continued to take blood from Caleb's neck before covering the mark with a plaster. Instinct demanded I lick the injury clean, but I remained where I was. If Caleb was open to it, I would bathe the wound later.

My mate trembled when someone grabbed his tail, trying to unwind it. Tails were sensitive for drakcol, Caleb's even more so, and I didn't like the idea of anyone but me touching his. Caleb's eyes turned glassy. I stalked forward, snarling at the technician, who yanked away, throat bared.

"Mate?" I asked.

He burrowed against my chest, nuzzling. I ran my fingers through his hair. I doubted he even knew why he was rubbing me, scent marking me. He was claiming his mate, which I was more than fine with. Everyone needed to know I belonged to him, and him alone.

"We need to scan his tail," the doctor said in a calm voice.

I kissed the top of Caleb's head. "I'm going to grab your tail."

Tears dripped down his cheeks, and the sight shattered me. I was trying to care for him, but he was overstimulated. There were too many sights and sounds in here. I wished he didn't have to do this, and I felt guilty for making him sit here, but I needed to know how to help him.

I unwound his tail as carefully as possible, kissing the brown-haired tip, and his breath sharpened. The technician ran a scanner over the appendage. When he was done, I stood, and Caleb wrapped his tail around my wrist, tugging me. I settled in between his legs and drew him into my arms.

The doctor raised an eyebrow at my position, but she didn't remark or ask me to step aside. Caleb burrowed against my chest, and the examination continued with more scans and tests that made him cringe and me growl.

When they finished, the doctor told us, "We will have the results in a week or so."

"Thank you," I said. I cupped Caleb's cheeks. "Let's go back to our quarters."

"I want to see the garden."

"Come." I led him out of the palace and to the terrace garden. The ever-present wind blew around us, ruffling Caleb's hair. He jerked, then frowned, trapping the locks. "Perhaps you should cut your hair?"

"Yolkeltod had it long."

"But it's your hair now." The straight brown strands were several shades darker with a red tint than Caleb's original hair color. Had those curls been soft? Would they have wrapped around my fingers?

"It's not," Caleb snapped.

"What?"

Caleb yanked out of my grasp. "This is not my body."

"It is," I said, but my mind went back to his human form.

"It's not. I'm not me. I don't know who I am anymore."

I reached out to him, and he drew back. Hurt, I asked, "Mate?"

Tears slid down his cheeks, and his wings hugged his shoulders while his tail curled around his ankle. The wind blew, and he barked, "I hate how everything feels and smells. I hate it all. I hate being touched."

A shard of ice stabbed my soul. I'd done nothing but touch him. I hadn't even asked. I'd assumed Caleb desired my touch as I did his. Permissions hadn't come up, and they should have. Of course, they were different now that he had a body. We were different. Our relationship was different.

Guilt, strong and cold, swept through me, and on its tail was self-loathing. I was failing him again. Utterly and completely. I was longing for Caleb's human body when he was struggling to exist.

"I want to go back," he cried. "I can't do this anymore, Fyn. I want to go back."

"Caleb," I whispered, unsure of what to say. I couldn't desire that. Not ever.

He shook his head and started to run away, body stiff.

"Caleb!"

"Leave me alone, Zoltilvoxfyn," he shouted, limping out of the garden.

Caleb

I ran until my body screamed for me to stop. My back throbbed, my legs trembled, and my head pounded. I couldn't believe I'd said those words. I sounded like an ungrateful, whiny bastard. I was given a second chance—a chance Yolkeltod had never gotten—and here I was complaining because my senses were driving me to the brink.

Sunshine probably thought I hated him. I didn't. I loved him, desperately. He was the one thing I was completely sure of. I didn't even know who I was, but I knew him and what he meant to me.

Fyn was everything.

But I wanted to go back. I wanted to be a ghost again. It was easier; it was what I knew. Though, at the thought, my stomach churned and my chest throbbed in a weird thrumming. To not be able to touch Fyn again, to not know how amazing he smelled or how warm he was against me would be torture. I couldn't exist like that again.

Going back wasn't an option, but the here and now was so hard. And I couldn't help but wonder what if.

What if I'd been human? What would it have been like? What would we have been like? I could ask Seth, though he'd probably die from embarrassment if I asked what Kal's dick felt like plowing him or what he tasted like.

Did it even matter? If I knew, it wouldn't change anything. I was a drakcol now, not a human, though, at the same time, I wasn't. I was neither and both.

God, everything was so damn confusing.

"Caleb," a calm voice said, making me start.

Monty stood in front of me, expression peaceful. His long silvery white hair hung around his broad shoulders, and he was dressed casually in a high-collared black sleeveless shirt and black pants.

"Monty." I scrubbed the tears off my cheeks. "Hello."

"Did you and Zoltilvoxfyn fight?"

"No." I shook my head, then nodded. "Yes. I don't know."

He gestured to the path, and I moved to his side. Monty walked at an even pace beside me. He was my height, which was on the taller side for drakcol. "How are you?"

I shrugged, freezing as the upper part of my spine twinged.

"I have no knowledge of what that human movement means."

"I don't know how I'm doing." The damn wind blew, wrapping around me and stirring my hair. I yanked the strands back in place.

Monty paused. "May I?"

I cringed.

"I won't touch you." When I agreed, Monty grabbed my hair and tied it in a loose knot, securing it with a band.

"Thanks."

"How long were you a spirit?" he asked.

"Uh," I said, blinking at his blatant question. "Over twenty cycles."

"I understand."

"What?" I asked.

"You are overburdened with these new senses."

"What?" I mean I was, but still, what?

Monty gestured to my tail, then my wings. "Your body is radiating terror and stress. Normally we do not hold our legs, nor do our wings hug our shoulders."

"I couldn't feel or smell anything as a ghost, and now…" I helplessly trailed off.

"It's everything."

I ran a hand down my silky shirt. "This is not my body. I have appendages I don't know how to use. I'm gigantic. Everything is different."

He started moving again toward the cathedral with the Crystal looming in the distance. "You are correct. That is not your body."

For some reason, tears dripped from my eyes.

Monty didn't react.

"Sorry," I muttered.

"You are allowed to mourn, Caleb. You died. You wandered. You lost Zoltilvoxfyn. And now you're in a foreign body in a foreign world. Of course, you are experiencing some grief. It's natural."

Was that what I was doing? Grieving? I didn't believe I'd even taken a moment after my death to be sad. I just moved forward (well, after a shit ton of anger). Now, all these years later, it rushed back to me. Rolling down the staircase. The sharp crack, then nothing. I'd hovered over my body as my brother screamed my name over and over again.

More tears slid down my cheeks as I sniffed.

Monty didn't say anything as I wept and kept leading me to the massive cathedral before directing me inside. The Crystal thrummed with energy in the center. My lips curled in a silent snarl at the sight of it. That stupid fucking rock had thrown me into a body I didn't know what to do with. It should have given Yolkeltod his body back. It should've saved him and not me.

I swallowed the sudden surge of emotion. I was alive; I was with Fyn, and I was so damn grateful. I couldn't be happy, though, because that was so damn selfish. Tinlorray was suffering,

Yolkeltod's friends were pissed, and it was his body that I stole. How was any of this fair?

"Why?" I demanded.

"Why what, Caleb?"

"Why did the Crystal put me in this body? Why, Monty?"

He looked at the glowing rock that peacefully hummed. "I don't know."

"Aren't you the purest spiritual soul? Shouldn't you know?"

Monty glanced at me. "I don't have all the answers. But I don't think there is a reason why. Not one we would understand, anyway. It was Yolkeltod's time, and it wasn't yours. He is dead, and you are not. It simply is, Caleb."

I stared at him, heavily reminded of the conversation I had with Yolkeltod before he passed on. There were no answers. I asked, "What now?"

"You learn to live." He rested a hand on my sternum, making me wince. "This is your body. Your mind. Your soul. You must find a way to live with it."

"Perhaps I can ask the Crystal, and it will tell me what to do."

His tail flicked. "It spoke to you?"

"It asked me why I was trying to reaffirm what hadn't been made yet."

His mouth fell open. "The Crystal spoke to you?"

"Doesn't it talk to everyone?"

"No," he said. "Never. We spiritual souls have an understanding of it, but it doesn't speak to us or anyone."

My heart throbbed. "Why me?"

"I don't know, Caleb. I shall have to ask Seth if the Crystal spoke to him as well. You humans might be more in tune with the Crystal than we drakcol."

"Can I touch it again?" I asked.

"No," Monty said, swiveling in front of me. "Tradition dictates that you cannot until you reaffirm your bond with Zoltilvoxfyn. The two of you haven't even forged the genetic link yet. You will have to wait."

Even though I could go my whole life without hearing that otherworldly voice again, I needed direction. Something. Anything.

"I imagine the Ranks will desire to speak with you more than they already do," Monty continued.

I *really* didn't want to do that. Hopefully, Seth had also heard the Crystal so we could talk to them together if we had to at all. Kal was fairly vicious in his protection of Seth, and Fyn wasn't far behind him regarding me.

My Fyn would keep me safe and away from anyone I didn't want to speak to. Though we had just fought, and he might not be pleased with me at the moment. I couldn't believe I'd run from him; I shouldn't have, but... I couldn't breathe.

Monty gestured to the door. "You should find Zoltilvoxfyn."

Had he heard my thoughts? "H-how did you know?"

"A feeling. He needs you, Caleb. More than you know."

"I don't know what to do."

"Try the truth."

"I hurt him."

"Then apologize and start again," he said. "That's what life is, Caleb—a series of choices, mistakes, and decisions. We always have a chance to start again. With every breath, our life starts anew."

I needed to return to my Sunshine's side, but at the same time, I felt so guilty. I hadn't meant to pop off at him. The words had built in my gut until I exploded.

Tinlorray appeared in my thoughts. I hadn't spoken to her since she and Seth had freed me from the locked ward. I'd tried, but she hadn't responded. Maybe it would be better to see her in person? Yet how could I see her when I'd stolen her brother?

"Caleb?" Monty said, drawing me from my thoughts.

"I'll talk to him," I lied. I needed to see Tinlorray to make sure she was okay. I'd promised Yolkeltod, and it was literally the least I could do. I left Monty and slipped, rather easily, out of the palace and snuck into the city.

Chapter 46

SILENCE IS AN ANSWER.

Caleb

I wound through the streets, head down. I had to see Tinlorray; I'd promised Yolkeltod. Selfishly, I hoped she would alleviate this all-consuming guilt that wouldn't abate. I needed to be able to breathe without suffocating or thinking I'd stolen something precious. How could I live my life like that? Monty said I needed to make peace with it, but how could I do that when Tinlorray was devastated and her brother was gone?

I kept close to the buildings until I made it to the port where I boarded the shuttle that would take me to where Tinlorray lived. The second I crossed the threshold, my muscles froze and my breathing harshened. I had no idea why; shuttles had never bothered me before.

In the past, I would've talked to the strangers next to me. I would've bounced around investigating. I would have... I stopped that train of thought. The past was the past. I might be me, but I was different. Now, the thought of being near someone or having them talk to me made me anxious.

The reality of my life had changed, and I had to adjust.

With every shake and vibration of the shuttle, I fought back tears. I needed off, and I needed it now.

When it finally docked, I pushed through the crowd to the exit. The drakcol stared at me, some even growled, but no one said anything about my rude behavior.

By the time I'd reached Tinlorray's complex, my knees shook and my chest ached. I started to pant and my vision wavered as if I was going to pass out. I pressed a hand on the side of the building, half-bent over, and tried to breathe. God, the pain was horrible. It was everywhere, throbbing, aching, stabbing, so many different types all demanding my attention.

"Yo—Caleb," a voice said from in front of me.

"Tinlorray," I said, voice rough.

She had her arms wrapped around her waist and her tail thrashed, eyes glassy with emotion. Otherwise, she appeared well enough in clean clothes with her neatly braided hair.

I gave her a shaky smile. "I'm here to check on you."

"You need to leave."

"What?" I straightened, my heart pounding so hard I feared it would rip out of my chest.

Tinlorray's hands curled into shaking fists. "I didn't answer you, Caleb. I don't want to see you, I don't want to talk to you, and I don't even want to receive notes from you. You are not Yolkeltod. You are not my brother."

"Tinlorray." I didn't know what to say.

"Stop. Just stop," Tinlorray snapped. "I helped you, alright? I helped you be with your soulmate. I don't want to see you anymore. We aren't friends. We aren't family. We are nothing."

"Yolkeltod asked me to take care of you."

A vicious roar ripped out of her throat as her wings sprawled. I cowered, shuffling back to get away from her, but I moved too fast and tripped, collapsing to the ground. Fiery knives shot up my spine, stealing my breath.

"Don't say his name. You are not him." Tinlorray breathed slowly, remaining silent until her wings settled against her back. "I am trying to move on, Caleb, and seeing you reminds me of what I've lost.

"I won't speak against you or Prince Zoltilvoxfyn for what happened, because I know neither of you tried to do this. It's not your fault. But the fact remains that you, not Yolkeltod, inhabit that body."

"I'm sorry."

"I don't need your apologies. I need you to leave me alone."

I nodded, then stopped, remembering drakcol didn't do that. "I can do that, but, Tinlorray, please remember I'm here for you and I would like to be friends."

She did not respond.

"Please, Tinlorray."

"Go, Caleb, and don't come back." Without a second glance, she walked away.

Something snapped within me. I felt oddly abandoned. Tears dripped down my cheeks. "Tinlorray," I begged, but she didn't stop.

Zoltilvoxfyn

I stared at the door, unable to pull my gaze away. Caleb had been gone since this afternoon. I thought it might help him to have some space, and truthfully, I hadn't known what to say to him—I still didn't. Now, the sun was beginning to set. Clearly, I'd made yet another mistake.

My instincts demanded I search for him, or at the very least ping him, but Caleb didn't want me to. At least I didn't think he did. I truly didn't know. I didn't know anything anymore. My mate was a stranger, and it was my fault. I hadn't even asked him what he needed; I'd assumed, like an idiot. Which I was. Everything, absolutely everything, was my fault. I'd sworn to keep him safe, and yet he was somewhere without me, possibly in danger.

He had a touchstone. If he needed me, he would ping me or I hoped he would. Caleb would, wouldn't he? He knew he could rely on me, didn't he? I shoved my hand through my hair, tail thrashing. I didn't know anymore. I had failed my mate so completely again that maybe he didn't trust me anymore. He would be justified.

No. I closed my eyes. Much as my mate-brother Seth had said, not everything was about me. Yes, I had made mistakes, but Caleb had also chosen to leave. Though, I should have been more careful. I shoved a hand through my hair. It was hard to fight the cloud of worthlessness. Everything inside of me felt as if I alone bore the guilt, but it wasn't that simple. I knew it. In this situation, there was no blame. It was simply hard for both of us.

My touchstone warmed as a deep voice echoed in my ears, "Zoltilvoxfyn."

"Caleb," I shouted, yanking the stone out of my pocket. "Where are you?"

"Sunshine," he said breathlessly.

"Where are you, Mate?"

"I went to the city." He panted, stopping.

"Are you injured?" I asked, racing out the door, my wings spreading.

"I went to see Tinlorray. She doesn't want to see me. She doesn't want to talk to me. I feel so guilty. She was crying, Fyn, and I couldn't do anything. It's all my fault. This is all my fault. I'm a fucking thief."

I heard the tears in his voice.

"I walked around for a while before heading back."

"Where are you?" I demanded, a moment away from finding his location and sending a local patrol to him.

"I tried to make it back, but I can't."

"What's wrong?"

"I hurt, Sunshine. I can't go any further. Please, help me."

My soul thrashed. "I'm coming, Mate." I moved toward a monitor, refusing to disconnect from Caleb. "NAID, where is Caleb?"

"Unknown name," it replied. He hadn't been added yet to the system, but there had to be dozens of Yolkeltods.

I banished the silhouette and logged into Kalvoxrencol's system. "Edith."

"Hello, Prince."

"Where is Caleb? I am speaking to him currently."

Edith put his location on the map.

"Send a local patrol. I'm heading there now."

"Understood."

"Mate," I said, but Caleb didn't respond. "Caleb!" Nothing came from the other side, and the touchstone was inactive. I raced to the open window, and my wings flapped, lifting me into the air.

Time passed so slowly that every second was agony. I would not lose Caleb a second time. He was here with me, and I intended to keep him for the rest of our lives. We would find a way through the problems. We would grow used to his new body. We would be together.

I dove to the ground, sweeping the street for my mate. My soul stuttered when I spotted him. Caleb was lying on the steps of a multi-dwelling building.

I dashed to his side, falling to my knees, heedless of the hard ground. "Caleb. Mate." I cupped his cheek. "Wake up."

His eyes fluttered open, and he smiled, though it was shaky. "You came."

"I will always come for you." I stroked his cheek, and he groaned. "Are you well?"

"I hurt."

Gently, I helped him to a seated position. "You did too much."

"I didn't mean to."

I gathered him into my arms and took a deep inhale of his floral fragrance. That plus Caleb's solid form in my embrace soothed my tension. I rubbed my forehead against his neck, scent marking him. I needed to claim him, and for everyone to know, that this wayward soul was mine wherever he wandered.

"I would've taken you to see Tinlorray, Caleb."

He pulled back. "I can do things by myself."

Cupping his cheeks again, I said, "Then I would have arranged a shuttle or showed you how to do so. You cannot wander this far, Little Soul, not anymore."

Tears gathered in his eyes, and claws raked my chest. I hated being the cause of his suffering. I was his mate, and drakcol cared for our mates, but I was injuring mine.

I brushed the tears away before kissing his cheek, then froze. Caleb had said he hated to be touched. I slid back. "My apologies. I shouldn't have touched you."

He dragged me closer, wincing. "I didn't mean you, Sunshine. Hold me."

I hooked my arms around him, settling him against my chest as we waited for the patrol. They would take us back to the palace, so Caleb didn't have to walk any further.

"I don't know much right now, Fyn," Caleb said. "I'm confused and upset, and I don't even know who I am, but I am completely certain about one thing."

"What?" I asked, stroking his back.

"That I love you."

My soul thrashed against my ribs as heat washed through me. “I love you too.”

Chapter 47

HONEST CONFESSIONS.

Caleb

I lay in bed, waiting for Fyn to snuggle next to me and surround me so I could fall asleep. After we'd been dropped back off at the palace, he'd taken me to the medbay for a quick checkup. The doctor had thought I was merely exhausted and recommended rest. As soon as we got back to our bedroom, Fyn had helped me lie down before taking a shower.

I wished I could join him, licking his cock. How would he taste? I'd wondered as a ghost, but now, I could find out for myself. My cock started to stiffen at the thought, but I was exhausted. Also, if we fucked, I might freak out in the middle; that would be beyond embarrassing.

Fyn came in, running a towel over his long hair. He threw it into the laundry before crawling into bed. He didn't bother to put on clothes, which I appreciated, because it allowed me to run my hands over his tight muscles and shiny scales.

He was lovely.

I swallowed as an urge to cover my scars burned through me. My wings hugged my sides and my tail coiled up my leg, making me grimace.

Fyn pulled me into his arms. "Breathe, Mate."

"I am." I swore I was, though I did forget at times.

He smoothed a hand over my back, and I shivered, groaning. I gently tugged on one of his nipple rings, and his breath sharpened. Monty had suggested the truth, and he was right. As much as it was easier to hide behind sex and smiles, that didn't make for a healthy relationship, and me and Fyn were it, so serious talking. Fun.

"I'm overwhelmed," I confessed. "I'm not used to everything. Every sense is stronger than ever, and I have no idea what to do with my wings or tail."

"Do you want me to stop touching you?"

"No," I said, moving closer. My hips slotted against his, and my hard cock pressed against him.

"Caleb," he groaned, breath rushing over me.

"I just..."

He pushed my long hair back, and I fought a cringe. "What?"

"I can't help but wonder what this would be like if I was in my human body. I know that's impossible because I died a long time ago. Like a very long *long* time ago. God, my body is probably withered or gooey... I shouldn't have thought about that, because I feel gross now."

"Caleb," Fyn said, drawing me out of my random thoughts.

"Anyway." I shrugged, ignoring the ache the movement created. "What if? The question never stops circling my head. I try not to... But I can't help it."

"Can I be honest without upsetting you?"

"Yeah," I said, even though I wasn't sure it was the truth.

"I wonder too."

"You do?"

"I do," he said, kissing my forehead. "I am so happy and grateful you are here, Caleb. Beyond happy. I never want to be without you ever again. Not even for a day. But I think about how you used to look because that's what I'm used to. I wonder how your human form would have felt against me. How kissing you would have felt. What hugging you would have been like. How falling asleep with your much smaller body in my arms would have been. How fucking you would have felt. I think about all of it."

Fucking hell, I was crying again. Why? I had no idea. "I thought about asking Seth, but I don't think he will answer."

Zoltilvoxfyn laughed, tail curling around my leg. "I think you're right."

Rocking my hips into his made his rare laughter break off as his breath caught. I said, "I want to have sex, but I'm afraid of how I'll react."

"We can wait."

I didn't want to wait, but we might have to because of how sore I was. At least for tonight. Still, I worried my body wouldn't handle it when Fyn fucked me, but maybe it would be worth the pain or we could find a position that didn't hurt? I wasn't sure. This was new to me. Then again, so much was.

"I want you to fuck me," I said, kissing his jaw. "But maybe nothing penetrative tonight. I'm tired and not used to this body."

"We can do whatever you want."

A frown tugged at the corners of my lips. Fyn hadn't told me what he wanted, and his wants and needs were as important as mine, and lately, everything had been about me. In fact, now that I thought about it, he'd been over-solicitous and catering to my every need. He rarely said what he thought.

"What do you want, Fyn? I need to know. You've been very careful with me lately, which I love, but I also love you being you. We haven't even talked about how you are doing or how you're handling everything." I didn't know if he was comfortable with me bringing up his depression, but I knew Fyn hadn't seen his doctor since I'd come back, which wasn't good.

His fingers slid into my hair again and made me shiver. The silky strands of Yol—my hair made me wince from the tickling. Fyn moved up and started to massage my scalp, and I groaned, rutting into him. His hard cock brushed mine, and I swore. That was beyond nice.

"I worry," he confessed.

"About?" I knew the answer or I thought I did, but he needed to say it.

"You. I'm scared to lose you again, Caleb." He met my gaze. "I couldn't live through that again. I would rather die. I'm scared I'll say something wrong or that I'll upset you. I'm terrified I will fail you even more than I already have."

My forehead crinkled. "When did you fail me?"

His eyes slid away.

"No." I shifted on top of him, straddling him, and shockingly, my back didn't even twinge. "Talk to me."

He cupped my hips, and I became acutely aware of his very hard cock beneath my ass, pressing against my balls and taint. I forced it away, focusing on Fyn. He played with the delicate scales across my hip bones as he kept his eyes on my chest. I waited; he needed to get this out. We both did.

"When you vanished. Before you vanished. After you were reborn. Every time in between."

"What?" I asked.

"I failed you, Caleb," he said, finally looking at me. "You stayed. You risked your soul. Then I made you touch the Crystal against your wishes. Now you're back, and I still don't know how to help you."

I smoothed a thumb over his cheekbone. My poor Fyn. He felt as if the weight of everything was his to bear. I carefully bent down, ignoring the twinge the movement caused, and pressed my lips to his in a gentle kiss. I kept the pace slow and soft to convey how much I loved him. I pulled back, flicking his septum ring with my tongue.

"You did not fail me," I said in a hard voice. When he opened his mouth to protest, I grabbed his chin and repeated, "You did not fail me, Zoltilvoxfyn."

"I did."

"No. I chose to stay. And neither of us knew what touching the Crystal would do. Besides," I said, gesturing to Yolkeltod's body, "I think this would have happened anyway."

"I don't know how to help you."

"I don't know how to help *me*," I replied. "This is a unique situation, Sunshine. No one knows what to do. But you are helping me by being beside me. I need you, but I also need to know what's going on with you. I love you."

"I love you too."

I lowered again, so my face hovered above his. "What does my Sunshine want?"

"I want," he said in a low voice, "to fuck my mate."

Chapter 48

US. JUST US.

Caleb

"We should discuss our permissions," Fyn said. "Things are different now, and we've never discussed physical ones when..."

"When I could touch you and you could touch me," I finished when he trailed off. I didn't mind talking about my previous ghost state. It simply was.

"I would also like to talk about this," Fyn said, lifting my hand and kissing the wide palm. "How you feel about this body. I think we have both been so worried about sounding ungrateful for this blessing that we've neglected to talk about how you feel. This is a change, Caleb, and this," he gestured to my body, "is not going anywhere."

I burrowed against his neck, and Fyn gathered me close, forcing me to reposition against his side again. Our cocks had softened with the changing conversation. I took a few deep breaths, lungs expanding and pulse slowing.

“I feel horrible,” I confessed.

“How so? Physically? Emotionally? Mentally?”

“All of the above.”

He paused for a second, and I didn’t think he quite understood what I said. Apparently, he hadn’t had multiple-choice tests in school. But his hand continued its journey up and down my back, fingers teasing the sensitive scales between my wings with each pass.

“Explain it please, Mate.”

“It’s hard to, Fyn, and you won’t ever truly understand. You can’t know what it’s like. I was a ghost for a very long time. I’d forgotten what it was like to touch, taste, or smell anything. Even now, I can’t tell you what it was like to be a living, breathing human.

“Now, I’m not human. I’m not drakcol either. I’m a...” I couldn’t even think of a word for what I was. “I’m in a body that aches all the time. All of these senses are driving my brain to panic. I’m overstimulated, and I don’t know how to cope.

“I think...” I trailed off. “I think I’m lost right now. Just really lost.”

His hand slid up my spine, flattening to hold me securely. “You *are* my wayward soul.”

I smiled, hiding against his chest. “I like that.”

Fyn kissed the top of my head. “I am with you, Caleb. I always will be.”

I peeked up at him. “You are the one thing I’m certain of, Sunshine, the only thing that’s keeping me in place so I don’t rip apart.”

He cupped my chin and angled it until his lips brushed mine. The shock from the light touch raced down my spine, making the tip of my tail tingle, and settled in my cock that bucked. Fyn kept the kiss soft as he traced my lips with his, nibbling them. He nipped my bottom lip, ripping a low groan from me. His tongue darted out to steal any sting.

With a feral groan, I mashed my mouth to his. His tongue dipped into mine and slid over me. Our tongues tangled in a slow dance, twining and tasting. I wrapped my arms around him and my tail instinctively coiled around his, and Fyn held me back, keeping the pace unhurried.

I didn't know if this kiss was leading somewhere or not, and I didn't care. At the moment, my anxieties had quieted and the overwhelming pressure of everything had vanished.

It was just us. Just me and Zoltilvoxfyn. Nothing else.

My hips canted forward, and my cock rubbed against his stomach. I jolted from the roughness of his scales dragging over my shaft. Fyn slowed, probably fearing I was becoming overstimulated, but I wasn't; I wanted more. I wanted him.

I pressed forward, chasing his lips, and rutted against him. The movement jarred my lower spine, but not enough to hurt, as long as I didn't go too fast or hard. Fyn growled, gripping my ass. He kneaded the cheeks, pulling them apart, making my pucker twitch.

"Fyn," I cried, one iota away from begging. "I need you."

"We need to talk about permissions."

We did—things were different now—but I didn't want to. My cock felt as hard as a rock, throbbing with need as pre-cum leaked from the tip and slid down my shaft. I couldn't stop now.

"Can we jerk each other off?" I asked. "No fucking. Just coming together. Please."

"Soft or hard?" he asked.

"Soft." I was not opposed to hard, but I couldn't take it right now.

"Can I be in control?"

"Yes." I trusted Fyn implicitly; besides, I didn't know what felt nice or not. Fyn did.

His lips pressed against mine, claiming me. Carefully, Sunshine rolled me to my back, and my wings sprawled over the bed. His white hair caressed my cheeks and the hard metal of his nipple rings dragged over my scales as he rocked into me.

Fyn slid his cock along mine, both slippery with pre-cum, and I ripped my mouth away from his. "Fuck," I bit out, clutching his back. "Fuck, Sunshine."

"Should I stop?"

"Don't you dare."

He chuckled, head bowing toward me. "I love you."

"I love you too, but hurry the fuck up. I'm desperate."

Kissing the column of my neck, tongue flicking out occasionally, Fyn thrust his cock against mine. I arched, matching his movements as well as I could. His ring dragged against my cock, hitting the sensitive head, and made me whimper.

My tail at some point had switched to his leg and practically strangled Fyn's calf while I clutched his back so tight that I worried my claws would puncture his scales.

He lifted off me to wrap his fingers around the base of our dicks and jerked up. I shifted my hands to his shoulders, squeezing, and looked down. There was something so erotic about seeing mine and his cock pressed together as Zoltolvoxfyn pumped us in long, unhurried strokes.

Our pearly pre-cum mixed and slid down, easing the glide of his palm as he pleased us. He slid up, then his thumb teased the head of my cock, and I groaned. The ring of his piercing pushed into the crown with each pass and had me seeing stars.

A fire started in the base of my spine as my muscles clenched and my balls hugged the base of my shaft. The tension grew, and my cock felt so hard it was painful. I whimpered, shaking.

"It's alright, Caleb," Fyn whispered. "Let go. I'm right here. Come for me, Mate. Let me see it."

My mouth opened as a loud cry ripped out of my throat. My hearing turned to static as intense pleasure swept through me like electricity. My hips arched, and ropes of cum shot out of my dick, painting both of our stomachs.

Zoltilvoxfyn kept working our cocks, extending the wildfire consuming me. I heard a crash, followed by a thump of something flying off the wall—my fault probably—but I paid no attention because Fyn released a low snarl that rumbled in his chest. His lips smashed into mine as cum splashed onto my stomach and his movements on our dicks turned frantic.

When he finished, he practically fell onto me, panting, but he still supported a good amount of his weight. I released my death grip on his shoulders and saw green blood slide down his black scales.

"Sunshine. I cut you," I said, horrified.

He shut my mouth with a harsh kiss that softened almost instantly, then said in a shaky voice, "I am fine, Mate."

I wrapped my trembling arms around him. "I don't want to hurt you."

"You'll learn how to wield your strength. Don't trouble yourself over a few drops of blood."

It was more than a few, but I let the matter go because I couldn't see any more blood escaping. An odd urge to lick the cuts swept through me, making me swallow. Something primal insisted I bathe the injuries and soothe away any pain that I might have caused.

I glanced at Fyn, who breathed heavily above me. I swallowed, fighting the urge, but in the end, I was unable to. I arched up and dragged my tongue over one of the punctures, tangy blood filling my mouth. Fyn's breath went jagged.

"I'm sorry," I said, yanking back.

He fisted my hair, drawing my mouth back to his injured shoulder. "I like it. Don't stop."

Unable to resist, I licked the other nicks my claws had left behind, bathing each one thoroughly. When I moved to his other shoulder, I asked, "Why do I want to do this?"

"Instinct," he answered. "Drakcol care for our mates, and we have the instinct to clean any injury."

"Did you ever wish to do this to me?"

"Yes. After the doctor took your blood."

"Why didn't you?"

"You were so stressed, Mate. I could hardly add to it."

"You should've asked," I said, cleaning the other small cuts. Fyn groaned with each swipe of my tongue, and his desperate noises had my cock twitching in interest, though it didn't rise to the occasion.

"Always tell me what you need, Fyn. Don't hide from me," I muttered against his scales. "I want to be the one who knows you best, the one you run to, the one who holds you. I love you."

He didn't answer, panting.

Finished, I kissed Fyn's forehead, unable to stop my smile at a random thought. I'd never been the bigger lover in bed. I'd often draped over past partners, but never the reverse because of how small I was. This was nice, him resting on me, his hair covering me, his tail wrapped around my ankle. It was nice—though I could tell he wasn't putting all his weight on me.

Trying to keep my pressure gentle, I slid my fingers up his spine, over his shoulders, and down his sides. "We'll make it, right? We'll get past this, right?"

"Yes," Sunshine said, his deep green eyes meeting mine. "We are forever."

"We are endless. Life or death, it will just be us."

Zoltilvoxfyn pressed a kiss to my lips, making my words a promise. We would be alright, in time.

Chapter 49

I DON'T WANT TO LEAVE.

Zoltilvoxfyn

I loathed to leave my mate, for even a single breath, but Father and Mother had summoned me. I was fairly certain they were going to talk about when Caleb and I would be officially bound. Knowing Mother, she probably wished to make it an elaborate ceremony since she'd been deprived of that with Kalvoxrencol and Seth. No doubt, they also planned to discuss the unrest Caleb's rebirth had caused.

My eyes remained on him, and his stayed on me. Caleb had said, more than once, that he was fine by himself, but the tension in his body told me differently. His wings were hugging his shoulders, and his tail was coiled around his leg. He'd been fine this morning, but when I'd told him Mother and Father had sent a note requesting to speak with me alone, he'd immediately tensed.

A large part of me wanted to refuse them. Caleb had been back in my life less than a week, and I needed more time with him. The logical part of my brain acknowledged that my parents had left me and Caleb alone during the budding unrest while also protecting us from the Council of Seekers and the Ranks.

I had to go, even if my instincts told me to never leave my mate's side ever again.

I buried my fingers in his hair, and he shuddered—not a good one—so I pulled away. I was getting better at deciphering his good and bad shivers. This one came from his hair. While I rather liked long hair on him, Caleb couldn't tolerate it. Most of the time he asked me to pull his hair up. I'd suggested he cut it, but he refused. My mate still struggled to accept this body as his, and I wasn't going to pressure him.

Nudging up his chin, I kissed him. "I will be back shortly."

"I'm fine, Sunshine."

He said that, but he didn't act like that. Perhaps it was a pride issue. He'd wandered the universe by himself, and now, he was afraid to be alone for a few minutes.

I settled beside Caleb and drew him against me. A single flash of wondering how he would've felt as a human went through me before it disappeared. I nuzzled his head, scent marking him; this was my mate.

Caleb slid a hand beneath my shirt to rub my side and the gland there. I swallowed at the sudden burst of arousal that it triggered. I needed to cover my mate in my scent and claim him.

We had stroked each other off a few times now, and I'd tried to suck Caleb once, but he hadn't liked it—it had been too much for him. We hadn't fucked yet, and I was desperate to be inside of him, filling him with my seed, but he wasn't ready, and I would wait for as long as it took.

He started to nuzzle and rub me. Caleb was exceedingly possessive most of the time, and I loved it. The longer he marked me, the more he calmed. He kept pushing me until I lay back on the couch and he was on top of me. I slipped under his shirt to trace his scales. When I brushed his bare skin, Caleb jerked, and his cock started to harden.

Drakcol skin was exceedingly sensitive, as it was meant to be covered in scales. I made sure to oil his side and the bare spot on his head daily. Both would have to be covered in extreme weather to keep him safe.

"Need you," Caleb said. "Now. I need you now. Right now. I can't wait."

My cock lurched, eager and ready.

Caleb licked his lips. "Can I taste you?"

I needed to go, responsibilities to attend to, but I didn't care. I cupped his cheek, running my thumb over his bottom lip. Caleb sucked the digit into his mouth and bit it. Hard. I winced.

He pulled back. "I hurt you again. I keep hurting you. I'm sorry. I didn't mean to. You probably don't want me anywhere near your cock. I mean, I did bite you. I'm sorry, Sunshine."

I grabbed the back of his neck and yanked him to my mouth, claiming it. Caleb moaned, and I forced my tongue into his mouth, fucking him until he was panting and shaking.

"I am not afraid of you, Mate."

He bit his lip, and I licked his chin and up to his mouth. Caleb started, then laughed. "I don't want to hurt you."

"You won't."

"Permissions?" he asked, and I flushed with pride. We hadn't had one comprehensive conversation, but rather small ones regarding what we were doing. Also, Caleb varied in what he wanted to do, depending on how overwhelmed he was.

"You can lick and suck me. No blood or biting. I do like my piercing played with. Same with my testicles. You can touch or lick my hole, Mate, and I like it, but I don't like anything inserted, even your finger." This wasn't something we'd discussed. I did not like to be fucked. I'd tried multiple times in my youth, but I didn't enjoy any aspect of it.

"You don't (human word)," Caleb said, and NAID didn't translate. It had a hard time with his garbled human speech. Edith did better, but I was *not* inviting her into our sex talks; she would have an opinion, several in fact.

"I don't understand."

"You like to be the one who fucks," he said.

"Yes."

Caleb grinned. "I like to be the one who's fucked."

"Excellent."

"I used to like it rougher," Caleb commented, palming my erection through my trousers. I arched up to grind into his palm, craving friction. I wanted him on my scales with no cloth between us, but I wouldn't rush my mate. He did better when we went slow.

"What?" I asked, struggling to focus.

"Before I died. I used to like it rougher. Sex. When other guys sucked me, I liked being nipped and teased."

I stopped moving, struck by the thought of anyone else touching *my* Caleb.

"You're growling," he teased. I paused and realized he was right. "Are you jealous?" Caleb brushed his fingers along my straining shaft.

"Yes," I snarled. "You're mine, and I don't like anyone touching you besides me."

He laughed, head landing on my chest. He kissed my neck, stealing any sting his laughter might have caused. He rested his chin on me and met my gaze. "You've fucked other people too, Fyn. I don't want anyone else. I'm a drakcol, sort of, now. I have one mate. You."

Any jealousy I had was soothed at his easy assertion. "I love you."

His eyes turned wet, and he pressed against me again, brown hair falling all around him. Sometimes Caleb would turn emotional for seemingly no reason. Was it because this body was more emotional than he used to be? We couldn't ask Tinlorray—she wasn't talking to Caleb and nor should she be forced to, even though I knew it would ease my mate's worry. Or it could be because Caleb was constantly stressed due to the overstimulation.

I massaged his scalp, and Caleb groaned, the sound reigniting the fire of arousal in my gut. I wanted him, but I didn't want to pressure him. Still, I could not tread lightly around my mate forever. He'd asked me to tell him of my desires, and I had to trust he would say no if he was no longer interested.

"Little Soul," I murmured, rocking my hips against him. "I need you."

Caleb kissed my neck, then nuzzled his way down my body. "I'm desperate to taste you. I've always wondered what you tasted like, and now, I get to know."

Caleb hadn't tasted me yet, despite the past times we'd pleasured each other. I'd figured he hadn't liked it, but maybe he'd been nervous. I reached out to touch his cheek, love burning my soul at the same time worry gutted me. I couldn't lose him. Never again. That agony was something I would rather die than experience again.

"Don't ever leave without me," I said.

He paused in undoing the ties on my trousers. "I won't."

I didn't think he truly understood, but it didn't matter.

Caleb yanked my trousers and undershorts off in one go as I lifted my hips to assist him. My cock slapped my stomach, the tip wet and ready for him. He held my shaft loosely, biting his lip.

"You won't hurt me, Mate."

"I might," he muttered, but Caleb didn't allow me a chance to respond. He flattened his tongue and dragged it over the crown, teasing my piercing. We both moaned at the same time. "You taste so good," he said right before he sucked the tip into his mouth.

I lost all thought as his tongue circled and prodded the slit. His teeth latched onto my ring, and he tugged softly, making me cry out.

"Like that," I forced out, to reassure him I was enjoying what he was doing.

Caleb grinned, and I saw a shadow of the spirit he used to be. Though his form was different, he was my Caleb.

He sucked me down, taking far more of me. I moaned at the wet heat of his mouth and the tight pressure he kept around me. The head of my cock hit the back of his throat, and he gagged. I started to shift away, but he gripped my butt, keeping me in place as he swallowed, breathing through his nose.

"Caleb!" I howled as the muscles of his throat worked around me. He slid up my shaft, releasing me with a pop. Caleb twisted and played with my ring, making me growl, before placing open-mouthed kisses down the shaft, tongue flicking me.

When he reached my testicles, he forced my legs further apart and I complied. Caleb nuzzled my sack, taking a deep inhale. "You smell good."

My breath was too harsh to respond, but I was his mate—of course, I smelled good to him.

His tongue dragged over the seam between my balls, then he sucked one into his mouth, slowly licking and sucking on it. Caleb brushed my shaking thighs, moving inward, making me shiver and grunt, and pressed a knuckle to my hole, circling in slow movements.

"Mate, I need your mouth on me." My orgasm was building with every second. I needed release.

He kissed the soft scales between my hole and balls, and I moaned, fisting his hair. Caleb chuckled, his breath rushing over me, making me shiver at the sudden chill from the wetness of his saliva.

"Same as humans." His tongue dragged from my hole to my balls, and I panted, trying to stop the building pleasure. I was so desperate for him that I threatened to unload without him touching me.

Caleb took pity on me and sucked me into his mouth again, teasing my ring with his tongue. My orgasm swelled as he bobbed up and down on my cock, hands playing with my balls.

"Prince," NAID said, and I started. Caleb paused, glancing at me, tail flicking, then sucked my cock harder, playing with my balls. I moaned.

"Prince," NAID said again.

"Y-yes," I forced out.

"The emperor would like to speak to you. You are late for your scheduled meeting."

My mate didn't slow; if anything, he picked up speed. I whimpered, moments from release.

"I'm unavailable," I yelled. My hips rocked up, driving my cock deeper down his throat. Caleb grabbed my butt and yanked me toward him, encouraging me to fuck his face. I rutted upward, chasing my pleasure.

"Prince, the emperor insists."

Stars, my father had bad timing. I could not speak, because my pleasure raced down my spine, and I came with a snarl, thrusting into my mate's waiting mouth. He swallowed around me, drinking my seed.

I panted, shakily cupping the back of his head. Caleb sucked up and off my softening cock and smugly smirked at me. I chuckled. "You liked that someone might have seen us."

He kissed my cock and it twitched in interest, though I would not be ready to go again for some time yet. Caleb glanced at the monitor, and NAID was still there; the computer didn't care.

"Tell my father I will be there soon," I told it.

"Understood." NAID vanished.

I cupped his cheek. "Shall I suck you?"

"No. Not yet. At some point in the future, yeah, but not right now," he said.

Pulling him up so he was on top of me, I undid his trousers enough to pull his hard cock out. Caleb gasped. I pumped him, harder than I normally did, testing my mate's reaction, and Caleb moaned, pressing his forehead against mine. I brushed my thumb over his leaking crown, listening to him whimper; I loved finding exactly what he did and did not like.

"I want your seed on me," I said. "I need to smell like you."

"Fuck, fuck, fuck."

From his gasps and rolling hips, I knew he liked that I worked him fast and hard. I scratched him gently with my claws to make him sting, and Caleb whimpered, tip leaking pre-seed. It did not take long for Caleb to tumble over the edge. Spurts of his seed coated my stomach, and I groaned at the sight. Something primal inside of me needed to be claimed by my mate in such a way.

He collapsed against me, boneless, and I swallowed a grunt. Caleb was heavy, even heavier than me, and he was still underweight for his frame. He wasn't small anymore, and I wouldn't be able to hold him like this for much time.

I kissed the top of his head. "I need to go."

"No," Caleb protested, but he moved off me.

"I'll return as soon as possible. Maybe we can go on a date later?"

"I'd like that."

Chapter 50

MEETINGS, STAR TREK, AND INTERRUPTED DATES.

Caleb

I lay on the couch, sated from my and Fyn's earlier fun, but tension vibrated in my muscles. I didn't like being alone, which was weird. I used to be alone all the time, but now, I needed Fyn here. All the time. I felt like I would disappear or become a ghost if someone didn't assure me they saw me and that I was alive. Though part of me still hated being alive.

My brain was a mess.

A face suddenly appeared on the monitor in front of me, making me start. Wings sprawling, I half fell off the couch as I scrambled to get away. A pot crashed off the shelf, and I whimpered.

"It's me, Caleb," Edith said.

"Fucking hell," I whispered, hand over my racing heart. "Don't suddenly pop up," I said in English.

"I'm sorry."

I glanced at the broken pot that held a seedling. I broke another one. My inner fire came in spurts, usually when I was experiencing powerful emotions. No one had started teaching me to control it yet because I wasn't particularly strong, and I already had so much going on.

"How are you?" she asked.

I started to clean up the mess I'd made and answered, "Better, though not great."

"That, I believe, makes sense. I have been researching your situation, and the human medical texts have not provided a satisfactory result. You do not have body dysmorphic disorder in the traditional sense nor do you have body dysphoria. Then again, I lack the credentialing or experience to make an official diagnosis."

"Ghosts don't go into brain-dead bodies on Earth as far as I'm aware," I remarked.

"True. That is why I searched for another species that might have something similar to you."

I paused, shards of pottery falling to the ground. "Did you find something?"

"The Mosvoye of Mauute. They have a ritual to trade bodies. The consciousness leaves one body and enters another. It is done when they mate. They believe that you can only be truly one if you live in your chosen mate's body. They trade every year for the rest of their lives. Elderly mosvoye have documented they often forget which body they started in."

An urge to whip out my tablet and research them raced through me. I wanted to see their planet, live among them, and figure out exactly what made them tick. "Did they have good advice for me?"

"Yes and no," Edith replied. "This is a natural phenomenon for their species that pre-dates technology or written recordings. But they do extensively talk about the first switch, and how overwhelming it can be. I have already collected the information and sent it to you."

Tears burned the backs of my eyes, and I wiped them away, heedless of the dirt I was spreading. "Thanks."

"I wish to help," she replied quietly.

"I know, and I appreciate your friendship."

A huge grin crossed her face. "We are friends."

"We are."

The door rang, and I waved goodbye to Edith, who gave me a cheeky wink. Fyn had assured me no one from the Ranks or the Council of Seekers would bother me, and I trusted him, so I wasn't concerned about whoever was on the other side.

"Kal." I glanced around him. "Where's Seth?"

"He's with Wyn and Urgg today."

I could finally meet Urgg. I should've thought about it earlier. I *knew* we would be great friends.

"You said you liked *Star Trek*."

"I do."

"I have everything Edith got from Earth. Shall we watch it together?"

It was an offer of friendship, one I appreciated, but Kal had hated me since I'd gotten this body, and I needed to know why. "Why?"

"We both like it," he answered, tail flicking.

"I mean, why don't you like me anymore? You've been distant. You were nice before. Was it because I wasn't really here?" Shit, I sounded needy, but I refused to take the words back.

Kal ran a hand through his silvery-blue hair. "It's not that I didn't or rather don't like you, Caleb. I do. You are my mate-brother."

I blinked at the word. I hadn't heard it before. I assumed it meant something similar to an in-law.

"I am very protective of Zoltilvoxfyn and all of my siblings."

I knew this.

"He was inconsolable when you... left, were reborn, I'm unsure of how to phrase it. Then you returned, and I feared he would be injured again. There is also the matter of instincts and body language. I know you don't understand that you are threatening me or my Seth when you growl or extend your wings, but my instincts see you as an outsider who is a potential threat to those who are mine. Logically, I can accept you are Caleb, but it is taking time for me to truly understand that. It was never about you. My apologies. I never intended to hurt you."

So he, like me and Fyn, was struggling with the newness of everything. I got that. He was protective of his brother. I got that as well. I had two choices: make him work for my forgiveness or move on. I was so damn tired of struggling, and right now, being friends with Kal sounded nice.

This was hard on everyone, and honestly, I wanted to move forward.

"So do you want to watch *Star Trek*?" I asked.

He smiled. "I do. Seth doesn't like it."

"What? Who doesn't like *Star Trek*?"

"I know. If my mate has a flaw, that would be it."

We sat on the couch, and I smiled to myself. This. I'd wanted this for so long. Friends, family, and a place to belong. I'd wandered away from home so many years ago, and now, I'd come back. Though it looked different, and I looked different, it was still home.

Zoltilvoxfyn

I entered my parents' quarters and both Mother and Father were on the couch. Father was reading something on his screen while Mother was rewiring a circuit board. They both looked up at me, and Father's expression remained the same calm mask he often wore, so similar to the one Dontilvynsan often had, but Mother gave me a tight smile.

This wasn't going to be a pleasant meeting.

I took a seat on the stools across from the couch. Neither of them spoke, and I remained silent, arms crossed. If they wished for a battle of silence, I would come out the victor.

Eventually, Father asked, "When are you and Caleb officially bonding?"

I couldn't, not yet. I needed more time to assure myself that Caleb wasn't going to disappear the moment I lost sight of him. The thought of days, if not weeks depending on how grand Mother and Father wished to make the ceremony, without seeing him or having him by my side was too much to bear. Besides there was the matter of Caleb's health. He still struggled to stand for long periods and required my help.

No. The official bonding would have to wait.

"Not yet," I said, but I couldn't stop my tail from thrashing in agitation.

Mother stood and placed a hand on my chest, above my pounding soul. "You don't want to be away from him."

"I can't," I whispered.

"I understand," she replied. "I truly do."

Father moved to my side and hugged me tight; I allowed the contact, tensing for all of one moment before wrapping my arms around him. He held me tight, and Mother smoothed my hair.

"Your Caleb is not going anywhere," Father said. "He is going to stay right beside you."

"You cannot promise that."

"You are correct," he said, "but I doubt your mate desires to leave you any more than you desire to leave him."

That was true. Caleb loved me as much as I loved him.

"Your fear is reasonable, Zoltilvoxfyn. You lost your mate and now have him back. Of course, you wish to stay by his side, but this cannot go on indefinitely."

I pulled back. "I do not need it to be indefinite. I need it for right now."

Father said, "For now, then."

My parents exchanged a glance, and I asked, "What?"

"There has been some unrest," Mother answered.

"I am aware." Having a human soul come back to life in a drakcol body was new, and not only that, shocking.

"The Council of Seekers wishes to speak with you because they are curious to see if such a thing can be replicated. The Ranks wish to speak to you and Caleb to find out why he is so special and why the Crystal chose him. The Ranks, of course, oppose the seekers trying to replicate this occurrence, as they believe the Crystal alone could or should do this again."

I was with the Ranks in this matter. I'd seen how much Caleb was struggling to adjust. While I was grateful my mate was alive and with me, I didn't think spirits coming back to life in the body of another was a wise thing. Also, how many viable brain-dead bodies were lying around? Not many, I presumed.

"There is a faction of our people," Father said, "who are displeased that the Crystal placed Caleb, your mate, in Yolkeltod's body instead of reunifying him."

Which was why Caleb, I, and hopefully Tinlorray were remaining quiet about the fact Caleb had spoken to Yolkeltod prior to him passing on.

"To flaunt what happened in the face of some of our people's suffering would not be wise or fair," he said.

"That is why we are remaining here in the palace," I replied.

"Yes," Mother agreed. "Indeed. But when you and Caleb choose to officially bond, we believe it would be far wiser to have a small ceremony over something grand."

I understood now. When Hallonnixmin took Gilvaxtin officially as his mate, the announcement had been huge and viewable by our people via screens, and they weren't genetically bonding like Caleb and I would, as they were not Crystal-bound mates. Doing the same right now was insensitive at minimum and cruel at worst.

"That's fine." I hated the thought of anything large, and anything sizable would upset Caleb.

Mother and Father both relaxed. "Truly?" Father asked.

"Yes."

"We love you," Mother said. I knew that already, and I didn't need something elaborate when I bound my mate to my side forever to prove that.

I returned to my quarters, eager to see my mate again. When I opened the door, I paused briefly. Kalvoxrencol and Caleb were on the couch together, talking as they watched something on a screen.

"I love this part," Caleb said, shaking Kalvoxrencol's arm.

"Quiet," Pest replied with no bite. They both fell silent before laughing.

Warmth flooded my soul at the sight of my mate and my brother laughing. Caleb was getting rooted in my family with ease, and I knew that this was something he wanted—no needed. He needed to be a part of a family once again, and I was honored he would be a part of mine.

I sat beside my mate and ran my tail over his arm. Caleb shivered, a good one, and leaned toward me. "Hey, Sunshine," he said. Kalvoxrencol grunted in welcome, tail flicking at me.

"What are you watching?" I asked, trying to understand the humans in colorful uniforms on the screen.

"*Star Trek*," Caleb replied shortly.

"What?"

"Quiet," Kalvoxrencol said.

The play, or whatever it was, was confusing. I didn't understand why my mate or Kalvoxrencol enjoyed it, but both were engrossed. I frowned at Kalvoxrencol. He needed to leave so Caleb and I could go on a date.

"Where is Seth, Pest?" I asked, hoping to distract him.

"With Urgg and Wyn," he replied.

I fought a growl. I glanced at Caleb and brushed my tail down his spine before coiling around his. I asked, voice low, next to his ear, "How long is this... play going to continue for?"

"It's a (human word), Sunshine. And for a while."

He wasn't hearing the desire in my voice. I didn't want to keep my mate from having fun, but I also craved time alone with him. I pressed against his side, and Caleb leaned against me. I nuzzled his cheek, but he didn't react.

I surrendered. I wouldn't win this battle, so I kept my arms around my mate and let him enjoy his human play.

It was late by the time Kalvoxrencol had left. Seth had eventually come for Kalvoxrencol, and only then did they stop watching their show. Now Caleb was stretched out on the bed, lovely in his bare scales.

I snagged the oil for his skin and started to rub a decent amount on. He moaned, tail coiling around mine before flicking away. I spread a generous amount of the oil on his side, then moved to the exposed skin on his head.

"Did you have fun with Kalvoxrencol?" I asked.

"Yeah. It was nice to watch *Star Trek*, and there are new ones I haven't seen, which is awesome. I can't wait. Kal agreed to watch everything with me."

I massaged his skin while I inspected for dry spots. "I'm glad you two are getting along."

Caleb sat up, snagging my hand and pressing it to his chest. My soul sped up. He rubbed my palm on him. "I love you."

"I love you."

He lay back down and reached for me. I came willingly and snuggled against his side. His arm wound around my waist, followed by a wing. I trailed my fingers over his chest, and Caleb groaned. His tail tickled my ankle and slid up my leg, creating a fire in its path. The tuft tickled the swell of one of my cheeks, and I planted a firm kiss on his chest, the edge of my mouth brushing his nipple.

"Are you more comfortable?" I asked.

"About?"

"This," I said, patting his chest that was still far too thin.

"Hmm." Caleb fisted my hair. "I don't know. Sometimes I am, and other times, I'm not. Sometimes I feel like this is me, then I see myself in the mirror and I'm... not."

"You could speak to someone professional about it."

"Maybe. Edith got me some information I'm going to read."

I kissed him, licking the scales around his nipple and making him whimper. "Did you want to be husbands?"

"What?"

"Husbands like Kalvoxrencol and Seth." 'Husband' as I understood it was the human equivalent of mate, and Pest and Seth enjoyed the term. I wanted to give Caleb whatever he needed or wanted.

"No, I don't."

Pain stabbed me, and I ducked my head so he wouldn't see it.

Caleb rolled, and I grunted in surprise when he lay on me, his weight nearly crushing me. He bit my chin and met my gaze. "I love being your mate. I want to spend my life, my second life, my next afterlife, whatever time I have with you. But using the word 'husband' is too (human word) for me. Some people like it, and that's great for them, but I don't."

"I don't understand."

"I'm not sure how to explain this in a way you'll understand. When I grew up, people like me, men who liked other men, couldn't become husbands by law. We had our own terms. Being called 'husband' is too straight presenting for me."

"I don't understand why you're using the word straight."

"It's for people who like the opposite gender."

I was just as confused, but I knew from Kalvoxrencol that not all humans were like us. Most drakcol did not have a sexual preference regarding gender. Occasionally, there were people like Hallonnixmin who were only attracted to women, or Kalvoxrencol who were only attracted to men, or people who were not attracted to anyone.

"I want to be your mate, in every way possible, but I don't like the word 'husband.'"

"That's fine," I said, and it truly was. I didn't care if we called each other husbands or not. Caleb was my mate.

"I don't want children either," he said. "We never really talked about it, but I don't want them, Fyn. I swear I will be an excellent uncle to whatever nieces and nephews your brothers have, but children are not something I desire for myself. We should have talked about this sooner. I can't believe I didn't bring it up. Why didn't I bring it up? I should have."

I covered his mouth to stop his panicking. "I don't want children either."

"Truthfully?" he asked against my palm. "You're not just saying that for me?"

"I'm being truthful."

"Good."

We hadn't had the date I wished for, but this was perfect—just me and him.

Chapter 51

THE PERFECT DATE FOR AN EX-GHOST.

Zoltilvoxfyn

I sat near the end of the bed, waiting for Caleb to wake up. We hadn't gotten to have our date yesterday, and I was determined for us to have one today. In a way, Kalvoxrencol interrupting us had helped me because I planned a different outing for us—one that I thought Caleb would enjoy far more. After a quick consultation with Edith, who'd insisted on getting involved and dragged Wyn into the conversation as well, I had my plan set. All I needed was for Caleb to wake up.

Today, unlike usual, he was deep asleep.

Carefully, I crawled up the bed and settled next to him, staring at him. With my gaze, I traced the slopes and planes, lingering on his long eyelashes, then his perfectly straight nose, and luscious lips. I still missed his human aspect, but I found Caleb as a drakcol exceedingly attractive.

A heavy breath rushed out of his lips as his tail twitched in his sleep. I dragged my nose along his, nuzzling his forehead. Caleb took a deep inhale and calmed once more. I didn't know for certain if Caleb was having nightmares, because he didn't recall dreaming when he woke up, but sometimes he would thrash in his sleep.

With a gentle kiss on his forehead, I guarded his sleep as I studied him, memorizing every detail.

After the morning had started to bleed into the middle hour, Caleb stretched, reaching for me. I went into his embrace, rolling him to his back. He smiled up at me, muscles relaxed beneath me.

"Good morning, Mate," I said before claiming his mouth. Caleb groaned, his fingers tracing their usual pattern over my back before finding purchase on my butt as he ground me into his hard cock. My own started to awaken from his arousal and the taste of him on my tongue, but I pulled away before this became something more.

"Fyn?"

I nipped his nose. "I have a surprise for you."

"Is it sex in our bed because that sounds nice right about now?"

"No," I replied. "But you will like this surprise."

"Will it be fun?" he asked, tail starting to wiggle as his voice grew in volume.

"Yes."

"Have I done it before?"

"I do not believe so."

Caleb beamed, and something in my soul settled. This was Caleb. My Caleb. With every smile, touch, word, and action, Caleb showed me he was the same person I'd fallen in love with. The same spirit who was easygoing, loved learning, had an insatiable curiosity, and loved me in return.

"Come, my Mate," I said, sliding off him. "Allow me to take you on a date."

Caleb

I followed Fyn on shaky legs through the palace, unsure where we were going, but I was excited. He guided me to a lower floor I'd never been to before. Fyn palmed a door open and directed me inside with a flick of his tail. I frowned at the empty space.

He must have seen my expression because he stated, "It's an experience suite."

My mouth dropped open. On the Admiral Ven, I'd popped into a few experiences, but I'd never gotten to interact with them (this was the closest to a holodeck I'd ever get; of course, I was desperate to try it).

Snagging the back of his neck, I drew Fyn against me to capture his mouth in a quick kiss. "Thank you, Sunshine."

He rewarded me with a slight quirk of his lips, which sent my pulse racing.

Fyn thumbed through the choices on the terminal near the door before he rejoined me. The blank white walls and floor flickered before an entire jungle appeared. Mountains were towering above us, riddled with caves. Palm-like trees, though gold and brown, filled the jungle, forming a canopy around us. Sunny yellow ferns and spidery plants grew over the dark brown ground that was covered in fallen palms.

"It's beautiful," I commented.

"I thought we'd explore." Fyn gestured to a tree. "Walk through it."

I knew how experiences worked. Force fields and light made everything, but they would stop me from passing through anything. Besides, just yesterday, I'd crashed into the bedroom door because I'd forgotten I wasn't a ghost anymore.

Still, I stepped forward and put my hand on the trunk; I slid right through. I yanked back, heart thrashing against my ribs. My wings sprawled as I scrambled back, losing my feet.

A solid arm caught me before I fell. "You're safe," Fyn said against my ear. "I promise, my Little Soul. You are here. With me."

When I felt him behind me, I calmed. Pushing out of his hold, I approached the tree again, fingers disappearing inside. I gaped, realizing for the first time that I didn't hear much. There were no scents beyond mine and Zoltilvoxfyn. No touch besides my clothes and the floor beneath me.

He'd made me into a ghost again.

Sunlight burned in my gut. I whirled in a circle, beaming. My knees shook and I tilted dangerously to the side. Fyn snagged me, and I wrapped my arms around him. "Thank you."

He smiled—a true one. "Wyn and Edith helped me reprogram this exploration experience. I thought it might help."

It did. There was less. So much less.

"Explore, my Mate. I have you." Fyn lifted a black device that had a ball in the center. It must control where we were going. Unlike holodecks, experiences only went as far as the room's edges, nor did they create texture, smell, or taste. The latter three were a major benefit for me.

Stepping forward, I explored the jungle until my legs burned and my lungs struggled to take in air. Eventually, I sat down to rest, watching a waterfall of green water that fell into an emerald pool, encrusted with huge glowing crystals.

Fyn sat behind me, legs bracketing me, and supported my weight. I sagged against him, marveling at the nothingness around me. The sights were lovely, but my brain felt calmer than it had since I'd come back into this body.

"Are you well?" Sunshine asked, nose against the nape of my neck. His breath rushed over my scales, making me shiver and snuggle into him.

"Yes." It was like the volume had finally been turned down. "Can we do this again?"

"As many times as you'd like."

I sighed, content for the first time in a long time.

We remained in the experience until I could barely stay awake, and then we headed back to our apartment to nap. My steps were slow and hesitant with my exhaustion, but Zoltilvoxfyn supported my weight with an arm around my waist. My eyes wandered over the open windows, and I spied Seth and Kal in the garden. The remnants of a picnic were around them, and Kal and Seth relaxed on the grass.

I wonder where that gray-scaled drakcol is? He'd followed Seth around a lot. Like magic, I spotted him hunkered down near a towering tree with black bark and red and gold leaves. I swore he hadn't been there a moment ago.

"Who's that drakcol?" I asked Fyn.

"Who?"

"The one in the garden."

"Kalvoxrencol?" Fyn asked slowly.

"Sunshine, I know what your brother looks like. The other drakcol."

"What other drakcol?"

Could Fyn not see him? I pointed. "The gray-scaled one crouched near the tree. He has a screen, and he's watching Seth and Kal."

Fyn blinked. "I'm not sure how I didn't notice him. But no, I don't know him. He has to have clearance to be here, so he's not a threat. I'm sure it's fine. I'll talk to Kalvoxrencol about it later. Now, you need to rest, my Mate."

I nodded, watching the strange drakcol until he disappeared from view.

Chapter 52

THE GREENHOUSE OR A LOVE SHACK BY ANOTHER NAME.

Caleb

Zoltilvoxfyn lay beneath me, a gentle smile on his lips. We'd napped before spending a lazy day in bed filled with cuddling, dozing, snacking, and *Star Trek*. As darkness started to descend, I'd asked to go outside to the terrace. Fyn, being Fyn, had been worried about me getting sore, so he'd gathered up blankets and pillows aplenty, making a comfortable nest for me.

I started out looking at the stars above me, but now need pulsed deep in my gut. I wanted him inside of me, claiming me. In anticipation of this hopeful outcome, I'd snuck some lube into the mass of items Fyn had carried down. I rubbed my forehead on his, and my floral fragrance flooded my nostrils. Fyn massaged my sides, making even more of my scent fill the air.

"I want you," I muttered, trailing soft kisses over his face. I dragged a finger down his chest, stroking his stomach before seizing the hem of his shirt and tugging it up. Fyn lifted his arms, allowing me to strip him. I didn't stop there and quickly pulled off his shoes and pants.

Finally having him bare beneath me, I grabbed his shaft. Fyn gasped, hips arching to follow my movement as I shuttled up and down his steadily hardening cock. When he was fully erect, I slid one of my fingers through the ring in his cock and played with it. He grunted, hips rutting.

"Permissions," he ground out as I pumped him, careful not to squeeze too hard. I was much stronger now and still not used to it. I'd injured him multiple times, and I felt hella guilty for each one.

I kissed his neck. "You know I don't top. I like to be fucked, hard, but this body will not take it right now. I love to be tied up. And I love being spanked, or well, I assume I still do. That's the extent of impact play I like, though. I don't mind biting or nipping, but no blood. You can touch me whenever or wherever you want, even in front of people, especially in front of people. I love it when you touch me, but sometimes it overloads me, so please be patient. I love fucking when I know people can possibly see me, but I don't share. I don't want anyone else to fuck me or for you to fuck anyone else."

"I'm all for hard fucking, but you need to heal first," he said. "And of course, we will not fuck anyone else. We're mates."

I'd forgotten; drakcol didn't do polyamory, sharing, or consensual cheating. They had nothing against any of it, but they mated once. That, and they were possessive, which suited me fine.

"What do you like?" I asked.

"You."

I grinned. "Seriously?"

He said, "I don't mind tying you up, but I have no interest in being tied up. I would enjoy spanking you, but it's not something I enjoy for myself. I like having sex in the tub, so eventually, I would like to try it with you. I do enjoy light pain."

I sharply tugged on the ring in his cock, and Fyn moaned, a bead of pre-cum sliding down his shaft. "You like that?"

"Yes."

"Good."

"I don't enjoy tasting my seed, but I am more than happy to drink yours."

So no cum swapping. I could live with that. I paused. Wait a fucking second. "You've tasted yourself in front of me, Fyn."

His eyes skirted to the side, hiding from me, as he commented, "I didn't want to disappoint you. You couldn't taste me then."

I swallowed a sigh. Permissions were a drakcol thing and he'd crossed one of his limits. I realized something as I stared at my mate—he struggled to put himself first, especially if he thought I would be disappointed. I didn't know if it was him, his depression, or something else entirely, but Fyn had a hard time saying what he needed, like he wasn't worthy of anything.

"I wouldn't have been mad, Sunshine. I don't like you doing things that upset you."

"I understand," he said.

I very much doubted that, but this wasn't something that I could fix with a few pretty words. This was going to take time, and we had as much as we wanted. And I would wait patiently. By his own words, Fyn didn't like to speak about his depression, though he had nothing to be ashamed of. One day, though, I trusted he would feel comfortable enough to talk to me, and I would be here, arms open. Until then, I would meet my mate where he was at, showing him just how much I loved him, and how valuable he was.

I asked, "Anything else?"

"I am utterly desperate to fuck you among my flowers right now."

"Then fuck me, so everyone can see who I belong to."

His eyes darkened, and more pre-cum slid down his shaft. I stood, with his help, and lifted my arms. His lips quirked, but he complied, slowly undressing me. He took his time, fingers dragging over my scales as his possessive eyes roved over me.

I took his hand, kissing his knuckles. Fyn snagged the blanket and some pillows. He shook his head when I held up a container of lube, grinning, but he took it from me. Fyn didn't fight me as I led him to the greenhouse, both of us naked. It was dark outside and people were unlikely to see us, but the thought of someone catching us butt-naked, cocks hard, in the garden made my dick harder than ever. I slowed my steps to a snail's pace, almost hoping someone would.

We stepped into his greenhouse that would offer us a semblance of privacy, and I moved to kiss him, bending slightly, and captured his mouth. A groan broke free at the contact. His tongue swiped at my lips, and I opened for him, both of us too impatient to drag this out. His burning hot tongue wrapped around mine, and I moaned at the scratch of his scales.

His hands slid down my sides, teasing where the scent glands were, before gripping my ass, kneading and separating my cheeks. One of his hands pulled back, and he slapped the fatty part of my ass, making me jolt from the sting.

"Like that?" Fyn asked.

"Harder."

He smacked me again, much harder, and I growled, cock twitching in need, before he went back to kneading my cheeks. Fyn attacked my mouth, rubbing his cock on my thigh, as he occasionally spanked me. My thoughts whirled, arousal clouding me.

My tail lashed suddenly, smacking into the metal leg of one of the tables with Fyn's many plants. I jerked back, breath jagged.

"We don't have to, Mate."

"It's not that." It was the fucking table. My cock was so hard, it hurt. I needed relief. I needed him.

"I don't want to hurt you."

Lips pursing, I ordered, "Lay down."

He complied, though he took a minute to arrange the pillows and blankets into a comfortable nest. His cock was hard, the tip glistening with pre-cum. I swallowed as the bead landed on his taut stomach. Carefully, I lowered to my knees. I stroked his thighs, and Fyn spread them further apart with a groan.

This wasn't going to be the most energetic fuck I'd ever had, but I had to make it good for Fyn. And I needed this. I needed to feel like this was my body, like this was my life, not one I'd stolen. I needed to belong to Fyn, and to know in turn that he belonged to me.

"My Caleb," he said, "it's alright if you can't."

I licked the head of his cock, making him snarl, and groaned at the sweet taste. "You taste amazing. How do you taste this good? I can't get over it."

I sucked the head of his cock into my mouth, relishing him on my tongue. Fyn fisted my hair, though he was careful not to pull too hard on the strands or shove me down onto his cock, but part of me liked the idea of him impaling me on his cock as he used my mouth. Later. We would try that another time.

I slid my hands up his thighs, spreading them even wider to circle his hole. Sunshine sharply inhaled. "Caleb, my Mate. That feels so good."

I took him as deeply as I could manage before sucking up and pulling on his ring with my teeth.

Fyn panted, arching beneath me. "Caleb." His thumb stroked my chin as I sucked on his cock, fingers cupping his heavy balls. My cock bounced between my legs as I increased the speed, cheeks hollow with the force I was exerting. I took him all the way into my mouth and fought back a gag, but I swallowed, focusing on breathing through my nose. When my throat relaxed around him, I moaned.

He filled me perfectly.

"Mate," he growled. I looked up at him and whimpered; he was playing with the golden ring in one of his nipples. Pulling, tugging, teasing, he worked the nub, shaking. It was so fucking hot.

I swallowed again, squeezing his balls. Hollowing my cheeks, I went for the kill, ready to make him fall apart beneath my tongue.

Fyn caught my chin and forced me up and off of him.

"What?" I asked, breath harsh. "What did I do wrong?"

"Nothing, Caleb. I want to come inside you."

Heat barreled down my spine as my cock twitched, pre-cum escaping the slit. Zoltilvoxfyn sat up and helped me lay down, shoving a pillow under my ass to help support my back, before his lips found mine. He kissed my mouth open and his tongue thrust inside, fucking me. I moaned, sucking on him.

"I'll be careful," Fyn whispered, kissing my jaw. "If I hurt you or you need to change positions, tell me."

When I didn't reply, he nipped me, making a sharp sting bloom on my chin. "Yes, Sunshine."

He kissed down my neck to my chest, tongue tasting me. He sucked on one of my nipples, laving the sensitive nub, and I jerked as electricity shot straight down to my cock. He sucked and nibbled, making me writhe.

I grimaced, and he stopped. "Are you well?"

"Keep going." God, this was going to be the most basic fuck in the history of fucking, but I hurt too bad to do anything. Despite it all, I was desperate for him. I swallowed as tears started to gather, making me bite back a swear. I wanted it to be good for Fyn, and I couldn't do anything. This wasn't me or my body.

What was I doing?

Fyn stopped, chin resting on me. "What's wrong?"

"Nothing."

He bit my stomach, and I groaned at the sharp sting. He licked the same spot soothing it away. "Talk to me."

"I'm sorry."

"For?"

"Not being able to do anything. It's pathetic that I can barely please you."

His brow furrowed. "Caleb, I love you, and I'm not wishing for more nor am I disappointed. Stop fretting." He kissed my stomach, tongue circling my navel. "This body is all yours, and I love it." His lips moved over the scars on my waist, tongue darting out to taste my skin.

I groaned. The skin beneath my scales was beyond sensitive. I panted, fisting his silky hair as pre-cum leaked from my slit and dripped onto my stomach.

"I love everything about this body. It's you, Caleb. Every part is you."

I swallowed. Was it?

He kissed each of my fingers. "Your perfect hands." Then he moved up my arm to my shoulders. "Your broad shoulders." His lips whispered down to one of my wings that spread out as much as it could. "Your glorious wings." He kept kissing and naming each part of *my* body. Tears slid down my cheeks. He lapped up the liquid before kissing my lips. "I love you, my Caleb, and this body is yours. I don't need or want more than you can comfortably give."

"I love you."

"Let me *love* you."

Zoltilvoxfyn kissed his way down to my weeping cock and rubbed the tip on his cheek, making my breath harshen. "Can we try?"

We had in the past, and it overwhelmed me to have Fyn's mouth on me, but I wanted it. I wanted everything. I nodded, but he waited until I said, "Yes. Yes, Sunshine. I need you."

He didn't waste any time and sucked me into his mouth. I cried at the wet heat, hips arching, which made my spine creak.

Hand on my hip, he kept me in place as he sucked me down to the root. His tongue worked the underside of my cock as he bobbed up and down. When he slid up, his scaled tongue circled my crown, and I swallowed at the erotic sight. His lips wrapped around me again, and I couldn't pull my eyes off my mate, slurping me down until my head hit the back of his throat.

Each swipe of his tongue drove me toward the edge. My wings stretched out as far as possible, hitting the tables, and my tail strangled his wrist. His name was on my lips with every breath.

When he sucked off me, I protested. He nipped the head of my cock, making me whimper. More pre-cum oozed out and my balls hugged the base of my shaft.

"More," I demanded. "I need more."

"Soon." He opened my legs, and I spread them as far as possible without straining myself. He licked my balls, and I groaned, hand going to his hair. He spread my cheeks, thumbs keeping me open, and with a flattened tongue, he licked my opening. My hole twitched, and my jaw clenched as a strangled noise ripped out of my throat. Fyn blew on my now wet hole, and I shrieked, gripping his hair in a stranglehold.

"You are going to bring someone with all your noise," he muttered.

The thought of someone seeing Zoltilvoxfyn eating me out, made me whimper. I lifted my legs, drawing my knees up. I held the backs of my thighs, opening myself up for him. The thought of someone seeing how my mate made me scream and come for him turned me on. I wanted someone to stare, wide-eyed, as Fyn claimed my ass with his mouth, then with his cock.

"Please," I begged.

He licked my rim. "Are you desperate for me?"

"Yes."

"You're a needy thing, aren't you?"

I moaned. "I am. Please. Fuck me. I need it. I need you."

Zoltilvoxfyn returned to licking me over and over again. Each one made pleasure build and stole moans from my lips. His tongue prodded my hole and slipped inside. I tried to wiggle downward to get him in deeper, but the movement sparked something in my spine.

"Let me do the work, Mate." His mouth returned to my hole, tongue prodding my ass. He slipped inside, fucking me as deep as he could. I lowered one of my legs to his shoulder so I could grab my cock, pumping it. My balls tightened even further, and my breath turned jagged with need.

"Fyn," I begged. I was getting close. He grabbed the container of lube, then slung my other thigh onto his shoulder. "What about your claws?" I asked breathlessly.

"They will not hurt you. Trust me."

"I do."

He slicked his fingers up, and I braced myself for the burn as he prodded the tight pucker of my ass, but it slid in with little resistance. I blinked. Was it supposed to be like that? As a human, I remembered some discomfort. He thrust his finger in and out a couple of times before adding a second. There was a moment of stretch before it faded on waves of bliss and pleasure.

My head leaned back as I moaned. "Don't stop."

He kissed the inside of my thigh, then licked the crease of my groin. "I won't. It will not take much to prime you."

A third finger joined the others, and I swore, fisting the blanket. He spread me, sliding in and out of my desperate hole and drawing whimpers from my lips. It was so good. I could not believe how good it was.

"Please, Sunshine. I need your cock. I can't wait."

His fingers retreated, and I couldn't stop the desperate whine that came out of my lips. Fyn handed me the lube, panting. "Why don't you ride me?"

Keeping my back straight was easier.

Fyn helped me up, then he lay back, I scooped up some lube and slicked it over his thick cock, shaking. I breathed, trying to calm down so I didn't explode the second he was inside of me. When his cock was nice and shiny, I settled on his lap. Lifting on my knees, I reached back and guided his cock toward my hole. I slid down, unable to stop the moan of pleasure that ripped out of my throat. He was stretching me perfectly, and I had zero problem taking him in deep.

"Fyn," I whimpered. "You're so perfect, so utterly perfect. I've never felt this good."

Clutching my hip, he grunted as he rocked up. I cried, head going back. His scales scraped on my walls as he stretched me while his piercing hit something deep within me that had me seeing stars.

"You're so warm, Caleb."

I squeezed, and he shivered.

"*Ungh.*" Fyn moaned beneath me as he planted his feet wide and thrust up into me. "So tight."

I clutched his shoulders and slid down on him until my ass landed on him. Our rhythm was slow and steady, each thrust bringing me closer to release.

Panting, I claimed his mouth, shoving my tongue between his lips, desperate for him. He groaned into my mouth, rutting into me. For the first time since I'd awoken in this body, it felt like mine.

My cock turned to steel, pre-cum leaking out and smearing all over our stomachs. The scrape of his scales was enough friction for my cock; that and Fyn kept hitting that spot deep within me. Both had my orgasm barreling down my spine. Everything tightened as I whined his name.

My whimpers and his growls filled the hot air of the greenhouse. I bounced on his cock, chasing my growing pleasure. My hole clenched as my balls scrunched up tight. I moaned. I was going to come. I tried to contain it because I wasn't ready for this to end, but I couldn't.

"I'm coming," I ground out.

"Let me see it, Mate."

He gripped my hips and pounded up into me, going faster and harder. I rode his cock, barely noticing the jarring movement as my orgasm built to extreme heights. I crashed over the edge with a howl against his lips, fingers digging into his shoulders, claws pricking him. White noise filled my ears as everything clenched in painful pleasure.

My ass squeezed Fyn's cock, and he snarled, fingers digging into my hips, as he continued to fuck me. One, two, three more thrusts, then his cock jerked and flooded my insides with molten heat.

When the blinding pleasure dimmed, I sagged on his chest, panting. My heart thudded and my muscles trembled. Fyn stroked my back, his cock softening inside me. He did not pull out, and there was no discomfort nor did I need him to slide out. I did remember as a human, I hadn't liked my partners to stay inside of me afterward; it had been uncomfortable. Some dudes liked that full feeling outside of sex, but I hadn't.

Drakcol were apparently different.

I rubbed my face on him. "I love you."

"And I you."

I nuzzled his neck, cheek, and everywhere I could reach, needing it in a way I didn't understand.

"I am yours, my Caleb. You may scent mark me as much as you like, but I am yours."

"Can I?" Unable to stop myself, I kept rubbing my forehead on him and pulling his hands to my sides, relaxing with each breath. My wings spread over him and my tail hung loosely over his legs.

"Yes."

I took him at his word and continued to claim him. He was fucking mine after all.

His fingers traced my spine, claws scraping my scales. "Are you feeling better?"

"I feel more like me."

"You are you." He kissed my temple. "We need to be honest with each other. This is going to be an odd transition, my Caleb, but we can get through it."

"We can." I took a deep breath and snuggled against my mate's chest. We could get through this; we could get through anything.

Chapter 53

HOME AT LAST.

Caleb

Three Months Later.

I stood on the beach and ran a hand through my short hair. The crash of the waves on the purple sand made me smile. The warm air no longer bothered me; instead, it relaxed something inside of me. I loved the salty brine and the sand against the scales on the bottom of my feet.

It had taken me three months to get here after Seth and Kal's invitation, but I didn't begrudge the time. Much had changed. For a couple of days after the greenhouse, Fyn and I had hidden in our apartment, fucking like rabbits. We only left when the doctor had the results from the tests they'd run.

The damage Yolkeltod had received in the shuttle accident was irreversible. There were things the doctors could do to help mitigate the pain, but my mobility was always going to be affected, and my scales would never regrow on my waist nor the scales or hair on one side of my head. I had started physical therapy, and it had helped, but they were almost positive I would never fly, which honestly I was okay with. I was pretty sure it would've been too much for me, and I was easily distracted, which probably wasn't good when flying.

The physical therapy also helped me adjust to my new body. Discovering how it moved had helped me accept this was *my* body. I'd also started to see a therapist. Not Fyn's, but another one. The thought of my towering purple doctor with horns and four arms was enough to make me relax. He was consulting with a mosvoye physician on how to help me cope with a new body, and it was helping, at times. Sometimes, though, I didn't recognize the person in the mirror.

Tinlorray still wouldn't see me. I'd tried multiple times, even though she'd asked me to leave her alone, I owed it to Yolkeltod, but she wasn't ready. Seeing me was too hard, and naturally, she was angry at me. It wasn't my fault I was in Yolkeltod's body or that he'd passed on, but she was mad, and I got it. We'd exchanged a few messages in the last month, and I was hopeful, in time, that we would have a semblance of a relationship.

Seth and Kal had left the capital not long after Monty found out the Crystal had spoken with me. The Ranks had finally corralled a meeting with me and Seth, wondering if Seth had also heard the Crystal. Apparently, he had, and the rock had called him *chosen* and that it had been waiting for him. The Ranks had hounded him day and night until Kal whisked him and Lucy away to their country home (rich people).

In his absence, I'd become better friends with Wyn, who was shy at heart but so funny, and Serlotminden, who loved languages. I was teaching him English with Edith's help while refining my accent so NAID could understand me. Wyn had also introduced me to Urgg, and I was right. Me and the barbarus were a match made in heaven. We'd drank until I'd passed out, and I ended up in the medbay because alcohol and I no longer agreed. Still, it had been fun for me, not for Zoltilvoxfyn; he'd been furious and worried.

Days ago, Fyn and I were bound. He'd refused to go through with the ceremony, because of the separation in the interim, so I decided to plan everything with Urgg (I ignored their suggestion about a fight to the first blood), Wyn, and Edith. I'd told Fyn about it a few hours beforehand. Vyn had called me efficient while Kontolmakqilnen called me presumptuous. Both made me smile. I was getting along with my in-laws, and now that they knew about me and had met me, they loved me.

We'd been bound in his terrace garden with his family and our friends around. It had been perfect.

Most of all, my sensory overstimulation had gotten better. My mind had finally adjusted to being alive, and my brain was filtering out excess stimuli like it was meant to. At times, I would become overwhelmed, but it was better, and I knew to avoid my triggers.

Arms came around my waist, making me jolt, moments before kisses trailed over my neck, followed by a hard bite. I pushed back into Fyn's embrace and groaned in pleasure. His very touch made me content.

"Sunshine, we have an audience."

"I don't care, nor do you."

True, but everyone here was his family, and Seth cared. He got flustered so easily—it was adorable. I was often tempted to poke his red cheeks or squeeze him; I never did, but hell, I was tempted. However as I looked down the shore for him, hoping not to embarrass Seth too badly, I stopped worrying. Kal had Seth slung over his shoulder, threatening to drop him into the water. Seth was yelling, but there wasn't an ounce of fear in it as he blushed profusely. Hal picked up his mate Gilvaxtin and chucked her into the ocean without hesitation. She came up sputtering and whirled on him, tackling him into the sand, snarling.

Mindy hooted, cheering her on as she wrestled her husband. Gil, I'd found, was a warrior soul like her husband and she was equally fierce. She loved to gamble, so Seth and I had taught her poker. She beat us every time. We no longer played with her unless we were prepared to lose money or random shit she claimed from our apartments.

Kontolmakqilnen shook his head at their antics and carried his young grandchild, Farrittenmon, Hal and Gil's second child, along the shore, cooing to him. Vyn wasn't far behind with Jonyontinlok, Hal and Gil's eldest son, who chased a harried crab the size of a lobster with massive spider legs.

Vyn was a seeker soul like me, and she loved engineering, taking things apart and putting them together. She was easier to talk to and get to know than Kontolmakqilnen, but I liked him too. He loved his kids, me and Seth included, he was just reserved.

The only ones missing from the family gathering were Don and Monty. Both had duties on their respective ships.

My family. This had become my family, and I was so grateful for it. I came from a large family in my first life, and now I had one again in my second life. For years I'd wandered from one end of the universe to another, searching for something I didn't understand.

My home. My mate. My love. All housed within Zoltilvoxfyn. I had searched without knowing what I was trying to find. Now that I'd found him, I didn't intend to let him go.

This life might be full of chaos, but I wanted it. I wanted to be here with him, with my family. I'd wandered from home all those years ago, to come back to my home. Now, my wandering was over, and I was more than alright with that.

"Little Soul, what are you thinking about?" Zoltilvoxfyn asked.

"How happy I am."

He smiled against my scales, and I wound my tail loosely around his leg. "So am I," he muttered. "Happier than I ever thought possible."

I turned in his embrace to wrap my arms around his neck and kissed him. His tongue slipped into my mouth, making me groan. Maybe death hadn't been so bad, but life was sure great. I highly recommend it.

Bartholomew

Life could be better, I randomly thought as the shuttle I was on careened toward a planet in a death spiral. I'd been abducted from Earth by creepy-ass aliens, then sold at what can only be described as a cattle market, only to be forced to work cleaning up bodies in a fighting ring. Now I was on a ship with a white-haired, purple-scaled alien who "claimed" to be rescuing me.

If this was a rescue, he left a lot to be desired.

I glanced at the alien who frantically pushed buttons and yanked on a yoke. Serlotminden, he said his name was. He really needed to get better at this whole rescue thing.

Afterword

I didn't plan to write this book (of course I hadn't planned on writing the first one for more than fun). But when I finished *Cosmic Husband*, and Andra was convinced I needed to publish it, I started thinking about all the other brothers. The "phase variance" in the first book was originally planned just to be a funny stressor for poor Wyn, but when I got serious about writing the other books, I reworked it to be Caleb (yes, I did finish writing this book before *Cosmic Husband* was even published).

My idea for this book came from simply wracking my brain to figure out who Zoltilvoxfyn should get together with. Then I was like, "Ghosts. Aliens. That makes sense to me," and boom this book was born... Well, after a lot of drafting, tears, and what-the-hell-am-I-doings.

In the first draft, Zoltilvoxfyn's depression was more severe, but it triggered my own depression, and I ended up in a bad depressive spiral. So for my mental health, I ended up editing out some of the more depressive aspects. I really wanted to focus on his depression, like I had Seth's anxiety, but it was too triggering for me.

One thing I wanted to remark on is that depression (whether treated or untreated) is different for everyone. Fyn's depression was modeled after my own (barring some of my regular extremes), but mine looks different than others with depression. So when in doubt, be kind and accept people where they're at.

During the process of editing this book, Andra and I figured out how much she hates certain ghost romances (i.e. ghost gets shoved into a body)... so that was fun! A major thanks to Andra for powering through and poking so many holes in my book, I felt like Swiss cheese. Thanks to Etheric Designs for my gorgeous cover (seriously, they went all out for this one).

And finally, thank you for reading this book. It seems inconceivable that there are people I've never met reading *my* book! You are making my dream come true, and I am beyond grateful. Thank you, my Martians, whether you're new to this series or picked up *Cosmic Husband* first. I appreciate every single one of you! I would hug all of you, but you know, germs.

I'll catch you in the next book or on my socials!

PS. I am beyond excited for you to read Serlotminden and Bartholomew's story, so stick around.

PPS. I know Lucy wasn't as prevalent in this book, but I couldn't logically put her in more (No, Andra, I really couldn't). BUT you can see pics of Monster, who Lucy was modeled after, on my socials.

About the author

Mars Quinn is many things (a potato masquerading as a human—quite possibly), but first and foremost, he's an obsessed cat dad to his horde of cats. As a transmasc author with mental and chronic health issues, he tries to write characters who face similar things. All in all, he's a boring hermit who never leaves his house unless forced. Usually, you can find him on his couch writing, reading, or gaming.

Made in the USA
Coppell, TX
15 February 2026

71307401R10267